TRANSIT OF
MERCURY

TRANSIT OF MERCURY

Simon Jones

Matador
9 Priory Business Park,
Wistow Road, Kibworth Beauchamp,
Leicestershire. LE8 0RX
Tel: 0116 279 2299
Email: books@troubador.co.uk
Web: www.troubador.co.uk/matador
Twitter: @matadorbooks

ISBN 978 1789016 277

British Library Cataloguing in Publication Data.
A catalogue record for this book is available from the British Library.

Printed and bound in Great Britain by 4edge Limited
Typeset in 12pt Adobe Garamond Pro by Troubador Publishing Ltd, Leicester, UK

Matador is an imprint of Troubador Publishing Ltd

For Betty
and for Alan and Mary

Simon Jones studied classics at the University of Oxford. He worked and travelled in the Far East before qualifying as a solicitor and now lives on the Welsh borders in Herefordshire. *Transit of Mercury* is his debut novel.

'Orpheus would have brought Eurydice up from the Underworld… if he had not looked back.
Thus the principle of real life is the death of the life that is unreal.'

Lorenzo de' Medici.

AUTUMN

———◈———

1

London – 21 September 2005

THE RAIN FELL lightly as Tom Talbot stared at the glass. Tiny flecks of water appeared out of the emptiness: some remained solitary and still, some combined with others and began to glide slowly down the carriage windowpane, only to stop part way, as if exhausted or blocked by some insuperable barrier. Now and then a droplet succeeded in reaching the bottom of the pane, only to hit the sill and cease to be. Tom watched this process impassively from within the cocoon of the stale, airless carriage. As the external world grew dark, his attention passed from the watery ribbons to the wry reflection staring back at him. How unfamiliar it seemed, this apparition on the surface of the glass. Was this really him: the man who, just a few short hours ago, still had a career, a future to look forward to? He sank back wearily into his seat and closed his eyes, reliving the day's events.

It had certainly started off normal enough, right down to the early-morning train from Bristol being late 'due to leaves on the line'. 'I suppose they don't have trees in Switzerland,' one disgruntled commuter had carped. 'All conifers, sir,' the ticket collector had shot back in a lilting Welsh accent, much to his own amusement.

Emerging as usual from Bank tube, Tom had battled his way through the blustery, autumn drizzle, dodging the spokes of wayward umbrellas and the spray from cowboy bus drivers. Yet, no amount of rain could dampen the unfailing sense of achievement which, every weekday morning for the past three years, had accompanied him up the steps of No. 8 Lombard Street. The monolithic edifice of pale Portland stone housed the London branch of the Banca de' Bianchi, the exclusive Italian private bank where he worked. Though small by city standards, it nevertheless enjoyed an enviable reputation as the financier of choice to the scions of some of Europe's wealthiest elite. At the top of the steps, massive bronze doors, sporting imperious lion's-head door-knockers, reinforced the bank's impregnable image. Liveried footmen, looking like figures in a glockenspiel clock, opened them precisely at nine every morning and closed them again each evening on the stroke of five. Most staff had to enter the building via an anonymous side door, but the bank's senior management (and a few young high-flyers like Tom) enjoyed the privilege of using the main entrance.

He glanced up at the bank's insignia: back-to-back capital Bs, picked out in white on a square of black marble that stood proud of a granite lintel. But on that particular morning something else caught his eye: a weathered, sandstone plaque just above the lintel. He had not noticed it before, but then it was virtually invisible beneath a thick layer of city grime. He could just make out some round shapes on a shield and a few letters: 'Le Tem...', but the rest was illegible. Maybe it was 'Le Temps Perdu', a French version of 'Tempus Fugit'? Below the shield was a single word, carved in raised capitals and somewhat more legible. It read: 'SEMPER'. Though Tom's degree was in modern languages, he had enough Latin to know that this meant 'Always'. Some Victorian precursor of the modern mission statement, he guessed, exhorting workers to keep their noses to the grindstone.

In the lobby, Joe, the club-footed cockney porter in his traditional red tailcoat and top hat, had been watering a pair of neatly trimmed laurel bushes in bulbous urns that garnished the ends of the reception desk. He greeted Tom cheerily as ever with his customary 'Morning, Mr T'.

'Morning, Joe,' Tom had responded in a tone that, in recent weeks, betrayed just a quiver of envy for the older man's apparent contentment with his humble, uncomplicated lot.

A whisper-smooth lift, guarded by an old-fashioned concertina grill and brass fittings, whisked Tom to the third floor. His office lay at the far end of a large, open-plan area. 'Hi, Tom, how are you today?' a well-manicured voice with an Australian twang rang out as he passed by.

'Fine, thanks, Carrie. Are you going out this evening?' he answered, noticing his secretary's unusually revealing outfit.

'Sure am. Off to a birthday party with a couple of the other girls. Want to tag along?'

Tom grimaced. 'Sorry, got to go home and feed Jasper.' Jasper was his dog, a large shaggy beast with mastiff ancestry and as stubborn as the proverbial mule. He had always been

Tom's dog but, after he moved away to university and then to the City, Jasper had remained with his parents. They had both been killed a few months earlier in a car crash and Tom, as the only child, had temporarily had to abandon his bachelor pad in the Docklands to sort out their old house, a chocolate-box cottage in the depths of rural Gloucestershire. What to do with Jasper was a decision he had yet to face. The cottage was ideal for animals with expansive outdoor needs, but not so good for people whose work and social lives were defined by the Square Mile and the West End. Tom's love life had been one of the first casualties of this enforced exile. His girlfriend, a Russian financial analyst, could not stand spending every weekend in the middle of nowhere with not a Michelin-starred restaurant or glitzy nightclub in sight. Such backwaters were too reminiscent of mother Russia.

'You definitely need help,' Carrie remarked, only half-jokingly. Having worked at the bank for six months now, she had reluctantly concluded that Tom was not her type. Though he had plenty of plus points – deep blue eyes, athletic build and a boyish charm – he was rather too serious and reserved for her high-spirited tastes. 'Oh, by the way,' she added, 'Poison Ivy rang down just now. He asked if you could pop up to see him as soon as you got in.' ('Poison Ivy' was the nickname the secretaries had given to Max Woodcock, the branch general manager, who was wont to linger at open doors, eavesdropping on gossip and spying on indiscretions.)

'Damn! What does he want now?' Tom muttered.

Carrie inspected her freshly painted nails. 'No idea,' she said. 'Maybe he needs his shoes shined.'

'Ha, ha! Very funny,' Tom groaned as he headed back to the lift. He liked his first hour or so in the office to be undisturbed so he could get ready for the day ahead, sifting through the pile of emails and faxes that had inevitably built up overnight from around the world. He balked at these peremptory summonses to discuss God-knows-what topic, but that was Woodcock's style. He hoped that his boss might finally want to discuss the draft report that Tom had sent him in a sealed envelope the previous week: a report which had raised the spectre of fraud at the core of the bank's business. It had given Tom a lot of sleepless nights of late. But Woodcock had not even deigned to acknowledge receipt.

Woodcock's office was on the top floor and had panoramic views from the Mansion House to the Monument. The gleaming mahogany door was wide open. Tom entered with a polite tap. Dark oak panelling spread gloomily in all directions, and a mixture of old leather and stale cigar smoke assailed his nostrils. Woodcock was enthroned on a high-backed armchair that was slightly too wide to fit between the pedestals of his vast rosewood desk. 'Good morning, sir. You wanted to see me?' he proffered.

Woodcock said nothing, seemingly engrossed in whatever was on the computer screen in front of him. Tom eyed him critically. His copious double-breasted jacket accentuated rather than softened his portly figure, while his charcoal-grey tie matched his funereal air. As Tom stood waiting for an acknowledgement, he sensed another presence in the room, but saw no-one.

After a minute or so Woodcock finally spoke, without looking up. There was a trademark hesitation in his voice, as if double-checking every word before letting it slip from his fleshy lips. 'Hmm, Talbot, yes. This is most distasteful so I'll keep it short. I'm sure it will come as no surprise, you must have known you'd be found out sooner or later.'

Tom frowned. 'Found out? I'm sorry, I don't quite follow what…'

'Oh, come on, don't play the innocent with me. I haven't spent thirty-five years in banking not to recognise a fraudster when I see one. You people always imagine you can pull the wool even when the game's up.' The general manager sighed deeply and clasped his hands magisterially across his rotund midriff. 'There was a spot check on all UK accounts over the weekend. It's so much more fruitful to do these things unexpectedly when the staff are out of the way, don't you agree?' Woodcock chucked a thick computer printout across the desk. 'The check turned up some extremely disturbing discrepancies in your portfolio. It's all there,' he snarled, gesturing at the pile of paper. 'All those bogus, offshore special purpose vehicles, into which you've been systematically siphoning funds from your client accounts. It's quite disgraceful.'

Tom picked up the printout. He was startled to find that it looked very familiar: indeed, it was identical to the one he had appended to the draft report he had sent to Woodcock – except that the references were now to *his* client accounts, not those of others. How could that be? He had been investigating the subject matter of the draft, unofficially, in his spare time, ever since noticing a sudden, and very unusual, surge in bank transfer activity at the end of the previous month. He had discovered inexplicable anomalies in the bank's accounting system.

Large, and apparently unauthorised, money transfers were being wired to accounts in the names of brass-plate companies in Liechtenstein, Antigua, Cyprus and other jurisdictions notorious in banking circles for their dubious anonymity. Moreover, these companies were unknown to any of Tom's colleagues as being clients of the bank. No-one acted as their account manager or had any contact with their directors or other personnel. Yet, over the last few weeks, several million pounds had been credited to their accounts without any corresponding receipts or debits. Initially intrigued, his curiosity had turned to alarm as he gradually pieced together parts of the jigsaw and found that the money was being systematically siphoned off from a large number of important accounts. He had gone to Woodcock with his initial findings. Woodcock had congratulated him on his detective work and instructed him to produce a draft report as soon as possible so that he, Woodcock, could present it to the bank's board. 'But,' the general manager had impressed upon him, 'don't mention this to anyone else. It must remain strictly between us for now. If such matters leaked out prematurely, irreparable harm could be done to the bank.' These words were ringing in Tom's ears when that same pompous voice barked across at him: 'Well? Hurry up, man! What have you got to say for yourself? I haven't got all day. The bank's chairman, Count Scala, is flying over specially from Florence to see me. His plane's due in any time now.'

Tom was too intent on Woodcock's outrageous accusations to notice his boast. 'But these records have been altered,' he objected. 'The correct originals were appended to the draft report I sent you last week: the one you yourself asked me to produce.'

Woodcock banged his fist on the desk. 'Don't you try to implicate me in your contemptible dishonesty!' he shouted.

Tom shook his head. 'You can't be serious. This is some sort of joke, right?'

'It's no joke, Talbot,' answered a voice behind him. He spun round: Jackson, the uniformed head of bank security stepped forwards from behind the office door. 'If you'll come this way, I'll escort you off the premises.'

Tom stared at him in disbelief. His stunned silence must have given the impression of intended resistance. At any rate, Jackson swiftly took hold of his arm and nudged him firmly towards the door.

'Don't make a scene, Talbot,' Woodcock warned. 'You're lucky the bank doesn't need this dirty linen washed in public. But you try and make any trouble and our friends at the Serious Fraud Office will hear of it. Got that?'

Tom was too shocked to respond. Jackson took him down to the ground floor via the back stairs, away from prying eyes. A few moments later he found himself unceremoniously ejected into the alleyway at the rear of the building, soon to be joined by his rifled briefcase and mangled brolly.

As Jackson slammed the cold, steel door in his face, a sickening knot twisted in the pit of his stomach. The three years he had spent working his guts out for the bank flashed before him: the long days that had become even longer nights negotiating multi-million-pound loans; the endless training courses and seminars the bank required all junior executives to attend; the Christmas parties and summer barbecues, the friends and colleagues, the familiar daily routine –

everything, in fact, that had become the very fabric of his existence, now terminated in an instant. He gathered up his scattered belongings and stumbled past the bulging rubbish bins that lined the alley. Stopping at the street corner, he looked down at a tramp stretched out on the pavement: they both had nowhere to go.

2

BEADS OF PERSPIRATION ran down Max Woodcock's forehead as he lumbered along Pall Mall and up the steps of the Athenaeum. It was well past noon. He was late for his appointment with the Banca de' Bianchi's chairman, Count Giovanni Scala di Colle di Val d'Elsa, to give him his full Tuscan title; a title which Woodcock had been assiduously repeating to himself ever since the count had announced his impending visitation.

Woodcock had never been inside the Athenaeum: why should he have? As a temple to the Goddess of Academe, this was the ivory tower par excellence. It had no place in Woodcock's world: a world of bonds and loans and lending rates, of deals and swaps and blunt Anglo-Saxon. Unsurprising, then, that Woodcock did not pause to admire the gilded statue of Athena towering above the club's Doric propylaeum, much less the copy of the Parthenon frieze that crowned its roof. Nor did he notice the flames from the gas braziers, burning at the corners of the first-floor balcony to signal some special gathering that afternoon. Blundering through the glazed front doors, his unfamiliarity was spotted at once. 'Can I help you, sir?' the porter who guarded the entrance enquired with a disdainful sniff.

Woodcock stopped and caught his breath. 'I'm meeting someone... Count Scala di...' he spluttered, wiping the sweat from his brow.

Before he could finish his sentence, the porter had shot to his side, his whole demeanour transformed at the mention of the count's name. 'Do please come with me, sir,' he fawned as he relieved Woodcock of his wet raincoat and ushered him across the marbled hall towards a sweeping staircase. Halfway up, where the stairs split into twin curving arms, Woodcock squinted at a large, round clock set in the wall. There was something not quite right about it. The porter knew that look of old. 'Don't worry, sir, you're not seeing double,' he said. 'The clock does have two sevens.'

'Why?' asked the bemused banker, hoping he did not sound too much like Alice in Wonderland.

'There are a number of theories, sir, as you might expect in a place like this. But no-one really knows. The reason's lost in the mists of time, as you might say.'

The porter's pun was wasted on the distracted Woodcock, who now found himself entering an immense drawing room, populated by huddles of coffee-sipping, biscuit-munching academics. An abrupt hush fell upon the scene. He felt a dozen pairs of eyes peering over half-moon spectacles, observing the interloper like some specimen of Homo erectus from the Lower Palaeolithic. He and his escort hastened to the far side of the room. Scholarly periodicals slumbered on the side tables: *Bulletin of Byzantine Prosopography, Journal of Medieval Dialectics,*

Quantum Mechanics Quarterly. Woodcock looked in vain for his favourite mag – *The Telephoto Photographer.*

'Count Scala is just over there, sir,' whispered the porter, nodding towards a solitary figure who occupied one of a pair of studded leather armchairs set in front of an ornate fireplace. Between the chairs, a coffee table boasted a crystal decanter and two matching glasses already charged with wine. The count was sitting at an angle, facing away from Woodcock, apparently engrossed in a copy of the *Financial Times.* But even with that partial profile Woodcock instantly recognised him from the photograph on the bank's website. The high forehead topped by jet-black hair, the aquiline nose and the prominent cheekbone were unmistakable.

Woodcock had spent the previous evening poring over the count's curriculum vitae. He had never met the bank's top man before and you did not go in cold to a first meeting with someone of his rank. His credentials were certainly impressive: he traced his aristocratic forebears all the way back to a fifteenth-century Florentine chancellor, whose family seat was a palatial villa in the Tuscan hills. The count himself had studied politics and economics at the University of Pisa before following in his father's footsteps to the Banca de' Bianchi's headquarters in Florence. Climbing rapidly through the ranks, Scala was now the guiding hand behind all the bank's major policy decisions. To have received a summons from such an exalted figure was indeed a rare, if risky, opportunity to make an impression.

Woodcock sidled softly across the thick-piled carpet until he was standing just behind the count's chair. Now he could fully appreciate the fine lines of the expensive silk suit, the gleam of gold links on the monogrammed shirt cuffs, and the eye-catching diamond ring. Entranced by such exotic opulence, he failed to notice his own reflection in the large mirror above the fireplace. Without a word, Scala cast the newspaper aside and tapped his gold Rolex.

'Oh... umm... sorry. Sorry I'm late, Count Scala di Colle di...'

'I expect results, Woodcock, not excuses,' Scala spoke in clear, fluent English but with a strong, gravelly accent that was redolent of his earthy Tuscan origins. 'I'm due to attend a talk on equinoctial precession in the library in precisely ten minutes.'

Woodcock wondered if those starched lips and chiselled features were even capable of a smile. 'Oh, precession... yes, right. The securitisation boys often use it in subordinated debt restructuring, I believe.'

Scala regarded him for the first time, his piercing black eyes appraising the portly bank manager from double chin to beer-belly, like a chameleon perusing a fly. Then, tiring of his inspection, the count turned his attention to the black attaché case lodged firmly under Woodcock's armpit. 'Ebbene, you have brought me the report, yes?'

Woodcock hurriedly unzipped the soft leather case and handed over the dossier which Tom Talbot had sent him the week before. Scala flicked cursorily through the pages before placing the document in the hand-tooled Morocco briefcase propped against the side of his chair. 'There are no copies?'

'None, Count. I had Talbot's office thoroughly checked and his computer's been wiped clean.'

A cloud briefly crossed Scala's brow. That name, 'Talbot', rang a distant bell. But he let it pass. It was no doubt a mere coincidence: the name was not uncommon. 'And the "domestic arrangements"?'

'All taken care of, sir. Your man came in last Friday, and I personally handed him the sealed package you sent over. I also gave him the address of Talbot's apartment in London as well as his parents' house in the country. He'll have been in there as soon as Talbot left for work this morning.'

'Benissimo,' Scala purred, changing his tone with autocratic ease. 'You did well to inform me immediately about this matter; you shall be duly rewarded for your discretion. Do please be seated.'

As Woodcock settled himself on the armchair opposite, the count raised the nearer of the two glasses of wine from the table and invited his colleague to do likewise. 'Now, my dear Woodcock, since your name was unfortunately omitted from the Founder's Day guest list, you must at least join me in a toast, here in London, to our bank's illustrious founder.'

Woodcock was well aware that, as a mere Englishman, he had reached the pinnacle of his career at the old-fashioned Italian bank: he would never be 'fortunate' enough to be invited to the hallowed Founder's Day service, which took place every September in some fancy Florentine church. Still, that did not stop him being eligible for an annual bonus, based on 'performance'. So, although his usual tipple was a pint of bitter rather than white wine, he took up his glass with gusto.

'To Averardo de' Bianchi: may he rest in peace!' declared the count.

'Everard dee Banki!' Woodcock echoed with a hearty slurp of the free booze, relieved that the count had volunteered the founder's name, since he had not the slightest idea who the bank's founder was: it was all ancient history to him. All he knew was that, at the beginning of each year, the bank's chairman would announce the date of the Founder's Day and, on that day, every branch of the bank throughout the world would close. 'Bloody waste of time and money!' as far as Woodcock could see.

And that was a sentiment privately shared by virtually all the bank's senior executives, in Florence and London alike, as the count knew only too well. But he was not concerned. In fact, he was delighted that his colleagues had such scant regard for history. Otherwise they might have questioned why the original date of the bank's founding (on 27 September 1397, being the feast day of the founding family's patron saints) had been moved to coincide with the autumnal equinox. But that was all part of the master plan. Shortly after the family's expulsion from Florence by the Pope and his supporters in 1494, the count's forefather, the chancellor of Florence at the time, had secretly resurrected the defunct bank. At first, it was just a small finance house on the Via Porta Rossa, supposedly established by a fictitious merchant-adventurer, 'Averardo de' Bianchi', a name concocted from the founding family's primogenitor and the Bianchi – a Renaissance nickname for the mercantile nouveaux riches. But now, half a millennium later, the bank had finally achieved a status worthy of its true parentage, and soon the real purpose behind its resurrection would be revealed to an astonished world. Nothing and no-one would be allowed to interfere with that.

'Do you like the wine, Woodcock?' Scala enquired. 'It is a Vermentino di Bolgheri from the Guado al Tasso estate of the Antinori family. They have been making wine in Tuscany since the twelfth century.'

'Really? Well, it's certainly aged well,' Woodcock chortled, presuming that a shared drink signalled an invitation to greater familiarity. The count's pursed lips should have told him that his attempt at bonhomie had not found favour, but Woodcock was too eager not to lose the moment. 'By the way,' he said as casually, as if he were talking to an old golfing buddy, 'I'm throwing a little dinner party for some of our best London traders at my place tomorrow evening. Why don't you join us? It would be a great opportunity for you to get to know us Brits a bit better.'

Scala winced. He had no desire to get to know Woodcock and his cronies any better than he had to. He had his own man in London: the one who had effected the fraud which the troublesome Mr Talbot had stumbled upon. 'You are too kind, Woodcock. But regrettably I have to return to Firenze this afternoon to prepare for the Founder's Day service tomorrow.'

Woodcock was crestfallen but made light of it. 'Well, I do hope you haven't set your watch by that weird clock on the stairs. The double seven is like something out of Lewis Carroll.' For a moment he thought he detected a tremor of unease in the count's chill features, but it quickly passed.

'Ah, yes, the clock.' Scala nodded, glancing at the solitaire ring on his right hand. 'I was told that the eight was replaced by seven to allow the Duke of Wellington, who was habitually late for dinner, to claim that he was in fact early.' Woodcock chuckled: the duke was obviously a man after his own heart. Then Scala added as an afterthought: 'But I think perhaps the clockmaker had something else in mind.'

'Oh?'

'Yes. You see, eight is an esoteric symbol for eternity. What clock could possibly measure that?' A gong sounded somewhere beyond the drawing room's doors. Scala snatched up his briefcase. 'I must go. The talk is about to start.'

Woodcock made to get up as well but the count patted him back. 'No, no, Woodcock, per favore. Stay and finish your drink, I insist. You deserve it.'

'Most kind, Count Scala, most kind,' Woodcock gushed, adding with a sly wink: 'And of course I'll keep you posted on any "developments".' Scala inclined his head and waved his loyal minion goodbye.

Woodcock relaxed. A self-satisfied grin larded his face as he emptied his wine glass and helped himself to a top-up. He relished the thought that, however high and mighty the count might act, it was he, Max Woodcock, who was now privy to secret knowledge of the bank's innermost workings. And knowledge, as Max well knew from his years in the City, was the key to power. Sure, he had not been born with a silver spoon in his mouth, but he was nobody's fool. He had taken photocopies of Talbot's report – and of the letter in that sealed package he had steamed open. They were both safely tucked away in his desk, along with numerous other compromising documents he had acquired over the years, ready to be hauled out when the time was ripe.

Woodcock checked his watch: it was nearly one o'clock. If he hurried he could just catch the 1.25pm to Guildford. He awarded himself a rare half-day off: 'In honour of old Everard the banker.' He would have lunch in the Pullman dining car and get to Worplesdon in time for a quick round of golf before driving the short distance home. As he got up to leave, he noticed the newspaper which the count had cast aside, still open on the page he had been reading so avidly. It had a large photograph of the pyramids on it. Salivating with anticipation, Woodcock scoured the newsprint for that nugget of financial insight which was surely the only thing that could have grabbed the undivided attention of the bank's chairman. But his excitement subsided as he found the entire page to be devoted to the story of a three-thousand-year-old mummy from which undamaged DNA had been successfully extracted. 'So what?' he huffed, chucking the paper back on the floor and fleeing the Athenaeum's rarefied atmosphere.

It was as he crossed the concourse at Waterloo station that Woodcock began to feel dizzy. At first, he put it down to the count's heady wine. But then the pavement started to spin; nausea churned his stomach, and his heart throbbed against his ribs. He tottered and swayed like a drunk before the sharpest pain he had ever felt engulfed him. Crying out in agony, he sank to his knees and keeled over. An off-duty nurse ran to his aid. With the help of another passer-by, she managed to roll him into the recovery position. She felt for a pulse, but there was none. 'Someone call an ambulance!' she screamed as she gave him the kiss of life. But, after a minute or so, she stopped. It was no good.

Woodcock's dilated pupils stared at the small crowd that had now gathered round in morbid curiosity. He was dead, seemingly the result of a massive heart attack. He was overweight, middle-aged, smelling of alcohol and rushing for the train. Classic indicators. No reason to suspect foul play. The post mortem would be routine; the death certificate would confirm the obvious diagnosis. No trace would be found of the odourless, colourless poison, a favourite concoction of Maître René, Catherine de' Medici's obliging parfumier, which Scala had surreptitiously dripped into Woodcock's glass before he arrived. Max's knowledge of secret things would perish with him and, whatever material rewards such knowledge might otherwise have bestowed, it afforded not a crumb of solace at the moment of his demise.

3

THE CARRIAGE DOORS banged behind the last of the passengers on board the delayed 5.20pm to Bristol. Tom half-opened his leaden eyelids, roused for a moment from his ruminations on the day's traumatic events. His head ached, as did his feet. After being chucked out of the bank, he had spent hours wandering around the City, racking his brain for answers: how far did the fraud extend? Should he go to the police? Where was his evidence? Where was his career? Despair had led him to The Red Herring and an unaccustomed single malt, followed by another at Hennessy's and another at Balls Brothers. It was almost six by the time he got to Paddington, but he was still in time for the Bristol train, 'delayed due to signal failure' in darkest Berkshire. 'At least some things don't change,' he thought. Chancing on a pair of unoccupied seats, he had collapsed on the one by the window and slung his briefcase on the one beside him. As his eyes closed again, he succumbed to the alcoholic drowsiness which the rhythmic lullaby of train on track would hopefully soon ripen into sleep.

'Hello, Tommy Talbot.'

He woke up with a start. Seated opposite, an old man, dressed like a Tibetan monk, fixed him with a piercing gaze. 'I'm sorry,' he blinked, 'what did you say?'

'Where does Tommy think he's going?' the old man demanded.

Tom's head felt like sawdust. He was in no mood to be interrogated by some weirdo in a peaked hat and purple robe. 'Look,' he said, 'I don't know who you are but...'

'I am Rinpoche, of course,' the monk replied, as if this were the stupidest question he had ever heard.

Tom wondered if the guy was on drugs or just unhinged. 'Go away and annoy someone else, will you?'

But the monk took no notice. 'In the next carriage up,' he said, 'another young man, from Libya, is sitting in seat 24A.' Tom folded his arms and shut his eyes. Maybe now this nuisance would get the message. The monk squinted at an oversized gold watch which dangled from his bony wrist. 'In two minutes', he continued, 'this train will leave. Twenty-eight minutes later, at six-thirty, the Angel of Death will appear with fiery mane and silver skull.' Now Tom was sure the man was a nutcase. 'At six-thirty-six, as the train approaches Reading station, the Libyan will hurry to the last carriage. He will wash his hands in the toilet, say a prayer and tap a number into his mobile phone.' The monk paused, letting a moment's silence lend gravity to his next words: 'At six-thirty-nine precisely, the bomb in the blue holdall he left under his seat will detonate.'

Tom reopened his eyes. The old man was so calm, so matter-of-fact. Maybe he was not just a nutter: maybe he was a psychopath in cahoots with a bomber? But a psychopath dressed as a Tibetan monk? That was too ludicrous. Then it struck him: this was all some elaborate hoax. The whole thing, right from his inexplicable sacking that morning to this weird encounter on the train home. It was all one big set-up, part of some new employee evaluation programme dreamt up by the bank's dreaded human resources department. 'Okay,' he chuckled, 'I get it now. You can drop the Dalai Lama impression. How much is the bank paying you for this Oscar-winning performance?'

But the monk was not laughing. 'Life is a series of choices, Tommy boy,' he said. 'Here is yours. Option one: get off the train now and run away to safety and eternal regret. Option two: do nothing and die within the hour. Option three: accept the call of destiny.'

A hand tapped Tom's shoulder. He looked up. A scruffy student, in a soaking wet parka with the hood still up, was hovering over the aisle seat next to him. 'Anyone sitting here, mate?' he asked accusingly, as rainwater dripped from his threadbare rucksack onto Tom's designer-label briefcase. Exhaling his irritation, Tom heaved his briefcase into the overhead rack. The student unzipped his parka and crashed out on the empty seat. Tom turned to resume his exchange with the mystery monk. 'What the…' he gasped when all that met his eyes was a pinstriped City gent who gave him a puzzled stare. Tom cleared his throat and looked away. 'Shouldn't have had that last double Scotch at Balls Brothers,' he thought, as the monk and his musings were filed away under alcoholic hallucinations.

The train squealed into motion and the lights of Paddington receded into the gloom. Other, more pressing, matters crowded Tom's brain: how would he find another job? The bank might be persuaded to give him a reference, since they did not want this scandal to come out, but it would not be a glowing testimonial, that was for sure. Anyway, why should he have to go begging to the bank that had so unjustly sacked him? Surely he would have a cast iron case for unfair dismissal? But what about the evidence that someone had clearly gone to a lot of trouble to fabricate against him: how would he explain that? Who was the real culprit? He needed a lawyer. He had several friends who worked for big City practices. He would call one of them first thing in the morning.

He was drifting off to sleep again when a jarring staccato sound jolted him back to consciousness. A statuesque redhead strode through the automatic door next to the student, stabbing the floor with six-inch stilettos. A dizzying whiff of musk wafted over him as she stalked down the aisle, gold bracelets jangling, crimson talons flicking her long, glossy tresses. When she reached the door at the far end of the carriage, she stopped and looked back for a second, smiling at the swell of ogling that always attended her passage. Tom too was transfixed, but not by her looks. His eyes were riveted on the bulbous silver skull which hung from her neck and the words blazoned in rhinestones on the lapels of her black leather jacket: 'Hell's Angel'. Could this be the monk's 'fiery-maned Angel of Death'? He checked his watch: it was exactly six-thirty.

The train's tannoy crackled into life: they would shortly be arriving at Reading. The student jumped up, intent on beating the queue to get off. As he threw his rucksack over his shoulder and sped down the aisle, a slip of paper fluttered onto Tom's lap. It was a flyer for some lecture or other. Tom called after him but he was already beyond earshot.

The train started to slow into the last half mile before the station as the glow of street lights illumined the darkness outside the carriage window. Tom told himself to get a grip. The redhead model had been just that, a model. The Tibetan monk was just a bad dream, a figment of booze and stress. Premonitions were for little old ladies who read the horoscopes in fashion magazines. He tried to relax, watching with mild amusement as a group of doddery pensioners readied themselves to disembark, fiddling with recalcitrant raincoats and fussing over bulging shopping bags. Then the automatic door at the other end of the carriage slid open once again.

Hopes of the stunning model making a repeat appearance evaporated as a clean-shaven young man of North African extraction entered. He stared dead ahead, avoiding all eye contact. Slipping past the pensioners, he hastened towards Tom's end of the carriage. Odd, Tom thought, that the guy should be moving to the back of the train when they were approaching the station. As he reached Tom's seat, the train wobbled over a point and he put out a hand to steady himself. The hand was clutching a mobile phone. Tom checked his watch again: it was 6.36pm. 'Oh my God,' he gulped, 'it's the Libyan!' What were the monk's three options: escape, die, or act? The first had expired; the second did not appeal. He had just three minutes to take the third. The Libyan had already disappeared through the rear carriage door. Tom had to go forwards and find the bomb – fast.

'Bloody lunatic!' shouted an old codger standing in the aisle as Tom leapt to his feet and made for the forward door. Bursting into the next coach like one possessed, the other passengers stared in alarm as he darted from row to row, madly examining the seat numbers on the luggage racks. 1A, 1B, 1C. 'Damn!' he was at the wrong end of the carriage. He barged his way as fast as he could down the congested aisle. 6D, 9E, 13C – green Harrods bag, grey mackintosh, brown Gladstone, black pilot's case, all noted and dismissed. 19A, 20A: he was getting closer. Here were two striped canvas sacks bursting at the seams and bearing airline tags. A jacket hung down beneath the sacks obscuring the seat number. More shopping bags, missing seat numbers. A rucksack and the number 26D below it: he had gone too far. What time was it? 6.38pm. He stepped back a row. Two orthodox Jews sporting skullcaps and wispy dreadlocks had scriptures spread out on a table. An elderly lady sat opposite them. The seat next to her was vacant. Tom ducked under the table and peered into the shadows: something bulky was stuffed under the seat. He lunged forwards. The rabbis frowned; the old dear clasped her handbag. He grabbed the object and yanked it into the light: it was a blue holdall.

The train's intercom crackled again: 'Reading. This is Reading.'

Empty sidings rolled into view outside the windows. In a few seconds they would reach the platform. There was no time to think. Knocking a bemused City trader for six and scattering a gaggle of West End secretaries like ninepins, he launched himself and the holdall in a single bound to the end of the carriage. The student was standing in the external vestibule; he had already lowered the window of the exit door and had a hand on the outside handle, ready to open it as soon as the automatic lock was released. Pointing frantically at the holdall, Tom shouted 'bomb!'. The student rapidly stepped aside. Tom was just about to throw the holdall out of the opened window and into the last of the empty sidings when he felt an arm coil round his neck. Instinctively, he rammed an elbow into his assailant's ribs. The arm lost its grip. He spun round: it was the Libyan. Tom's intervention had somehow disrupted the phone signal. The Libyan had rushed back when the bomb had failed to detonate. But now he was on his mobile again: one jab and, at this range, the signal was bound to get through. The holdall was balanced half-in, half-out of the window. Tom gave it an almighty shove.

There was a blinding flash, followed by a deafening bang. The train shuddered; the lights went out. A hail of nails and ball bearings struck the carriage. A piece of shrapnel shot past Tom's head, missing him by millimetres. The train's brakes screeched as if in sympathy with the screams of its passengers. Moments later, the wounded juggernaut ground to a halt at Reading station.

Pandemonium erupted. Tom realised at once that he had to get away. He had no credible explanation for his knowledge of the bomb. 'Well, you see, officer, there was this guy dressed like the Dalai Lama who appeared to me and told me what was going to happen…' And what about the money the bank would say he had siphoned off abroad: all part of an Al Qaeda money laundering operation no doubt.

The crowds were pouring off the train and stampeding through the ticket barriers. No-one was stopping them; no-one could have stopped them. Tom joined in the throng. As he squeezed through the turnstile he suddenly caught a glimpse of the Libyan just a few yards ahead. He could not just let him escape to try again another day. He dodged through the crowd until he was right behind his quarry.

They were now on the street outside the station. The Libyan was about to cross the road towards the bus terminus. As he stepped off the kerb Tom stuck his foot out in front of him. The Libyan stumbled. Tom jumped onto his back and flattened him to the ground. The would-be killer groaned as blood streamed from a deep graze on his forehead where it had hit the tarmac. Tom looked around for help: there were some taxi drivers standing on the other side of the road. 'Oi,' he called, 'give us a hand! I've caught the bomber.'

Two of the taxi drivers ran to his aid but, just as they reached him, the Libyan lashed out, catching his left eye with a glancing blow. Tom reeled backwards but the cabbies grabbed his opponent before he could escape. 'You'll 'ave a real shiner there tomorrow, pal!' chortled one of them.

Tom rubbed his bruised cheek. He told the cabbies to keep hold of the bomber while he went to fetch the police. As he raced off down the nearest side street, he hoped that the Libyan would soon find himself being questioned at Paddington Green. But that was no longer his problem. His problem was how to wake up from this nightmare.

4

New York – 21 September 2005

MIRANDA MADDINGLEY SKIPPED triumphantly down the
steps of the US Bankruptcy Court for the Southern
District of New York. Against all the odds, she had persuaded
the chief judge to grant financial protection to her client, an
oil company incorporated in Saint Petersburg but owned by
a Russian billionaire living in Manhattan. He was the subject
of a politically motivated attempt by the Russian government
to force his company into bankruptcy and thus effectively
nationalise it. For Miranda this was not only a significant
legal first which would be reported in glowing terms in the
New York press, but it would surely also seal the deal on her
partnership bid. Ever since joining the prestigious law firm of
Delaney & Pratt three years earlier, she had set her sights on
becoming the youngest female lawyer ever to make partner in
the 125-year history of the firm. Even before today's success,
she was already well on her way to achieving that goal. A

highly regarded associate of the firm, she had come top of her class at Harvard Law School, and now routinely worked one hundred-hour weeks to become the firm's star performer in corporate bankruptcy and restructuring.

To celebrate her victory Miranda decided that a small treat was in order. She crossed the street to her favourite coffee shop, sat at her usual table by the window and ordered a warm strawberry jam doughnut and large cappuccino. Then she turned on her Blackberry. When attending court, the rules required that all mobile devices be switched off. Normally, however, she would keep her Blackberry on at all times, even in the bathroom. It was vital not to miss a client's call for help; if you did, your dear colleagues could confidently be relied upon to snap him up. She scrolled through the usual dross of emails: travel deals, seminars on the latest laws of Outer Mongolia, and yet another update from some junior typist confirming to all and sundry that Mary-Lou (whoever she was) and her new baby Angelina (7lb 4oz) were doing just fine. Miranda exhaled impatiently: for her, marriage and children were a long way down the road.

A waitress brought over the coffee and doughnut. Miranda was about to put her Blackberry back in its leather holder and take a sip of the chocolate-topped cappuccino when her mobile's familiar jingle – 'Hail to the Chief' – rang out. The screen flashed up an out-of-town number which she did not recognise. 'Maddingley,' she announced crisply.

'Would that be Miss Miranda Maddingley of Messrs. Delaney & Pratt?' a male voice enquired in an unctuous Southern drawl.

'Yes, this is she.'

'Ah, good morning, ma'am. Your secretary gave me your number. I trust this is not an inopportune moment?'

'That depends on what you want,' Miranda answered guardedly. Unsolicited calls from 'wealth management consultants' touting tax-free offshore funds were the price of success on Wall Street.

'Oh, don't you worry, Miss Maddingley,' the soapy Southerner reassured her, 'I'm not trying to sell you anything. The name's Winslowe, Kenneth Winslowe. I'm a probate lawyer down in Newport, Tennessee.'

There was a pregnant pause. 'Yes?' Miranda prompted. She hated being kept in suspense.

'It's concerning your uncle, Mr Edward P. Maddingley III. I'm very sorry to have to apprise you of his recent demise.'

Miranda put a hand to her lips. She was not so much shocked as surprised by this news. She had last seen her uncle at her father's funeral, three years earlier, when he looked in pretty good shape for a man in his eighth decade. Since then, he had taken to sending her a card at Christmas, but that was all. He had always been a fairly remote figure in her life. Her father, who was his much younger, and much poorer, little brother, had always accused Uncle Ted of being a skinflint. The two men were not close. There had been some family rift long before Miranda was born. Nevertheless, her father could never understand why Ted, rich and childless as he was, had not helped his only niece through college. Miranda, for her part, could not have cared less. She was an only child and her own woman; what others did with their money was a matter for them. She would never stoop to moral blackmail to try to force someone to give with a grudging heart. Still, the news of her wealthy uncle's 'demise' did cause her a frisson of guilty anticipation. 'Oh… I see. When… how did it happen?'

Winslowe explained that he had had a serious heart attack three weeks earlier and passed away in his sleep the previous Saturday night. 'I know this must come as a terrible shock to you, Miss Maddingley, but your uncle gave express instructions that you were not to be informed of his illness. He was – How shall I put it? – somewhat eccentric.' A fair description, Miranda thought; at least it was if her father's opinion were anything to go by. Still, she did feel a pang of regret that he had died alone, without family around him, and that pang manifested itself in irritation at her uncle's choice of lawyer. Who was he, this dinosaur from a bygone era, with his fusty bedside manner and cloying delicacy?

'I assume then that you're calling me as my uncle's only surviving relative,' she responded brusquely. 'Am I the executor of his estate?'

'Well, no, Miss Maddingley, I'm afraid you're not…'

'Not his executor?'

'Not his only surviving relative.'

Now here was something Miranda really did find shocking. She listened closely – her impatience abated – as Winslowe told her about another uncle named Jack: Ted's elder brother. She had never heard of him but he seemed to have had a pretty colourful life. He had gone travelling in Europe shortly before the outbreak of World War II. Apparently, he had ended up in Italy and got involved with Mussolini and his Blackshirts. By the time the war ended, he had disappeared, presumed dead. However, it had recently come to light that he had survived, found work as a jobbing actor, married an Italian and had a son. 'Your cousin, Frankie, Miss Maddingley.'

As she digested the startling news that she had a previously undreamt-of Italian cousin, Winslowe informed her that there were a couple of other things they needed to discuss. 'They're rather delicate matters. Best if we speak in person.' Having arranged to meet the following evening at the Plaza Hotel on Fifth Avenue, where he would be attending a conference, Winslowe signed off. Miranda gazed at her untouched doughnut and cold cappuccino. The Plaza? Probate must pay a hell of a lot better than she had imagined.

5

Tom's Audi TT sport (bought for the initials as much as the performance) grunted to a halt outside the red-brick garage adjoining his parents' cottage. As the car's indicators winked goodnight, he stretched, drinking in the cool, pre-dawn air. It had taken forever to find a taxi to ferry him the seventy-odd miles from Reading to Bristol Parkway, where he had left his car the previous day. Endless queues had blocked the exit roads out of Reading as police cordons and wailing ambulances held up the traffic. It had been a similar story at Bristol, where the streets were clogged with commuters whose trains had been cancelled. But now, as his shoes crunched on the gravel path of his old home, its ivy-clad walls bathed in gentle moonlight, he finally felt able to relax. A hot shower and soft bed beckoned. He went to insert his key into the front door but it swung open at his touch.

He stepped cautiously over the threshold; an unfamiliar draught greeted him. As he switched the hall light on, the door to the dining room banged shut. Heart pounding, he turned the doorknob. A crack of light penetrated the inner gloom: something moved at the back of the room. Throwing the door wide open, he saw the velvet curtains on the French windows billowing in the breeze. The panes were shattered: he had been burgled. He dashed back across the hall into the study. A sickening sight confronted him: furniture had been upended, family photos smashed, books and files strewn across the floor. The display cabinet which had housed his father's prized collection of oriental snuff bottles was bare. The emptied drawers of the writing bureau gaped mutely. He turned to the corner where he had installed his computer: it was gone.

'The perfect end to a perfect day!' he groaned, sinking onto his father's old captain's chair and swivelling round, surveying the chaos. As the chair slowed, he pressed his foot to the floor to launch into another dazed rotation, but his shoe slid sideways. There was a dark red smear on the polished wood parquet. He poked his fingertip into the sticky, viscous liquid: 'Blood!' he gasped. A trail of red spots led him back into the dining room and the broken French windows. 'Jasper!' he called into the darkness. Nothing. He ran across the lawn to the low wall that separated the formal garden from what his mother had disparagingly referred to as 'the Wilderness': half an acre of weeds and long grass, interspersed with saplings of silver birch and wild cherry. Jasper would spend his days here, patrolling the boundary hedgerows, on the lookout for wild rabbits and farm cats, neither of which, in his tenth year, he had any hope catching. Tom called out again. Nothing. He jumped the wall and stood stock-still, straining his senses for the merest movement, the slightest sound. Dawn was just breaking when he spotted a curious glint in the middle of the Wilderness. Tramping through the damp vegetation, he came upon a stone pillar, half-hidden in the undergrowth and crowned by a battered copper sundial. Drops of dew, sparkling in the sun's first rays, dripped like verdigris tears onto the body lying motionless beside it.

'Jasper!' he cried as he reached down to touch the dog's thick, wheaten coat. A patch of matted blood marked the spot where the fatal blade had struck. He dropped to his knees, hugging the limp pile of fur that he had loved more than he knew, breathing in that old familiar scent of fresh grass and dusty earth. Suddenly the massive head lifted, revealing fearsome canines stained red from goring the intruder's flesh. Big brown eyes opened one last time and looked straight into those of their speechless master. Then the head slumped back and Jasper was no more.

It took over an hour to dig the grave. When he had finished, Tom leant, exhausted, on his shovel. Lack of food, lack of sleep and the strain of the last twenty-four hours finally overcame him. He tottered backwards and caught his head on the baleful column that now served as Jasper's headstone.

***

It was past midday when Tom recovered consciousness. The mellow autumn sunshine warmed his stiff limbs. He felt the bump on his head: it was sore, but not bleeding. His lips were dry and his mouth parched. Still groggy, he stretched out a hand to lever himself upright. Something jabbed against his palm. At first he thought it was a stone but, on closer inspection, it turned out to be a cufflink with a broken spindle. It lay just a few inches from the spot where he had discovered Jasper's body. Turning it between his fingers, he could see that it was no ordinary cufflink: weightily crafted in gold, it boasted a hexagonal shield with seven balls, six red and one blue one in the middle that sported a golden fleur-de-lis. The design reminded him of the faded shield above the doors of the bank he had noticed the previous morning. Coincidence? he wondered. The burglar had taken his father's snuff bottles, but he had also stolen his computer – which had contained a copy of the fraud report he had sent to Woodcock.

Tom struggled to his feet and returned to the cottage, intent on calling the police. It was only when he got inside that he focussed on the small matter of the bomb. That could not possibly have been anything to do with the bank. If they had wanted to get rid of him permanently there were far less spectacular ways of going about it. But it did pose a serious problem in terms of contacting the authorities. He did not know whether they were yet aware of his involvement and, if they were, how they viewed it. Was he still an anonymous commuter or a terror suspect? He sighed: his head hurt and his stomach demanded attention. He retreated to the kitchen. Having devoured a plate of baked beans, he turned on the television and watched the one o'clock news over a mug of hot coffee.

Film footage of mangled tracks and a battered railway carriage flashed up as the newscaster reported that a Libyan national had been detained in connection with the bombing of a Great Western train at Reading last night. Twenty-one people were injured, none seriously. That was the good news.

The bad news was that the police were anxious to trace a second man who was seen with the suspect. Tom's heart sank. It sounded as if he had been helping the damned bomber rather than trying to stop him. Those cabbies at Reading station must have got suspicious when he did not come back. They would have given the cops his description – as would that student who actually witnessed him carrying the exploding holdall. How could the cops not suspect him? Probably the bomber himself was even now pointing the finger at him: it was he who had been trying to stop Tom, not vice versa. He took a deep breath and told himself to keep calm. 'Okay, so they've got your description, but so what? It all happened so quickly, the descriptions are bound to be pretty vague. There must be thousands of yuppies like you commuting to and fro to London every day in their regulation suits and ties. The police are looking for a needle in a haystack. No, even with a description, they are no nearer knowing who you are or where you live.' The knot in his stomach began to unwind; he gulped down the last of the coffee. But then another thought bubbled up: what about the taxi he took to Bristol. Would the driver recognise the description, vague though it might be? Had he said or done something to arouse suspicion? No, he had said very little and snoozed most of the way. The cabby had dropped him off at the station car park and driven away. No, wait, he had not left immediately – he had stopped in a lay-by near the barrier. Tom had driven past him as he exited the car park: 'God, did he clock my registration number?'

His imagination went into overdrive. What was that helicopter doing, buzzing so low across the valley? Was that a car pulling up outside? Were those footsteps on the gravel path? He had to get away. He reached for his car keys, but that was no good: if the police did have his registration number, or even just the make and colour of his car, he risked being stopped. But what was the alternative? He could not get far on foot and there were no buses in this rural backwater. He would have to chance it and call a taxi. The local directory was kept by the phone in the study. Despite the chaos wrought by the burglar, the directory was still in place. Tom quickly looked up the number of a local firm. But, as he put the receiver to his ear, he could hear no dialling tone: the phone wire had been cut. He reached for his mobile, but the holster on his belt was empty. Then he remembered: his mobile was in his briefcase. And his briefcase? He slapped his forehead in disbelief: he had left it on the train.

Despair set in. The game was up. It was only a matter of time before the police matched his unclaimed briefcase with the man they were so anxious to trace. And the mobile would lead them straight to him. Cursing his luck, he kicked the leg of the captain's chair, which was sent spinning on its castors and crashed into a small table, knocking a silver photo frame onto the floor. The glass cracked, disfiguring an old photograph of him as a baby. As he bent down to pick it up, a much smaller photograph slipped out from the back of the frame. Tom found himself looking at three strangers: a young man in a boater and blazer, and two young women. But, wait, who was that behind them? No, it couldn't be!

6

A NOTICE IN THE Plaza's glitzy lobby announced the National Association of Probate Lawyers' Annual Conference and Charity Ball. Miranda felt distinctly underdressed in her sober black skirt and jacket, as she squeezed through the maze of tuxedos and evening gowns. When she eventually made it to the Oak Bar, Winslowe waved to her. 'Ah, Miss Maddingley, a pleasure to meet you at last,' he gushed, admiring her flowing chestnut hair and bright, hazel eyes. 'The photograph on your firm's website doesn't do you justice. Can I get you a drink?'

Miranda did not reciprocate the flattery. Winslowe looked exactly as he sounded over the phone: slick, fat and slippery. 'Sparkling mineral water will be fine, thank you,' she replied, perching demurely on the bar stool next to his and taking care to tuck her long legs well beneath the counter.

Winslowe motioned to the bartender and ordered a Perrier. 'May I first of all extend my deepest personal condolences, Miss Maddingley,' he began. 'It must be very upsetting…'

'Mr Winslowe,' she cut in, 'I'm a bankruptcy attorney; you're a probate lawyer. We're both in the business of unhappy endings. So, please, spare me the exequious patter and tell me what was so "delicate" that you couldn't mention it over the phone.'

He gave her a wry smile and took a slug of the Jack Daniel's he'd been nursing when she arrived. He proceeded to relate the details of her deceased uncle's estate. He had inherited the Maddingley family business, Dolphin Enterprises Inc., in the aftermath of World War II. It was just a small trading company then, but her uncle had turned it into a multi-million-dollar import–export corporation. By the time of his death his personal shareholding was valued at $75 million 'net of tax'.

Miranda almost choked on her Perrier. She had expected her uncle to have a million or two stashed away, maybe a little more. But $75 million? That was seriously rich.

Winslowe drank another shot of Tennessee rye: now for the hard part. 'You recall I mentioned yesterday your cousin Frankie?'

She nodded. Of course she remembered the news that she was not the only surviving member of the Maddingley clan. She had actually been intrigued to learn of an exotic Italian branch to the family and was quite sanguine at the prospect of having to share her uncle's estate. After all, $75 million was more than enough for two. Winslowe applauded her generosity but unfortunately there was more to it than that. Following his heart attack, her uncle had altered his will, not just to include his new-found nephew but to make him the sole beneficiary. Miranda did not get a dime.

'Frankie!' she exploded, causing the barman to give her a quizzical look. 'But that's ridiculous,' she said, swiftly lowering her voice. 'I thought you said Uncle Ted lost touch with his elder brother sixty years ago. How could he have suddenly changed his will and left everything to some Italian who appeared out of the blue, claiming to be his nephew? It's complete and utter madness!'

'Miranda – you don't mind me calling you by your first name, I hope?' Winslowe soothed. 'I've been in this business a long time and I've seen people do the strangest things when the grim reaper comes knocking. I'd been your uncle's lawyer for over twenty years. I helped him, though I say so myself, through some pretty tough times. He worked damned hard for his success and I admired him for that. But after the heart attack he changed, changed completely. Curious thing, though,' he added, scratching his smoothly shaven jowls.

'What?'

'Oh, just that his housekeeper swore that he suffered his heart attack right after he got off the phone with Frankie. I guess the shock was too much for him.'

Frankie was beginning to sound like bad news all round, Miranda thought to herself. And this impression only strengthened as the probate practitioner droned on about medical certification of the deceased's mental capacity and his specific instructions not to notify his niece of his illness, nor to investigate Frankie's bona fides, but to do everything necessary as quickly as possible to ensure a smooth transfer of the estate to his long-lost nephew. 'You don't mean to say that Frankie has already got his mitts on my uncle's money, do you?'

Winslowe whirled the ice cubes around the bottom of his glass. 'Well, no, not quite yet,' he said vaguely. 'But it's only a matter of time. Just some minor formalities to be completed.'

Miranda felt sick. She had unknowingly been the heiress to a fortune, only to have it snatched away by some foreigner who, as far as she could see, had all the hallmarks of a classic conman. How could such a successful businessman as her uncle have been so easily duped? 'So, let me get this straight, Kenneth,' she said, spitting his name out like a mouthful of corked wine. 'Your client gave away $75 million bucks to some guy in Italy he'd never met on the strength of a single phone call?'

Winslowe's eyes darted towards the exit. His conference colleagues were filing into the ballroom. 'I'm sorry, Miss Maddingley, but I'm afraid I have a dinner engagement. I've told you all there is to tell.'

Miranda grabbed his arm. 'Not yet you haven't. What about the funeral? When is it? Will dear Cousin Frankie be there as mourner-in-chief? I'd so love to meet him.'

Winslowe hurriedly downed the last drop of Jack Daniel's. 'Funeral was last Monday. No mourners. Your uncle's strict instructions.' Pulling his arm free of Miranda's grasp, he slithered off the bar stool.

'But I have to talk to Frankie,' she pleaded. 'How do I contact him?'

'This is all I have,' he replied, taking a slip of paper from his wallet and handing it to her. 'Take my advice, Miss Maddingley,' he added darkly. 'Don't try to contact your cousin. Sometimes it's better not to know.' He turned to go, but then paused. 'Oh, I almost forgot, your uncle did leave you one thing.' With a final wave of his hand, he deposited a small, red leather box on top of the bar and left.

Miranda watched, shell-shocked, as Winslowe scuttled across the lobby and vanished through the double doors into the ballroom, where he would partake of a banquet and call it charity. At length she unfolded the piece of paper he had given her. It was a compliment slip from a law firm in Rome called Studio Legale Albizzi. All it said was: 'Frankie Maddingley, Assistant Archivist, Biblioteca Apostolica Vaticana, Roma.' No phone number, no fax, no email.

She turned her attention to the red leather box on the bar. It looked like a presentation case for a ring, or maybe earrings. Sure enough, when she pressed the little brass pin on the front, the lid popped open to reveal a ring. Disappointingly, it was not made of gold, not even gold plate, but cast in bronze with a chunky, masculine band culminating in a heavy, oval setting. It looked antique. A black, onyx intaglio stood slightly proud of the setting. The engraving depicted two vertical dolphins, in 'S' and reverse 'S' formation, framing dagger-like Christian crosses.

Was it the company seal of Uncle Ted's 'Dolphin Enterprises'? Perhaps. But why leave her this of all things? Why this and nothing else? Nothing about her uncle's death made any sense. She snapped the box shut. Kenneth Winslowe esquire might be used to getting his own way back home in Hicksville, Tennessee, but this was New York and she was not about to give up $75 million bucks without a fight. She would track down the elusive Frankie and uncover the truth, no matter what.

'Excuse me, ma'am,' the barman called after her as she stood up to leave. 'That'll be $20 for the drinks.'

'Gee, thanks, Ken,' she sighed.

7

THERE COULD BE no mistake: there, staring out at Tom from the photograph, was the Tibetan monk he had seen (or dreamt he had seen) on the train. But who were the others: the guy wearing a boater and the two young women in summer dresses, standing next to a sort of spherical sundial? And why had the photo been hidden behind one of him as a baby? He turned it over. There was a note on the back: 'Sophia, Stella and me with Rinpoche by the armillary sphere. Milton, June 1978.'

'Rinpoche' – that was what the monk had called himself, but the other names meant nothing to Tom. He went back into the kitchen and looked up the family address book, which his mother kept on a shelf among assorted recipe books and herbals handed down from mother to daughter across the generations. He drew a blank under 'T' for Talbot and 'P' for Payne (his mother's maiden name), so he tried looking for a 'Sophia' or a 'Stella' under any other surname. But again nothing. Then he noticed an entry that had a line through it but was still legible beneath the crossing out: it read 'Aunt Stella S'. He frowned: as far as he knew, there was no aunt named Stella in the family. The entry gave no surname (apart from the inital 'S') or phone number, but there was an address: '9 Milton Street, Oxford'. Yet, where did that get him? The entry was clearly old and the photo had been taken over twenty-five years earlier. What were the chances of this Aunt Stella person still being alive, let alone still being at that address?

He opened the back door and breathed in the fresh air, pondering his next move. The paved patio was strewn with parched, russet-red leaves from the chestnut tree in the middle of the lawn. The leaves swirled up in a sudden crosswind, raising a cloud of dust and causing him to sneeze violently. Fishing for a tissue in his trouser pocket, he pulled out a piece of paper: it was the flyer which had fallen from the student's knapsack on the train. He must have absent-mindedly stuffed it in his pocket. He perused the crumpled print. It was advertising a lecture entitled 'The Hermetica and The Primavera'. It sounded pretty abstruse but then two names leapt out at him. The lecture was to be held at Milton College, Oxford, and the lecturer was one 'Dame Stella Stockton, Emeritus Professor of Hermetic Philosophy'. He looked at the date: 'Thursday 22 September at 4.15pm'. But that was... today!

***

The timeless bells of Oxford were already striking four as Tom drove across Magdalene Bridge. He was late. What should have been an easy ninety-minute journey had taken over two hours in his mother's battered old Peugeot. He had remembered it was in the garage under a pile of tarpaulin. Road works and Oxford's labyrinthine road system had then conspired to delay him still further. At last he turned into Milton Street and, it seemed, into another era. Tarmac gave way to cobblestones, over which the Peugeot rattled alarmingly, and a sudden downpour engulfed the college's walls in medieval gloom. Parking as close as he could to the porter's lodge, he ran through the rain and tucked in behind a group of other late arrivals.

The lecture theatre was packed. A tall, slim woman with sharp blue eyes was in full flow on the podium. She paused while the latecomers shuffled into the last remaining seats in the topmost tier of the auditorium. 'Time, as I was saying, is of the essence,' she resumed pointedly, to a chorus of muffled laughter. 'Of the essence of the physical plane, that is. But, as Ficino's landmark Latin translation of the Corpus Hermeticum made clear to the intelligentsia of Quattrocento Florence, the soul can, if sufficiently self-disciplined, break free of time and dwell among, if not beyond, the stars.' She signalled to an assistant, and the lights dimmed, allowing the title page of a richly illuminated incunabulum to fill the screen behind her. 'Such ideas concerning the true nature of man,' she continued, 'appealed not only to quasi-humanists like Ficino but also to proto-syncretists like Pico della Mirandola. They mirrored in large degree Neoplatonic, and indeed oriental, beliefs as well as those of certain heterodox Christian sects. By the same token they were, of course, anathema to Rome.'

Though he knew nothing about the subject matter of the lecture, Tom was soon spellbound by the speaker's erudition as well as her bubbly enthusiasm. A feeling of pride also welled up inside as he contemplated his aunt – an Oxford professor, no less – expounding the complexities of ancient texts and their impact on the Renaissance to a clearly captivated audience.

She nodded once again and the image on the screen duly changed. 'Now let us examine these Hermetic themes in the Primavera,' she said, aiming a laser pointer at the new slide. 'Superficially, Sandro Botticelli's masterpiece seems a straightforward depiction, in mythological terms, of the coming of spring. Venus, the goddess of love, stands in benediction at the centre of the scene. To the right, Zephyr, the west wind, blows the pallid, almost bare, earth nymph, Chloris, towards her mother, Flora, the golden-haired, fecund goddess of spring, as she enters an orange grove.'

Tom watched the laser's red dot hopping around the painting. He was struck by the contrast between the demure, Madonna-like figure of Venus, and Flora, who could have been the archetype of every wedding-dress model who had ever appeared in a modern fashion magazine. Bedecked in flowing white dress with pink garlands, and escorted by beautiful bridesmaids ('The Three Graces dancing in a circle in the foreground'), she floated on a carpet of wild flowers towards the handsome, dark-haired groom ('The young god Mercury driving the clouds away with his wand on the left of the picture.'). Yet there was nothing glossy or kitsch about the painting. On the contrary, the more Tom looked at it, the more he felt its extraordinary energy, as if the figures were caught on the very cusp of movement, about to burst into life. He could well believe, as he heard his aunt explain, that the painting was commissioned for a wedding in the Medici family, the fabulously wealthy

Renaissance bankers. He recalled seeing a portrait of the family's patriarch (Cosimo, was it, or some similar-sounding name?) during a management training course at the Banca de' Bianchi's head office in Florence the previous year.

'But remember,' Professor Stockton continued, 'that it was Ficino who guided Botticelli's hand in executing this work and therefore we must go beneath the surface and view it, not with the physical eye but with the mind's eye, as the Hermetic teachings enjoin.'

Now the academic theories flowed thick and fast: from the mythological to the metaphorical, the literal to the allegorical, the obvious to the esoteric. Chloris and Flora became symbols of the soul's journey from wintry death back to spring's rebirth, returning to the ever-circling dance of life, represented by the Three Graces. Meanwhile, the god Mercury was supposed to be there in his capacity as Psychopomp, the Guide of Souls. He apparently bore a likeness to Cosimo de' Medici's grandson, Lorenzo the Magnificent. Similarly, Flora was said to be a famous Florentine beauty with whom both Lorenzo and his brother had fallen in love. However, whilst admiring the meticulous scholarly ingenuity which had clearly been lavished on this one painting over the years, it all sounded pretty far-fetched to Tom.

'And so,' his aunt concluded, 'I leave it to you, the latest generation of scholars, to decide for yourselves the true meaning of the Primavera. For me, the enigma is epitomised in Flora's smile: the only smile Botticelli ever painted on the face of a woman.'

After she had finished and the queue of students plying her with questions had dissipated, Tom went up to introduce himself. 'Excuse me, Professor,' he said, 'my name's Tom Talbot. I believe we're related?'

His aunt brushed back her long, dark hair. Like her flawless skin, it shone with a youthful beauty which Tom, seeing her now close up, found surprising given that she surely had to be approaching fifty if that old photograph of her and the others was taken in 1978. She displayed no emotion as she studied him intently, exploring his thick, wavy locks, his deep-set eyes, the straight ridge of his nose, the jovial curve of his lips, the firm contours of his chin. 'So, Rinpoche is back,' she said at last and smiled at Tom's stunned expression. 'You've much to learn, Tom Talbot,' she said. Then, touching him on the arm, she asked if he knew the young man near the exit who had been staring at them for the last few minutes.

He caught his breath: it was the student from the train. He was talking excitedly into his mobile phone. 'I've got to get out of here!' he blurted.

His aunt picked up the urgency in his voice. 'This way,' she said, pointing to a door marked 'Staff Only'.

8

Aunt Stella took Tom through the lecture theatre's kitchens and out into a sequestered quadrangle. Striding across the lawn with accustomed disdain for a 'Keep Off The Grass' sign, she led him down a narrow hallway to a studded oak door. 'Do sit,' she said as they entered her study.

Looking around for a seat, Tom wondered if the professor's invitation was more of an intellectual challenge. There were books piled everywhere: on the sofa, on both armchairs, even on a three-legged stool. The only unoccupied space seemed to be on a window-seat set into the opposite wall. But as he sat down a long, ginger tail lashed out from behind a curtain and an angry hiss announced its owner's displeasure.

'Marmaduke, you naughty boy!' Aunt Stella scolded the large tomcat, which, disturbed from its afternoon nap, now leapt across Tom's lap and scuttled off beneath the sofa.

'It's ok,' Tom shrugged. 'Cats and I never get on.'

'Well, you wouldn't, would you?' his aunt replied inscrutably. 'So,' she said as she poured them both a dry sherry, 'are you going to tell me why we had to leave the lecture theatre in such a hurry? Is it to do with that bruise below your eye?'

Tom felt his cheek; the bomber's parting gift no longer hurt, but it was obviously still visible. Sipping his sherry, he briefly related the previous day's events, from the weird encounter with Rinpoche to reading the flyer which the student had left on the train. 'And finally,' he said, handing her the photograph which had first put him onto her, 'finding this.' He noticed just the faintest quiver of emotion as his aunt gazed into the past. 'Ah, dear John,' she sighed, sinking onto the arm of the sofa. 'He was engaged to my younger sister, Sophia. That's the three of us standing by the armillary sphere,' she said, pointing to the window.

Tom looked out at the archetypal lawns and flower borders, so characteristic of Oxbridge colleges. The spherical sundial he had seen in the photo stood proudly on a tall rectangular pillar, next to an ancient mulberry tree, propped up on iron stanchions. The dial's arrow-tipped pointer glinted in the evening sun; it reminded him of Jasper's grave. 'Were the three of you studying at Oxford?' he asked.

'John was head of art history and conservation at the Ashmolean Museum. Sophia was one of his students. I was doing my doctorate here at Milton. We were all collaborating on an archive of ancient Buddhist texts and paintings which the explorer Aurel Stein had deposited at Milton before the First World War. He discovered them in caves along the Silk Road.'

'You mean the old trade route between Europe and China, as per Marco Polo?'

'Yes, though Polo's travels were many centuries later.

In fact, John and I were very interested in what Polo had to say, especially about Persia and the Fire-worshippers – Zoroastrians, that is.'

Tom shifted impatiently in his seat. Somewhere nearby a bell was chiming a quarter after six. Fifteen minutes had passed since the student had spotted him in the lecture hall. 'And how did you come across Rinpoche?' he prompted. She said that John had been working late one night in the library and had chanced upon an incense burner buried among the scrolls which Stein had brought back from Dunhuang. 'If only he hadn't lit it,' she sighed, 'he might still be alive today.'

'Was there a fire?'

'No, not a fire.' She brushed the corner of her eye. 'He was shot outside the Uffizi Gallery in Florence, a few weeks after this photograph was taken.'

'Shot?' Tom echoed incredulously. He listened with increasing unease as his aunt explained how John had gone to Italy to assist in preparatory work for a major restoration project involving various old masters, including Botticelli's Primavera. 'The official line was that it was a mugging gone wrong,' she snorted, her voice dripping with scepticism. 'When news of his death reached us, Sophia was inconsolable as well as…' she broke off, unable to bring herself to say the word. Instead, she walked across the room to a side-table on which an antique coromandel writing slope stood. As she opened the lid, a bundle of correspondence, bound in red ribbon, fell out. 'There were post-natal complications,' she said, undoing the ribbon, 'Sophia died a week after giving birth to a little boy.'

Tom downed the remainder of his Amontillado. Odd, he thought, that his parents had never mentioned this family tragedy to him, but then he had never heard of Aunt Stella either. Maybe his mother and his aunt had fallen out years ago and never made up, hence her deletion from his mother's address book. 'What happened to the baby?' he wondered.

His aunt picked out a brown envelope from the unbound bundle of letters. 'Sophia entrusted this to me before she died,' she said, handing the envelope to Tom. 'It was in John's breast pocket when he was shot.'

Tom poked a finger through the neat round hole in the middle of the envelope. A wax seal was fringed with dried blood. It was broken, but the outline of a hound was still visible. It dawned on him that his family connection was not so much with Aunt Stella, but rather with John. 'Talbot' was an old name for a hunting dog, and the pun on his surname was only too familiar from the signboards of many a city tavern and country inn. However, the strange name written on the front of the envelope was not one he recognised at all. 'Who's "Dorje"?' he queried.

'John was a lot older than Sophia,' his aunt replied, side-stepping his question. 'She was far too young for him.' She gave Tom a glare, as if he was somehow to blame for her younger sister's folly. 'When they announced their engagement, our father was furious. He disowned her. After she died, John's brother adopted the baby; his wife couldn't have children, so they brought the little boy up as their own.' She paused and poured Tom some more sherry. 'You're going to need that,' she said.

The sherry glass froze in his hand: he guessed what was coming. And when she confirmed that John's brother's name was the same as that of the man he had always called father, his world shattered before his eyes for the second time in as many days. All the old certainties were gone; every answer had suddenly become a question. The clatter of hobnailed boots in the corridor outside his aunt's study jolted him from his daze.

'Quick, Tom, out the window!' she cried.

He scrambled over the stone sill and onto the lawn below. 'Which way now?' His aunt pointed at the armillary sphere. 'Go over and touch the arrow-tipped gnomon with John's letter,' she ordered, 'then run anticlockwise round to the other side of the stone pedestal.' He looked at her as if she had gone mad. 'Just do it, Tom!' she hissed.

9

New York

MIRANDA SAT UP in a cold sweat. She lit the bedside lamp: it was 3am. The familiar surroundings of her bedroom were reassuring, yet her nightmare was still vivid.

She was on a wooden galleon, like the pirate ships in children's picture books or swashbuckling B-movies, except this one flew a large red cross rather than the skull and crossbones. Dolphins were swimming alongside the ship's bows, forming a tight-packed escort. But they were not the friendly, acrobatic creatures that entertain visitors to marine parks. These dolphins sported grotesque masks with maniacal grins and emitted ear-splitting screams as they leapt above the waves. Miranda, now a little girl again clutching a rag doll, ran through a door and down a flight of stairs, seeking refuge in the captain's cabin. But here another, even stranger, sight awaited her. The body of a young woman lay on a bare table, her face covered in a white shroud, her long golden hair hanging to the floor. Two men in white robes, their faces hidden under hoods, were standing on either side of the corpse, pulling at its lifeless limbs as if in a tug-of-war. Suddenly, a swarm of angry wasps billowed up from the shroud and drove the two men up on deck. As they reached the open air, a dolphin jumped right over the ship's bow, knocking one man into the sea, where the rest of the pod dragged him screaming beneath the waves. The other man rushed to the gunwale, calling to his unfortunate companion but, as he did so, a giant magpie swooped down from the sky and snatched him up in its claws. Cawing and screeching, it carried him off towards the coast. But, when it got to the shore, the man drew a sword and stabbed the monstrous bird, forcing it to release him. He fell onto a sandy beach and dragged himself to his feet. The last thing Miranda could remember was watching him brandish his sword at the water's edge, shouting and cursing as she and the ship and the dolphins disappeared over the horizon.

She slumped back on her pillow, exhausted. She had had nightmares before, of course, especially after late business dinners where blue cheese and port rounded off the evening. But this one was different; it was so real, so intense, and she had not eaten late. Gradually, she relaxed and her eyelids began to sag. As she reached across to turn off the lamp, the old ring her uncle had left her glinted in the little red box which she had left open on the bedside table.

Florence

Count Scala sat apart from the congregation, to the right of the high altar, on a throne normally reserved for the archbishop. His gaze wandered upwards to the choir of Florentine saints that adorned the dome of San Lorenzo. As he listened to the closing benediction of the Founder's Day service, it seemed to be absorbed into the very fabric of the ancient basilica. Slowly, his gaze descended to the congregation of Armani-suited bankers and their trophy wives. He had files on them all. Files packed with the proclivities that gnaw at probity, the peccadilloes that ruin reputation, the passions that destroy lives. The organ struck up the Lux Aeterna and his colleagues took their leave in a procession of deferential nods and false smiles. How they coveted his job. But his was not a job; it was a mission, a mission beyond their wildest imagining. And tonight, he felt sure, that mission would commence its final chapter. The long years he had had to endure this annual charade, this requiem for nobody, were coming to an end. He longed for the real ceremony to begin.

The Prior of San Marco, who traditionally officiated the service, approached wearing the white tunic and black mantle of the Dominican Order. Silent and unsmiling, he made the sign of the cross before vacating the predella and processing down the nave to the west door. As he passed the last in a row of side-chapels he stopped and glanced inside. Scala watched him, but it was another prior whom he saw: a fanatical friar who had gone to the stake centuries earlier on the orders of a corrupt pope. What poetic justice, he mused, that the devil who had single-handedly brought Florence to her knees was burnt in the very same piazza where he had previously consigned half of her books, her music and her paintings to the so-called Bonfire of the Vanities. Was it not on this very day, the Feast of St Matthew, five hundred years ago, that the demon in saintly guise had prophesied the end of the world? Was it not it here, in San Lorenzo, that he had invoked the Sword of God upon the heads of Florence's noblest sons?

Scala's index finger tapped impatiently on the arm of his gilded chair; the diamond solitaire on his ancestral ring flashed in the candlelight. This was the night when that ancient wrong would finally be righted, when the curse of Savonarola would at last be lifted from his beloved city. Yet, neither Savonarola nor the Vatican had achieved their real objective: the recovery – or incineration – of a secret from the dawn of Christianity, the key to the ultimate mystery.

Now the Dominican was at the west door. He turned and looked back at the count, seated like some pagan emperor on the throne of St Peter. Softly, the Dominican recited the prophet Isaiah: 'Woe unto the crown of pride. It shall be trampled underfoot.'

Oxford

Tom could not believe he was actually doing as his aunt had instructed: tapping a sundial with an old envelope and running round behind its plinth. He prayed that anyone observing his antics would presume him to be just another of the potty academics who, he was now convinced, had to be the primary inhabitants of Aunt Stella's world.

The minutes passed. He peeked round the side of the plinth. The window he had jumped out of was now firmly shut and there was no sign of the boys in blue or of anyone else for that matter. In fact, the whole garden had fallen silent: no bird, no bell, no breath of air disturbed the stillness. His thoughts turned to the letter; a letter written before he was born, by a father he had never known, contained in an envelope handled by a mother whose touch he could not recall. Of all the blows he had suffered these past two days, this was by far the bitterest. The broken seal crumbled in his fingers as he lifted the flap and gently tugged on a blood-spattered sheet of paper. The writing was crabbed, as if scribbled in haste:

> '*Soul of my soul,*
>
> *There isn't much time. Rinpoche warned me that my life is in danger. If you are reading this, you will know that he was right.*
>
> *He first appeared to me out of the smoke. He said he had waited two thousand years for me to light those joss-sticks in that ancient censer. He translated one of the scrolls from the Dunhuang Caves. The translation is enclosed. Read it and remember what once you knew. It will seem insane, but the truth must be tested in the forge of courage, not on the anvil of convention.*
>
> *I have found a lock which has no key. It holds the secret to what happened to perhaps the world's most precious treasure, certainly its most dangerous. Yet the time is not ripe. You must take up the baton. Listen to your heart. Follow your destiny. Do not falter or the world is lost.*
>
> *John Talbot, Florence, July 1978.*'

Tom scratched his head. The letter said nothing about the mysterious 'Dorje' to whom the envelope was addressed. Nor did it explain who exactly Rinpoche was. And what lock had no key, what treasure was so precious and yet so dangerous? Maybe the translation of the scroll would shed more light. He opened the envelope again. There were two more sheets of paper inside, both tattered and bloodstained. He teased them into the waning daylight and laid them on the grass, attempting to read the half-obliterated script:

'Alexander... Egyptian Oracle... went in search... ends of the Earth... Heavenly Mountains... forced to turn back... Many years later, in a cave among the clouds, Rinpoche... about to enter Nirvana... entrusted to Yingsel, the devoted... and Dorje, the faithful... casket... symbols... cursed treasure... They to... wise monk Nagasena in the land of King Milinda. But in the trackless Taklamakan... bandits... death... Sogdian merchants... Chang'an... Emperor Wu... embassy to Parthia... gifts to King Mithridates... Augustus sent Ourania, beautiful Etruscan slave, to the court of Great King Phraates... Treachery... theft... Guardians of the Sacred Flame... Persepolis... turn of the kalpa... Guided by Tishtrya... to land of...'

The rest of the first sheet was illegible. He moved on to the second. But, just as he picked it up, a gust of wind snatched it from his hand and blew both the translation and his father's letter across the lawn and up a bank. Tom jumped to his feet and raced after them, ignoring the risk of being spotted by the police in his eagerness to save those precious scraps of paper. But, as he reached the top of the bank, a breeze wafted the frail sheets over a low wall and out of sight. Shouts rang out behind him: 'Come back, Tom! Don't go near the edge!'

But he was already on top of the wall. A chasm-like drop opened up in front of him. The light suddenly faded and the air was ice-cold. His head spun, his legs no longer connected with his feet. Someone screamed: 'Tom, watch out! Beware of Deadman's Walk!'

10

THE THUD OF an iron bolt reverberated in the cavernous
silence of San Lorenzo. Emptied now of its Founder's
Day congregation, vespers' echoes had long since been stilled
in the stony symmetry of its sequestered chapels; only the
martyred or the damned were left to brood on darkness and
decay. Then a flame touched seven candles in seven golden
candlesticks set above the altar, and cast a cowled shadow
down the nave.

A bell tolled the third quarter before midnight. The
shadow descended the predella until, stopping on the bottom
step, it raised a white-robed arm and aimed a long black
wand towards the dome. 'Avanti, Frati della Compagnia
del Diamante!' boomed a gravelly, baritone voice. At once,
six more white-robed figures appeared, three in the north
aisle, three in the south, each bearing a candle, floating like
phantoms between the crepuscular colonnades. On reaching
two bronze pulpits that flanked the transepts, they turned
towards the central crossing. Then, drawing themselves up
on each side of a large square, outlined in black on the marble

pavement, they hailed their summoner: 'Salve, Maestro della Compagnia del Diamante!'

'Brothers of the Company of the Diamond,' declared the maestro, addressing them in heavily accented English, 'we meet, as always, under the aegis of Cosmas and Damian, the patron saints of medicine and of the greatest family ever to tread the blessed streets of Florence. I speak of the Medici: progenitors of popes, fathers of kings, mothers of queens, benefactors of the Renaissance, architects of capitalism, defenders of the dignity and liberty of man. What a debt does mankind owe them.'

'Vivat Domus Medicea! Long live the House of Medici!' chanted the hooded brethren.

'Every year,' the maestro continued, 'on this night, in this place and at this spot, our Brotherhood has gathered for over five centuries, bound by a sacred and unbreakable vow. Neither the fires of the mad dog Savonarola nor the bombs of the retreating Nazis could stop us from keeping faith and remembering. But, though we are Brothers, we are also strangers, for none of us knows the identity of any of the others. Thus it was ordained by our founders in order to preserve and protect our Brotherhood until the appointed hour. As each generation passes, so it is the solemn duty of each Brother to bequeath this great honour and responsibility to his successor. And he must choose that successor on the basis of pre-eminent merit, true friendship and absolute loyalty, on pain of death.' The black wand tapped the cold marble floor, punctuating the air. 'Therefore, Brothers, do we now stand in San Lorenzo, the church of the Medici and the most ancient of Italy's basilicas. A Christian place of worship since the fourth century of Our Lord, it was before that the site of a Roman temple of Demeter and her daughter, Persephone. Their secret mysteries were celebrated here on this very night, the night of the autumnal equinox.' He paused and pointed to the Crucifixion and the Resurrection, sculpted at the behest of the Medici, on Donatello's bronze pulpits. 'They bear a message,' he said, 'a message that this building is the embodiment of an enigma, the mystery of life and death, the riddle that gives meaning to existence and renders all else ultimately futile.'

He let his words fade into silence before raising his wand heavenwards again. 'Let us give thanks to God,' he prayed, 'for the life of Averardo, founder of the Medici dynasty.'

'Deo gratias,' came the response.

'And for the life of our patron, Cosimo, born on the feast day of Cosmas and Damian, above whose hallowed tomb we now humbly stand.'

'Laudamus Dominum.'

'And lastly for Cosimo's grandson, the greatest Medici of all: Lorenzo, Il Magnifico.'

'Gratias Deo in excelsis.'

'Requiescant omnes in pace; may they all rest in peace,' intoned the maestro before stepping down onto the floor of the basilica to join his brethren at the boundary of the black square. 'Brothers,' he said, directing his wand towards the centre of the square, 'here at our feet is Cosimo's tomb marker. Let us take our appointed places.'

Each man promptly stepped forwards onto a circle of white marble which was enclosed within the black square. At the circle's cardinal points, offshoots curved inwards to form a symmetrical pattern of roundels, ellipses, vesicas and cartouches; these were picked out in dark green serpentine or deep red porphyry, so that the whole design resembled the face of some elaborate, yet unfinished, timepiece whose numerous dials lacked their hands. Two of the Brothers took up position to the right of the maestro, at seven and eleven o'clock on the circle. Between them, at nine o'clock, a broad, porphyry cartouche bisected the circle along its horizontal axis; here a third Brother took his place. Similarly, the three Brothers to the maestro's left stood opposite them, at one, three and five o'clock. Then the maestro himself moved to the top of the circle, where a vertical cartouche cut across its horizontal counterpart to create a sort of rounded cross. At the centre of the cross a white-edged square mirrored the outer black one which now encompassed them all.

The maestro tapped the floor with the tip of his wand. This was the signal for the Brothers on his left to recite the inscription inlaid at the chancel end of the vertical cartouche: 'Cosmus Medices Hic Situs Est Decreto Publico Pater Patriae' ('Cosimo de' Medici lieth here, by public decree the father of his country'). Then the maestro tapped his wand a second time and the three Brothers to his right read out the words inlaid at the western end of the cartouche: 'Vixit Annos Septuaginta Quinque, Menses Tres Dies Viginti' ('He lived seventy-five years, three months and twenty days').

'Fratres,' declared the maestro, 'short indeed is the life of man when measured against the millennia. Just as the Earth is merely a speck in the infinite and eternal cosmos, so does Cosimo lie beneath the square within the cross that is the immortal measure of the never-ending circle of time.'

At this point the Brothers stretched out their right hands. On each man's index finger a diamond sparkled on a broad-banded gold ring, a ring they wore but once a year. All the rings were identical but not so the diamonds. One was bright yellow, another lustrous orange, three were brilliant white, and one was the colour of blood.

The maestro resumed his monologue: 'The diamond is the quintessence of geometric symmetry. It is matter in its most indestructible form and yet it is also the purest conductor of that energy we call light. The Medici chose the diamond ring as the symbol of eternity, of man's place in the universe, and of his indomitable spirit. So let us, the Order of the Diamond, end our commemoration, as always, with a conjoining of body and soul.' With that, the maestro thrust his wand into the centre of the conclave, exposing as he did so his own diamond ring, and thus completing the diadem of twinkling jewels which now hovered over Cosimo's tomb.

At that precise moment the great bell of Florence's Duomo tolled twelve midnight. Suddenly the white marble circle of the tomb marker began to glow, getting brighter and brighter until a curtain of white light shot up into the centre of the great cupola two hundred feet above. Then the maestro's diamond started to change colour, going from aquamarine to deep indigo and firing dark blue beams in all directions. Tremors shook the building and the Brothers were thrown to the floor, crying out in terror as they tried to shield their eyes from the blinding light.

And then, with equal suddenness, the light was gone and the tremors ceased. As they uncovered their eyes, the Brothers were aghast to see the maestro bent double on the ground, clutching his right hand. They rushed to his aid but he pushed them away. 'Where's my ring?' he cried, rubbing a band of burnt flesh on the finger where his ring had been. 'It must be found!'

They all began scouring the floor. The missing ring was soon spotted; it lay in the middle of the tomb marker, gleaming darkly. The maestro pounced on it like a panther on its prey, before anyone else could touch it. He ran to the altar and held it up to the candlelight. The ring appeared undamaged; indeed there was nothing to indicate that, only a few seconds before, this small solitaire had displayed the power of a dwarf star. But then, as he inspected the ring's inner band, a gasp of recognition escaped his lips. Wincing, he slid the ring back onto his blistered finger. 'Brothers,' he said in a voice trembling with emotion, 'my dear, dear Brothers, we have just witnessed a miracle, a sign from God; confirmation that the day will soon dawn for which our Brotherhood has waited so long. We must prepare. Be at the Grand Hotel Villa Medici at 6.30pm on 7th November. Until then, guard your rings with your lives. And remember,' he added with a hint of menace, 'the secrets of our Brotherhood are sacrosanct; cursed be the man who betrays them.'

The Brothers nodded their cowled heads and returned in silence to the side-chapels. There, behind the drawn confessional curtains, they disrobed and prepared to re-enter the mundane world once more. The maestro meanwhile sank to his knees, his gaze fixed on the tomb marker's interlacing patterns. They resembled, he thought, the intricate workings of a Byzantine lock, a lock to which he would soon have the key.

One by one, the Brothers departed as anonymously as they had arrived, following the instructions which each had received when assuming the mantle of his predecessor.

As the church door closed behind the first, so the second, hearing the sound, emerged from the next side-chapel, and proceeded likewise. And thus followed the third, fourth and fifth men until, after the door had shut for a sixth time, the maestro himself, now in a suit and carrying a black Malacca cane, snuffed out the altar candles. With the aid of a torch, he too made his way to the exit. The brisk tip-tap of his cane had receded some distance along the deserted streets when another figure slipped from the basilica's side door and vanished silently into the night.

11

MIRANDA'S MOTHER GRIMACED. 'Ugly looking thing,' she said as she returned Uncle Ted's bronze ring to her daughter. Miranda had hoped her mother might recognise its peculiar design. It was not the logo of Dolphin Enterprises: she had checked. But, no, Mom had no idea of the ring's significance, if any, nor could she tell her much about her father's family history. 'Your Pa's family was pretty dysfunctional, Mandy,' she said. 'I never took to any of 'em, your uncle Ted least of all. So full of bullshit. Didn't even come to our wedding. Thought your father had married beneath him. Huh!' she sniffed. 'At least my brothers fought *agin'* Hitler, not *fer* him.'

Miranda sighed. Her Halloween weekend trip back home was proving just as fruitless as her attempts to contact Cousin Frankie. The law firm in Rome which represented him had responded to her enquiries with delay, evasion and finally silence: tactics she knew of old from her dealings with dodgy defence attorneys. They had even refused to pass on her messages, citing conflict of interest, for Heaven's sake!

Her approaches to Frankie's employers at the Vatican had met with even greater obfuscation. At least the Roman lawyers used phones and email. With the Vatican all communication had to be by post. She imagined ranks of tonsured monks in labyrinthine catacombs scribbling on vellum with quill pens. It was rapidly becoming clear that the only way she was going to get answers was in person, face to face, in Italy. And, for that, she would need her own employer's agreement to a leave of absence: not easy when you were conducting a fast-moving litigation practice. 'Mussolini,' she said, correcting her mother. 'It was Mussolini's Blackshirts that Pa's brother joined, not Hitler's.'

Her mother rolled her eyes. Sometimes she worried that all that college education had spoilt her daughter's chances of finding a husband. Men did not like girls who were too clever. 'Hitler, Mussolini, whoever,' she shrugged. 'The point is your uncle supported them just like...' She hesitated, reluctant to rake over the past.

'Just like...?' Miranda prompted.

'Well, Pa was pretty right-wing too. Don't you remember how he used to go on about having blue-blooded ancestry and how his family went way back beyond the Pilgrim Fathers and the *Mayflower*?'

Miranda remembered; of course she did. But only in the way that she also remembered her father's support for the Boston Patriots or being a John Wayne fan. It was part of his quirkiness, an idiosyncrasy so familiar it became unremarkable. 'But that was just bluster, Mom,' she objected. 'An old family folk-tale. There wasn't anything to it, was there?'

'Maybe not. But he sure believed it. I reckon that's why he kept that old model ship up in the loft all those years.'

Miranda knotted her brow. What ship was this? She had never heard of it. She had to see it. They went upstairs. Having helped her mother to lower the loft-steps onto the landing, she climbed up through the hatch and into her family's tea-chested, boxed-up past. Specks of dust floated in and out of the weak October sun whose rays shone wanly through a skylight. Miranda picked her way amid the gloom, dodging the low rafters while, at the same time, trying to avoid putting her feet through the ceiling of the room below. Having resisted the temptation to lift the lid of the battered tin trunk she had used in her college days, and the covers of her high school yearbooks stacked beside it, it was the sight of some tarnished metal studs that stopped her in her tracks. She recognised Smokey's old collar at once. The huge Alaskan husky had been the inseparable companion of her childhood. As she breathed in the familiar smell of his fur, she was back among the green fields and dirt trails where they had run and played and shared a bond as precious as it was timeless. Reluctantly, she lowered the wrinkled leather from her cheek and spied, in the semi-darkness beyond, the distinctive curve of a billowing sail. Crouching down, she lifted her father's model ship from a sea of cobwebs, imagining herself a Greek goddess rescuing her hero's vessel from the briny deep. But this was no Greek trireme: this vessel bore an uncanny similarity to the galleon of her recent nightmare.

'Did Pa make this?' she called back to her mother, who was now standing at the top of the loft-ladder with her head poking through the hatch.

'Hell no! That's an old family heirloom from way back when. The closest your father ever came to carpentry was when they put him in that pine box three years ago.'

Miranda smiled. Her mother, though a regular churchgoer, never let sentiment get in the way of reality, a trait which Miranda had inherited and to which she attributed much of her own lawyerly toughness. 'So, it's probably not the *Mayflower*,' she mused, casting her eye along the deck to a little door at the stern which, somehow, she knew led to the captain's cabin. 'Maybe it's Columbus's ship. What was she called – the *Santa Maria*?'

Her mother shook her head. 'No, your dad always said Columbus only discovered the West Indies. That ship was the other guy's. You know, the one who actually found America, the one the USA is named after. Amerigo something...?'

'Vespucci.' The name tripped off Miranda's lips: those history lessons at the local elementary school had not been wasted.

'Yeah, that's it. And I think the ship's name was somewhere on the front.'

Miranda was tempted to say 'prow', but just managed to stop herself correcting her mother a second time. 'I'll check,' she said, puckering her lips and blowing along the ship's side. This resulted in a bout of violent sneezing and she had to blink her eyes several times before she could read out the name which had emerged from the dust: '*La Bella Simonetta*,' she snuffled, before sneezing again.

'Bless you both!' cried her mother. 'It's All Souls' Day tomorrow. I'll ask Father Benedict at St Mary's to include Simonetta in his prayers. After all, whoever she was, she must've been pretty special to have a ship named after her.'

But Miranda wasn't listening. She had seen something else on the ship's prow: a figurehead in the form of a gold-banded wasp.

12

T OM FELT A hand pull him back from the precipice beyond the garden wall.

'What do you think you're doing? You could have fallen to your death.' Aunt Stella panted breathlessly.

'My father's letter,' he lamented. 'The wind's blown it away.'

'That's Deadman's Walk down there,' she said, pointing into the darkness below. 'Not a place to be on All Hallows' Eve.'

Tom gave her a quizzical look. 'Halloween? But it's only September.'

'It was until you went clockwise instead of anticlockwise round the armillary sphere.'

He frowned. Okay, so he had gone round a garden ornament the wrong way. What could that possibly have to do with the date?

'Do you hear that?' his aunt asked as the chapel bell tolled seven o'clock.

'Yes.'

'Then why is it already dark?'

He gulped. It was less than half an hour since he had jumped out of his aunt's study window when a warm evening sun was still well above the horizon. Yet now stars twinkled in frost-laden air and he was shivering with cold.

A group of students trooped past on their way to the college bar. They gave Tom and his aunt some queer looks as he stood on top of the wall with her holding onto his jacket. 'We can't talk here,' she said. 'My house is just down the street.'

**

Tom sat cross-legged on a goatskin rug and sipped the mulled, homemade blackberry wine which his aunt had given him as an antidote to the bone-chilling Oxford frost. Flames danced on logs in the wood-burning stove whose doors opened out like the wings of a miniature theatre. It took him back to the fires of his childhood, where sprites and goblins leapt out from glowing caves in the hearth and hurled crackling sparks from their world into his.

'If I spoke of magicians and alchemy,' said his aunt as she draped a tartan blanket across his back, 'or talked of the elixir of life and the philosopher's stone, of ether and the spirit world, most people would scoff and consign my words to the realm of fairy tales and gobbledegook, would they not?'

'More than likely,' Tom smirked, contemplating his own undoubted inclusion among the sceptical majority.

'But let me go on television and expatiate on scientists and quantum mechanics, on genetic engineering and nuclear transmutation, on black holes, dark energy and parallel universes: wouldn't those same people be agog with deferential awe?'

'I suppose,' he yawned.

'And yet, though they wouldn't realise it, I'd be talking about the very same things, the very same ideas. And that's because the fundamental questions haven't changed, merely the terminology. The astrophysicist's equations and formulae are no less incomprehensible today than were the alchemist's spells and incantations yesterday. It's all a matter of perspective.'

Tom leaned back against the seat of an armchair and closed his eyes for a moment. He could see the force of her logic, but how did it relate to the armillary sphere and the apparent loss of a whole month? And what was all that stuff in his father's letter about Rinpoche and a cursed treasure? If only the wind had not blown the translation away before he had finished reading it. He reached back and scratched his head. 'Ouch,' he cried as sharp claws dug into his skin.

Aunt Stella chuckled. He was leaning against Marmaduke's favourite chair. He shifted to a safer spot, whilst Marmaduke resumed his imperious repose. 'And so,' said his aunt, taking up her narrative again, 'that armillary sphere you hid behind occupies a spot where space-time is warped. A place where a mini black hole (as predicted by Einstein) may occur when the continuum wears thin: at the equinox, for example, or the solstice. That's when Rinpoche appeared in the old photograph you found. Such occasions are known as "liminal points".'

'Sorry, what points?'

'Liminal. From the Latin for threshold. Doorways from

one world to another, one dimension to another. But they need a trigger: sometimes a birth, sometimes a death, sometimes, as with Rinpoche, a transcendent being.' She paused and picked up a small figurine from the table beside her. It was jet-black, with a man's body and a jackal's head. 'This is Hermanubis,' she said, passing it to Tom. 'He's a synthesis of the Greek god Hermes and the Egyptian Anubis.'

Tom stroked the statuette's smooth basalt surface. He felt a tingling sensation in his fingertips as if he had tapped into some unseen energy. 'Is it very old?'

'First century BC, I believe. Rinpoche gave it to your father; told him it was his guardian spirit.'

He gazed into the jackal's blank eyes. 'And it's connected with the liminal points you mentioned?'

'Hermes and Anubis are both liminal beings. Hermes was believed to escort the souls of the dead from this world to the next, whilst dogs, wolves and jackals have universally been associated with death. Think of Cerberus, the three-headed mastiff who guards the entrance to the Roman underworld, or the four-eyed dogs of Yama, the Hindu god of the dead.'

'But there was no birth or death at the armillary sphere, nothing to trigger this black hole of yours.'

His aunt smiled. 'Your father's letter,' she said. 'The bullet went straight through it into his heart. It's drenched in death.'

Tom could not disagree with that. And it explained why she had told him to tap the letter on the sphere's pointer. But what about the clockwise/anticlockwise conundrum? She explained that that was due to the autumnal equinox, when time flowed backwards. By going clockwise he had gone against the flow and thus jerked the clock forwards, so to speak. Had he gone anticlockwise, as she had instructed, time would simply have stood still, as far as he was concerned, for a few vital minutes while the police were about. As it was, he was catapulted forwards to the next liminal window: Halloween, also known as Samhain, the druidical festival of the dead. That was when she had come back to wait for him to reappear. She had an answer for everything. 'I suppose Deadman's Walk is some kind of black hole too?'

'Possibly. The college wall is actually part of Oxford's old city walls. In medieval times, funeral processions passed beneath it on their way to what was then the Jewish cemetery, but is now the Botanical Gardens. Hence the sobriquet "Deadman's Walk". A place where the occasional ghost is still said to walk abroad.' Aunt Stella peered at her watch, like someone waiting for an overdue train. 'So, yes,' she went on, 'the college wall may well be a boundary between the world of the living and the dead, though which side is which is a moot point.'

Tom blinked: why was she staring at him like that? Why was the room spinning? Why… But he had lost consciousness before he could finish the question.

13

Count Scala watched the sunset from the balcony of his beloved Villa Luna, high in the Tuscan hills. The sound of tinkling fountains washed over the villa's russet walls and crossed green-carpeted lawns before melting among the shadows of umbrella pines. For a moment he caught the scent of irises and orange blossom and heard his wife's laughter beneath an August moon. How he wished they could have witnessed together the great events that destiny was about to unfold. Then a chill wind blew down from the Apuan Alps. Storm clouds were gathering over the distant Ligurian Sea: it was November and his wife was dead. He went inside to prepare.

It was just after 7.30pm when the custom-built Maserati limousine which had collected the Brothers of the Company of the Diamond from the Grand Hotel Villa Medici passed through the gated archway into the count's estate and swept down the long, cypress-lined drive. As it drew up in front of the villa, a brace of burly footmen stepped forwards and opened its doors. The Brothers were glad to leave the claustrophobic saloon in which they had spent the last hour eyeing one another in wary silence. Breathing in the fresh, upland air, they adjusted their bow ties, straightened their dinner jackets and tugged at their double cuffs whilst gazing, with obvious admiration, at the four-square Tuscan grandeur of their host's mansion.

'Buonasera, Signori. This way, if you please,' called a gruff voice from the steps of the floodlit portico. It was Fabio, the count's butler. He came of Sardinian goat-herder stock: hard as an ancient holm oak and loyal as one of his island's fearsome shepherd dogs. With a wave of his white-gloved hand, he ushered the guests into a glittering reception hall, where his cousins doubled as waiters serving chilled Vermentino and warm bruschetta.

The count appeared on the stroke of eight. Tall and aloof, he introduced himself to each man in turn with a firm handshake and fixed smile. Then, at the sounding of a gong, he led the way into dinner. Surrounded by Cellini bronzes and Gobelin tapestries, he invited the Brothers to take their seats at a large oval table. Beside the immaculately laid settings, arrayed at seven precise intervals, gilt-edged cards bore each guest's name and title. None of them ventured to question this, though they all recalled the maestro's insistence on the strict anonymity of their Brotherhood at that last, eventful conclave in San Lorenzo, six weeks before. Scala glanced around the table. A motley crew, he thought: an Englishman, a Greek, an American and a Serb. Only two Italians left (excluding himself) after five hundred years. Some looked younger than he had expected, but then looks could be deceptive. The Serb, for example, reminded him of an Orthodox Church father, with his thick black beard and high forehead, staring up at the painted stucco ceiling, as if in prayer. 'Trust an astronomer to be interested in the patterns overhead, Professore Jankovic,' Scala remarked.

The professor scratched his patristic whiskers. 'How did you know I'm a...'

But, before he could finish, the count launched into an exposition of the various motifs adorning the ceiling, all of which turned out to betoken the Medici. There were the interlocking diamond rings which signified the dynasty's aspirations to eternity: a favourite motif of Lorenzo the Magnificent. His father, Piero, on the other hand, had preferred the peacock's feathers since the peacock's flesh was believed to be incorruptible, thus symbolising immortality. 'Sadly, Piero was racked with gout, the Medici's hereditary curse, and died an untimely death.'

'Too fond of peacock perhaps,' quipped the young man seated to Scala's left.

The count regarded him icily. 'Only a saint or a fool mocks death,' he replied. 'Which are you, Mr Radopoulos?'

The Greek laughed nervously. 'Oh, I'm just a poor teacher,' he said, 'despite my parents naming me Gorgias after an ancient Athenian orator. They hoped I'd become a rich lawyer.'

Scala grimaced. 'I'm afraid your parents got it wrong. Gorgias wasn't an orator; he was a sophist, a man who peddled cleverness and called it wisdom. The philosopher Plato despised such men.'

'Whew! If only my parents had known. Still, at least these days sophistry isn't a career option.'

'On the contrary, today sophists rule the world. They have merely reinvented themselves as spin doctors and advertising agents and... journalists.'

Radopoulos shifted in his seat; the count seemed to have touched a nerve, but the moment passed. A flurry of waiters emerged from the kitchen bearing dishes laden with a steaming risotto of truffles and shredded rabbit, accompanied by decanters of vintage Chianti. After toasting the Company of the Diamond, Scala informed his guests that they were about to sample a favourite dish of Queen Catherine de' Medici. He had just stabbed his fork into a particularly juicy truffle when he felt a nudge at his elbow.

'Going back to the motifs on the ceiling, old boy,' gurgled a bluff, broad-shouldered man through his handlebar moustache, 'are those laurel branches I can see up there?'

Scala flinched at his neighbour's boorish manners. 'Ebbene, Colonel Hawkwood…'

'Oh, it's Hawkeye to my old chums,' the Englishman butted in, clapping a bear-like hand on the count's shoulder with surprising familiarity.

Radopoulos could hardly contain his amusement at the look of consternation on Scala's face. Yet, the count seemed at pains to indulge his other guest, calling him immediately by his nickname and explaining that the branches were not in fact laurel – the symbol of Lorenzo Il Magnifico – but olive, the symbol of his younger brother, Giuliano. 'Olive, you see, is "Julea" in Latin, and "Giuliano" is "Julianus" or "Julius"…'

'As in Julius Caesar,' Hawkwood interrupted again.

'Whose fate Giuliano shared,' commented a slim, weasel-faced man seated next to him.

'I'm impressed, Signor Rossi,' said Scala. 'I thought your expertise lay in art, not history?'

The man's perfectly manicured fingernails patted his neatly coiffed hair. 'But my dear Count, surely every Italian knows the tragic story of Giuliano de' Medici, the handsome young prince brutally murdered on the steps of the Duomo?'

'I doubt it,' Scala sighed gravely. 'Yet, I for one shall never forget Giuliano's murder by his treacherous friends as he was going to Mass, that Easter of 1476. They would have killed Lorenzo too if he and his companions hadn't fought them off. A more despicable, cowardly, blasphemous crime it is impossible to imagine!' The count's wine glass suddenly shattered in his hand.

The ubiquitous Fabio discreetly disposed of the broken glass whilst Scala, who had sustained only a minor scratch, quickly regained his composure and summoned service of the main course: Tournedos Medicis (this time a favourite dish of Queen Marie de' Medici), accompanied by a Brunello di Montalcino. 'A '97, gentlemen. One of the finest post-war vintages.'

'Exquisite,' Rossi gushed, rolling the deep red liquid extravagantly around his palate. 'But now I too have a question about the ceiling motifs: that oval shield with six red balls surrounding a blue one in the centre.'

Scala arched his eyebrows. 'But surely you recognise the Medici coat of arms?'

'Oh, but of course, your Excellency, as no doubt does Dottore Gatti.' Rossi beamed at the young man sitting opposite him. At the mention of his name, Gatti dropped the place-card he had been twirling between his fingers (thus enabling Rossi to read the name) and fixed the art dealer with a suspicious stare. 'However,' Rossi continued unabashed, 'our foreign friends, Colonel Hawkeye and Mr Radopoulos and...' he glanced at the place-card of the white-haired man seated to his right, 'Mr Sarachin here –'

the man nodded politely '– may not be so familiar with the history of the Medici insignia. In any case, I'm sure I don't know everything there is to know about it. In particular, I've long been curious to know why the number of balls varies so greatly?'

This time Radopoulos could not stop himself snorting at his foppish fellow guest's interest in balls, Medici or otherwise. But he avoided another rebuke from Scala thanks to Mr Sarachin, who now decided to speak. 'I should indeed like to know the history of the Medici crest,' he said in a croaky whisper, explaining that a sore throat made it painful for him to talk or, even more regrettably, partake more fully of the delicious banquet laid before them. Hawkwood recommended a large double whisky but Sarachin demurred, being teetotal. The colonel shrugged and, downing yet another glass of wine, declared that he, at least, was very familiar with the Medici's crest. Scala winced at his jarring accentuation of the second, rather than the first, syllable of the Medici name. It was a common error among the Anglo-Saxons, but it grated all the same.

'As a military man,' Hawkwood puffed, 'I know the importance of badges and such like. In fact I recently received a splendid pair of cuff...' He broke off abruptly, coughing and covering his mouth with his right hand, displaying as he did so a deep scar from what looked like an animal bite. Fabio once again came to the rescue, this time with a tumbler of water. 'Sorry... sorry,' the colonel spluttered, shooting a glance at the count. 'Old war wound, you know. It was in the Falklands...'

'You're absolutely right, Signor Rossi,' Scala intervened. 'I should say something about the Medici coat of arms on an occasion such as this.' And, as dinner progressed from steak to zabaglione and on to the local caprino goat's cheese and figs, he discoursed on the various theories and legends associated with the Medici balls ('or "palle" in Italian'). Some said they represented coins, alluding to the Medici as bankers, others that they were medicinal pills ('a pun on "Medici"'), and yet others held that the palle were the dents on the shield of Averardo, a Carolingian warrior and founder of the Medici dynasty, who defeated a giant called Mugello in single combat.

'So, that explains why the Medici's ancestral village of Cafaggiolo is here in the Mugello, the region named after the giant,' Rossi noted enthusiastically. 'But what about the number of the palle, Count Scala? Why do they vary so much?'

'Ebbene, the number varied over the years, depending on the whim of the Medici ruler at the time. However, according to my family's archives, Cosimo and Piero kept the number to six, whilst Lorenzo, for reasons which I will explain later, increased it to seven.'

Up to this point the previously tight-lipped Dr Gatti had managed to contain his growing frustration, but no longer. 'Rather than discussing balls, Count Scala,' he said pointedly, brushing aside an unruly blonde forelock which kept lolling over his thick, black-rimmed spectacles, 'I should much prefer to know the answer to a question which must have occurred to all of us, but which the others are apparently too polite to ask.'

Scala pondered his response. He had not expected such boldness from the pale, crab-shouldered academic. 'Perhaps, Dottore,' he said, 'your fellow guests subscribe to the librarian's motto: "Vincula da linguae vel tibi lingua dabit."'

Gatti flushed. The count had not only guessed the nature of his question but also thrown down a challenge. But the dottore was up to it. 'Bite your tongue or get bitten,' he translated. 'But we're not in a library now. Yet, you obviously know that I'm a librarian, just as you know the names and professions of everyone else around this table. How can that be, when you expressly stated in San Lorenzo that none of us knows any of the others?'

Just then a clock struck 11pm. Scala rose from his seat and, with a wry smile, announced that it was time to repair to the library.

14

MIRANDA SLAMMED HER office door. The meeting with her managing partner had not gone well. Unsympathetic to her request for a leave of absence, his sole concern was the disruption and inconvenience it would cause. She had two major trials scheduled for December: there was no-one available to take on the extra workload at this late stage. She was being unreasonable, selfishly pursuing her own interests at the expense of her clients, her colleagues and the firm which had so generously nurtured her. Okay, so her rich uncle had left all his money to her cousin instead of her. Tough. Maybe it was not fair, but was it worth risking her career for? Surely this 'flight of fancy' to Italy could wait till the New Year. If she insisted on going now, she would forfeit a month's pay and have to quit her job for good. So much for her past successes, she thought, all that empty praise which had been heaped upon her. When the chips were down, nothing trumped the interests of the firm.

She sat at her computer and sulked. Caught between ambition and anger, she had no appetite for work. On a whim, she searched 'Amerigo Vespucci' on Wikipedia. She found that he had been born in Florence in 1454, the son of a notary. 'Another darn' lawyer!' she huffed. Educated by his uncle, a Dominican friar and friend of the fanatical preacher Savonarola, Amerigo had initially gone to work for Lorenzo de' Medici, who despatched him to be his agent in Seville. Then, after Lorenzo's death in 1492, he had entered the service of the kings of Portugal and Spain, taking part in several pioneering voyages to the New World (later named 'America' after him). Miranda yawned: nothing particularly remarkable so far. She scrolled further down till a name caught her eye: Amerigo's cousin-in-law was one 'Simonetta Vespucci'. Could this be the 'Bella Simonetta' of her father's galleon?

She clicked through to the entry for Simonetta. Born in Genoa, her parents had married her off when she was just sixteen to a well-connected, but dull, Florentine called Marco Vespucci. The wedding was celebrated in the private chapel of the Palazzo Medici, with a reception at their villa near Careggi, on the outskirts of Florence. A real *Vogue* magazine party no doubt, Miranda smirked. Indeed, Simonetta was apparently such a paragon of beauty and wit that she became the object of intense rivalry between Lorenzo de' Medici and his dashing younger brother, Giuliano. The latter had even tied her colours to his lance at a famous joust, which he won, clad in shining armour of course. Thereafter, Simonetta was acclaimed the most beautiful woman in Florence, if not in all Italy. Yet, just a year later she was dead, cut down by consumption at the age of twenty-three. The whole of Florence had turned out for her funeral, calling out her nickname as the cortège passed by: 'La Bella Simonetta'. Miranda punched the air: 'Snap' she cried.

But what did the beauteous Simonetta look like? The website had a photo of Botticelli's 'Birth of Venus', for which she was said to have been the model, but no-one really seemed to know for sure. Her lover, Giuliano, on the other hand, was portrayed in a couple of Botticelli paintings. Miranda could not help admiring Simonetta's Prince Charming, with his shoulder-length hair and youthful good looks. But he too was a tragic figure, assassinated by enemies of the Medici on the steps of Florence Cathedral, where he had been about to say prayers at Easter for his beloved's soul: two years, to the day, after her death. Miranda sighed. Saccharine tales of doomed romance usually left her cold, but this one touched her somehow. Or was it her own dispirited mood projected onto it? In any case, the story brought her no closer to understanding why a model of Amerigo's ship should have become a family heirloom, nor to explaining the significance, if any, of her recent nightmare. Maybe she had forgotten seeing the model as a child and her subconscious had resurrected the memory and woven it into a nightmare, triggered by Uncle Ted's curious dolphin ring. But where did those two white-robed men come in and why the unusual wasp mascot on the ship's prow?

'Hi Miranda,' chirped a buxom woman whose head now popped round the office door. 'Care for a coffee and a slice of home-made sponge-cake just like my mama used to make?' It was Maria, the Italian tea lady; she had been trundling her trolley along the firm's corridors since no-one could remember when. Her sing-song Neapolitan voice always lifted Miranda's spirits. 'You bet!' she responded eagerly.

Maria scooped a generous portion of cake onto a paper plate and poured steaming hot coffee into a china mug. 'I hear you're going to my old country,' she said with a knowing grin.

Miranda gurned. Lawyers treated client confidentiality like priests treated the confessional, but their penchant for in-house gossip was second to none. And Maria had a knack of always being within earshot. 'Well, it's not settled yet,' she mumbled through a mouthful of cream and sponge. 'But, yes, maybe I will go to Rome sometime soon.'

The trolley-lady's eyes lit up. 'Ah, La Citta Eterna,' she pined, clasping her hands to her bosom as if in the grip of a beatitude. 'I went there once when I was a girl, to St Peter's, to see the Holy Father. So beautiful. But,' she said with a sudden wag of her finger, 'watch out for those cheeky Italian boys asking you to go for a ride on their Vespas.'

Miranda almost choked on her cake. 'Vespas?'

'Oh, you're too young,' Maria laughed. 'You don't remember Gregory Peck and Audrey Hepburn on that scooter in *Roman Holiday*.'

Miranda wiped the sticky crumbs from her lips. She knew the classic film alright. It was hearing that word 'Vespas' which had sparked her curiosity. It sounded so close to Vespucci. Why were motor scooters called Vespas? The question had never occurred to her before. Presumably it was like vacuum cleaners being called 'Hoovers' after their manufacturer or inventor?

'No, no,' said Maria. 'It's that terrible buzzing noise the scooters make, like "le vespe", like wasps.'

15

THE VOICE KEPT repeating the same instruction: 'Go back, Tom, back to the time before you were born.' And it kept asking the same questions over and over again: 'What do you see? Who is there? What are they saying?' He looked around but everything was shrouded in a dense fog. Suddenly a jet-black figure stepped out in front of him. He shuddered as the jackal-headed Hermanubis beckoned him into the mist, parting it down the middle, like a stage curtain. A sea of white peaks stretched to the horizon. An old man, hunched over a crooked staff, was standing on a snow-covered ledge, near the entrance to a cave. 'Farewell, Yingsel, farewell, Dorje,' he called into an oncoming blizzard.

Tom's heart skipped a beat: 'Dorje' again, and 'Yingsel'. Both were mentioned in the translation his father had enclosed with his letter.

'Guard the casket with your lives,' the old man cried. A girl looked back through the swirling snow. She was pushing a sled. Her companion was somewhere ahead of her, but the snow was too thick to see him. The girl gave a brief wave as the blizzard closed in and she too disappeared from view. Tom put out a hand and touched the old man's shoulder. He turned and smiled in recognition: it was Rinpoche. Then, before Tom could utter a word, the curtain of mist came down again.

Hermanubis reappeared and conjured another scene. It was night-time, in the desert; stars were sparkling overhead. Three men in black robes stared into a blazing fire. Veils covered their faces, masking all but their troubled gaze. Beside them a wooden casket lay empty, its lid flung open.

'Ourania has taken the gold and the jewels,' said one, mentioning another name which Tom recognised from his father's letter: 'Ourania', the 'beautiful Etruscan slave' sent to the court of a 'Great King'. But in that case, could these three be the 'Guardians of the Sacred Flame'?

'Ah, Queen Ourania!' sighed the second of the three. 'The slave who stole the King of Parthia's heart to gain an empire has now gained a curse by stealing a king's riches.'

'Like all thieves, her greed blinded her to the real treasure she left behind,' said the third. 'Yet, I fear the scroll is also missing. We must ensure that its secret knowledge endures for good, lest it fall into Ahriman's evil hands.'

Somewhere nearby, a wolf howled. 'Hark,' whispered the first, 'Tishtrya, loyal servant of Ahura Mazda, summons us.'

'And behold,' said the second, 'tonight his star shines brighter than all the rest.'

'As he leads the dead to Mithras across the Bridge of Souls, so may he guide us across the desert to the land of the Saoshyant,' prayed the third.

Tom had heard of Mithras from a school trip to Hadrian's Wall, where a ruined chapel was dedicated to the guardian god of Roman legionaries. But who or what was the 'Saoshyant'? He tried to move closer, but once again a curtain of mist descended and all went blank.

Later (he had no idea how much later), Hermanubis returned one last time and raised the curtain on two more actors whose names resonated. One was tall and in his prime. He wore a full-length woollen cloak which rustled on fallen leaves as he followed an older, shorter man down a narrow path. The taller one beamed with a swarthy intelligence as the flaming torch he was carrying lit up his face. 'What a splendid dinner party that was, Master Ficino,' he enthused, his vowels moulded deep but harsh by the long, flat-ridged nose that matched the rugged firmness of his jaw.

The older man glanced back, his eyes like pools of watery blue. 'I'm s-so glad, Prince Lorenzo,' he stuttered. 'Your lovely villa, here at Careggi, was the perfect s-setting for our academy's re-enactment of the divine Plato's s-symposium on the true nature of love. I do s-so hope that it has lifted your s-spirits after the terrible events of earlier this year.'

The prince shook his head. 'I shall be on Charon's bark crossing the river Lethe before that memory is washed from my soul. I see it even now: poor Giuliano's skull, split in two by Francesco de' Pazzi's treacherous sword on the very steps of the Duomo.'

'But the people of Florence rallied immediately to your defence and hung the traitor's naked corpse from the battlements of the S-Signoria.'

'It was the least that butcher deserved for the injuries he and his cowardly conspirators inflicted on my little brother: his eyes stabbed out, his nose smashed, his flesh torn to shreds.' The prince clenched his fist. 'As I cradled his broken body in my arms,' he snarled, 'I swore to obliterate the Pazzi from the face of the Earth.'

Tom watched the two men approach a small wooden gate. Ficino fumbled with the latch. 'And you have been as good as your word, Lorenzo. Virtually the whole Pazzi clan has been executed or exiled and s-stripped of their property.'

'Yes,' Lorenzo answered, shutting the gate behind them. 'And anyone left who bears their accursed name must, by law, change it or face banishment.'

Tom trod softly behind them as they passed through an orchard of peach and plum trees, the branches now bereft of fruit and all but a few brittle leaves. 'The Pazzi are like these trees,' observed Ficino, 'bare and anonymous. Even their coat of arms has been erased from our public buildings.'

'I wish I could say the same of their foreign paymasters, Pope Sixtus and Count Riairio, not to mention their Dominican henchmen.' A large dog suddenly bounded past Tom and barged into Ficino, causing him to grab hold of Lorenzo's arm to stay upright. 'Buontempo, come back here!' Lorenzo shouted angrily as his hunting hound chased a rabbit into the bushes.

'Ah yes, the Domini Canes,' Ficino exhaled as he recovered his balance. 'More God's hyenas than his hounds.'

A few paces more and they arrived at the door of a modest cottage. 'Welcome back to Montevecchio,' said Ficino as they entered his study, joined once more by the boisterous Buontempo. 'This house was your grandfather Cosimo's greatest gift to me. A place of solitude and tranquillity where I could complete the research that enthralled us both.'

'And did it ultimately make you happy or sad?' asked Lorenzo, pointing at a fresco of two philosophers, one laughing whilst the other wept.

'Democritus and Heraclitus are two s-sides of the s-same coin,' Ficino replied. 'My own motto is "be happy with the present".'

'My present is nothing but absence,' Lorenzo grimaced. 'The two people I loved most in all the world are gone. Assassins have robbed me of Giuliano just as disease took Simonetta before him.'

'And if you could bring just one of them back to life again, which would it be? Your beloved brother or the woman you loved?' Tom wondered if Ficino had overstepped the bounds of friendship with such an intimate question. But Lorenzo merely smiled and said: 'Didn't Orpheus try that once?'

Ficino looked at him strangely. He said he had something to show him, something that Cosimo had instructed him to reveal when the time was right. Something so secret that no-one else, not even Cosimo's trusted chancellor, Bartolomeo Scala, knew about it.

Scala! The name hit Tom like a thunderbolt. There had to be a connection with the chairman of the Banca de' Bianchi and surely, therefore, with his own dismissal from the bank. In his excitement he shouted the name out loud, and instantly Ficino and Lorenzo, Buontempo and Montevecchio were gone. All that remained was that voice, just as insistent as before, except now it was telling him to wake up.

16

'AFTER ALL THAT talk about symbols and the Medici,' yawned Colonel Hawkwood, puffing on a cigar and cradling an Armagnac, 'you must tell us, Scala, old man, the meaning of your own intriguing coat of arms. We all noticed it on the gates of the villa as well as on the dinner service and the wine labels. And now, by golly, I see it's even engraved on your bookcases too!' The colonel waved a hand vaguely around the count's magnificent library. Rows of finely bound books, some dating back to the dawn of printing and beyond, glimmered in the subdued lighting, bearing witness to Scala's ancestral thirst for knowledge as well as riches.

Hawkwood's fellow guests glared at him. He had obviously overindulged in the count's hospitality; not only did he seem unduly familiar towards the 'maestro', but he also appeared to have forgotten the purpose of their gathering that evening. They, on the contrary, were keener than ever to hear what it was that the count had to tell them about the strange happenings at San Lorenzo and why it had taken him so long to bring them all together again. They also wanted to hear his response to Dr Gatti's still-unanswered question: how did he know their names and professions when he had stated at San Lorenzo that none of them – including himself – knew any of the others?

But Scala was in no hurry to provide answers. He crossed to the centre of the room and casually brushed a celestial globe into motion, studying the spinning constellations intently before finally turning to his audience. They sat in hushed anticipation; the only sounds were those of rain lashing against the window panes and a grandfather clock tick-tocking towards midnight.

'Patience is a rare virtue these days. Don't you agree, Brothers?' Scala began at last. 'People demand instant responses, immediate gratification, quick fixes, rapid results, bullet points, sound bites.' He spat the words out like pips from a bitter lemon. 'Saving time has become an end in itself. And what do we do with all that spare time? Why, we fill it as soon as possible with even more activity, like hamsters running ever faster on an ever-spinning wheel.' He paused and sipped on a glass of amaretto. 'But our Brotherhood,' he went on, 'has waited patiently for five hundred years for this moment to arrive. Today, planning or even thinking on such a scale would be incomprehensible to the philistines who squeeze the last ounce of profit from their companies, corrupt their governments and consume the world's resources in an orgy of self-indulgence worthy of Nero himself, fiddling while Rome burns.' The count's amaretto shook in his hand as he spoke, and his audience feared another breakage. But they need not have worried; he had never been more in control. He took another sip before continuing. 'When the Company of the

Diamond was formed in Quattrocento Florence, things were very different. In those days, men planted olive groves and oak woods, not for themselves, but for generations yet unborn.'

He turned and pointed his glass towards Hawkwood. 'Brother Hawkeye here has asked me to explain my family's coat of arms and I shall do so, since my ancestors' story is as good an introduction as any to the things you all need to know.' He took a deep breath. It was not easy to give voice to things concealed for half a millennium. 'Ebbene, my ancestors came from a small town in southern Tuscany: Colle di Val d'Elsa. They were poor. They owned no land and had few possessions. But they were honest and worked hard as tenant millers making flour for the people's bread. Then, in the year 1430, a son was born to them. His name was Bartolomeo and his portrait hangs over there.'

The Brothers looked across to the huge granite fireplace, above which a gaunt, hollow-cheeked man watched them with cold, uncompromising eyes. He bore little resemblance to his sleek, well-nourished descendant, save that they shared the same air of sombre zeal.

'He was clever and ambitious,' Scala went on, 'and fortunately for him the authorities in Colle encouraged learning, even among the poor. He studied hard and was eventually accepted into the University of Florence to study law and oratory.'

'Not to be confused with vulgar sophistry!' Radopoulos whispered to Gatti.

Scala glared at him before adding that Bartolomeo had risen rapidly to become Cosimo de' Medici's private secretary and then chancellor of Florence, holding the post until his death in 1497.

'So the coat of arms came with the chancellor's job,' Hawkwood remarked, stifling another yawn.

'Certainly not, Hawkeye. Bartolomeo was invested with the insignia of a knight of Christendom entirely through his own merit. The Pope himself bestowed the honour on him in St Peter's Basilica on Christmas Day 1484.' The count went over to the fireplace and pointed to a shield in the top right-hand corner of his ancestor's portrait. 'My family's coat of arms,' he said, 'comprises two staircases: a play on the name "Scala", which means "stairs" in Italian. Below the stairs is a seven-sailed flour mill, which recalls both our humble origins and the seven balls of the Medici crest. Finally, the twin torches of knowledge and wisdom burn at the top of each staircase, reminding us that knowledge is its own wealth and wisdom, its own luck.'

'Very interesting,' commented Gatti, joining the count beside the fireplace, 'but it still doesn't explain how you know who we are.'

'Nor why you summoned us here tonight,' Radopoulos threw in.

Scala took another sip of amaretto, savouring its sweet aftertaste. 'Don't worry, Gorgias,' he said, 'the end of the story will come soon enough. But first let me answer the dottore's question.'

With everyone's attention riveted on the count, no-one noticed Radopoulos quietly slide a finger behind the lapel of his dinner jacket and activate a tiny digital recorder.

'It's really quite simple,' Scala began. 'After our conclave in September, it was clear to me that the time for anonymity was over. Now, as the final stage of our sacred enterprise draws near, I needed to weed out any "rotten apples" in our five-hundred-year-old harvest.' As he spoke these words he shot a withering look at Radopoulos. 'After the original Medici bank was destroyed by Savonarola and the papacy in 1494, my forefather Bartolomeo secretly resurrected it, lending money at a table on the Via Porta Rosa.' He gazed up at Bartolomeo's portrait and explained how his ancestor had given the bank a different name and a fictitious founder. 'But, from that small seedling,' he declared proudly, 'the Banca de' Bianchi grew back, like Lorenzo de' Medici's eternal laurel, into the great institution of which I am now chairman.'

'So that's why the conclave always takes place after that boring Founder's Day service,' Professor Jankovic grumbled, 'forcing us to hang around for hours on end in those bum-numbing confessionals.'

'Well,' Hawkwood chortled, 'I don't mind the hard seats as long as there's an envelope on them each year with a banker's draft for fifty thousand dollars.'

Scala nodded. His forefather had instituted the annual honorarium to facilitate the Brothers' loyalty. 'The payees of those Banca de' Bianchi drafts are of course anonymous, but we bankers know how to trace the accounts into which such funds are paid.'

One or two of the Brothers fidgeted uncomfortably at this revelation. Hawkwood, however, blew a circle of cigar smoke into the air. 'Disloyalty, disobedience and cowardice, the Roman soldier's three cardinal sins,' he mused. 'The penalty was garrotting, you know.'

Scala glanced at Fabio, who was standing at the back of the room, just behind Radopoulos. 'I believe the Sardinians still inflict a similar punishment,' he said, 'for breaches of "Omerta".' Fabio's eyes flashed with menace at the mention of his island's ancient code of honour. 'You Greeks, on the other hand,' Scala continued, focussing now on Radopoulos, 'have always admired cunning and deception, have you not?'

The young man stiffened. 'Well, I... I...'

'Oh, come, come, Gorgias, we've all heard of the wily Odysseus, Homer's hero, who tricked the one-eyed Cyclops and dreamt up the Trojan horse. What profession, I wonder, would suit a modern-day Odysseus? A lawyer, perhaps? A private detective? Ah yes, I have it: an undercover journalist.'

Radopoulos blanched. He tried to stand up, pleading nausea and the need for some air. But Fabio's hand was already on his shoulder and held him firmly in his seat. Hawkwood too was soon at his side. 'Don't worry, old chap, we'll look after you,' he smiled as he loosened the young man's collar and pressed a blade discreetly against his ribs.

'Ach, he'll be okay,' Jankovic snorted. 'Just another youngster who can't hold his drink. Now let's cut to the chase, Count Scala. You saw something didn't you? Something on your ring after it lit up so spectacularly in San Lorenzo. What was it you saw?'

Scala spread his right hand. Slipping the diamond ring from his index finger, he proceeded to read out an inscription which had miraculously appeared on its inner band:

'"IN LUNA PRIMUM QUAERITE OCCULTA MAGORUM. PLATONIS D.N.M.D."'

'It's all Greek to me!' Hawkwood smirked at Radopoulos.

'It's Latin actually,' Gatti corrected him.

'Si, Dottore,' Scala agreed. 'It's a Latin hexameter, the metre of Virgil and Lucretius. Perhaps you would be good enough to translate it for us?'

Gatti pondered for a moment. 'Let me see: "In Luna"...
in the moon... "primum quaerite"... first seek... "occulta
magorum"... the secrets of magicians...'

'What nonsense is that?' Jankovic scoffed. '"Seek
magicians' secrets in the moon"? I've been observing the
moon for years and I can tell you there aren't any magicians
there, nor any little green men for that matter.'

'It was just a literal translation,' Gatti smarted.

Scala raised a calming hand. 'Gentlemen, please. It's
quite understandable that the dottore should miss the real
meaning. He wasn't to know that "In Luna", literally "in the
moon", actually refers to this house, the "Villa Luna".'

'And what magicians' secrets does the Villa Luna hide?'
demanded Jankovic.

Scala looked up at his ancestor's portrait again: he too
wore a diamond ring on his hand, the very ring which the
count now held in his. 'The Company of the Diamond,' he
said, 'was named after the great Medici diamond known as Il
Libro, one of the largest diamonds ever found.'

Jankovic sat up. 'Is it hidden somewhere in here?' he asked,
his eyes darting eagerly around the library. But he slumped
back in his chair when he heard that it was long since lost:
looted, like so many Medici treasures, during Savonarola's
reign of terror. 'Guilds and religious brotherhoods were
common in Renaissance Italy,' Scala told them, 'but virtually
all died out or degenerated into vulgar drinking clubs. Yet
the Company of the Diamond was different. To this day,
it has never been legally dissolved.' He paused, hesitating
to turn the key in a long-locked door. Then he revealed
that the name "Compagnia del Diamante" had only been
adopted after Lorenzo de' Medici's death, to avoid unwanted

attention from Savonarolan fanatics. 'But originally ours was a religious fraternity, a brotherhood formed to perform the last burial rites of its members. Its original name was "Compagnia de' Magi" – the Company of the Magi.'

'Magi?' Jankovic harrumphed. 'So we're back to magicians again?'

'No, not magicians, but Magi: the Three Wise Men of the Nativity tale, to be precise.'

'You can't be serious, Count? The Wise Men are just a fairy tale, like Santa Claus.'

Scala eyed the bewhiskered Serb: for all his Eastern Orthodox appearance, he was obviously an apostate. 'That's precisely what the modern sophists want you to believe, Professore, but the Magi were indeed flesh and blood.'

'And their relics are still venerated in three golden sarcophagi in Cologne Cathedral,' Rossi added.

'More to the point,' Scala went on, 'the Magi and the Medici had much in common. The Magi were wealthy men who nevertheless entered the Kingdom of Heaven. They were associated with medicine, astrology and magic: subjects which fascinated the Medici. Even better, there were three of them: the sage Melchior, the king Balthazar and the young prince Gaspar. A perfect match for the Medici dynasty of Cosimo the grandfather, Piero the father and Lorenzo the son.'

'Okay, okay,' Jankovic shrugged. 'I get the picture. But what about the "secrets" of the Magi? What are they?'

Scala ran his hand along a nearby bookshelf and took down a thick tome, bound in white vellum. 'This is the first edition of the *Theologia Platonica on Immortality*,' he announced, 'by Marsilio Ficino.'

'Marsupial who?' Hawkwood gurgled into his Armagnac.

Gatti sniggered as Rossi leapt to enlighten the tipsy Englishman. 'Marsilio Ficino, my dear Colonel, was one of the greatest humanist scholars of the Italian Renaissance. He was the first person to translate Plato's works into Latin. And, if I am not mistaken, he was another Medici protégé, the son of Cosimo's physician.'

'That's right, Riccardo,' Scala confirmed. 'Ficino's father wanted him to become a doctor too, but Ficino decided to minister to men's souls, rather than their bodies.'

Jankovic dabbed a handkerchief on his glistening forehead. 'But what's Ficino got to do with the Magi and their secrets?'

'Everything. Ficino revered Plato, the mystic philosopher who had been read in Greek Byzantium for nearly two thousand years but only became known in the Latin west when Byzantine scholars fled the Turks in the fourteenth century.'

'I thought we were the Brothers of the Company of the Magi, not Plato,' Gatti carped.

Scala raised an eyebrow: 'Surely, Dottore, as a Vatican scholar you know that Plato's esoteric teachings on the soul were ultimately derived from Zoroaster, the Persian magus par excellence?'

A hint of red tinged Gatti's cheeks. 'Well, of course I do, but...'

'And so did Cosimo de' Medici,' Scala pressed on. 'That's why he revived Plato's ancient academy of Athens here in Florence. He appointed Ficino as its first maestro, and its members included the artist Botticelli, the poet Poliziano, the cabbalist Pico della Mirandola and the sorcerer Pulci, as well as my forefather Bartolomeo and, after Cosimo's death, Lorenzo Il Magnifico himself.'

'Seven in all,' Rossi remarked. 'Just like the seven palle on Lorenzo's coat of arms.'

'And seven of us,' noted Jankovic.

'At last you see it, Brothers,' Scala smiled. 'Within the circle of the Company of the Magi there was an inner circle of the Platonic Academy. And every year, on Plato's birthday, those great men would hold a secret banquet in Lorenzo's villa at Careggi.'

'So that's it!' Rossi exclaimed. 'Those last letters on your ring – "Platonis D.N." – they refer to Plato's birthday, his "Dies Natalis".'

'That's a no-brainer,' Gatti sneered. 'I knew that from the start. The real problem are the other initials: "M.D.". I don't suppose Plato was a doctor, was he?'

Scala shook his head. "M.D" referred to the fact that Plato died on the same day of the month on which he was born. 'So his birthday was also his "deathday" or "Mortis Dies", eighty-one years later.'

'The square of nine,' Sarachin croaked from the other side of the room, overcoming his sore throat. 'The perfect number according to ancient numerology.'

'Yes,' said Scala. 'And every year, on the anniversary of Plato's death, Magi were said to come from Persia to visit his tomb in ancient Athens. Who knows, maybe they still do.'

Jankovic stopped dabbing his forehead and scratched his whiskers instead. 'But how did the Magi know the date of Plato's birthday? Was it recorded somewhere?'

Scala slid his diamond ring back on his finger. 'Like you, Professore, the Magi read the heavens. Plato's birthday was written in the stars, midway between the autumnal equinox and the winter solstice.'

Jankovic made some quick mental calculations. 'But that would mean…'

'Yes, another seven,' Scala smiled. 'The very day in 1482 on which Ficino first published his *Theologia Platonica*: the seventh day of November. In other words, today.'

17

HER ONE-BEDROOM APARTMENT in Brooklyn Heights felt welcoming as ever as Miranda threw off her shoes and clicked on the television remote to catch the late-night news. She had lived there for three years, ever since she got the job with Delaney's. The rent ate up half her monthly salary but the location, a well-appointed, red-brick block in a highly desirable district, was worth it. Pouring herself a generous glass of merlot, she went to the window and looked down at the promenade three storeys below. All was quiet; it was almost midnight on a weekday, after all. She had left the office early for once and spent the evening wining and dining with friends, her mobile switched off, trying to forget for a few hours the dilemma that confronted her. The promenade overlooked Lower Manhattan, its lights twinkling in the clear night air. In the distance, the waters of New York Harbour shimmered under a full moon.

How could she possibly give all this up to go looking for some chancer of a cousin in Italy? Sure, he had snatched a multi-million-dollar inheritance from under her nose, but he had done it legally, with Uncle Ted's conscious, and apparently considered, approval. And she had not actually been expecting anything anyway. No, it would be stupid to throw away all that she had worked so hard for, her career, her lifestyle, the bright future that awaited her: and for what? Even if she managed to track Cousin Frankie down, what then? He was hardly likely to greet her with open arms, let alone volunteer a share of his legacy. She had no evidence of wrong doing, merely a suspicion which (she could already hear his lawyers objecting) was founded on fantasy and driven by envy.

A fanfare trumpeted the start of the news. She turned to watch. It was all the usual stuff: a bomb in Baghdad, a sex scandal in London, a minor rally on Wall Street. Her attention wandered to the newscaster's chunky designer necklace and matching earrings. Too showy, she sniffed, stretching her arms and yawning. She was about to press the off button on the remote and head for bed when an item of 'breaking' local news came on. A body had been discovered at the bottom of a disused lift shaft at the Plaza Hotel. It was badly decomposed but documents found in the clothing indicated that it was that of Kenneth Winslowe, a lawyer from Tennessee who had been reported missing six weeks earlier. He had been stabbed to death.

The remote fell from Miranda's hand, killing the television as it hit the floor. Gripped by a sudden panic, she ran to the front door and bolted the security chain. Then she doused the lights and crossed back to the window. The promenade was still deserted; no unfamiliar vehicle was parked opposite, no stranger loitered in the shadows. Yet the scene had altered radically. She suddenly felt threatened. The safe, comfortable home of a few minutes ago had become the target of an unknown enemy. Winslowe must have been murdered that night when she met him at the Plaza. The two events had to be connected: her family's previously unguessed-at past had come back, not just to haunt her nightmares but to invade her reality. She slammed an angry fist against the window's thickened glass. Damn Cousin Frankie! What the hell was he mixed up in? Damn him for making her cower in the dark like a frightened child, afraid of a knock at the door, afraid of a bully-boy boss. Outside, high above the distant harbour, black streaks now scarred a piebald moon and cast dark shadows across the deep. A brightly lit cruise ship glided into view, sounding its foghorn in farewell, as it slipped out towards the open sea. Yet, it was no ocean liner that Miranda saw; it was Amerigo Vespucci's wooden galleon, her sails at full mast, her flags flying boldly in the wind. She took a deep breath: undaunted by danger, Vespucci and *La Bella Simonetta* had crossed the Atlantic and discovered a new world. Miranda now resolved to do likewise and rediscover an old one.

18

'AH, AWAKE AT last,' Aunt Stella chirped. Tom blinked up at the sunbeams dancing on a crystal chandelier. He was lying on the floor, wrapped in a blanket with a cushion under his head. 'Sorry, you were too heavy for me to lift onto the sofa,' his aunt apologised as he struggled to sit up. His back and shoulders were so stiff he might have been wearing a straightjacket. He had fallen into a deep sleep, she told him, and seemed to be having nightmares. Did he recall any of them? she wondered. His head felt like lead, as though he had had an all-night boozing session. He could not remember what day it was, never mind nightmares. He shook his head. She smiled. Dreams were like that, weren't they? She told him to help himself to whatever he could find in the fridge and feel free to use the guest bathroom at the far end of the corridor. She had to go out for a while. Her once-a-week college cleaning lady ('"scouts" we call them at Oxford') was not due till the following day, so he should not be disturbed. 'However,' she warned, 'it would be unwise to venture out. The police are still prowling around.'

Tom heard the front door shut. He went to the window and watched his aunt open her green umbrella and dissolve into the pastel murk of a foggy Oxford morning. Across the street his mum's old Peugeot was still parked where he had left it the day before, though its windscreen was unexpectedly festooned with parking tickets. The sight reignited the throbbing in his head, so he turned away from the window and concentrated on the gnawing in his stomach. He was famished, as if he had not eaten for a week. The well-stocked fridge in the kitchen fortunately provided him with a hearty breakfast of bacon, tomatoes and scrambled eggs. He made a mug of black coffee and, pivoting on the rear legs of a Windsor chair, leant back against the kitchen wall. His eyes drifted along rows of willow-pattern plates on a stripped-pine dresser, then dropped down to the gleaming electric oven and polished steel worktops adjacent to the spotless sink. His aunt's domestic life appeared to be one of well-ordered solitude, undisturbed even by the surrogates of television or radio, of which there was no sign, either in the kitchen or, now he came to think of it, in the living room. His attention wandered back to the breakfast table: a book lay open opposite him. He had noticed it before but, till now, his dull head and biting hunger had stifled his curiosity. Leaning forwards, he dragged it across the tabletop and swivelled it round. A face stared up at him, and suddenly his nightmares hit him like an avalanche. That flat-ridged nose, the jutting chin, the pensive gaze: Lorenzo de' Medici's portrait was unmistakable. Now he could see in his mind's eye Lorenzo walking behind Ficino down a narrow path, entering Ficino's cottage, and the hound Buontempo bounding in front of them. It all came back to him, every detail of their dress, every word they exchanged and, above all, the name that echoed into his own time: Scala.

He looked at the book's front cover: *The History of the House of Medici*, and there, at the centre, was the same shield with six balls surrounding a seventh which had topped the entrance to Scala's bank and been engraved on that cufflink he found beside Jasper's body. Turning the pages, he read quickly, thumbing through the centuries with a strange familiarity, as if he was merely being reminded of things past, rather than learning anything new. True, bits of the dynasty's early history had already figured in his dream: the villa at Careggi, the Platonic Academy, the Pazzi conspiracy, even Prince Lorenzo's love of dogs and Marsilio Ficino's stutter. But how come his dream bore such a close relation to what, for him, had been previously unknown history? And, anyway, that did not explain his peculiar feeling of déjà vu about the rest of the Medici's incredible story: their rise to become the first international bankers of Europe, perhaps even the founders of modern capitalism. First there was Cosimo, manipulating the government of Florence for his own ends, like some precursor of a Mafia godfather, and creating a banking empire that stretched from Rome to London, Bruges to Geneva. Then came his grandson Lorenzo, said to be the model for Machiavelli's infamous prince, yet hailed as 'The Magnificent', patron of Leonardo da Vinci and Michelangelo, and himself no mean poet.

What particularly struck Tom was how the Medici's influence had percolated down to the present day and into his own daily life. The scrambled eggs he had just eaten had been introduced to France, and thence to the rest of Europe, by Lorenzo's great-granddaughter, Queen Catherine, along with ice-cream and artichokes. Lorenzo's son, Pope Leo X, had made Henry VIII 'Defender of the Faith', and the initials 'F.D.' still appeared beside the Queen's head on the pound coin he took from his pocket.

As he put the coin back, he noticed the tip of a ginger tail whipping moodily to and fro, inches from his left foot. 'Oh no you don't, Marmaduke!' he cried, jerking his foot back onto the rung of his chair. The cat poked its head out from under the table and gave him the dirtiest of looks. 'I'll bet you were a real duke in a previous life, weren't you, Marmy, old bean?' he taunted his thwarted tormentor. 'Yes, you could easily have been Alessandro, Duke of Florence, Il Magnifico's great-grandson by a Moorish slave-girl, debauching his way through the city's convents, poisoning one rival only to be murdered by another.'

The cat let out a strangled hiss, somewhere between a growl and a meow. 'What's that you say? You don't agree? Well, maybe you're right. You were probably someone much grander than that.' Tom thought for a moment. 'How about Cosimo, the first Grand Duke of Tuscany? Of course he was only from the cadet branch of the Medici family – Il Magnifico's side died out with Queen Marie of France. She was Charles II's grandma, don't you know?'

Marmaduke rolled over onto his back, stretching his paws carelessly in the air like some sated marmalade sultan in his seraglio, completely indifferent to Tom's mockery.

'I know,' said Tom, warming to his theme, 'you're Gian Gastone. Grand Duke Cosimo's great-grandson, the fattest man in Florence. Never up before noon, always drunk by sundown, stuffed himself silly at lunch and threw up over his guests at dinner. Died in bed in 1737, too bloated to move.

No wonder the Medici line fizzled out a few years later.'
Marmaduke stood up and stalked out of the room in disgust.

As Tom washed up the breakfast things, his thoughts were
still with the Medici. What was it that Ficino had been about
to show Lorenzo when his nightmare (or was it a vision?)
ended so abruptly? What was so secret that Cosimo had not
even told Scala, his trusted lieutenant, about it? And could
all that really be connected with the current Count Scala and
his own trumped-up dismissal from the count's bank?

Having dried the dishes, Tom returned to the living
room. He briefly scanned the array of invitation cards on his
aunt's mantelpiece (a dinner at All Souls, a luncheon at the
Royal Academy, a talk at the Athenaeum), before grabbing
the backpack he had retrieved from the boot of the Peugeot
the previous evening. He always kept it at the ready, filled
with all the essentials for last-minute business trips. He was
about to head for the bathroom when the front doorbell
rang. Assuming his aunt had forgotten her keys, he went to
let her in. A sharp-eyed woman with thin lips and pointy
nose confronted him, mop in one hand, bucket in the other.
Apparently the college scouts had changed the cleaning rota
without informing his aunt. Tom saw a flicker of suspicion
cross her face as he explained his aunt's absence and his
own presence as an unexpected visitor. The charlady peered
distrustfully into the room behind him before bustling off to
her next call, saying she would come back later.

Tom resumed his search for the bathroom. The first door
along the corridor was locked but the next one opened without
a problem, revealing a white-tiled bathroom as pristine as
the kitchen. He showered and shampooed, luxuriating in the
warm droplets that simultaneously relaxed and invigorated

his limbs. After the shower, a shave. Stroking his chin, he could not believe how thick the stubble had grown in one night, nor how long his fingernails looked in the mirror above the washbasin. He opened the small cabinet next to the mirror to look for a socket for his electric shaver. An array of pill bottles crammed the shelves; all bore his aunt's name and address. Realising he was in the wrong bathroom and swearing under his breath at the prospect of having to explain the wet towels and steamy shower to his hostess, he was about to close the cabinet door when a label caught his eye. It was on a small box that stood out among the glass bottles. The label said: 'Pentothal (Thiopental Sodium)'. Surely that was the truth drug beloved of spy thrillers? What was it doing in Aunt Stella's bathroom? A shiver ran down his spine. He recalled the glass of mulled wine she had given him the night before and how the room had begun to spin shortly afterwards. He also recalled the shrill, insistent voice interrogating his dreams. Something was not right. Throwing on some fresh clothes, he decided to take a closer look around his aunt's lodgings.

19

'INCREDIBILE, MAESTRO!' ROSSI effused. 'To think that we have just held a birthday party for Plato without even knowing it.'

'And become heirs to the Platonic Academy,' Gatti beamed, straightening his ready-to-wear bow tie.

Scala basked for a moment in the wonder which his revelations had aroused, but there was more to come. He motioned to Fabio and, seconds later, the lights went out. As the warm glow of a flame-effect electric fire illumined the gloom, outlandish shadows danced along the library's bookshelves. 'Behold, gentlemen,' declared the count, 'how the majority of mankind experiences reality. They live in a mental cave, believing mere shadows to be real. Only a few Great Souls, the "Makropsychoi", as Plato called them, are able to perceive the truth and know the secrets of the universe.'

'And what might they be?' questioned Jankovic.

Scala's grip tightened on the vellum tome he had earlier removed from the bookcase. 'Ficino,' he said, 'devoted his life to translating Plato's works and other esoteric texts rescued from the collapsing Byzantine Empire. And in so doing he uncovered a secret so tremendous that he had to ensure its concealment until...'

'Until "Le Temps Revient" – "The Season Returns",' Gatti interrupted. 'That was the motto on Lorenzo's coat of arms, wasn't it?'

Scala's eyes widened in surprise. His dossier on the backroom Vatican archivist had not indicated such intimacy with the details of Medici history, but then he had only recently been incepted into the Brotherhood and personal information was not easily extracted from the Holy See. 'Yes, Dottore,' he replied, 'that, together with "Semper", or "Always", was indeed Lorenzo's motto, expressing his undying faith in the perennial renewal of the House of Medici. And it was also Lorenzo who instructed Ficino to cast the seven solitaire rings which we are all wearing tonight, one for each member of the Platonic Academy.'

'What about the rings' inscriptions?' Gatti continued. 'Are they Ficino's work too?'

'Ficino was a master alchemist. Aided by the sculptor Donatello, he somehow contrived for the inscriptions to become visible when the diamonds were energised in certain places on certain dates, thus leading our Brotherhood to the greatest secret of all.'

'Ah,' sighed Rossi, admiring the gem sparkling on his finger, 'so my ring might once have graced the hand of Botticelli.'

'And maybe I've got Lorenzo's ring,' Gatti exclaimed gleefully. But his joy evaporated when Scala disclosed that his own ancestor, Bartolomeo, had been entrusted with Lorenzo's ring after the latter's death, having undertaken to ensure the due transmission of all seven rings down the ages. 'Which is why,' said the count, 'Lorenzo's ring has passed down through the Scala male line until, at last, it came to me.'

As he finished speaking, the grandfather clock began to chime midnight. Suddenly, a ray of blinding light shot from the diamond ring depicted in Bartolomeo's portrait and struck Radopoulos's solitaire. The young Greek screamed as the diamond on his finger shone like a splinter of sunlight, and stroboscopic beams filled the room with staccato silhouettes. Shouts and thuds peppered the air. Then, as suddenly as it had started, the display ceased. When, at last, someone turned the lights on again, Radopoulos was lying on the floor, motionless.

Rossi rushed to his aid but Hawkwood was already there. 'It's alright,' he yelled, pressing Radopoulos's neck to feel for a pulse. 'He's fainted, that's all.'

Fabio and two of the waiters lifted him off the floor, and Scala instructed them to take the poor fellow to the guest suite where his doctor would attend to him first thing in the morning. As they bore Radopoulos out of the library, Scala removed his ring, quietly noting the thin red line that encircled his throat.

'What does the ring say?' excited voices clamoured, as all thoughts of Radopoulos exited with him.

Scala read out the inscription with slow deliberation:

'"NIGRORUM O FRATRES MONACHORUM CELLA PETENDA EST XXXIX. N.B."'

'I think it's another hexameter,' Rossi proffered.

'Never mind the poetics,' grunted Jankovic. 'What the hell does it mean?'

'Simple,' Gatti jumped in at once. 'It translates as "O Brothers of the Black Monks cell 39 must be sought".'

'What about the "N.B." at the end?' Rossi queried.

Gatti sucked his teeth. 'Surely everyone knows that "N.B." stands for "nota bene", don't they?'

'I doubt that's the case here,' Sarachin's hoarse voice piped up. 'The initials on the count's ring referred to a date, so I'd expect those on Mr. Radopoulos's ring to do so too.'

Scala agreed with him and pointed out that, in classical Latin, "N.B." could also stand for "Nox Brumalis": the winter solstice.

'That would be December 21st,' said Jankovic. 'But what's all this about cell 39? Is there a prison in Florence?'

Scala paced the floor. The Museo Nazionale del Bargello had functioned as a prison for hundreds of years during the Medici era, but it had been turned into a museum more than a century before. Cell 39 had to be somewhere else.

'I say,' Hawkwood boomed, 'you don't suppose it's got something to do with *The Thirty-Nine Steps*, do you? You know, the First World War spy story? The steps were on the Thames, near Blackfriars Bridge.'

'Don't be ridiculous,' Gatti scoffed. 'The clue was inscribed in the fifteenth century, five hundred years before the First World War.'

But Hawkwood's reference to Blackfriars Bridge gave Scala an idea. 'I think Dottore Gatti's translation wasn't quite right,' he said. 'He attached the genitive "Nigrorum Monachorum" to "Fratres" but it actually goes with "cella".'

'Ouch! Schoolboy howler, what!' Hawkwood crowed, grabbing the chance to get back at Gatti.

Gatti scowled at him. 'So what? It still makes no sense.'

'On the contrary, Dottore,' said the Count. 'Instead of referring to "the Brothers of the Black Monks", it actually refers to "the cell of the Black Monks" or rather the Blackfriars: a nickname for the black-cloaked Dominicans.'

'So?'

'So the Dominicans have a monastery, the Priory of San Marco, right here in Florence, just up the road from the Palazzo Medici.'

'I still don't see what that has to do with the clue.' Gatti sulked.

Scala explained that Cosimo de' Medici had paid for the monastery to be rebuilt and, in gratitude, the Dominicans had let him have his own room or 'cell' to pray in: cell number 39.

'Another multiple of three,' noted Sarachin.

But Gatti remained unconvinced. 'How could Cosimo have been so friendly with the Dominicans? Didn't their leader Savonarola hate the Medici?'

'With a vengeance,' Scala replied. 'But the mad monk was not yet born when Cosimo died. In Cosimo's day, the Medici still enjoyed good relations with their Dominican neighbours. And now I come to think of it,' he added after a moment's thought, 'the Company of the Magi had its headquarters at San Marco. It was there, on the night of the 5th of January each year, that they would begin their annual celebration of the Epiphany.'

'But the ring refers to the winter solstice, not Epiphany,' Gatti persisted.

Professor Jankovic's hand shot up. 'I think I can answer that one,' he said. 'All the dates we have been given so far – the autumnal equinox, the winter solstice and Plato's birthday as the midway point between the two – are astronomical, not ecclesiastical, reference points. So, it seems to me that we are dealing here with a secret which predates the Christian era.'

'That's very true,' Rossi agreed. 'And it's well known that the Church chose many of its holy days, as well as its places of worship, to coincide with and replace earlier pagan ones. Christmas, for example, occurs at the same time as the old Roman winter festival of the Saturnalia.'

'No,' rasped Sarachin, struggling to clear his throat, 'the Saturnalia was before Christmas. Christmas itself is celebrated on the birthday of the Roman god Sol Invictus. But, yes, most religious festivals, Christian or otherwise, do reflect changes in the heavens or the seasons.' He broke off, coughing loudly. Fabio, who had by now returned from dealing with Radopoulos, offered him a glass of water. After a couple of sips, he recovered his voice: 'In Egyptian mythology, for instance, Horus, god of light, was born at the winter solstice, and so was Mithras, the divine mediator between God and Man, according to the ancient Iranian calendar. But of course,' he emphasised, 'all such festivals are merely the physical manifestation of metaphysical constructs by the psyche.'

Scala could not help chuckling at this last remark. 'If I didn't know it already, Leo, I should by now have no doubt that you're a Jungian psychoanalyst by profession. But I'm sure that you and Rossi and the Professore are all correct. Whatever the solution to this mystery may be, it is one that goes far back in time.' He looked at his watch: it was well past midnight. 'Gentlemen,' he said, 'my chauffeur will now return you to the city. We shall meet again at San Marco on the night of the winter solstice.'

20

Tom raced out of the bathroom. He did not have much time: Aunt Stella could come home any minute. He went back up the corridor and stopped by the locked door he had mistakenly tried earlier. He turned the handle again: there was a loud click and, this time, it opened easily. How or why, he could not stop to speculate.

Inside, it was dark: blinds covered the windows. He flicked on a light switch. A desk and chair occupied the centre of the room, with a bookcase on one side and a full-length mirror on the other. Opposite them was a museum-style display case. Intrigued, he took a closer look. Inside the case, what looked like a goatskin was held taut on stretchers: it seemed to be a map of some sort, with a variety of crudely drawn monochrome figures populating an antique landscape. A strange, spidery script wound in between the drawings while, here and there, another hand had penned brief notations in English. Starting at the left-hand edge, he saw a temple with massive columns covered in hieroglyphics and framed by palm trees. The notation read: 'The Oracle of Siwa, Egypt. Alexander learns of the treasure which will make him master of the world.'

'Egyptian oracle', 'Alexander': these were two of the names Tom had managed to decipher in his father's blood-spattered letter. With growing excitement, he followed a dotted line which led out of Egypt, across the desert, past Babylon, Persepolis, and the Hindu Kush, until it arrived at snow-capped mountains captioned "The Mountains of Heaven". In the midst of the mountains stood a bent figure, waving to a girl with a thick braid down her back. She was pushing a sled with a wooden chest on top. A large dog (or was it a wolf?) was pulling at the front. Tom gasped: this was the scene in the first of his 'nightmares'. The old man had to be Rinpoche, and the girl Yingsel, but where was the one called Dorje?

The dotted line moved south into another desert. The sled was now on its side, bereft of its cargo. Yingsel lay face down in the sand, an arrow in her back, and the wolf howling beside her. Again, Tom recognised the scene: it was not from his nightmare but from the translation enclosed with his father's letter. Yet seeing it, depicted so graphically, he felt a terrible rage well up inside him. 'Calm down,' he told himself. 'It was only a dream, wasn't it?' The feeling subsided and he followed the dotted line once more, through Central Asia to China and back again towards Persia. Suddenly a sharp voice crackled behind him. 'What are you doing? How did you get in here?' It was his aunt. He had been so engrossed in the map he had not heard her come home. 'I took the wrong door,' he answered, which was half-true.

Aunt Stella walked over to the display case. 'It's Rinpoche's map,' she said with a pained smile. 'I'd gone to look for John, your father, that night when Rinpoche appeared to him in the library. John had fallen asleep. The incense burner was still smoking. Rinpoche came out of nowhere and asked me to show him the *Corpus Hermeticum*.' She explained that Milton College's medieval library contained one of the earliest surviving texts, which she had studied for her thesis. 'Rinpoche looked through the text and claimed it was incomplete.' She poked her nose in the air: the monk's effrontery still rankled. 'Then he produced this map from his knapsack. He thought I could help him complete it.' She gazed down at the map, recalling her puzzlement when Rinpoche had begun talking of Tibetan caves, robbers on the Silk Road, murder and stolen treasure. 'They sold the treasure to merchants who traded it for silk at the court of the Chinese emperor. But he, being warned of a curse, sent it to Babylon as a "gift" to the Persian king, Mithridates. That's where the Magi came in.'

Tom followed his aunt's gaze to the end of the map where three veiled men sat by a campfire in the desert, staring at an empty casket. 'Who did you say they were?'

She looked him in the eye. 'You know as well as I do, Tom.'

She was right. As soon as she had spoken that name, something had clicked, just as it had when he read about the Medici earlier that morning. The Magi were somehow a part of his own personal history. He shuddered. It was too much to take in.

She put her hand on his shoulder. 'Don't worry, I felt the same when I remembered.'

He frowned. 'Remembered what?'

'That I was not who I thought I was.' Her hand slid from his shoulder and she went back across the room to the free-standing mirror. 'Rinpoche triggered my astral memory, quite unintentionally of course.' She paused to admire her reflection, squaring her shoulders and fluffing up her hair. 'He thought that I could complete the story, plug the gaps between the first century and the twentieth.' She turned from the mirror and let out a little giggle: 'When he realised his mistake, he dropped the map and fled as if he had seen a ghost – which, in a way, he had.'

Tom ran his hand impatiently through his still-damp hair. He did not like the way she ridiculed Rinpoche, though he could not fathom why. 'For God's sake, stop talking in riddles!'

'As you wish,' she replied archly. 'Rinpoche showed me the map in the expectation of resurrecting his disciple. Instead, he lifted the veil on a curse which has doomed me to two thousand years of loveless lives and barren spinsterhood.' Her voice seethed with an ancient bitterness. 'Your father,' she spat, 'was *my* fiancé first. Sophia stole him from me. I should have been your mother, not she.' She broke off, almost choking on her anger, and had to grab hold of the mirror to steady herself. When she spoke again, her fury had turned to ice. 'But now, thanks to you, I shall soon be free of the curse forever.'

'Thanks to me?'

'Let's stop pretending, shall we, Tom? You broke into my study and you found the map. You wouldn't have done that unless you'd also been into my bathroom and discovered the sodium pentothal.' Tom gulped: she knew he knew about the truth drug. It was, apparently, a leftover from her time with MI6. She had been recruited as an undergraduate and spent some years as a spy behind the Iron Curtain before returning to academia. Using the drug in conjunction with the haunted Hermanubis statuette, she had infiltrated the depths of Tom's psychic memory. His last 'nightmare' about Lorenzo de' Medici had confirmed what she had long suspected: that the Medici, being not only great fans of the Magi but also bankers to the Vatican, had taken as collateral from a spendthrift pope a fabulous treasure. 'A treasure which Rome has been trying to recover ever since.'

Tom looked back at the map and at the body of Yingsel lying beside the overturned sled. What on Earth had been inside that stolen casket? he wondered.

'Then, last night,' Aunt Stella concluded, 'after days of regression, you finally spoke the name I most wanted to hear: Scala.'

Tom rubbed his cheek: no wonder he was growing a beard, he had been drugged for days. 'You know Scala?'

'The latest descendant of the Medici's staunchest supporter? Of course I've heard of him. And seen his photograph in society magazines. That's how I spotted him at the Athenaeum in September, attending a talk on the Precession of the Equinoxes: it had to be significant.'

'Why?'

'A man like Scala could have only one reason to be interested in such an abstruse subject.' She shifted the mirror on its castors until she could see Tom reflected in it. 'I told you before that the equinoxes are liminal windows, portals in time and space through which liminal beings from Merlin to Nostradamus have peered or passed in their search for truth. This cheval glass,' she said, addressing herself now to Tom's reflection, 'is another such portal. It belonged to Ruggieri, Catherine de' Medici's astrologer. Why don't you come and take a look.' He was about to do so when the front doorbell rang. 'Drat!' she scowled and scurried off to repel the unwelcome caller.

Tom listened at the study door. It was probably the charlady returning as promised, he thought. But the voice at the front door was male, and it sounded official. There had been a report, someone acting suspiciously, someone matching the description of the person being sought in connection with the September train bombing. Tom's heart pounded: the charlady had gone to the police. Then he heard a whisper: 'Tom, over here.' He swung round but saw no-one. 'No, here,' urged the whisperer impatiently. It was coming from his aunt's magic mirror. He looked into the glass and froze.

'No time for questions,' said Rinpoche's disembodied face with a Cheshire Cat smile. 'Get away now. Follow Marmaduke.'

'Marmaduke?'

'You going deaf as well as dumb, Tommy boy?' the face snorted. 'Your old self was so much smarter. When things calm down, come to Montevecchio. I'll be waiting for you.' With that, the face vanished and Tom was left staring at his own startled visage.

By now the police were inside the house: 'Check the kitchen,' he heard one of them shout. He closed the study door as softly as he could. As he did so, a ginger streak bolted through the gap and up behind the window blinds. Marmaduke was equally keen to escape the noisy intruders. A well-practised paw deftly lifted a latch and moments later the canny cat was outside on the pavement, a few feet below. Tom followed suit and landed right next to him.

A blanket of fog engulfed them both. Archways loomed, locked gates were jumped and railings scaled; winding passageways eventually led to green lanes and on to the water meadows beyond the university walls. Marmaduke slipped away as the riverside mist became punctured with the calls of relentless coxswains and the splash of rival oars. Tom followed the towpath, though by now he had no idea where he was headed. After half an hour or so, a low bridge came into view, then a village pub – The Trout – with an old red telephone box next to it. The good news was that the phone was working; the bad news: he had no coins and could not risk trying to get change in the pub for fear of being recognised again. He would have to make a reverse-charge call. But who to? Who could he trust? There was only one person.

WINTER

21

THE TAXI FROM Fiumicino Airport sped up the long straight avenue towards St Peter's Square as if the apostle himself were about to slam the Pearly Gates. As they wove in and out of the traffic, honking at unwary cyclists and straying pedestrians, Miranda wondered if insanity were a prerequisite to driving in Rome or merely a consequence. But neither her cowboy driver nor the jet lag from the overnight flight from New York could dull the splendour of St Peter's basilica, basking in the mid-morning sun beneath a sky of duck-egg blue. As a schoolgirl at the local Catholic High, she had often imagined herself gazing up at Christ and his disciples, arrayed in white marble above that vast piazza. And now here she was, passing right in front of it, caught for a moment in the embrace of Bernini's twin colonnades. But that embrace had long since soured into a snare; the small-town schoolgirl had grown up. There was no room for faith in the world of well-heeled bankers and white-shoe lawyers. It was no pious urge to pilgrimage which had brought her to the nerve centre of the Catholic Church but a visceral indignation at the thought of a cheat prospering, of bullies winning, of crime evading punishment. And that, she recalled wryly, was what had first attracted her to the law.

Bernini's masterpiece slipped round the curve in the road; the towering walls of the Vatican loomed ahead. Miranda turned her attention to the brief missive which she had received just two days before:

'Dear Madame,
    You are hereby granted an audience with Fr. da Forli O.P. Present this letter, together with your passport, at the Cancello di Sant' Anna on 8th December, 11.30a.m.
    Yours in faith
    The Office of the Prefect of the Vatican Archive
    The Holy See of Saint Peter, Roma.'

The letter bore the stamp of the Papal Court. The image brought back childhood memories of the old family bible in her parents' front parlour. Her father used to compare the mitre and cross-keys embossed on its front to the skull and crossbones, much to her mother's annoyance. But the stamp on the letter had an additional Latin tag: 'Archivum Secretum Apostolicum Vaticanum'. She took this to be a department of the Vatican Library, and certainly, she thought, a 'secret archive' was just the kind of place the elusive Frankie might be found.

A short distance down the Via di Porta Angelica the taxi pulled up in front of high, wrought-iron gates. Miranda alighted (with relief) and handed her letter and passport to the Swiss Guard who strutted forwards in his carnival-coloured doublet and breeches. Had Venice come to the

Vatican? she mused, as he waved her through and into the custody of another particoloured sentry. But, as she fell in behind her unsmiling escort, she quickly sensed that there was no carnival atmosphere in this place. The noisy streets of Rome faded into a subdued hush of introverted courtyards and lofty, unlit windows. Despite her respectful navy-blue headscarf and knee-length raincoat, she could feel the displeasure of unseen eyes, as if the apostasy in her heart had been branded onto her forehead.

A plain stone plaque was the only clue to their arrival at the Archivo Segreto. Vases of white lilies dotted long corridors, scenting the air with a melancholic sweetness. At the top of a narrow staircase, the Swiss Guard tapped on an anonymous door. 'Avanti,' squawked a harsh, parrot-like voice from within. The room was cold, bare and definitely unwelcoming. Only the faint smell of cigarette smoke jarred with the otherwise monastic scene. A man was seated at a table; sunlight streamed in through an open window behind him. Raising her hand against the glare, Miranda could make out the profile of an almost comical Humpty-Dumpty figure, complete with pot-belly and egg-shaped head whose baldness was made all the more emphatic by the long strands of grey hair drawn punctiliously across it. His eyes were hidden in shadow whilst a thick white tunic and black mantle cloaked him from the neck down. Two podgy hands stuck out from the sleeves; they were clasped over a file. With a cursory nod, he motioned her to a low wooden stool on the opposite side of the table.

As she sat down, she could feel the man's furtive gaze and kept her knees firmly together, pulling the lapels of her mackintosh tight across her bosom. 'Thank you so much for seeing me, Monsignor,' she ventured, attempting to thaw the glacial silence. No answer. She tried again: 'Oh, do forgive my ignorance, I'm not sure if that's the correct form of address to the prefect of the Vatican Archive?'

'The prefect is abroad on papal business,' the cleric replied. 'I am one of his adjutors… his assistants.'

'Oh I assumed from the letter…'

'Assumptions are the sign of a lazy mind, my child,' he interrupted, adding with a sanctimonious sigh: 'You may call me Father Vincenzo.'

She decided to cut the small-talk: 'I understand that my cousin, Frankie Maddingley, works here in the Vatican Library. Does he report to the prefect or to the Vatican librarian?'

The adjutor drew himself up in his chair, explaining, as if to one who could not possibly appreciate the subtleties of high office, that the prefect *was* the Vatican librarian, a post in the direct gift of the Pope. He nodded towards a painting on the opposite wall. 'That is a copy of a famous fresco,' he said. 'It commemorates the appointment of the first Vatican librarian, Platina, by Pope Sixtus IV, the Pope who commissioned the Sistine Chapel.'

Miranda glanced over her shoulder. There, lording it on a gilded throne, was a swarthy, square-jawed man who looked more like a corporate chief executive than a Pope, chairing a meeting of shifty-eyed sycophants, cooking up a boardroom plot. If those guys swapped their cardinal's robes and tonsures for lounge suits and crew-cuts, she thought, they'd be right at home on Wall Street. 'Awesome,' she enthused politely. 'I guess that's the librarian kneeling in front of the Pope's throne. But who are the other men standing next to them?'

Her question prompted a brief spark of enthusiasm into the adjutor's voice: 'On the left is Count Girolamo Riario, Lord of Imola. The others are Cardinals Raffaele Riario and Giuliano della Rovere with his brother Duke Giovanni. They were all,' he said with a sly grin, 'the Pope's "nephews".'

Miranda raised an eyebrow. She was not shocked by worldliness in a priest, but there was something distinctly unpleasant about da Forli's innuendo, something that put her even more on guard. 'Father Vincenzo,' she said, fixing him with a determined stare, 'I'm here, as you know, to see my cousin. Where can he be found?'

Vincenzo reverted to funereal gloom. 'He's gone,' he answered flatly, brushing a speck of dandruff from his black cloak.

'Gone? Gone where?'

'I've no idea. He was just a part-time porter. He left quite suddenly, without giving notice.'

'When?'

'About two months ago, I believe.'

Miranda got to her feet, unable to contain herself any longer. 'Look,' she said, raising her voice and slamming her hand on the table, 'I haven't flown halfway round the world to see my cousin only to be told that you don't know where the hell he is!'

The adjutor rocked back in his seat. He clearly was not used to such temerity, and certainly not in a woman. 'Please, Miss Maddingley, do calm yourself,' he croaked, nervously tapping his fingers together. 'I don't usually deal with personnel matters. There are so many neophytes passing through the Holy See. Most stay for just a few months before deciding that the Church is not for them.'

'But you must have an address on record, surely?'

He drew a deep breath and lifted the cover of the slim file in front of him. Licking a nicotine-stained fingertip to turn the pages he discovered, as if for the first time, that Mr. Maddingley had rented a flat in one of the poorer parts of the Trastevere district. When he failed to turn up for work for several days, efforts had been made to contact him, but without success. He had vacated his lodgings without leaving a forwarding address or paying the rent. 'There's nothing more,' he said, shutting the file firmly. 'I'm afraid you've had a wasted journey, my child.'

There was a distinct note of schadenfreude in that last remark. 'What about his family and friends?' Miranda demanded. 'There must be someone who knows where he is?'

Vincenzo shook his head. Her cousin was apparently an only child. Both parents were dead. 'As for friends,' he shrugged, 'I really can't say. Our records don't go into such details.'

At that moment the door to Vincenzo's office burst open and a rosy-cheeked young man in a blue habit tumbled in, balancing a pile of books in his arms. 'These are the authorities you wanted for the meeting this afternoon, Father,' he declared breathlessly. 'Sorry it's taken so long to find them all.'

Vincenzo glared at him. 'Brother Andreas, how many times have I told you to knock before entering? Can't you see I have a visitor?' The novice peered over the tower of books and gawped at Miranda as if she were a creature from another planet. 'Now you see, Miss Maddingley,' groaned the adjutor, 'what imbeciles I have to put up with.'

Brother Andreas stammered an apology but Vincenzo cut him short, barking a command in Italian. The novice immediately set the pile of books down on the table, then stood by the door in silence.

A solitary bell started to toll in the courtyard outside. 'Ah, the Angelus calls,' Vincenzo exhaled, rising from his chair and making it clear that the audience was at an end. Miranda seethed with frustration but she realised that further protest was futile. Thanking him for his time, she made for the door, eager to get away from the creepy cleric, though she had no idea what to do nor where to go next. Vincenzo instructed Brother Andreas to escort his visitor back to the Cancello di Sant' Anna. 'After all,' he said darkly, 'we wouldn't want you to get lost, would we, my child?'

Miranda and Brother Andreas walked, in what she now took to be the customary silence, back down the stairs and along the corridor that would return them to the open air. Outside, fluffy clouds were scudding across the sky, but the sunshine did nothing to lift her spirits. Vincenzo was right: she had hit a dead end.

'Signorina... Signorina,' Brother Andreas whispered nervously as they got outside. 'Forgive me, but I heard the adjutor call you Miss Maddingley just now. Are you by any chance related to Frankie Maddingley?' Miranda stopped in her tracks. 'No, don't stop!' the novice urged, looking round anxiously. 'You don't know who might be watching.'

She glanced up at the windows behind them and just caught sight of a podgy hand hurriedly closing the only one that was open. As they walked on, she avoided eye contact with her escort whilst explaining that she was indeed Frankie's relative – his cousin. 'Do you know him?' she asked hopefully.

'A little. He was Dottore Gatti's assistant. Dottore Gatti is a lay conservator in the Persian and Oriental Manuscripts Department. He's a friend of my eldest brother, Roberto.' The young man said that his brother, a wine merchant in Florence, would send Gatti a case of his favourite Tuscan wine every Christmas. 'The dottore is quite a connoisseur,' he chuckled.

'And Frankie worked with this Gatti guy?'

'*For* him, yes. Frankie would fetch and carry books and run errands. The dottore is very learned but also rather shy and reclusive. His nickname is the "Blonde Bookworm",' he said with a bashful smile, 'because he has blonde hair and loves spending all day in the cellars reading dead authors.'

'Sounds like fun!' Miranda quipped. 'But tell me about my cousin,' she said as they crossed a courtyard which she did not recall crossing on the way in.

The novice gurned. 'He never said much. He always had that serious look. No friends, as far as I know. Didn't drink or do drugs – yes, it happens even here, Signorina,' he said, waving at their surroundings. 'He seemed to live in a world of his own, disappearing for hours down in the storerooms of the Archivo Segreto. That's the Holy Father's personal library,' he added, pre-empting the question that every first-time visitor asked.

'I see,' she nodded. 'And the prefect in charge of the Archive reports directly to the Pope.'

'Why, yes, but how...'

'Father Vincenzo,' she smiled. 'He's a mine of information.' Brother Andreas sniggered. She began to warm to the ingenuous novice and pressed him to tell her more. He pointed at the ground: two metres below their feet were eighty kilometres of shelves, containing the Pope's private collection of books and manuscripts. They came from all over the world, accumulated over the centuries and never on public show. Fascinating though this was, it was Frankie whom Miranda really wanted to know more about.

'Frankie was a streetwise kind of guy,' Andreas replied. 'I heard he'd had a very tough childhood. Yet, he knew how to turn on the charm, especially with the dottore.' Apparently, the good Dr Gatti had treated her cousin like the son he had never had; tutored him in languages, history and much else besides. 'Frankie was a quick learner. He wasn't lazy, that's for sure. He worked day and night at his two jobs.'

'Two jobs?'

'Yes. His day job was working for the dottore, as I told you. But one evening I saw him coming out of Father Vincenzo's office. He said he was assisting the father with a special project.'

Miranda cocked her head. 'What kind of "special project"?'

'I don't know. He wouldn't tell me – said it was "classified".'

'How long had he worked here?'

'I'm not sure. I've only been here nine months myself. I know he'd worked for several years in the Vatican before being moved to the secret archive. He told me Father Vincenzo got him specially transferred last year to be Dottore Gatti's full-time assistant.'

Miranda felt like she had struck gold. She now had confirmation not only of her cousin's unappealing character but also of Vincenzo's duplicity: he had clearly lied to her about not knowing Frankie. She had to find out what else he had not told her. It was time to go for the jugular. 'You didn't like my cousin, did you, Andreas? And you don't like Father Vincenzo either?' Her youthful escort's cheeks turned bright pink. She put her hand briefly on his arm 'It's okay. I shan't tell.'

'Father Vincenzo is a Dominican,' he replied. 'I, on the other hand, am a Sylvestrine. You can tell from the colour of my habit.' He pointed at his dark blue vestment. 'The Dominicans regard Sylvestrines as an inferior order: too soft and easy-going, lacking the Jesuits' mental rigour and physical discipline.' Miranda frowned. Vincenzo had not come across as the ascetic type, far from it. Andreas read her thoughts. 'Father Vincenzo isn't a typical Dominican,' he said, giving his beautiful companion a sheepish look. 'Did he show you the picture on his wall?'

'You mean the one of Pope Sixtus and his nephews?'

He smirked. Father Vincenzo claimed that one of those so-called 'nephews' was actually his ancestor, Count Girolamo Riario, Lord of Imola and Forli. Had the adjutor not mentioned it? She shook her head. He raised his eyebrows: Vincenzo apparently bragged to everyone about his aristocratic ancestry. 'Actually, Frankie started doing the same recently, though he never put a name to his supposed noble forebears. In truth, I think he had an inferiority complex: he was prematurely bald, you know.' Miranda recognised the family trait: both her father and her uncle Ted had been bald as coots for as long as she could remember. Luckily, she took after her mother's side of the family: they had all kept their hair well into old age.

As they turned a corner, Andreas pointed to a nearby building. 'That's the Tower of the Winds, Signorina,' he said. 'It's the Vatican's observatory. Dottore Gatti and Frankie spent a lot of time there recently.' She looked up in surprise as incongruous visions of clerics in cassocks peering at the stars through giant telescopes came to mind. Her guide swiftly corrected this impression, explaining that the building was largely of historical significance. A line of white marble in its floor marked the meridian. 'Every day at noon – if it's not too cloudy – the sun shines through a tiny hole in the south wall, striking the line at a slightly different angle each time, thus marking the passage of the seasons.'

'Why go to so much trouble?'

'To get the date of Easter right. In 1582, Pope Gregory saw that the sunbeam fell sixty centimetres outside the meridian at the spring equinox, on which the timing of Easter depends, and accepted that the old Julian calendar was two weeks slow. He fast-forwarded the date and instituted the Gregorian calendar, which we still live by today.'

'An observatory of the equinox,' Miranda mused. 'But why should Doctor Gatti and Frankie have been interested in that?'

Andreas shrugged. 'I don't know. Maybe the dottore was researching some ancient text. He told me that the secret archive contains many important Chinese and Persian astronomical and astrological records.'

They walked on in silence for a while, Miranda quietly observing her escort with a mixture of pity and incomprehension. She failed to understand how an intelligent, good-looking young man like this could closet himself away from the world, subjecting himself to the tyranny of the likes of Father Vincenzo. True, when she was a pupil at her Catholic elementary school, she had felt a certain affection for the kindly nuns who taught there, and even imagined herself as a Bride of Christ, devoted to prayer and good works. But that childhood daydream had rapidly evaporated in the heat of adolescence. They rounded a bend in the road: they were almost back at the Cancello di Sant' Anna. She stopped and grabbed his arm: 'Don't you have *any* idea where Frankie might have gone?' she pleaded.

He pursed his lips: there was one thing. On the day that Frankie had failed to show up for work, Dr Gatti had gone to Florence to attend a conference.

'So?'

'Well, that was very unusual. I told you the dottore seldom ventures outside the library, let alone the Vatican. That's where Frankie came in. He did everything for him, from posting his letters to collecting his passport.'

'Passport? I thought you said the conference was in Florence?'

'To go outside the Vatican City is to go abroad. The Vatican is a sovereign state within the state of Italy. It has its own government, its own embassies, even its own courts.'

'I'll bet there's no appeal from them!'

'Only to the Pope.'

'And the new Pope's a Rottweiler,' Miranda chuckled, recalling the Pope's nickname from a news item. Andreas looked at her aghast: the Pope was clearly not a subject for jocularity. 'Was there anything else that struck you as unusual?' she asked, back-pedalling fast.

Andreas nodded. 'Dottore Gatti still hasn't come back from Florence. Father Vincenzo says his sister has been taken ill and he's had to stay on in Florence to look after her. But that can't be right.'

'Why not?'

'Because the dottore is an only child. His friend, my brother Roberto, told me.'

Miranda agreed that this seemed strange. She wondered if Andreas knew where in Florence the conference was held. He did not, but he had noticed Gatti reading a brochure for the Grand Hotel Villa Medici, although he could not imagine how the dottore could have afforded to stay at such a luxurious hotel.

'It's a start,' said Miranda, hurriedly scribbling the hotel's name in her pocket notebook. By now they had reached the exit barrier. She was reluctant to let go of her helpful, and disarmingly earnest, chaperone. 'How about a coffee?' she asked, nodding hopefully towards a café down the street.

But even as she uttered the words, the monk was taking two steps back. 'Oh, mi dispiace, Signorina,' he demurred. 'I cannot go beyond the walls of the Vatican.'

'Why not? Will the Pope excommunicate you?'

He laughed. 'No, no. It's a condition of my novitiate.'

Miranda kicked herself for being so crass. 'Oh, I'm sorry, Andreas. I didn't mean to…'

'It's alright. You're not from here. You weren't to know.'

'But don't you sometimes wish you were free to go where you like? Do what you like, unconstrained by all those vows you have to take?'

'You see those clouds,' he said, pointing at the sky, 'they seem as free as birds, yet they are merely the playthings of every passing breeze.'

Miranda knew when she was beaten. She held out her hand to say goodbye, but the monk put his palms together and bowed. As he turned away, he glanced back and said: 'You should visit Raphael's tomb in the Pantheon, Signorina. Every day since his death in 1520, an unseen hand has laid a rose beside it. In Italy, you see, vows are made to last.'

22

CARRIE WILSON STOPPED her car in an unlit lay-by on a quiet country lane, shortly after exiting the Eurotunnel terminal at Calais. The late-night rail journey from Folkestone had gone without a hitch. She got out and ran round to the boot. 'For God's sake, Carrie, can you point that thing somewhere else?' Tom groaned as the boot swung open and a blinding torchlight shone in his face.

'Sorry,' his former secretary apologised, shifting the beam towards his doubled-up legs. 'This is my first time at people smuggling, you know.'

'Well, don't give up the day job just yet,' he grunted. Two hours of being crammed, foetus-like, into the boot of her bouncy old Alfa Romeo had left him, like the genie in the bottle, ill-disposed, even towards his deliverer. He unfurled his legs over the car's bumper, straightened his back and stretched his arms, as his breath billowed in the freezing December air.

'Here, drink this,' said Carrie, pouring some tea from the thermos she had filled before they set off from her London flat. The hot liquid lightened Tom's mood and, after a few sips, he felt sufficiently restored to go round to the front of the car and ease himself into the Alfa's passenger seat. 'Sorry I snapped at you,' he said as he squeezed his legs under the dashboard. 'You've done so much for me this past month, letting me lie low in your apartment. I really don't deserve such kindness.'

'Too right, Mr Talbot,' she came back at once in her chirpy Australian English. 'You owe me big time. But right now, you'd better try to get some shut-eye.' It would take three hours to drive to Paris. She put some guitar music on the CD player. Tom closed his eyes, drifting on the soft melodies, disturbed occasionally by the glare of oncoming headlights. How lucky he had been to get straight through to Carrie from that phone box outside Oxford. How grateful that she had rushed from work to his rescue, driving him back to her flat in London's Docklands. She had put him up in her spare room, bought him new clothes, made travel arrangements, even lent him her hard-earned savings. Over bottles of Aussie shiraz and takeaway pizzas, he had relived his bizarre existence since his sacking in what seemed a lifetime ago.

Carrie had listened with an unexpectedly open mind. She had never for a moment believed the bank's official line that Tom had 'resigned for personal reasons'. And her doubts had been reinforced when the police arrived a few days later and not only seized Tom's computer but also searched Woodcock's office. The news of 'Poison Ivy's' sudden and now, thanks to Tom's alleged terrorist links, suspicious death had shocked him. It was not just that it had happened on the same day as his sacking; it had been right after Woodcock's lunch with Count Scala at the Athenaeum, where Aunt Stella had said she had also been that day. Carrie agreed that these were indeed striking coincidences. But whether she believed in the reality of Tom's more 'psychical' experiences was another matter. As a girl, growing up in the Australian outback, she knew the stories the Aborigines told about the 'Dreamtime', the time out of time. She had visited Uluru and felt its primeval power. But she was nothing if not a down-to-earth Aussie, and thought it just as likely that this Rinpoche 'fella' was the product of stress and exhaustion, not to mention alcohol and truth drugs.

Nor was Tom entirely unsympathetic to that view. Premonitions were not unheard of, psychologically speaking, any more than telepathy or hallucinations. And Aunt Stella's drugs could well have disorientated his perceptions. But there were other things that he himself still could not come to terms with, things so alien he had not shared them, even with Carrie: Hermanubis for one, Dorje for another.

Carrie nudged his arm. 'We're there,' she said, as she pulled up a few hundred yards from the main entrance to the Gare de Lyon, well out of range of any CCTV cameras. He rubbed the sleep from his eyes and checked his train ticket: the overnight sleeper was due to leave in forty minutes, and would arrive in Florence the next morning. Carrie put her hand on his shoulder: 'Are you sure about this, Tom?' she worried. He knew that note of concern in her voice; they had debated more than once the pros and cons of going to the police and making a clean breast of things. But the cops would not believe all that Rinpoche stuff, let alone the true significance of Scala's involvement. Not that Tom fully understood it either. But, as he had explained to Carrie, you did not always have to understand the truth in order to recognise it. He put the train ticket back in his pocket and reached for the travel bag on the back seat. 'I have no choice,' he said.

Carrie gave him a quick peck on the cheek. 'Good luck, Tom,' she whispered as he closed the car door.

'I was born lucky,' he smiled, pulling his parka hood over his head.

23

'I'M SORRY, SIGNORINA,' said the demure receptionist. 'I've checked and rechecked. We have no guests by the names of Dottore Gatti or Frankie Maddingley.'

Miranda exhaled deeply. She knew they would not be there. She had phoned the Hotel Villa Medici before leaving Rome and had already been apprised of that fact. But the hotel was now her only hope of finding her cousin. His sudden departure from his job at the Vatican on the same day that his mentor Gatti had disappeared to Florence was too much of a coincidence: there had to be a connection. And she knew from years of interviewing witnesses that people were always more forthcoming when you were looking them in the eye, not talking down a phone line. But this time even her considerable charm could not elicit any more than a blank disclaimer. It was the hotel's strict policy not to disclose any details about its guests unless the request came from an official source. Accordingly, the receptionist could not tell her whether Dottore Gatti had stayed there previously, whether anyone had accompanied him or even if he had left a forwarding address. Her only option was to create a scene.

'This is utterly outrageous!' she screamed in her brassiest New Yorker accent. 'I'm investigating Dottore Gatti's whereabouts on behalf of the Papal librarian at the Vatican. I demand to speak to the manager.'

A deathly hush descended on the hotel's genteel lobby. The queue of well-heeled guests who, up till then, had been muttering at the delay caused by the pushy American, pricked their ears and exchanged curious glances. Miranda's name-dropping had the desired effect. A glossy little man in a shiny three-piece suit and pink, polka-dot bow tie hurried to the counter and ushered her, with a deluge of fawning assurances, into his office.

Ten minutes and a complimentary cappuccino later, Miranda emerged from the manager's office, though only slightly better informed than when she went in. Dottore Gatti had indeed stayed at the hotel, for just one night, on 22nd September. He had reserved a single, non-smoking room, where he had taken supper. He had not made any phone calls or used the internet. He had checked out early the following morning, using the hotel's express check-out system to pay his bill and dropped off his room key in a box at reception. There was no forwarding address or contact phone number, which was a pity, said the manager, as the dottore left behind a bottle of vintage Frescobaldi which he had specially ordered from the hotel's cellar. As for Signor Frankie Maddingley, no-one of that name had checked into the hotel. Once again, Miranda's enquiries seemed to have hit a dead end.

As the manager escorted the pensive, but thankfully appeased, American signorina back through the lobby,

Count Scala happened to be coming in the opposite direction with a group of male colleagues. His expression betrayed his ennui at the prospect of yet another tedious lunchtime seminar on marketing, to be digested with a dish of bland, mass-catered fodder, thus rounding off his dysphoria with a dose of dyspepsia. The sight of the tall, willowy brunette coming the other way was thus a welcome, if fleeting, distraction, but it was only when he overheard the manager's extravagant valediction that the count's attention was truly engaged.

'Arrivederci, dear Signorina Maddingley,' effused the oleaginous hotelier. 'So glad to have been of service. Please inform Dottore Gatti that his wine will be waiting here for him any time he wishes to collect it.'

Letting his colleagues go on ahead, Scala intercepted the manager as he returned to his office. 'Who was that young woman?' he demanded. 'What did she want with Dottore Gatti?' The manager recognised the count instantly and commenced answering his questions in laborious detail. Scala turned impatiently to look for the woman herself, but she had already disappeared among a throng of tourists being disgorged from a coach in the piazza outside the hotel. However, the hapless manager redeemed himself by producing Miss Maddingley's business card, on the back of which she had scribbled her contact address in Florence: a small pensione near the railway station.

24

'SI, SI. CAREGGI, Villa Medici,' the bus driver gesticulated in response to Tom's query. He stared dubiously at the concrete and glass monolith across the street; it could hardly have been more different to the palatial vision he had been expecting. Instead of green fields and wooded hills, it was surrounded by busy roads and noisy traffic in what was effectively a suburb of Florence, a few miles from the railway station where he had just disembarked from the Paris sleeper train.

Lightning flashed as the bus drove away, and rain mixed with hail started to hammer down. He sprinted to the shelter of some trees overhanging a long wall. Brushing back his dripping hair, he noticed a wrought-iron gate set into the wall. As he peered through the railings he could see more trees and lawns which were not visible from the street. Perhaps this was the Medici villa after all? His hand was on the handle of the gate when a gruff voice barked 'Chiuso'. A grizzled old man was observing him from a kiosk at the corner of the wall. 'Domenica, chiuso,' he repeated, his chin propped up on gnarled fingers.

Tom rolled his eyes: he had forgotten it was Sunday. The downpour began to ease off and he stood in the drizzle wondering what to do next. The custodian called to him again, this time in a disconcerting cockney accent: 'From England are yer, old son?'

'Er, yes, from London,' Tom replied warily.

'Thought so,' the custodian smiled. 'I used to run a café in the East End.' He lowered the kiosk's shutter and shuffled out. 'Course, that was years ago, before I came back here,' he said with a toothy yawn. By now the rain had stopped completely and the sun was breaking through the clouds. 'Come on,' he winked, 'it's time for my rounds. I could do with some company.' Looking like something out of a Keystone Cops silent movie in his black, stiff-collared jacket and peaked cap, the old man unlocked the gate and led Tom inside. A rainbow arched overhead as they walked together among Lebanese cedars and Spanish chestnut trees. The custodian explained that the Medici villa and gardens had been turned into a museum in the 1930s when a local hospital had acquired the Careggi estate. 'Funny, isn't it,' he chuckled, 'being as the Medici were supposed to be descended from a medic?'

Tom recalled from the book in Aunt Stella's kitchen that the Medici had claimed Charlemagne's physician as their primogenitor. He grimaced: East End irony was the last thing he had expected to hear in Florence.

Soon the trees gave way to flower beds and herb borders. Orange and lemon groves had apparently grown here in Lorenzo the Magnificent's day, together with olives and myrtle. 'And even,' the custodian added with an air of mystery, 'frankincense and myrrh.' His words evoked the map in Aunt Stella's study and her talk of the Magi. 'Course,' he chattered on, 'the Medici loved to dress up as the Three Wise Men. They headed a special fraternity that made sure you got a decent send-off when you snuffed it.'

After a few minutes, they turned a corner and there it was in all its Renaissance glory: the villa at Careggi. In Tom's dream it had been veiled in evening shadow, but now the rain-washed, morning sunlight warmed its ochre walls, revealing an impressive crenellated gallery which jutted out above rows of massive corbels. An open-air terrace graced the villa's upper storey, framed by slender Tuscan columns and a terracotta roof. A feeling of déjà vu flooded his consciousness, just as it had at Aunt Stella's. 'Care to take a butcher's inside?' asked the custodian.

Soon they were standing in the al fresco loggia where Ficino and the Platonic Academy had debated the nature of love and immortality over jugs of wine, to the music of a harp. 'Course, when he was a youngster, Lorenzo was a different kettle of fish,' the custodian chortled. 'Partial to a few jars down the tavern with his mates, he was, not to mention the barmaids, when grandpa Cosimo wasn't looking.' And with that, he broke into song:

> *'Naughty satyrs cast their net*
> *on pretty nymphs in grottoes wet.*
> *Just like Bacchus in full heat,*
> *they skip and dance until they're beat.*
> *Lovely youth so fine and fair,*
> *there's no time to stand and stare.*
> *Who cares what tomorrow brings?*
> *Enjoy today, that's the thing.'*

'That was one of Il Magnifico's less bawdy ballads,' he laughed. Then his mood changed and, looking Tom straight in the eye, he added gravely: 'All that ended when life stopped being a game.'

They left the loggia and entered another room, a bedroom with a much more sombre atmosphere. Tom did not need to be told that the black-draped four-poster in the centre of the room had served as a deathbed, both for Cosimo and for Lorenzo. He could feel their presence all around him: and not only theirs. Crossing the floor he noticed a book on the table beside the bed. Gently opening the ancient binding, he found its parchment pages littered with the signatures of visitors to the Medici's country estate. They read like a Who's Who of the Florentine Renaissance: Sandro Botticelli, Angelo Poliziano, Giovanni Pico della Mirandola and Luigi Pulci, as well as Marsilio Ficino and, of course, Bartolomeo Scala. Then came a page with a single name, scrawled in bright red ink: 'Savonarola'. The hairs prickled on the back of his neck. He felt a presence behind him: it was not friendly.

He spun round. A hooded shape floated towards him. Two malevolent eyes flamed from an otherwise vacant blackness and a high-pitched squeak filled his ears before slowly resolving itself into speech: 'Repent!' cried the hooded figure, standing over the bed, seeming to address some invisible occupant. 'Return what the pirate antipope Cossa pawned to your grandfather. Return the Holy Gifts of the Magi entrusted to Pope Sylvester by the Nazarene Church a thousand years ago.'

The bedsheets rustled and a dent appeared on the pillow. 'The Jews,' panted a frail voice, clearly racked with pain, 'gave the pope gold, nothing more. They wanted his support to persuade Constantine to lift his ban on them entering Jerusalem.'

'Liar! Cossa mortgaged the Gifts, together with the papal mitre and gold plate, to the usurer Cosimo, in order to pay for his lewd depravity.'

'Nonsense. If the Gifts existed, why didn't Rome reveal them to the world long ago?'

'Because they belong to God, not to man.'

'Nor to the Pope.'

The ghost bent down so that its hood was directly over the pillow. 'I know you have them,' it hissed. 'At the tournament to celebrate your marriage to a Roman wife, before you returned to your Florentine whore, you brazenly displayed the great diamond, Il Libro, on your shield. It was seen by Platina, Pope Sixtus' faithful librarian.'

'Sixtus! That fat Rovere swine. He served his own purposes, not God's.'

The ghost reared up, its outline quivering with rage. 'The arrogance of the Medici,' it ranted, 'presuming to know the mind of God. Go and join Cossa in the fires of hell; you'll receive no absolution from me.' As it darted from the bed, it hovered for a moment in front of Tom: 'Out of my way, you cur,' it screeched. 'The Swords of the Lord will do for you as surely as sin has done for your master. They shall restore the Holy Gifts to the House of God. I already have Botticelli's confession. Soon the Medici's Golden Age shall be reduced to ashes.'

So saying, the wraith dissolved away, but that was not quite the end of the encounter. 'Do not pine for me, Buontempo,' the dying voice whispered as the pillow lost its dent. 'The Holy Gifts are well hidden, thanks to Ficino and Sandro and the rest of our Brotherhood. Savonarola may burn our books, our music and our paintings, but not our soul. One day soon, he too shall burn in the very fire that he started. And from its ashes the House of Medici shall rise again in even greater glory: Le Temps Revient!' Tom gasped: so that was the half-obliterated motto he had seen inscribed above the doors of No. 8 Lombard Street.

25

SIMULTANEOUSLY EXCITED AND apprehensive, Miranda lifted the miniature bronze ladder which doubled as the door knocker to Count Scala's palazzo. The gilt-edged invitation to dine with an Italian count had been hand delivered to her pensione, just a few hours after her fruitless visit to the Villa Medici Hotel. Signora Melfa, the kindly padrona who owned the Pensione Fragola, had burst into a flurry of superlatives on seeing the count's name: the oldest, the richest, the noblest of Florentine families, living in the grandest palazzo on Via Della Scala. Miranda felt flattered, naturally. But why should a wealthy Italian aristocrat ask her to dinner, completely out of the blue? Did it have something to do with Dr Gatti or Cousin Frankie? And, if so, what was the Count's interest? What did he want? Was he friend or foe?

To boost her confidence she had followed Signora Melfa's advice and bought herself a little black dress from one of the exclusive boutiques on the Via de' Tornabuoni ('Firenze's Fifth Avenue' boasted the padrona). The evening was sunny and quite mild for the time of year so, eschewing a taxi, Miranda had walked the mile or so from the pensione to the palazzo. With coat unbuttoned and lightness in her step, she had braved the not entirely unwelcome attention of the young bucks who ogled her from the bars lining the Piazza Santa Maria Novella, and had arrived in good time at Scala's front door.

Hardly had the door knocker struck the antique oak when Fabio appeared. Taking her coat in his white-gloved hands, he confirmed that 'Signorina Maddingley' was expected. She followed the old retainer through a colonnaded atrium where crystal-clear water tinkled in an alabaster fountain and life-size bronzes gleamed in back-lit niches. Oil paintings filled the walls with mythological figures and idyllic landscapes like windows into another world. As she negotiated the marble staircase up to the palazzo's first floor in her black high heels, she imagined herself back in Renaissance times, being wafted to a lost age of high culture. At the top of the stairs a broad gallery was lit by gilded cherubs waving Olympic torches that served as wall lamps. But she was not so beguiled by the décor that she failed to notice the film of dust on the lid of a large walnut cassone: the house, servants notwithstanding, appeared to lack the feminine touch.

Fabio showed her into a spacious, high-ceilinged, salon in the middle of which was a candlelit dining table with two places set for supper. Having enquired if she would care for an aperitif and, assuring her that his master would be along presently, the indefatigable butler scurried off to get her the glass of sparkling mineral water that was her stock response in unfamiliar company, especially when she was, it seemed, the only guest.

Meandering around the room, she glanced at a pile of business cards which had been left on a silver tray. Impressive, she thought, on discovering that the count was not only titled but also chairman of a bank. What would he look like? she wondered. The portraits dotting the walls did not bode well: the men were uniformly dull and dour, the ladies haughty and disapproving. He's probably got grey hair and false teeth, she mused, visualising an old fogey with a walking stick and stoop. She was considering making a dash for the door when a fine baritone voice broke into song. It was an aria from Verdi, one of her favourite composers. She went over to an open window, assuming the singer was outside. But the street below was deserted and, in any event, the singing had stopped. Turning away from the window, she noticed a portrait which was much smaller than the ones she had seen earlier. It was of a young woman but, unlike the rest, she was quite a beauty. As she was admiring it, a hand appeared at her side; it was holding a glass of sparkling water but it was not wearing a white glove. Surprised, she spun round. A tall, well-built man with jet-black hair and dark, penetrating eyes was standing just behind her.

'Forgive me, Signorina. I didn't mean to startle you,' Count Scala apologised with a disarming smile. 'When I came in and saw you standing there in front of my wife's portrait, with your Titian hair shining in the candlelight just like hers, I imagined for one brief moment...'

'Oh there's really no need to apologise,' Miranda interrupted, eager to spare his blushes and also relieved to find that her host was not, as she had feared, an elderly, goggle-eyed pensioner. Rather, he exuded that same virile, self-assured authority which she had encountered in only the most successful (and ruthless) of New York lawyers and which, though she would never admit it, she found quite irresistible.

The count took her hand and lifted it to his lips: 'Count Giovanni Scala, at your service,' he said with a brief bow.

'Piacere, Count Scala,' Miranda reciprocated, unsure if a curtsey was not also in order. 'I'm…'

'Signorina Maddingley, of course,' he smiled. 'But, please, call me Giovanni. I do so hate standing on ceremony, don't you?' And soon they were both on first-name terms, chatting about the excerpt from *Il Trovatore* which he modestly admitted to crooning, Verdi being one of his favourite composers too. As they sat down to supper, Scala directed Fabio to pour some wine. Toasting his guest's health, he watched her swirl the black-cherry Ornellaia around her crystal glass before breathing in its cigar-smoke aroma and putting it to her soft, full lips. 'Delicious!' she exclaimed as she lowered the glass, now bearing a crescent of red lipstick.

'You have a discerning palate, Miranda,' the count remarked warmly. 'It's a very special wine from the Antinori estate.'

She was duly impressed. She regularly took her best clients to swanky wine-tasting evenings and had become quite knowledgeable about the different grapes, vintages and wine-growing regions of both the Old and the New Worlds. 'Mmm, yes, it's still so young and vibrant, with such powerful fruit and a long finish,' she enthused. 'Yet it's already amazingly well-structured and complex.'

'What a perfect description,' said Scala, looking deep into her eyes.

She blushed. Time to apply the brakes. 'A fine wine to go with a fine house,' she said, sweeping back the glossy tresses which had strayed a little too far down her bosom. She glanced at the portrait by the window. 'You and your lovely wife must do a lot of entertaining.' In Miranda's experience, mention of 'the wife' always had a telling effect on predatory married males. Either they would retreat into pathetic pleas for pity or, worse, retaliate with callous indifference.

But the count reacted in neither of these ways. Rather, the darkness which had cut short his earlier serenade now returned to silence him once more. He stared into his wine glass, lost in thought. The lights of the chandelier hanging overhead danced hypnotically on the wine's ruby surface as he recalled the dazzling soirées which, a lifetime ago, had filled the palazzo's grand ballroom with music and laughter. A sudden pang of longing in his breast reminded him what a stranger he had become to joy. In his darker moments he blamed fate for the passing of those days: it was God's retribution for the actions he and his forefathers had had to take in order to protect the secret long ago entrusted to them. The despatch of Radopoulos the previous month was but the latest in a long line of 'eliminations'. His first act when taking over as Maestro of the Compagnia del Diamante almost thirty years before had been to order the death of an Englishman who had stumbled across the secret of the Primavera. Yet, could it be that God's anger had finally been expiated? Dared he hope that this girl from America, who had seemingly crossed his path by sheer chance, was destined to join him in the momentous events which were now unfolding? 'My wife died many years ago,' he said at length. 'Leukaemia. The doctors could do nothing.'

Miranda wished the floor would swallow her up. 'Oh, I'm so sorry. How long had you been…'

'Married? Just a year.'

'Did you… I mean, are there…'

'No. Lucrezia was pregnant when she passed away but unfortunately the child could not be saved.'

Miranda extended her arm across the table and touched the back of Scala's hand. 'Well,' she consoled him, 'there's still time, Giovanni. I'm sure that one day this ancient palazzo of yours will ring to the patter of tiny feet.'

'Perhaps, one day, Miranda,' he replied with a wistful gaze. Then, changing the subject, he told her that the current Palazzo Scala was a mere two hundred years old and that his original ancestral home, on the Borgo Pinti, had been sold in 1585 to the last Medici pope.

'Awesome!' she blurted, kicking herself for sounding like a stereotypical American tourist.

'Yes. And now it's being converted into a luxury hotel!' They both laughed. And as the laughter subsided she decided to ask the question she was most curious to have answered: why was she here?

'Quite simple,' he said, explaining how he had overheard the manager referring to Dottore Gatti at the Villa Medici hotel. Gatti was an acquaintance of his and, as it happened, they were due to meet the following week. Miranda could hardly believe her luck. She had started to tell him the reason for her journey to Italy when Fabio entered, bearing a starter of green salad with anchovies and a selection of aspics.

'A favourite dish of Catherine de' Medici,' Scala announced proudly as he raised his glass and wished his guest 'buon appetito e benvenuto in Firenze!'

After clinking glasses and savouring a morsel of jellied veal, Miranda continued with the story of her visit to Italy, tailoring it somewhat as her lawyerly caution kicked in. Following her uncle's death, she had been amazed to learn of the existence of an Italian cousin, Frankie, and naturally wanted to meet him. She omitted the unsavoury details about his father and said nothing about the loss of her inheritance. She had visited the Vatican only to find that Frankie was no longer there and she desperately hoped that his former boss, Doctor Gatti, might know his whereabouts.

'But why come to Florence? Gatti lives and works in the Vatican, does he not?'

'I understand,' she replied, sticking to the official line, 'that he travelled to Florence in September for a conference but then had to stay on here to look after his sick sister.'

Scala looked puzzled but gave no indication that he might know otherwise. Miranda let the matter drop, buoyed by the promise of meeting Dr Gatti the following week. And so she spent the rest of the dinner enjoying fine wine and rich food, seasoned with lively exchanges about opera and the arts. She found herself increasingly attracted to the cultivated, intelligent, yet curiously enigmatic, man who, when they finished eating, played Chopin nocturnes on a grand piano whilst she reclined on a Louis XVI chaise longue, praying that she was not dreaming. And when he mentioned his box at the Teatro della Pergola, she did not hesitate to accept his invitation to join him for a performance of *Il Trovatore* the following evening.

It was gone eleven o'clock when Fabio reported that the signorina's taxi was waiting outside. (The count would not hear of her walking back to the pensione alone, nor she of his escorting her.) He gallantly lent her his arm as she tottered, a little tipsily, back down the marble staircase to the ground floor. As they reached the bottom, a metal door tucked away in a corner of the courtyard caught her eye. 'What's in there, Giovanni, a dungeon?' she giggled.

Scala glanced at the locked, temperature- and humidity-controlled storeroom. That, he explained, was where centuries of his family's archives were preserved: all the certificates of birth, marriage and death, the church and state appointments, the honours and privileges, the correspondence with famous artists, poets, politicians and film stars, contracts with builders, merchants, lawyers, stretching back to the dawn of the Renaissance.

'Wow!' Miranda gushed. 'It must be wonderful to be able to trace your ancestry so far back. I couldn't go back fifty years, let alone five hundred.'

The image of a letter, written on parchment in Cosimo de' Medici's own hand, flashed before Scala's eyes. It had sealed his family's destiny for the last half-millennium. 'Count yourself lucky, Miranda,' he sighed. 'History can be a burden as well as a blessing.' He was helping her into the taxi when he said: 'Miranda, I've a proposal to make.'

'Oh, and what might that be?' she asked with a coquettish grin.

'Well, I don't mean to be presumptuous, but I'm seeing you again at the opera tomorrow evening and then you'll also be coming here to meet Dottore Gatti. Surely it makes more sense for you to stay here at the palazzo?' He saw the doubts clouding her eyes. 'There's a separate guest suite with its own entrance, and my staff will provide you with all the services that you could possibly want. That place where you're staying now is too near the railway station. All sorts of riff-raff hang around there. It's not safe for a young lady on her own.'

Miranda was completely taken aback. 'That's extremely generous of you, Count... I mean Giovanni,' she spluttered, 'but I...'

'Excellent. That's settled then. My chauffeur will come to collect you tomorrow morning.'

'No, Giovanni,' she protested breathlessly. 'I really can't allow you to put yourself out for me like this. We've only just met. How could I possibly accept such hospitality? It's just...'

'Please,' he countered in an almost plaintive tone, 'give it a try. If at any time you are not entirely happy, Fabio shall return you immediately to the pensione or anywhere else you wish to go. And in the meantime, if you will permit me, I should love to show you the sights of my beautiful city. So please, Miranda, say that you will allow me to do this for you?'

Despite her misgivings, she could hardly refuse such an attractive offer. To stay in an Italian palazzo and go on a private tour of Florence with one of its leading lights was something she could only have dreamt of in her normal life. Moreover, there would hopefully be opportunities to find out more about Gatti and his connection with the count. Something told her that the more she knew about Gatti and Scala, the closer she would be to finding Cousin Frankie. The fact that she was flattered by the count's attentions did admittedly also have an effect, but not a significant one, she told herself. 'Okay,' she smiled as the taxi drove off.

26

'YOU ALRIGHT, OLD son? You look like you've seen a ghost.' The Italian custodian with the cockney accent was gripping Tom's arm as though fearing he was about to faint.

'Did you see it?' Tom demanded anxiously.

'See what?'

He described Savonarola's grim apparition. The old man was not in the least surprised. Florence was awash with ghosts, and Careggi especially so. Aside from its history, it was also now part of a hospital and they always attracted ghosts, according to local superstition.

'But this ghost signed the visitors' book. See for your...' Tom stopped mid-sentence. The visitors' book was nowhere to be seen.

They went outside for some fresh air. Back in the sunlit gardens Tom's thoughts turned to Montevecchio and his appointment with Rinpoche. Which way to Ficino's cottage? The custodian shook his head. Montevecchio was long gone. He pointed to a gap in the trees: the spot where it had once stood was down there somewhere. Tom was welcome to go and take a look, if he wished.

As he ploughed through the undergrowth, Tom wondered if he had misunderstood Rinpoche's instructions. How could the monk have chosen a place which no longer existed to be their rendezvous? And could this overgrown track really be the path he had followed Ficino and Lorenzo along in his dream? The ferns and brambles were getting thicker and taller and he was debating whether to turn back when he tripped over a half-buried rock and tumbled headlong into a deep hollow, hidden among the bushes. As the ground disappeared beneath him he braced himself for a crash-landing, but instead everything seemed to go into slow motion. It was as if he was floating, weightless in the minute interstices of time, his vision blurred and the world filled with the sound of the wind. And in the wind, a whispering of words: 'Plato's ear', 'Hermes' epilogue', 'equinox', 'seven diamonds', 'Sandro', 'locks', 'Scala'. Then, all too swiftly, the ground came hurtling towards him.

27

COUNT SCALA'S LIMOUSINE arrived at Miranda's pensione soon after 9.30am. As the chauffeur loaded her luggage into the boot, the car's tinted rear window lowered and, to her surprise and delight, the count himself bade her a cheery good morning. They drove off towards the heart of the old city but, as they neared the Via Della Scala, the count suggested they stop and go for a stroll: it was such a fine winter's morning. Miranda was well wrapped up in a beige poncho and matching hat, whilst Scala wore a cashmere overcoat, grey homburg and black pigskin gloves. They were halfway along the Via Del Porcellana, a narrow side street that led to the river, when the count pointed to a nondescript terraced house. This was where Amerigo Vespucci had once lived, he told her, the Florentine who had discovered her homeland.

Miranda caught her breath. She was looking at the house but saw only her father's model of Vespucci's galleon, *La Bella Simonetta*. Scenes from her nightmare flashed before her: the beautiful girl in the shroud, the two men in white tugging at her body, the mad dolphins that knocked one of them overboard, and the giant magpie which tried to carry off the other. And now to be so unexpectedly confronted by reality, to be standing in the very street where Vespucci had once walked, was quite mind-boggling.

As she came back down to earth she could hear Scala enthusing about another, similarly unremarkable, house a few yards further on. Apparently it had been the studio of Amerigo's contemporary, Sandro Botticelli. The count chuckled as he told her the story of how a cloth-maker had set up a workshop next-door to the great artist. The thundering looms shook his house and their constant din drove him insane. He pleaded with the cloth-maker to move but the man stubbornly refused, saying that he could – and would – do whatever he pleased in his own home. 'But Sandro was a great practical joker and his solution to this impasse was a masterly piece of poetic justice.'

'What did he do?'

'He had a giant boulder transported from the Mugello hills, just north of here, and used a wooden crane to balance it up there.' He pointed to a partition wall which separated Botticelli's house from the one next door. The wall protruded above the roofline and sloped slightly towards the cloth-maker's side. 'So, when the looms started up again, the vibrations rocked the boulder and it threatened to come crashing down at any moment onto the noisy neighbour's roof.'

'What happened?'

'The cloth-maker demanded that Botticelli remove the boulder, but he simply replied that he could – and would – do whatever he pleased in his own home. The cloth-maker packed his bags and left the next day.'

Miranda laughed. 'Botticelli wouldn't get away with that type of self-help today.'

Scala's expression changed abruptly. 'Oh, I don't doubt it,' he snapped. 'Today we live in a madhouse where the courts protect the villain while the victim is hauled off to jail. The whole system is a pusillanimous laughing stock. It needs to be swept away, consigned to the flames like the rotten heap of dead wood that it is.' His outburst took Miranda aback: his voice was suddenly so raw and deadly serious. But the moment quickly passed and they walked on.

Soon they reached the river where the sun's rays glimmered on the Arno's icy surface and mist drifted through the arches of the Ponte Vecchio. 'Oh, Giovanni, what a magical scene!'

'Florence is a bella donna, Miranda. She flashes her eyes at you and casts her spell for which there is no cure. You yearn to discover more about her, to know her ever more intimately. But, though she may grant you this favour or that, she will never reveal all her secrets. Always there is something hidden, something that will forever draw you back.'

They strolled along the embankment for a while and then peeled off towards the city centre. Soon they were in the cathedral square, the Piazza Del Duomo. Scala dismissed the basilica's baroque façade as an 'over-iced wedding cake', pointing out that it was at the doors of the cathedral that Giuliano de' Medici had been brutally assassinated.

'Ah, yes,' said Miranda, keen to show that she had at least some knowledge of local history. 'He was Simonetta Vespucci's lover, wasn't he?'

The count gave her a curious look. 'How do you know that?'

'Oh, it was just one of those romantic stories I read as a teenager,' she lied, aware of a sudden edginess in his voice.

'Well, I'm impressed,' he said, smiling again. 'Even Italians are very unlikely to know that tragic story these days. I must point out, however, that Giuliano's older brother, Lorenzo the Magnificent, was his rival for La Bella Simonetta's affections.'

Lorenzo's name was new to Miranda; it set her thinking. 'Did the brothers fight over her?'

'Fight? My dear Miranda, there was no contest. Giuliano may have been younger and superficially more handsome, but Il Magnifico was the illustrious ruler of Florence as well as a gifted man of letters. Simonetta could never have chosen Giuliano over Lorenzo.'

Miranda was about to question this typically male assumption when the count began reciting poetry:

'O brilliant star that with your ray
Put all your neighbours in the shade,
Why so brightly do you shine today?
Woe is me when in that place
Where rests that sweet, angelic face.'

Moisture glistened in his eyes: though the lines came from Lorenzo's sonnet on Simonetta's untimely death, it was a much more personal loss that affected Scala. 'He must have loved her very much,' Miranda said softly. He nodded and looked away.

They turned their attention to the nearby baptistery, an octagonal-shaped building which was much more to the count's taste than the gaudy Duomo. It was, he said, the oldest building in Florence, occupying the site of a

Roman temple of Mars. The temple had been erected to commemorate Rome's victory over Etruscan Fiesole and to celebrate the foundation of Florence. Passing through the baptistery's bronze doors, dubbed by Michelangelo 'the Gates of Paradise', he pointed to the middle of the marble pavement where an ancient font had once stood: 'For over a thousand years, generations of Florentines were baptised here every year on the 25th of March.'

'Why that day?' queried Miranda as she studied the zodiacal signs which encircled the floor.

'That used to be New Year's Day, as well as the date of the spring equinox, under the old Julian calendar.' His words reminded her of Brother Andreas and the Vatican observatory where Cousin Frankie and Dr Gatti had apparently spent so much time. Florence was proving to be full of odd coincidences.

Scala took her hand and led her to an imposing monument next to the altar. 'And now,' he said, 'if you are to become a true Florentine, you must swear allegiance before the tomb of Pope John XXIII, the only pope to die in Florence and one of her truest friends.'

'As long as I don't have to seal the oath in blood!' she giggled.

'Repeat after me: Vivat Florentia! Vivat Domus Medicea!'

As she duly complied, Miranda assumed that she was performing the equivalent of throwing a coin into the Trevi Fountain: just another of those quaint little traditions kept alive for the benefit of tourists. She had yet to learn that, in Count Scala's world, there were no tourists.

Leaving the baptistery, they listened to Giotto's campanile strike eleven o'clock and decided to head for Scala's favourite café in the Piazza della Signoria. They were crossing the piazza when Miranda's shoe got caught in a loose manhole cover. As she stooped to extract her heel, she noticed the initials 'SPQF' on the offending cast-iron plate. 'What does that stand for?' she wondered.

'Senatus PopulusQue Florentinus: the Senate and People of Florence. It's just like the "SPQR" you find all over Rome.'

She looked blank.

'Senatus PopulusQue Romanus. The initials that were emblazoned on Roman legionary standards. It means: "The Senate and People of …"'

'Rome. Yes, I get it.'

'Ah, but we Florentines have an alternative translation,' he whispered mischievously.

'You do?'

'Sono Pazzi Questi Romani: They're Crazy These Romans.'

'Hmm, if the Romans are anything like New Yorkers, I'll bet they have their own version of SPQF too.'

'Well, some say it should be changed to SVQF: Sono Volgari Questi Fiorentini – They're Show-Offs These Florentines.'

They laughed and Miranda found herself warming to her Count Giovanni. She had met many successful men with much less to boast about than he, who were far too insecure to laugh at themselves. They continued chatting light-heartedly as they entered the Café Signoria. A moustachioed waiter immediately showed them to the count's regular table next to the window. A sudden squall beat down on the glass panes; Scala recommended the speciality hot chocolate to warm them up. 'Ecco due ciocolate calde, per la bella signorina e il Conte,' beamed the waiter, setting down two steaming cups on the chequered tablecloth and tipping the count a sly wink.

'I hope you don't think I make a habit of this, Miranda,' he said, fearing that she would misconstrue the waiter's innuendo.

'A habit of what?' she teased.

He smiled, turning his gaze for a moment towards the hailstones dancing on the pavement outside. 'I sometimes sit here and imagine Lorenzo de' Medici and his friends supping wine in a corner of the piazza,' he said. 'In his younger days, Lorenzo was no stranger to the pleasures of the flesh, yet he never lost sight of what he called "gentillezia", or nobility of spirit.'

'Do you think men were nobler in his day?' she mused as she sipped her hot chocolate.

'Very few men, then or now, hear the call of destiny,' he replied. 'And if you are deaf to destiny, then, like every other quality which distinguishes man from the beasts of the field, nobility becomes incomprehensible.'

The squall passed and the sun came out again. Finishing their drinks, they set off refreshed and spent the rest of the morning, and much of the afternoon, in the Uffizi Gallery. Here, Scala was in his element, providing a running commentary on the development of Florentine art, from the iconic madonnas of Duccio to Botticelli's Venus. Though her feet ached and her stomach rumbled, Miranda's interest never flagged. She was enthralled by the miraculous beauty of what she saw, fascinated by the lives and foibles of the artists who had created it, entranced by the rich vein of biblical and mythological tales that animated it. And, gradually, her wonder at the narrative transferred to the narrator.

28

BRUISED AND SCRATCHED but otherwise unhurt, Tom slowly extricated himself from the clinging bramble thicket which had cushioned his fall. The sunken hollow he had tumbled into was a dense jungle of weeds and thorn-bushes encircled by crumbling walls of rock and earth. The least tricky way back was up the same slope he had just crashed down; it was steep but lower than the rest and there were decent footholds. He was nearing the summit when he noticed a broken marble stump jutting out of the long grass a few feet to his right: the cause of his fall, he guessed. The top half of the stump was lying flat on the ground next to it. He climbed across and brushed away the dirt encrusted on its surface. His pulse raced faster and faster as, one by one, letters emerged. Eventually a name appeared that made him recoil in shock: 'B' 'U' 'O' 'N' 'T' 'E' 'M' 'P' 'O'.

'Have you stumbled on the truth, Tommy boy?' a voice called down from above.

He looked up: there was the Tibetan monk in his familiar

purple robe, chuckling merrily to himself. 'Rinpoche! Is that really you?'

'Who else?' answered the monk, pulling a peaked cap from behind his back. Then his gaze narrowed: 'But the real question is who are *you*, Mr Talbot?'

Tom groaned: Rinpoche was talking in riddles again. Why the emphasis on his surname? He knew it had a long history; he had once traced it as far back as a knight who had fought alongside Henry V at Agincourt. But there was no obvious family connection; medieval yeomen often took the name of their lord. Then he recalled the seal on his father's bloodstained letter and the ancient hunting hound which shared the same name. He looked down at Buontempo's broken headstone: suddenly all the pieces fell into place. He experienced a truth he could not put into words, a truth at the very core of his being.

'So,' Rinpoche nodded, 'now you walk in the realm of truth, outside the bounds of time and space. Did your aunt reacquaint you with Hermanubis?'

Tom shot him a questioning glance: 'Who exactly is my aunt?'

The monk sighed. 'She is a witch I mistook for an angel. An Etruscan slave who became a Parthian queen. She has lived many accursed lives since your paths crossed in the desert long ago, and I fear they shall cross again.' His voice began to falter. 'Quickly, Tom, tell me what the ghosts of this place whispered to you.'

Tom ran through the snatched words he had heard as he fell into the hollow, before describing the deathbed confrontation between Savonarola and Lorenzo. Rinpoche nodded: at last he knew how the Catholic Church had acquired the Gifts of the Magi, only to lose them to one of the most powerful and secretive families in all of history. But the circle was not quite squared. 'Did the ghosts say anything else? Anything at all?'

'Tom took a few seconds to think. 'Well, there was one thing, but it made no sense.'

'What?'

'It sounded like "Plato's ear".'

The monk shook his head. 'Your old self had much sharper hearing,' he tutted. 'It's you that needs an ear, Tom, not Plato.' But, before he could go on, Rinpoche began to quiver; the contours of his body grew blurred and seemed to lose their solidity. 'The equinox!' he cried. 'Remember the equinox.'

Tom stretched out his arms. 'Rinpoche! Wait!'

But there was no reprieve: the monk steadily melted away, like a snowman in spring sunshine, until all that remained was the sparkle of his eyes. As they too dissolved, a rainbow appeared and a distant voice spoke: 'Time is running out. Find the Gifts before it's too late. Only the gremlin can stop the machine; only the joker can fox the pack. Destiny calls you: but you shall not fight alone.'

Tom scrambled like a madman to the top of the slope, but Rinpoche was gone. A peaked cap lay in the grass, grimy and torn, as if it had been abandoned there many years before. He picked it up and gently brushed away the dust before placing it beside Buontempo's gravestone. Careggi was indeed a place filled with ghosts.

29

MIRANDA'S WHIRLWIND INTRODUCTION to the treasures of Florence continued unabated in the beguiling company of her urbane, aristocratic guide. In the days that followed their first intimate supper at his grand palazzo, they meandered through museums, chilled (literally) in churches and posed in piazzas. In the evenings, they would attend the opera, seated in Scala's private box, listening to Puccini, Rossini or Verdi. Count Giovanni showed her much, though not quite all, of what he most loved and admired in the city of his birth: the Michelangelos and Da Vincis, the Cellinis and Donatellos. For light relief, they would wander among the grottos of the Boboli Gardens, sup on bean and sausage stews in the Mercato Centrale, or window-shop at the jewellers of the Ponte Vecchio.

Then, late one afternoon shortly before Christmas, they drove to the Piazzale Michelangelo, the spacious terrace on a hillside south of the Arno, overlooking Florence's most iconic panorama. Laughter and the clinking of glasses could he heard coming from a sapphire-blue marquee, twinkling with sequinned snowflakes, where the Florentine glitterati chattered over flutes of sparkling Franciacorta and swayed to the music of a live band. The Christmas cocktail season was in full swing. Such ostentatious functions were not Scala's natural habitat, but he usually put in a token appearance, for the sake of form. This time, however, it was different. He was different. He was actually looking forward to the loud music, the mingling and the small talk: he felt alive again. What surprise there would be on those smug faces when he entered with his beautiful young companion on his arm, what admiring glances as they passed by, what gossip after they left. But first there was something he had to do. Taking Miranda's hand, he led her to a stone balustrade that rimmed the edge of the Piazzale. 'I couldn't let you miss this,' he whispered.

'Oh, Giovanni, it's beautiful!' she sighed as she watched the setting sun launch the Duomo across a sea of fiery terracotta, and the silvery ribbon of the Arno slip serenely into the west.

'Beautiful beyond belief,' he echoed, gazing into her eyes.

She felt her cheeks redden as she adjusted the fur stole which Scala had insisted on placing across her shoulders: it had belonged to his late wife. 'How can I ever repay your kindness, Giovanni?' she said. 'You've shown me such wonderful sights this past week.'

He gave her hand a gentle squeeze. 'Actually, there is one more place I'd like to show you.'

'There is?'

'Yes. You see I belong to a somewhat exclusive little club.'

She snatched her hand away: visions of pole-dancers and drunken businessmen leapt to mind. 'Oh no, not that sort of club,' he protested. 'My club was founded in the Renaissance by the Medici. It promotes humanist art and ideals, preserving traditional customs and ceremonies.' She relaxed, kicking herself for having entertained such totally undeserved misgivings. 'And we always meet in some famous historical setting,' he went on. 'Tonight it's in the Priory of San Marco.' One of the club's members had passed away unexpectedly, and he needed someone to make up a quorum. 'It can't be just anyone, though. It has to be someone suitable, someone "simpatico".'

'But Giovanni I wouldn't know what to do, what to say. And anyway,' she hesitated, knowing her next words would probably not be welcome, 'I wasn't planning on staying in Italy all that long.'

Scala displayed no emotion. Any disappointment he felt was merely a spur: it was inconceivable that she would refuse him. 'I fear that your search for your cousin may take longer than you think, Miranda,' he countered. 'But, in any event, it's just one meeting, just as a temporary stand-in. And there's really nothing to it. We wear traditional white robes but, apart from that, you won't have to do or say a thing, just follow my lead.' Then he played his ace: 'Dottore Gatti is a member.'

She looked back at the view. Street lamps had begun to glimmer along the river bank, and Venus was shining brightly above the horizon. She needed time to think. It obviously made sense to go along with the count's wishes in terms of her search for Frankie and meeting Dr Gatti, yet this secret society stuff sounded rather weird, despite Giovanni's assurances. She turned to him, still hesitant. 'Miranda,' he said before she could speak, 'as a member of the club, you must also wear one of these.'

For a moment, she thought the Evening Star had fallen to Earth, such was the brilliance of the diamond which the count was holding up to the sunset's crimson embers. It seemed to sparkle with an energy all its own, an energy that touched her soul. She sighed silently to herself: 'Ah Miranda, Miranda! Furs and diamonds; where have your principles gone!'

As he slid the solitaire down her finger, Scala knew he need say no more.

30

THE INTERNET CAFÉ was in a suitably down-at-heel street close to the train station. A place where Tom could pass unnoticed amid the flotsam and jetsam of modern city life. It was not far from the cheap hotel he had booked into before taking the bus to Careggi. His first task was to look up Count Scala. Simple, he thought, until he discovered that the chairman of the Banca de' Bianchi was not on Facebook or Twitter or any other social media. His write-up on the bank's website was brief and gave away nothing about his private life. This was clearly not a man who liked to share his holiday snaps. In fact, all that an hour's internet search had turned up was the location of his palazzo on the eponymous Via Della Scala and his generous support of the arts, being a patron of the Uffizi Gallery, among numerous other museums.

His next search proved more fruitful: 'the land of the Saoshyant'. The phrase had been nagging at the back of his mind ever since his vision at Aunt Stella's of the three, black-robed men in the desert. It turned out to refer to a Zoroastrian prophecy of a saviour, a 'Saoshyant', who would be born to a virgin. This obviously chimed with the Gifts of the Magi, as whispered of at Careggi. 'Bingo!' he exclaimed, causing some curious looks from neighbouring internet surfers. But his excitement soon waned as he realised that it shed no light on those other ghostly whisperings: 'Plato's Ear', 'Hermes' epilogue', 'seven diamonds', and the rest.

He decided to search for 'Plato's Ear'. This drew a complete blank. Then he tried combining it with 'equinox'. Now the results flooded in. He realised that it was not Plato's anatomy, but his astronomy, that the ghosts of Careggi had been referring to. 'Plato's Ear', or rather 'Plato's Year', was an astronomical/astrological term mentioned by Plato, but going back to ancient Babylonia and Egypt. It was connected to another astronomical phenomenon: the so-called 'Precession of the Equinoxes'. Apparently, when the sun crossed the celestial equator at noon on the spring and autumn equinoxes, it did not pass through the exact same point every year. Rather, it moved backwards, or appeared to do so, thanks to a wobble in the Earth's rotation. So, when viewed from the Earth, the equinoxes occurred slightly earlier each year, as the sun followed a seemingly retrograde path through the zodiac: the 'Precession of the Equinoxes'. And the length of time the sun took to complete a circuit of the zodiac was a mind-boggling 26,000 years, otherwise known as Plato's Year.

Tom straightened his back and rubbed his dry eyes. He could not get the 1960s song 'Age of Aquarius' out of his head. Meanwhile, none of this New Age hippy stuff seemed to fit the image of a high-roller like Scala. If only he had had more time with Rinpoche. Suddenly, the incessant 'Age of Aquarius' lyrics were interrupted by a buzzing sound; it was the pay-as-you-go mobile phone Carrie had given him. 'Hello?' he ventured cautiously.

'Hi, Tom, how's it going?'

'Carrie, good to hear your voice,' he said, suddenly feeling the loneliness of a stranger in a foreign city. 'I've found out where Count Scala lives, but that's about all so far. Any news your end?'

'I'll say,' she answered excitedly. 'They're closing down the bank's City branch.'

'What?'

'Yes. And the cops have been round several times. The last time they came, they searched the whole building, seized all the computers. There's a rumour going round that the entire business may be going under.'

Tom's brain went into overdrive. Could the fraud he had uncovered really extend to the top of the tree? To Scala himself? If so, what was to stop the secretive Count doing a runner? Or being arrested? Either way, his chances of solving the mystery of the Gifts, and thereby his own strange predicament, would be scuppered. He would have to move fast.

'Poison Ivy's secretary told me something odd as well,' Carrie threw into the silence that had descended at Tom's end of the phone. 'The cops asked her about a copy of a letter they found in his desk. It was from Count Scala to someone called "Hawkeye". It thanked him for some "cleaning work" he was going to do and – get this, Tom – it enclosed a pair of gold cufflinks. How odd is that?'

Tom grimaced as he realised she had just told him the name, or at least the nickname, of the man who had ransacked his home and killed his dog. And not only that: she had also confirmed that the guy was acting on Scala's orders. He took the broken cufflink he had found next to Jasper's body from his pocket and stared at the Medici insignia: Scala had a lot to answer for. Then Carrie mentioned something about Christmas. 'Sorry, what was that?'

'The bank's last Christmas party, Tom, it's today.'

His heart began to pound. He looked at the date on the bottom of the computer screen: it was 21st December. The encounter with Rinpoche at Careggi must have triggered another of Aunt Stella's 'liminal points'. 'Happy Christmas, Carrie!' he cried and raced out of the café.

31

SHADOWS FLITTED UNDER a gibbous moon within the ancient walls of San Marco. A nod in the right quarter from Count Scala had left the priory door unlocked for the white-robed Brothers of the Company of the Magi. In the minutes before midnight, they had been careful not to disturb the residents as they by-passed the chapter house and the dormitory to reach the inner cloister. But now the moon was slipping behind the clouds and darkness began to leaven the imagination. 'They say the ghost of Savonarola haunts these precincts,' one whispered. 'See it, and you're dead before the year's out,' murmured another. 'What's that over there?' hissed someone else.

From the far side of the cloister a torchlight jabbed at a statue in the middle of the lawn, lighting up a stern forefinger pressed to stony lips. Scala had arrived and, like St Dominic, he required silence. The torch flicked forwards. The chastened Brothers followed its bobbing light in single file, unaware of Scala's young companion walking beside him in the shadows, holding nervously onto his hand.

At length they came to a flight of stairs which led to the oldest part of the priory: a museum of antique cells. Scala paused when they reached the top: dark passages stretched to left and right. He took the one to the right, checking the number on the wall of each cell as he passed. Some of the cell doors were open and exquisite frescoes of the raising of Lazarus, the Last Supper and the Crucifixion flashed in the torchlight like snatches from a dream.

They had reached cell 37 when the count shone his torch back down the line of hooded Brothers. Excluding Miranda, who still remained unseen at his side, there should have been five of them: he could see only four. Where was the fifth? He flashed the beam further down the passageway: no-one. Then a cowled figure raced out of the darkness, mumbling an apology about taking a wrong turn. 'Shh,' Scala hissed, before crossing to the other side of the corridor and directing his torch at a blue-circled numeral.

'But this is only number 38,' someone objected sotto voce.

'Cosimo had a double cell,' Scala replied, 'number 39 is inside.' The old wooden door creaked open. Dousing his torch, he lit a candle and led the way into the cell's outer chamber. It was small and bare, save for a fresco of the Crucifixion. He went straight to one corner and up some steps into the inner chamber: cell 39. 'So, Brothers of the Company of the Magi,' he said as they all filed in, 'this is the place where Cosimo de' Medici came to converse with God. A far cry from the lavish luxury of his palazzo, is it not?' There was a general murmur of agreement as they shivered in the cell's icy atmosphere. 'Cosimo,' he continued, 'though one of the richest men in Christendom, never forgot the paramount importance of his soul.' Moving to the opposite side of the chamber, he put his candle close to the wall: 'Behold, the only depiction of the Magi in the whole of San Marco.' It was another fresco, this time of the Virgin and Child, attended by a train of exotic figures.

'It's one of Benozzo Gozzoli's finest works!' enthused Rossi, whose shrill tones were instantly recognisable. 'Look at the range of pigmentation, the cinnabar reds, the azurite blues, the detail in those silk cloaks and extravagant Byzantine headdresses.' He paused to inspect the paintwork more closely: 'Ah, and see here, the bearded man in the malachite robe. Could that be Cosimo's Greek friend, Gemistos Plethon, Maestro?'

Scala confirmed the identification and asked Rossi for his opinion of another eye-catching figure: a magus in a vermilion robe and conical hat, with an armillary sphere floating behind his right shoulder. But before Rossi could answer, a scream rang out. One of the Brothers' rings was glowing so fiercely that it turned the cell's grey walls crimson. Seconds later, a laser-like ray of light shot out of it straight at the figure of the mysterious magus. To everyone's amazement, the figure seemed to come alive; its eyes rolled and its mouth opened and closed as if trying speak. The armillary sphere floated away from his shoulder and started to revolve faster and faster, until it was spinning so fast it was just a blur. At the same time a deep humming sound filled the tiny cell, causing its walls to vibrate with such intensity that they became transparent curtains of energy. The armillary sphere flew from the two-dimensional world of the fresco and buzzed madly around the room like a crazed gadfly until it finally came to a halt, hovering weightless in the middle of the cell. Then the humming stopped, but the diamond ring glowed ever brighter.

Without warning, it fired a second laser beam, this time at the armillary sphere, whose central orb burnt like a miniature sun before enveloping the whole sphere and imploding into a black dot. The dot catapulted into a small tabernacle at the bottom of the fresco, where Christ was shown rising from his tomb. The tabernacle burst open: a speck of silver glinted in the blackness. It seemed to be travelling towards them at an incredible speed from an unimaginable distance. Rocketing out of the tabernacle it froze in mid-flight, before dropping like a stone to the floor. Whereupon the diamond ring ceased to glow and Cosimo's cell returned to candlelight.

Scala was the first to shake himself free of the trance-like state into which he and his companions had fallen. He scoured the floor for the object which been ejected from the tabernacle. It was lying by the wall beneath the fresco. 'The Key of the Magi,' he gasped, marvelling at the gold tracery on its solid silver shaft.

'Stop, thief!' a voice suddenly bellowed behind them. All eyes shot back to the doorway where a ghostly figure met their gaze. 'Repent ye sinners!' the spectre commanded, raising a luminous crucifix in its skeletal hand. 'Repent ye magicians and sorcerers, ye moneylenders and usurers. Repent! Cast aside the rings of evil and surrender the key to forbidden fruit before it is too late. Beware the Sword of the Lord!'

There was a loud crack. A steel blade flashed down from the ceiling, missing Scala's head by millimetres. The Brothers froze in panic. But Scala was not so easily spooked. 'What chicanery is this!' he cried, snatching the sword from the floor and hurling it at the ghost. There was a sound like breaking glass and the apparition promptly vanished.

'Come, Brothers!' Scala ordered. 'We must leave at once.' They hurriedly retraced their steps out of Cosimo's cell, stumbling back along the unlit passageway. Eventually they reached the cloister again where, aided by the moonlight, they made good their escape. Back on the street outside the priory, the Brothers agreed to await their maestro's next summons before going their separate ways. Scala ushered Miranda (still incognito in her hooded robe) into the back of his waiting limousine. Before getting in himself, he turned to one of the Brothers, who was nursing his right hand. 'Come to my palazzo tomorrow morning,' he whispered, 'and bring your ring.'

32

TOM PACED UP and down the deserted street, pounding his arms against his sides to keep warm. It was well past midnight. Where had they gone, Scala and his beautiful companion? An hour earlier, he had watched them arrive at the count's palazzo in a gleaming black Maserati. From the way they were dressed – he in black tie and silk cloak, she in a stunning dress and fur stole – he guessed they must have been to some high society Christmas party. He had expected the count to be married with a family, but that was not the impression he had gained from this, admittedly brief, glimpse of the couple. The girl was young enough to be his daughter, though of course rich men often attracted young wives. Yet, her demeanour was not that of a wife, much less a daughter. And husbands never looked *that* pleased with themselves.

The little trattoria from which he had carried out his surveillance was conveniently located just across the road from the palazzo. He had stretched out his third espresso until the café closed at 11pm. Instead of going straight back to his hotel, he had hung around, watching the palazzo's lights come on and go off, hoping (if he was honest with himself) that the girl would come out again, alone this time. But it was not to be.

Around 11.30pm, the front door had opened and Scala and the girl had reappeared. They had changed their clothes. Both wore long white tunics with hoods at the back. The Maserati had come back and swept them off into the night. Where were they going, dressed like that? A fancy-dress ball? An hour had gone by since then, but there was still no sign of them. Freezing, Tom reluctantly set off back to his hotel, hoping that they were not making a run for it disguised as monks. He would return the next morning, in warmer clothes and with wheels.

33

MIRANDA WOKE WITH a start. The strange happenings at San Marco the night before came flooding back. The special effects had been pretty amazing. But what was she to make of the 'Brothers' in their white habits and hoods? Were they an Italian version of the Freemasons? There were plenty of those back home in the States who loved their resplendent robes and secret rituals. Or was the 'Company of the Magi' something more sinister? She had seen a different side of Count Giovanni Scala – a side which she did not find so appealing. He had been so deadly serious about the whole thing, fanatical almost. Was that a real sword that dropped from the ceiling? And what was that gold and silver key he had found on the floor?

She got up and pulled back the curtains. The morning sun caught her solitaire ring. Why was it so beguiling? She recalled reading somewhere that the only true memento loved ones leave behind is the sparkle of their eyes reflected in their jewels. Whose eyes did she see in this stone?

Across the street, office workers and tourists were busy grabbing breakfast in the local trattoria before hitting their desks or the museums. Motor scooters weaved in and out of delivery vans waiting at the traffic lights. Vespas, she thought, remembering her nightmare of wasps and dolphins which had recurred more than once since her arrival in Florence. What did it mean? Did that family heirloom, the model galleon in her mother's attic, relate in some way to Cousin Frankie? Perhaps Dr Gatti would provide an answer. He was her last hope of finding her cousin. She sucked her lip: whatever Giovanni and his 'little club' were mixed up in, she had no choice but to string along with it for a while longer.

When she got downstairs Scala had already finished breakfast. He had risen early, unable to sleep. Fabio had just poured him a second cup of coffee. It was a rich Yunnan, flown in every month direct from Hong Kong, together with cakes of vintage Pu-Erh tea. Over the years, the count had developed a taste for Chinese cuisine, thanks to regular business trips to the Far East. As he breathed in the coffee's mellow aroma, he too was pondering the events of the previous night. Extraordinary though they were, they were not unexpected: not, that is, until the 'ghost of Savonarola' had burst in upon the scene. He had guessed that it was some sort of 3-D virtual image as soon as he saw it: it was so amateurish compared to the fresco's truly miraculous display. More worrying was the fact that the contrivance could not have been put together without the knowledge and cooperation of San Marco's friars. It followed that they must know not only about the Company of the Magi but also, from the 'ghost's' threats, about the Brothers' diamond rings. Was there another traitor amongst his brethren? Or had the Dominicans been spying on the Company's annual gatherings at San Lorenzo, including that last momentous occasion in September? It was their church, after all. That would explain the ghost's reference to the 'Sword of the Lord'. Would the House of Medici never be free of the curse of Savonarola?

'Buongiorno Giovanni,' Miranda trilled, seating herself on the chair which Fabio instantly drew for her, opposite the count. He looked up, smiling as her iris-scented perfume wafted across the table, blending with the smell of the coffee. 'A penny for your thoughts,' she said impishly, hoping he might keep his promise to provide answers in the morning to all the questions she had bombarded him with the previous night, during the short drive back from San Marco.

Scala fixed her with his impenetrable gaze. 'Forgive me, Miranda,' he said. 'I was miles away. Did you sleep well?'

'Oh, sure. I always find creeping round a monastery at the dead of night, being attacked by ghosts and flying saucers, a guaranteed cure for insomnia.'

The count burst out laughing. Fabio looked at him as if he had gone mad. It had been a very long time since he had heard his master laugh. Life had become such a sombre business for the count ever since his wife's tragic death, so many years ago. It was good to hear laughter in the house again.

'Thank you, Fabio, that will be all,' Scala snapped on noticing his butler's bemusement. 'Miss Maddingley will help herself to breakfast.'

Fabio inclined his head. 'Si, Signore,' adding as he left the room: 'It's good to have you and the signorina home again.'

The count raised an eyebrow at this odd remark, as did Miranda, but their minds were elsewhere. 'It was an armillary sphere,' he said, passing her a basket of freshly baked bread from the local panneteria.

'Sorry, what?' she frowned as she dunked the tip of a flaky cornetto into her black coffee.

'An armillary sphere, not a flying saucer.'

'Oh, silly me! Of course it was. What else would be buzzing around a monastery at midnight?'

'I did warn you that you might find the proceedings "stimulating".'

'Stimulating? Most people would call having a sword almost lodge in your skull terrifying.'

Scala tossed his head back. 'I'm sure most people would,' he scoffed. To him, 'most people' was a category of mankind to which neither he, nor Miranda, could possibly belong. 'I suppose,' he conceded after a brief silence, 'I didn't tell you quite all there is to know about our Brotherhood.' Miranda took a boiled egg from a nearby dish and sliced off its top. As understatements went, that was on a par with Apollo 13 telling Houston it had a problem. Scala looked at his watch: it was ten to nine. 'Ah, Dottore Gatti will be here soon,' he said, abandoning his napkin and leaping to his feet.

'But Giovanni, you promised...'

'Patience, Miranda. I always keep my word.'

'How did you know?' she fired at him as he made for the door.

He glanced back at her with a puzzled expression. 'Know what?'

'That it was Gatti's diamond that gave us the light show last night. Our faces were covered by hoods, yet you knew it was Gatti that you told to be here this morning.'

Scala tapped his nose. 'Say nothing to Gatti about last night,' he warned before stepping smartly out of the room.

Miranda fingered her diamond ring. Should she remove it before meeting the good dottore? On the balance of probabilities, he would turn out to be just as evasive as his Vatican colleague, the mendacious Father Vincenzo. In that case, a flash of her diamond might unnerve and wrong-foot him. She decided to play it by ear. After all, the lawyer in her pleaded, only *speaking* of last night had been forbidden. She dipped a last morsel of cornetto in her boiled egg and waited for a knock at the count's front door.

***

'Dottore Gatti,' announced Fabio in his standard deadpan voice as he showed him into Scala's study.

The count was seated at a Chinese rosewood desk, examining a piece of parchment under a magnifying glass. 'Ah, Dottore, do sit down,' he said, gesturing at the armchair opposite.

Gatti threw his overcoat (which he had warily withheld from Fabio's clutches) over the back of the chair and perched stiffly on the edge of the seat. Behind his thick, black spectacles, Gatti's intense blue eyes followed Scala's hands as he locked the parchment in a drawer. 'That was quite an experience last night, Maestro,' he remarked. 'But I wonder who was behind the "son et lumière" at the end?'

Scala studied his visitor, wondering if the question was as innocent as it sounded. 'I'm not sure. Obviously someone outside our Brotherhood knew of our presence in San Marco and went to a lot of trouble to try to intimidate us into abandoning our mission. We must continue to be on our guard and be ultra vigilant.'

'Absolutely, Maestro. We mustn't let anyone, outside or inside the Brotherhood, compromise our quest.'

Scala frowned. 'Inside? Are you suggesting that one of us had something to do with what happened last night?'

Gatti pushed his spectacles to the top of his nose. 'Well I... Oh, it's nothing, I'm sure.'

'Let me be the judge of that,' the count insisted.

Gatti nodded and recounted how, when one of the Brothers had lost his way the previous night in the dark corridors of San Marco, he had heard someone talking on a mobile phone.

'What did they say?'

'I couldn't tell. They were speaking a foreign language. It sounded like Russian.'

Scala's fist tightened its grip on the arm of his chair. Only one of their brethren spoke a Slavonic language.

'You don't think Professore Jankovic...' Gatti began.

'I'll look into it, Dottore,' Scala cut in. Jankovic could be dealt with later, if that proved necessary. Right now they needed to concentrate on Gatti's ring.

The dottore stroked the burn on his right hand. 'I've been puzzling over the meaning of the inscription all night,' he sighed. He was just easing the ring off his index finger when there was a tap at the door and Miranda waltzed in. 'Oh, I'm sorry, Giovanni,' she breezed. 'I didn't realise you had a visitor.'

The count jumped smartly to his feet. 'Miranda my dear, permit me to introduce Dottore Umberto Gatti.'

Miranda perused the tight-lipped young man who did not bother to get up. His stubbly cheeks and pale complexion, combined with hunched shoulders and mop of rebellious blonde hair, all chimed with the solitary academic whom Brother Andreas had described, right down to his bulky jacket and baggy trousers. All the same, there was something incongruous about him, something she could not quite pin down: maybe it was his tense expression, or the stiffness of his posture. The wariness in those distrustful eyes reminded her of the hostile witnesses she had often had to cross-examine in court. 'Pleased to meet you, Dottore,' she chirruped, extending her right hand so that he could not fail to notice the diamond ring.

Gatti hesitated, but only for a moment. 'Piacere, Signorina,' he reciprocated with a brief nod, keeping his right hand firmly in his trouser pocket.

'Umberto,' said the count, 'this is my guest from New York. Miss Miranda Maddingley.'

Now even those thick glasses could not conceal Gatti's surprise. 'Maddingley?' he repeated incredulously.

'Yes. Is that name familiar to you, Umberto?'

'Er, yes… yes, it is,' he stuttered. 'My assistant at the Vatican Library is called Maddingley.'

'So it is you!' Miranda cried. 'I hoped it was when Giovanni introduced you. But now I'm sure of it. Dr Gatti: you're the reason I'm in Florence.' He stared at her like a startled rabbit. She quickly retold the bare details of her uncle's death and the discovery of a previously unheard-of cousin. 'I do so want to meet him,' she said, 'but all I had to go on was that he worked in the Vatican Library. So I flew to Rome and met with Father Vincenzo da Forli. I believe you know him, Dottore?' Gatti nodded vaguely. 'Father Vincenzo was so kind and helpful,' she lied. 'He told me that my cousin Frankie had worked at the Vatican for some years but left suddenly three months ago. The father had no contact details for him but suggested that you might be able to help.' She deliberately omitted any mention of Brother Andreas: she did not want to get him into trouble. 'The only problem,' she continued, 'was that you had gone to Florence to look after your sick sister. Fortunately, the name of the hotel you'd booked into was on file.'

Gatti's narrowed his eyes. 'Fortunate indeed,' he said with just a hint of irony, Miranda thought. 'But in that case,' he went on, 'how do you come to be here, at the count's palazzo?' Scala explained how they met. 'Ah, now I understand,' Gatti nodded. 'Well, much as I should like to help you, Miss Maddingley, I'm afraid I have no idea where your cousin is. All I know is that his father died recently and that unsettled him terribly. He did mention the possibility of his visiting friends in Australia. Or was it New Zealand? Anyway, one of the two. But that's as much as I can tell you, I'm afraid.'

'But he left on the very same day that you came to Florence.'

'Did he?'

'That's quite a coincidence isn't it?'

Gatti flicked his hair. 'I'm not sure what you mean, Miss Maddingley. I wasn't aware until now that he'd gone anywhere. But even if he did leave on the same day that I came to Florence, I don't see anything particularly significant in that.'

This line of questioning was getting nowhere. She decided to raise the stakes. 'Maybe not in itself,' she conceded, 'but the fact is you don't actually have a sister in Florence, sick or otherwise, do you, Doctor?' Gatti clenched his jaws. Was that anger or panic in his eyes? She could not tell.

'Miranda,' Scala interrupted, 'kindly remember that the dottore is a guest in my house. I won't have him subjected to the third degree.'

'It's okay,' Gatti muttered. 'She's right, I don't have a sick sister. I don't know how she knows, but it doesn't matter. The truth is,' he sighed, sinking back into his chair and staring at the floor, 'I invented a sick sister in order to get away from the Vatican. I've felt constantly under surveillance there these last few months. I suspected that Father Vincenzo had suborned her cousin –' he shot a withering look at Miranda '– to spy on me. I had to get away.'

'But why should Father Vincenzo want to spy on you?' Miranda questioned.

Gatti studiously avoided eye contact with the meddlesome American. 'I believe, Count Scala,' he said in a confidential undertone, 'it has to do with the matter we were discussing earlier.'

Scala ran his fingers down his chin. 'Miranda,' he said, 'I think Dottore Gatti has helped you all he can.'

She would dearly have liked to know what the 'matter' was which Gatti and Scala had been discussing and why the Vatican should be so interested in it. She guessed that it had to do with their 'club' and the previous night's events. But, recognising the finality in the count's tone, she thanked the dottore and apologised for any embarrassment she had caused.

'The Antipodes, Miss Maddingley,' he replied with a shrug, 'that's where you should look for your cousin.'

Scala ruffled some papers on his desk and indicated that he and the dottore had business to discuss.

'No problem, Giovanni. I was about to go out anyway, to the Uffizi to take another look at your favourite painting.' Scala looked puzzled. 'You know,' she said, 'the "Primavera", the one with all those mythological references and levels of meaning.'

'Oh, it's hardly my favourite,' he chortled, glancing at Gatti as if to say that Botticelli's masterpiece was the last painting he would put at the top of his list. But Gatti was busy adjusting the strap on his gold wristwatch and seemed not the least bit interested in either the count's taste in art or Miranda's plans for the day. 'Have fun,' Scala called to her as she left the room.

The study door had almost closed when Miranda poked her head back inside. 'Oh, Dr Gatti,' she said, 'I nearly forgot. The manager at the Villa Medici asked me to remind you about the bottle of wine you ordered.' Gatti's eyebrows knotted together. 'A special bottle of Frascati, wasn't it? Apparently you left it behind in your room when you checked out.'

'Oh, how remiss of me,' he exclaimed, tapping his temple. 'I completely forgot. I'll go and pick it up this afternoon.'

Miranda closed the door and frowned. Something did not add up.

34

As soon as Miranda was safely out of the room, Gatti removed his diamond ring and handed it to the count. 'Did you say you'd already looked at the inscription, Dottore?' he enquired.

'Yes, but I couldn't make much sense of it, Maestro.'

'Let's hope two heads are better than one!' Putting a jeweller's loupe to his eye, he read out the words etched five hundred years before:

'"SUSCIPITE O FRATRES ARCANA HERMIS TRIMEGISTI. DIES MAGORUM"'

Gatti immediately offered a translation: '"Take up O Brothers the secrets of Hermes Trimegistus. The day of the Magi."'

Both men lapsed into silence, pondering what the injunction actually meant. 'Shouldn't there be an "s" after the first "i" in "Trimegisti"?' Gatti ventured after a while.

Scala put the ring down for a moment and retrieved a classical dictionary from the pile of books on the floor beside his chair. 'Ah, it's as I thought,' he said. 'They're alternative spellings. Ficino used "Tri" rather than "Tris" in order to make the initial hexameter scan correctly.'

'Ah, is that all?' Gatti sniffed. 'I thought the reason might be less obvious than that.'

Reading further, Scala noted that Hermes Trismegistus, apart from being an icon of Neoplatonic philosophy, was also identified with Thoth, the Egyptian god of learning and magic. 'He, and the jackal-headed Anubis, brought men's souls to Osiris for judgement.'

'Where does that get us?'

Scala slapped the dictionary shut. 'Not very far, I'm afraid.'

'How about taking a look at Trismegistus' original writings? Ficino must have had his own copy. Did he perhaps leave it with your ancestor Bartolomeo for safe keeping?'

The count shook his head. There was a fourteenth-century Greek manuscript of the *Corpus Hermeticum* in the Biblioteca Medicea-Laurenziana, adjacent to San Lorenzo. He had consulted it several times in the past but, beyond the fact that it was the oldest known copy of Hermes' works and the one that Ficino had used to produce his famous Latin translation, there was nothing particularly special or secret about it.

Gatti thrust his hands in his pockets. 'So, what now?' he exhaled.

Scala's gaze wandered over the antique Persian carpet which covered the study floor, as if seeking inspiration in its colourful, intertwining patterns. But nothing came to him. He was looking in the wrong place. But what was the right place? There was nowhere in Florence, as far as he knew, which could claim a special connection with the ancient

Egyptian sage. Could it be that what they sought was not in Florence at all? No, the city was the heart and soul of the Medici. It was surely inconceivable that they would have hidden their secrets anywhere else. His gaze drifted beyond the carpet to the chess table standing in the window. The plain, rectangular symmetry of its inlaid ivory and ebony squares contrasted sharply with the curves and colours of the carpet. Suddenly, he had an idea. Rushing across the room, he knelt down next to a newspaper rack stuffed with glossy booklets and magazines.

Gatti looked on curiously as pamphlets and periodicals of all types and sizes were snatched up, glanced at and tossed aside. 'What are you looking for?' he demanded. But Scala just carried on with his madcap search until, at the very bottom of the rack, he found what he was seeking. 'Eureka!' he cried, waving a slim, paperback guidebook aloft. Gatti glimpsed a picture of a bearded man in a white robe on the front cover. He was wearing a conical hat, just like the one on the head of the magus in the fresco on the wall of Cosimo's cell at San Marco.

Scala stretched out his arm and invited the dottore, who was by now standing right behind him, to read the inscription which appeared on a tablet beneath the bearded figure's feet.

'"HERMES MERCURIUS TRIMEGISTUS CONTEMPORANEUS MOYSI"'

'That's right,' Scala declared as the light dawned in Gatti's eyes. 'It's a depiction of the magus Trimegistus himself. And his name lacks the first "s", just like your ring.'

Gatti bent down and squinted at the bearded Hermes. He was handing an open book to two other figures, one wearing a turban, the other cloaked from head to toe. The book bore a further Latin inscription: 'SUSCIPITE O LICTERAS ET LEGES EGIPTII'.

'Take up the letters and laws of Egypt,' Scala translated excitedly. 'The resonance with your ring is unmistakable.'

'Incredible, Maestro! Well done!' Gatti enthused. 'So, tell me, where is this picture of Trimegistus to be found?'

Scala retracted his arm and slipped the booklet into his jacket pocket. 'Not yet, Dottore,' he said. 'Remember what happened at San Marco. The Vatican's spies may have followed you to Florence, and it seems we may also have a problem with Professore Jankovic. I shall not reveal the location until we are all assembled here and all go there together.'

Gatti straightened up. 'As you wish, Maestro. But when will that be? When exactly is the "day of the Magi"?'

The count returned to his chair and Gatti's ring. Those last two words, 'DIES MAGORUM', were surely a reference to Epiphany, the feast day of the Three Wise Men according to the Church calendar. Yet, as Jankovic had pointed out at the dinner in November, all the dates that had so far been significant had been astronomical, not ecclesiastical.

Gatti flicked through his pocket diary. 'Aha!' he exclaimed, 'Epiphany will be on the sixth of January.'

'Of course it will,' Scala snorted. 'It's always on the sixth.'

'Yes, but look, the sixth of January 2006 is also the night of the moon's first quarter. Isn't that an astronomical event?'

Scala eyed the small crescent next to Gatti's fingertip, silently running through a list of lunar associations in his mind. He recollected that in ancient Persia, the homeland of the Magi, they had followed the lunar calendar, according to which each month began with the first sighting of the waxing moon. Also, in Babylonian mythology, the crescent moon was the symbol of the moon god, the 'Lord of Wisdom'. And the 'Lord of Wisdom' was an epithet of the Persian god, Mithras, who was often depicted slaying a bull. 'The crescent moon in Taurus,' he muttered.

'Taurus?'

'Oh, nothing, Dottore,' Scala responded vaguely. 'But I do believe you're right about the sixth of January. That's when the Company of the Magi must meet again.'

They both breathed a sigh of relief. The inscription had been deciphered and the next convocation of their Brotherhood would be in a fortnight's time. Their task completed, Gatti slid his ring back onto his finger. He was just gathering up his overcoat to leave when a copy of *La Nazione* fell from one of its large pockets. He had bought the daily paper on his way to Scala's palazzo but, being in a hurry, he had not had time to read more than the headlines. As he picked it up from the floor, he stopped suddenly, as if struck by paralysis.

'What is it, Dottore?' Scala demanded anxiously as all sorts of unwelcome news buzzed through his brain. Had the Dominicans reported the strange goings-on at San Lorenzo? Had that snake Radopoulos managed to report some sensationalist story to his paparazzi pals before he was liquidated? Or had the fraud at the Banca de' Bianchi finally come to light? He was aware that a police investigation was under way in London, despite his pre-emptive action. He snatched the paper from Gatti's frozen grasp. 'But there's nothing here,' he shrugged, rapidly scanning the headlines. 'Berlusconi accused of mixing pleasure and politics'; 'German Pope's wartime record under scrutiny'; 'Headless corpse found in the Arno'. It was all just the usual stuff.

Recovering his power of movement, Gatti gesticulated at the top of the paper's front page: 'The date! Look at the date!' he shrieked.

Scala frowned. 'It must be a misprint,' he said, trying to calm Gatti's nerves. But an alarm bell was already sounding at the back of his mind. He pressed a button on the underside of his desk. 'Fabio, what day is it?' he demanded as soon as his omnipresent butler entered.

'Thursday, Signore.' Fabio replied serenely.

There was a sharp intake of breath as the count refined his enquiry. 'I am aware what day it is, Fabio. What I want to know is today's date.'

'Ah,' he beamed, 'it is January the fifth, Signore.'

'Are you quite sure?'

'Si, Signore. Tomorrow is the festival of Epiphany.' Then he added hesitantly, 'Il Conte will doubtless recall that it is bad luck to work on Epiphany. I and my... ahem... "cousins" will be following the Cavalcade of the Magi, as usual, from Palazzo Pitti to the Duomo.'

Scala grimaced. It was most unfortunate timing. Apart from his Sicilian chauffeur, all his staff were Sardinian (Sardinians made terrible drivers). He liked to think of them as his personal Praetorian Guard, who might well be needed if the enemies of the Medici were planning something for the next conclave of the Brotherhood. But the Sardinians were a superstitious bunch and it would be a mistake to upset them. In any case, if the instructions handed down through generations of his family were to be believed, there were powers now unleashed which mere mortal hands would cross at their peril. 'Very well,' he said with a dismissive wave. The butler turned to go. 'Oh, just one more thing, Fabio. Earlier this morning you said that it was good to have me back home again. Why? Have I been away?' The butler glanced at Gatti. 'It's alright,' Scala reassured him, 'you may speak freely in front of the dottore.'

Fabio cleared his throat. 'Signore,' he replied, 'today is the first time that I have seen you since before Christmas.'

'What the hell's going on, Maestro?' Gatti exclaimed as soon as Fabio had left the room. 'It's surreal.'

The count shook his head. 'No, Dottore, not surreal, more supernatural or even miraculous.'

'Miraculous?'

Scala removed the stopper from a crystal decanter and poured them both a shot of single malt. 'What else would you call what happened at San Lorenzo in September or at San Marco last night, or rather last month?'

Gatti drained his glass in one. 'What are we going to do, Maestro?'

Scala looked at his watch. 'We don't have much time. Come back tonight at 10pm. And bring your robe. I'll call the others and tell them to do likewise.'

Gatti looked even more confused. 'But, Maestro,' he said, his voice trembling, 'Epiphany's not till tomorrow... Or is it already tomorrow today?'

Scala grabbed him by the shoulders. 'Prender corragio, Dottore!' he growled. The young man straightened his back and took several deep breaths. The count relaxed his grip. 'Yes,' he nodded, 'Epiphany is tomorrow. But tomorrow begins at midnight, and so will the day of the Magi.'

35

TOM JUST CAUGHT the movement in the corner of his eye. The curtains in the upper-storey window were being opened. A face looked down. It was that girl again. Every day since the night he had seen her with the count, he had come here to the Via Scala, first thing in the morning, and sat in the local trattoria, watching and waiting. He had become such a regular customer that he was on first-name terms with the owners, Giorgio, and his wife, Gina. The café had been in the family for three generations and they were a mine of information when it came to their rich neighbour over the road. They did not know the count personally, of course, but his butler, Fabio, and some of the other Sardinians often dropped in for a coffee and a cigarette. Smoking was not allowed inside the palazzo: 'Nor much else either,' Giorgio remarked wryly.

'The devil lives there,' Gina whispered, describing the late-night comings and goings she had witnessed over the years. But now the count's new American girlfriend seemed to be making a difference. Music, and even laughter, had been overheard escaping those dour walls.

Tom licked the cappuccino foam off his lips. At least the beautiful brunette was not married to the devilish Count, he consoled himself. Lowering his gaze from the window where she had made her fleeting appearance, he observed the passers-by; some with briefcases, some with shoulder bags, some chatting on mobiles, some chewing on energy bars. After a while, a guy in a heavy overcoat, with the lapels turned up, crossed the road right in front of the trattoria. He stopped outside Scala's palazzo and glanced around furtively before knocking on the front door. It opened almost immediately and he stepped inside. Nothing of note happened after that until, several slices of toasted bruschetta and another cappuccino later, the door open again. This time the brunette stepped out. She strode confidently along the pavement in tight jeans and brown leather boots. A diamond ring flashed in the sunlight as she adjusted a red beanie which bobbed jauntily on her chestnut hair. Tom decided to follow her.

After a brisk, twenty-minute walk, they arrived at the Uffizi Gallery. Tom lined up behind her in the queue and noted her distinctive New York accent as she asked for a ticket. Once inside, she stopped to check out a floor-plan posted on one of the walls. Tom looked away, pretending to be waiting for someone. When he looked round again, she had vanished. He stood on tiptoe, craning his neck over a regiment of silver-haired British tourists. A red beanie bobbed briefly in the distance before passing through a doorway and out of sight. Dashing past the stragglers of the British expeditionary force, he had managed to outflank their rearguard when the main body came to an abrupt halt and he found himself surrounded on all sides. Their leader, a dapper Englishman in blue blazer and cavalry twill, drew his troops up right in front of the doorway through which the beanie had flown. The Brits stood dutifully to attention as they were harangued with hyperboles about the wonder they were about to behold: a work of art to rival the Mona Lisa as an icon of female beauty. Meanwhile, Tom fought his way apologetically through the phalanx of tut-tutting pensioners and finally made it to the doorway. A moment later, he came face to face with the Birth of Venus.

But not even Botticelli's heavenly vision could distract him. His eyes darted round the room. It was remarkably quiet. He was now ahead of the hordes, as was his quarry. There she was, standing entranced in front of another Botticelli masterpiece: the Primavera. He recognised it at once. Soon after arriving in Florence, he had visited the Uffizi: the site of his father's murder. In real life the painting was incomparably more impressive than the slide in Aunt Stella's lecture. The canvas was vast, occupying virtually an entire wall, and the colours were so vivid, the figures so alive. Was this what his father had been shot for? Suddenly, the army of British tourists burst through the doorway. The Birth of Venus was their first target but it would not be long before they turned their attention to the Primavera. It was now or never: he approached the girl. 'Did you know that this is the only painting in which Botticelli put a smile on a woman's face?' Even as he uttered this opening gambit, he cringed at what must have sounded like the most contrived of chat-up lines.

Miranda turned and regarded the stranger with a mixture of surprise and suspicion. Surprise because, ever since her run-in with the infuriating Doctor Gatti earlier that morning, she had been totally preoccupied with trying to work out what to make of him: his story about being spied on at the Vatican, amongst other things. Suspicion because that was second nature to an attractive young woman who was no stranger to being propositioned. Still, she saw no malice or madness in Tom's deep blue eyes. On the contrary, there was something rather appealing about his boyish air and disarming smile. 'No, I can't say I did,' she replied, feeling slightly miffed that Count Giovanni had not mentioned this particular nugget of information during their recent visit to the Uffizi. 'Do you suppose,' she wondered with a mischievous twinkle in her eye, 'that Botticelli knew how to put a smile on a girl's face in real life too?'

Tom grinned: the girl had a sense of humour. 'Well,' he said with a nod towards the Birth of Venus, 'he certainly knew how to put one on a man's.'

Miranda laughed. 'Touché, Mister…?'

'Stockton. Tom Stockton.' His aunt's surname flew from his lips, realising as he did that Scala might recognise his real one. 'And you?'

'Maddingley. Miranda Maddingley. From New York, if you hadn't already guessed.'

He confirmed that he had, explaining in half-truths that he was taking a gap year from his job 'in finance' which often involved business trips to the US. And, yes, in answer to her further questioning, he had heard of the Banca de' Bianchi. Miranda then reciprocated with the 'amazing coincidence' that she was staying at the palazzo of the bank's chairman whilst searching for her newly discovered cousin. 'It was the count who introduced me to Botticelli and the Primavera,' she said, turning back to the painting. 'He says the figure of

Mercury is an idealised image of Lorenzo de' Medici. In fact, all the figures look so real, don't they? They seem to be frozen in the middle of some drama, ready to come back to life at any moment.'

Tom had to admit that there was something quite magical about the painting, something that drew the viewer deeper and deeper into its mysterious, inner world, as if it was not really a painting at all but rather a portal into some parallel universe. 'Actually,' he said, 'the figure of Flora is also supposed to portray a real person. A famous beauty called Simonetta Vespucci.'

Miranda's heart missed a beat. She had understood from her internet searches that Simonetta had been the model for the Birth of Venus. But she had been disappointed on seeing the painting in the flesh: Venus was too perfect to be real. She looked again at Flora. Those delicate features, that distant gaze, the hint of sadness at the corners of her smile: there could indeed be a real woman beneath the golden tresses and the flowery garlands. Was it Simonetta who scattered those rosebuds, all too soon to die? In a flash of insight, she realised that Botticelli had painted this portrait, not from life, but from memory. But then something else puzzled her: how come Giovanni had not mentioned such an intriguing identification in the painting he loved above all others (despite his odd denial in front of Gatti)? She turned to Tom: 'I guess you must know all the various theories about the Primavera too?'

'Oh yes: all the "als".'

'The "als"?'

'As in literal, metaphorical, mythical, allegorical, symbolical and anagogical: it is the very picture of a painting enigmatical!' he chuckled, reciting his aunt's list of hypotheses in mock Mikadoese. They both laughed and, as their eyes locked, there was a moment of recognition, though of what neither could yet fathom. A gruff harrumph broke the spell. The British tour group had arrived. A ruddy-cheeked man with bulging eyes was frowning at them, whilst his prune-faced companion gave them a glare which, Tom felt, could easily have rivalled Medusa's. He and Miranda pulled furtive faces at one another and moved swiftly on, sniggering like naughty schoolchildren.

The next painting they came to was very different from the Primavera. They stopped to read the blurb on the wall beside it:

'Botticelli's "Mystic Nativity" (on loan from the National Gallery, London). The Virgin Mary kneels over the Christ child while shepherds and the Wise Men look on. In the foreground, three angels embrace three men, often identified with Savonarola and two other friars, burnt at the stake in Florence in 1498. Demons hide in crevices in the rocks at the men's feet. The Gothic style and archaic iconography contrast with the lively exuberance of Botticelli's earlier works, indicating his abandonment of humanism after the fall of the Medici and his conversion to Savonarola's medieval brand of Christianity. The title "Mystic Nativity" refers to the mysterious Greek inscription Botticelli painted at the top of the picture:*

"I, Alessandro, painted this at the end of the year 1500, in the half-time after the time, according to the XIth [chapter] of Saint John, in the second woe of the

Apocalypse, during the release of the devil for three-and-a-half years; then he shall be bound in the XII [chapter] and we shall see clearly [illegible] as in this picture".'

Tom gazed up at the painting. 'Whew,' he exhaled, 'it's hard to believe that this is by the same artist who painted the Birth of Venus.'

'According to Giovanni...' Miranda began.

'Giovanni?'

'Sorry, that's the chairman of the Banca de' Bianchi I mentioned just now.'

'Oh,' he nodded, simultaneously pleased and disappointed at her familiarity with Scala.

'Giovanni says Botticelli's genius is his ability to combine different thought worlds and juxtapose normally unconnected ideas.' She pointed back to the Primavera and its intertwining of classical myth with echoes of Christian and humanist ideals. 'And so here,' she said, recycling Scala's comments, 'you've got the birth of Christ combined with the Second Coming, the Resurrection of the Dead, and even the Last Judgement.'

He looked again at the painting. He could see now what she meant. She, or rather her dear friend 'Giovanni', had put into words the subconscious impact of those images. But other things struck him too. The three angels on the manger roof, their hands joined in supporting the Bible, were oddly reminiscent of the Three Graces in the Primavera. Three angels, Three Graces, Three Magi: always three. And what about that strange inscription written in the year 1500: 'the half-time after the time'? Half-time to what? The blurb on the wall certainly chimed with what Savonarola's ghost had said at Careggi: that he had received Botticelli's confession. And if Botticelli had switched his allegiance from the Medici, did that affect the Platonic Academy and the secret which Ficino had imparted to Lorenzo, whatever it was? Of one thing, however, he was sure: none of those three men being embraced by angels looked anything like the grim-faced ghost he had seen hovering at Lorenzo's bedside.

Miranda prodded Tom's arm: the British tourists were heading their way. They were about to move on when Tom became aware of someone behind them. Glancing over his shoulder, he saw a gloved hand gripping a silver blade. With lightning speed he grabbed Miranda's arm and yanked her bodily towards him. The dagger missed her by a hair's breadth. But she, unaware of the danger, lashed out so violently against Tom's apparent assault that he lost his balance and fell to the floor with the American attorney sprawled on top of him. As she screamed and shouted at him to let go of her, the British tour group arrived en masse and surrounded the impromptu wrestling match with a chorus of outraged gentility. Meanwhile, a hoodie in a black parka slipped away through the crowd.

Miranda was the first to get to her feet. 'What the hell are you playing at?' she blazed at Tom, who was by now sitting up, trying in vain to spot her would-be assailant. Seething at his lack of response, she looked round for a security guard and saw Scala marching towards her, pushing the tourists imperiously aside. 'Giovanni!' she cried. 'Thank God'.

The count put his arms around her. 'Are you okay?' he asked anxiously.

She pointed an accusing finger at Tom. 'That man,' she blurted, 'he attacked me!'

'No, she's got it wrong,' Tom protested, clambering to his feet. 'Some guy just tried to stab her in the back with that.' He pointed at the painting they had just been discussing. Miranda gasped in horror as she turned and beheld a dagger embedded in the painting's gilded frame.

Scala dislodged the weapon from the wood and examined its inscribed blade and distinctive ivory hilt. He realised at once that Tom was telling the truth. 'Did you see his face?' he demanded.

Tom shook his head. 'He was wearing a hood.'

Scala turned to Miranda. 'Let's get out of here,' he said, guiding her gently but firmly towards the exit while she tried to apologise to Tom for having accused him so unjustly. Scala glanced back at him. 'Yes, yes. Thank you so much,' he muttered dismissively, as if he were tipping a cab driver. But Tom was not to be brushed off so easily and fell in close behind them.

As the unlikely trio hastened from the gallery, the prune-faced English tourist turned to her fish-eyed husband: 'Well, that's Americans for you!' she sniped.

36

'SHOULDN'T WE CALL the police, Giovanni?' Miranda questioned as she, the count and Tom hurried along the broad, central passage of the Uffizi's first floor. But involving the police was the last thing Scala wanted. 'No, no, my dear,' he scoffed. 'Italian policemen are nothing like your New York cops. They're pen-pushing bureaucrats who'd have us filling in forms till kingdom come. No, the Uffizi's security staff sadly have plenty of experience in dealing with madmen defacing works of art. They'll catch him, don't worry.'

'But that guy was aiming at Miranda, not the painting.' Tom objected.

'Don't be ridiculous!' Scala snapped. 'What possible motive could he have had?'

Tom had no answer to that and neither had Miranda. 'Well, I'm just glad you arrived when you did, Giovanni,' she sighed. 'I'd have waited for you if I'd known you were coming.' Scala confessed that he had been arranging a surprise for her. The Uffizi's curator was an old friend of his and, as a special favour, he had agreed to a private viewing of the Primavera for her and his little club.

Tom's ears pricked up. Could this 'little club' have anything to do with the fraud at the Banca de' Bianchi? He was hoping to hear more when the count stopped and removed a key from his pocket. He opened a door, tucked discreetly away between two statues. A broad, stone staircase swept downwards in a majestic curve. Locking the door behind them, Scala explained that, as a trustee of the Uffizi, he had privileged access to the Vasari Corridor. This private corridor stretched all the way from the Palazzo Vecchio, the old seat of the Florentine government, through the Uffizi and across the Ponte Vecchio to the south bank of the Arno. It was off limits to the general public, he said, shooting a disdainful glance at Tom. As they reached the bottom of the stairs, he told them how the great Medici Grand Duke Cosimo I had commanded the architect Vasari to design the corridor for his new wife, 'the lovely Eleanora of Toledo'. Tom grimaced as Scala mooned into Miranda's eyes: 'Eleanora couldn't stand the stench coming from the tanners, butchers and fishmongers of the Ponte Vecchio, which she had to cross to get to the new palace Cosimo had bought for her. So he had this elevated walkway built for their exclusive use. Now she could walk high above the heads of the foul-smelling tradesmen to the fragrant Boboli Gardens, where Cosimo arranged magnificent pageants, pageants which gave birth to Italian opera. Yet another of the Medici's glorious legacies to mankind.'

Tom listened to the count's Medicean eulogy with growing irritation. The conversation needed to be brought back down to earth. 'Shouldn't we at least check with the museum security people?' he said. 'Won't they need Miranda and me as witnesses? That guy could strike again, for all we know.'

'That's true, Giovanni,' Miranda agreed. 'And if it weren't for Tom's prompt action, who knows what might have happened.'

Scala eyed them both. 'Tom', 'Miranda': they were already on first-name terms. Up to that point, Tom had been just a nuisance; now he was beginning to sound like a potential rival. 'You're quite right, my dear,' he soothed. 'Perhaps I have been a little hasty. I'll make sure the authorities have our full details in case they need any help.'

'Thanks, Giovanni,' Miranda smiled. Then she had an idea. 'I know,' she said, 'let's take Tom out for dinner tonight, to thank him properly for what he did back there.'

Tom's eyes lit up, but Scala was having none of it. 'Regrettably we have a prior engagement.'

'We do?'

'Yes, the club is meeting this evening.'

'Again? So soon? But we only…'

'Yes, I know. All very last-minute, I'm afraid.'

'It's no problem,' Tom intervened. A meeting of Scala's club was just what he wanted. 'I've got something on this evening too. Maybe another time?'

Scala leapt at the bait. 'But of course. Call me when you're free,' he said, handing Tom his business card.

Vasari's Corridor wound serenely above the noisy streets before launching itself across the Arno, riding piggy-back on top of the goldsmiths' shops which had long since replaced the obnoxious trades that had so offended the Grand Duchess Eleanora. An imposing marble bust marked the start of the

Arno traverse. 'That's Cardinal Leopoldo de' Medici,' Scala noted. 'He was responsible for the wonderful collection of portraits displayed along the corridor.'

Countless pairs of eyes seemed to follow them as they passed row upon row of the wealthy and the worthy, painted by the great and the gifted. From Raphael to Rembrandt, Rubens to Velazquez: all were represented there. But it was the cameo views from the small grilled windows, set at regular intervals along each side of the corridor, that most attracted Miranda. Those to the left provided intermittent perspectives on the shimmering river, gliding down from the Ponte Delle Grazie; those to the right allowed her to spy on the constant stream of humanity crossing the Ponte Vecchio, some twenty feet below. She was taking one such peek when she suddenly let out a little shriek.

Tom rushed to the window. He just caught a glimpse of a fat, tonsured figure in a black cloak and white habit before he passed out of view. But it was the person following close behind him who really arrested his attention. He looked exactly like the hoodie who had attacked Miranda in the Uffizi: same height, same build and wearing the same black parka, with the hood still up. He was about to speak out but Scala elbowed him aside. 'What did you see, Miranda?' he demanded, putting his face against the glass pane.

'Father Vincenzo,' she replied. 'Doctor Gatti's boss. I'm sure it was him, just down there by the bust of Cellini.'

Scala moved aside to let Miranda point to the spot. As she did so, Tom noticed that her diamond ring matched the one on the count's right hand. Rings and diamonds, he thought, recalling Careggi.

'Well, I can't see him,' Scala exhaled as he pulled back from the window. 'Are you sure it was Vincenzo, my dear? One tonsured priest looks so much alike another.'

'I know what I saw, Giovanni.' she retorted. She had twenty-twenty vision and a marksman's certificate from the Brooklyn Rifle Association to prove it. It was Father Vincenzo alright. What was he doing in Florence? Looking for Gatti? And if Vincenzo was around, maybe Cousin Frankie was here too? She thought of the hooded knifeman: could he have been aiming at her after all, as the cute Tom Stockton believed? But why? Was her search for her cousin interfering with some Vatican plot? Was that why Winslowe had been murdered? Or was it to do with her friendship with the count and the weird happenings at San Marco? Was that why he did not want to involve the cops? Was he more concerned with protecting his 'little club' than with her safety? Scala tried to put a reassuring arm around her shoulders, but she shrugged him off and they continued separately down the corridor.

Tom watched their exchange with interest. Was that a sliver of suspicion in her eyes? Was her relationship with Scala not quite as close as those matching diamond rings might suggest? And who was Father Vincenzo, the merest glimpse of whom had triggered such repugnance in the feisty New Yorker? Was it just coincidence that he and the knifeman were crossing the Ponte Vecchio at the same time? Immersed in these thoughts, Tom fell a little way behind, his gaze idly flitting to and fro among the portraits that crowded the walls. Brass plates announced yet more Medici bigwigs. Here was Lorenzo de' Medici's son, Pope Leo X, looking ready for another feast; next to him was his cousin, Pope Clement VII,

Giuliano de Medici's much more handsome son. And then came someone who needed no introduction. Those brooding features, that nose, that jutting chin and lofty forehead: who else could it be but Il Magnifico himself. Here he was, in miniature, at the centre of a dusty plaque, surrounded by six other miniatures. Tom recognised the oval pattern instantly: it was the Medici crest.

He stopped to take a closer look. As he blew off the dust, individual portraits, executed in the finest detail, came to light, each bearing the name of its subject. At the top of the plaque, he found the pallid cheeks and questioning eyes of Marsilio Ficino. Below right, was a young, curly-haired Alessandro Botticelli followed by Luigi Pulci, Giovanni Pico della Mirandola, Angelo Poliziano and, finally, Scala's forefather Bartolomeo, chancellor of Florence. These were the very same men whose signatures he had seen in that phantom visitors' book at Careggi.

At the bottom of the plaque, below the miniatures, gold lettering traced another name: 'Accademia Platonica'. Tom's heart raced as the pieces of the jigsaw suddenly clicked into place. These seven men had banded together to protect the secret of the Gifts of the Magi from Savonarola and the Vatican. Theirs were the 'seven diamonds' whispered in the wind at Careggi. They were the original members of the Platonic Academy whose diamond rings had passed to their successors down the ages, right up to the present day, to the current Count Scala and to... He looked up from the plaque: the corridor was empty. He ran to the far end where a two-faced bust of Janus pointed to opposite exits. He chose the one to his left.

A blast of icy air greeted him as he emerged into a parkland of fountains and grottoes which a notice identified as the Boboli Gardens. Of Scala and Miranda there was no sign. He turned to go back inside the corridor, only to find that the spring-door he had just exited had no external handle: he was locked out. Heavy droplets began to fall from the sullen clouds overhead; he made a dash for the nearest grotto. Cold and wet, with only gargoyles for company, he stared out at the sheets of vertical rain and the neat paths suddenly reduced to muddy torrents. What an apt reflection, he mused, of his own grotesque situation. From the solidity of his City office to the absurdity of this Renaissance funfair: how had his world collapsed so swiftly, so completely? The more he thought about it, the more farcical the whole thing seemed. An involuntary giggle triggered another and another until, in the solitude of the empty cave, he was convulsed in hysterical laughter.

'So you're a follower of Democritan amusement, not Heraclitan despondency, as Ficino might have said,' a cut-glass voice remarked.

'Aunt Stella!'

'Don't look so shocked,' she smirked. 'Surely you knew I'd find you sooner or later.'

'But how? When…?'

'Ruggieri's mirror. Once it captures a person's image or some treasured possession of theirs it will seek them out eventually. But don't worry, what you see is just a projection. I shan't spoil your fun. I merely thought you'd like to know that I'll be watching, even if I can't join in.'

'Well,' he retorted, '*you* might like to know that I know who you really are, Queen Ourania.'

'Good,' she shrugged. 'Now neither of us will need to pretend when next we meet in person.'

He folded his arms. 'Once was more than enough, thank you very much.'

She laughed. 'I promise you, Tom, you'll be knocking at my door before the daffodils lose their bloom.' And, with that, she vanished.

37

'YOU'RE LATE.' FATHER Vincenzo hissed as Frankie Maddingley joined him in the tiny chapel of Santa Felicita, just south of the Ponte Vecchio.

'Sorry, Father.'

'Sorry? Pah!' the adjutor harrumphed as he settled his considerable posterior on the front pew. 'You've never been sorry in your entire miserable existence, boy. I sent you to Florence to keep tabs on Dottore Gatti. Why have I heard nothing from him or you since before Christmas? Lazy, incompetent dolt that you are. Must I do everything myself?'

Frankie stood in the aisle, his head hung low in sullen penitence, white-knuckled fists clenched behind his back. 'Sorry,' he whined again, 'the Doc didn't come back to his lodgings till last night. I lost him at San Marco. I guess he must've gone straight from there to his sister's for Christmas.'

'San Marco!' Vincenzo screeched. 'What a fiasco that was. Those bungling friars trying to frighten Scala with fairground toys.'

'Yes, Father. We'll do better next time, Father.'

'We? Don't get ideas above your station, boy. Just look at yourself: dressed like a yob in the House of God. Remove that hood at once.' The young man grudgingly unzipped his parka and pulled back the hood, revealing his prematurely bald pate. 'I despair of you, Frankie, I really do,' Vincenzo exhaled. 'Is this how you repay me for rescuing you from the gutters of Rome, where your wretched mother spent her days begging at the walls of the Vatican and her nights being beaten up by your drunk of a father?' Frankie shuddered as he remembered the beatings he had both witnessed and suffered at his father's hands. 'I saved you,' Vincenzo ranted on, 'from the drug pushers, the street gangs, the paedophiles. I gave you a job and a roof over your head; I provided you with an education. All you have, all you are, you owe to me. And don't you ever forget it.'

Frankie bit his lip. He had heard this sermon a thousand times before and long ago learned to let it wash over him. But inwardly he seethed at the bloated cleric's hypocrisy. His mother had been a good-looking woman, and taking her little boy under his wing had provided Vincenzo with the perfect cover for regular enjoyment of her favours over many years. She had finally confided her shame to her son the day before she committed suicide. Thereafter he had become Vincenzo's personal factotum, helping with all those little things that a middle-ranking Vatican cleric found too awkward to organise in person, like procuring prostitutes in the Trastevere.

Then, just over a year ago, things had changed. Vincenzo had set him an altogether different task: to be Dottore Gatti's full-time assistant. Frankie had welcomed this partial release from Vincenzo's clutches and learned much from the reserved, yet kind-hearted, scholar who had taken him under his wing and assumed the role of personal tutor. He enjoyed helping the 'Doc' search the Secret Archives for ancient manuscripts, though he had no idea what the goal of Gatti's research was, at least not initially. But, whatever it was, Vincenzo wanted to be the first to know when Gatti found it. He trusted no-one, least of all an unworldly academic so unlike himself. So he set Frankie to be his spy, reporting back to him every night on all the books that Gatti had consulted, as well as providing surreptitious photocopies of the journal in which Gatti recorded his findings. Eventually, Frankie had gleaned from these nocturnal meetings (during which he would ply his self-indulgent boss with generous schooners of Vatican port) that Gatti had recently been made a member of some crackpot medieval Brotherhood. It supposedly kept a dark secret which would one day be used to undermine the Catholic Church and plunge Europe back into paganism and black magic. However, one of the Brotherhood's founding members had turned traitor and informed the Vatican of their diabolical plot. Gatti was the latest in a line of the traitor's successors. Down the ages, they had, with the aid of Rome, kept the Brotherhood under surveillance, whilst doing their utmost to uncover the true nature of a secret known only to one man: the Brotherhood's maestro.

At first, Frankie had put this story on a par with all the other fantastical tales of demonic possession and miraculous cures promulgated by the Church. For him, religion was merely a means to an end. Belief in God was no different to believing in flying saucers or truth or justice or love, or any of the other fairy stories that parents told their dim-witted offspring and governments fed their gullible citizenry.

However, last September, he had received an urgent summons from the Sisters of Mercy hospice: the father who had walked out on him and his mother twenty years earlier was dying. He hardly recognised the old man in the cancer ward and felt only elation when, with his last breath, he whispered 'safe deposit'. Frankie wasted no time in ripping the key and gold chain from his dead father's neck. He rushed straight to the Vatican Bank, where, so his father had promised, a wondrous inheritance awaited him.

How great his excitement had been as he inserted the little key into the steel box: how bitter his disappointment when all that greeted him was an old ring and a scribbled note. The note had rambled on about ancient history and the settling of old scores, about a lost treasure and a family cheated of fame and fortune. Another fairy tale, he had thought; as preposterous as the one of which it was oddly reminiscent, the one which the Doc had pieced together from crumbling Persian scrolls and tattered Chinese silks. Frankie had deemed it so utterly ridiculous that he had not bothered reporting it back to Vincenzo. Luckily, he had followed the note's single injunction: to call an uncle in America he had never heard of and speak a name he had never spoken. As a result, he had become overnight the heir to a vast estate, subject to just one condition. But even that was topped a few weeks later when Vincenzo had ordered him to follow Gatti to Florence. There, on the night of the autumnal equinox, he had observed a display of unearthly power and realised that fairy tales really could come true. More than that, he had understood for the first time in his young life the full enormity of the injustice which the world had inflicted upon him and his family.

'Frankie, wake up, boy!' Vincenzo boomed.

'Sorry, what did you say, Father?'

'Don't you ever stop daydreaming, you imbecile? I asked you where Gatti is now?'

'He went back to his lodgings, Father. I got a mate of mine to keep an eye on him while I came over to see you.'

'Good. From now on you must keep me fully apprised of his movements. I've no doubt that Scala and his gang will get together again soon. But next time it will be the Swords of the Lord on his tail, not those doddery old friars at San Marco.'

Frankie looked bemused. 'The Swords of the Lord, Father?' he queried.

'I speak of things far beyond your comprehension, boy. Suffice to say that I have requested the assistance of an elite force to hunt down the Diabolists and retrieve a great treasure that was stolen from the Holy See.' Vincenzo brushed the dandruff from his black cloak and fingered the gold cross on his chest. 'How grateful the Holy Father will be,' he mused. 'You're almost certainly looking at the next Vatican librarian, Frankie, my boy.'

His young acolyte's face displayed a suitably wide-eyed wonder. 'Wow!' he gasped. 'That's fantastic, Father. I wish I could meet the Swords of the Lord. They sound really cool.'

Vincenzo's lip curled upwards, as if he had chewed on a lemon. 'Well,' he said, 'it appears that your wish is to be granted. The Swords want you to attend a briefing at the Cappella dei Pazzi. That's in the Church of...'

'Santa Croce. Yeah, I know the place,' Frankie swaggered, adding that the Doc had given him several history lessons on the churches of Florence and Tuscany.

'Really? Well, just make sure you're there this evening at five-thirty sharp. Now get back to your duties.'

Frankie pulled up his hood. 'Should I tell the Swords about Scala's new girlfriend, Father?' he asked casually.

The adjutor sat bolt upright. 'Girlfriend?' What girlfriend?'

'Oh, didn't I mention it, Father? I seen that pushy American lawyer come out of Scala's place this morning. You know, the one you told me came to see you, said she was my cousin, the lying bitch. I recognised her from the CCTV photo you sent me.' For a moment Frankie thought his boss was having an apoplectic fit as his cheeks turned purple and his mouth stretched into a horrified rictus. 'I knew it!' Vincenzo fumed. 'I knew she was trouble. I could see it in her eyes.'

'I bet it wasn't just her eyes you were looking at, you old lech,' Frankie thought to himself before delivering his bombshell: 'Yeah, and she was wearing one of them diamond rings, just like the one the Doc's got.'

Vincenzo's eyeballs looked ready to pop out. This was a totally unexpected, and most unwelcome, turn of events. Who was this interfering female who not only pretended to be Frankie's cousin but had seemingly infiltrated Scala's sacred Brotherhood? It put her visit to the Vatican in a wholly different light. Was she Scala's spy? Or was she working for other, unknown, interests?

Frankie shuffled closer. 'Maybe, Father,' he whispered, 'the Swords of the Lord could kill two birds with one stone.' Vincenzo gave him a bemused stare. 'I mean,' Frankie elaborated, 'what if the Swords grabbed the girl and the treasure in one go?'

The adjutor stroked his double chin: 'Go on.'

'Well loads of girls go missing don't they, 'specially foreigners? They're always being kidnapped, beaten up and tortured without anyone ever finding out what happened to them. And, even if they did, her boyfriend Scala would be the obvious suspect, wouldn't he?'

For the first time since entering the chapel, Vincenzo smiled. 'I was right about you, Frankie,' he said, 'you're quite incorrigible.'

38

THE OLD MEN crowded round the trattoria's battered television: Fiorentina were playing Roma. Cries of 'bravissimo!' and 'merda!' exploded in time to the commentators' crescendos. But Tom was oblivious to the excitement behind him; his attention was focussed on the quiet street outside. It was late and raining heavily. The reflection from the trattoria's interior made it hard to see through the plate-glass window, but in the pool of light shed by a nearby street lamp he had spotted five men arriving at Palazzo Scala in the last half-hour. The count's 'little club' was assembling. He was just debating how to get a closer look when a stretched black Maserati pulled up. Several hooded figures exited the palazzo. Two got into the front of the Maserati; the rest got into the back. Then the street lamp went out and everything descended into shadow. 'God, is there nothing Scala doesn't control?' Tom thought. A few seconds later, the limousine's headlights came on and it slipped off down the road.

Tom zipped his black leathers, snatched up his crash helmet and, dropping two euros on the table for his coffee, sprinted out to his hired Ducati. The bike roared into life as he revved the throttle. Flying down the road in a hail of spray, he spotted the limousine's tail lights ahead and slowed to a discreet distance behind it. Soon they were crossing the Arno and passing through the Porta Romana. Scala was heading south, out of town. When they hit the autostrada the count's chauffeur floored his accelerator, treating flashing speed cameras with characteristic Sicilian contempt. Tom did likewise but, strangely, for him the speed cameras slept.

As the rain pelted against his visor, he wondered if Miranda was in the car, cooped up with Scala and five other guys in fancy dress. If so, did she realise the danger she was in? He was convinced now that her assailant in the Uffizi was connected to the Vatican: it could not have been a coincidence that he was right behind that Catholic priest who had so spooked her when she had spotted him on the Ponte Vecchio. But why would the Vatican want to harm Miranda? Could it possibly go back to Savonarola and his imprecations against Il Magnifico? The fanatic's ghost had boasted that at least two of Lorenzo de' Medici's most trusted friends, Botticelli and Mirandola, would transfer their allegiance after Lorenzo's death. The painting of the 'Mystic Nativity' in the Uffizi was pretty conclusive evidence of Botticelli's change of heart. Maybe he had betrayed the secrets of the Platonic Academy to Savonarola's 'Swords of the Lord'. Maybe the diamond ring on Miranda's finger was all the spur they needed to attempt a stab in the back.

After forty minutes or so, the Maserati suddenly veered off the autostrada and down a tightly curving slip road. A signpost pointed to Siena. The rain started to ease off. Soon the halogen-lit asphalt of the motorway gave way to dim, cobbled lanes, looming tenements and high-walled courtyards. The count's car slowed to a crawl as it negotiated the entrance to a vast fan-shaped piazza in the centre of the old city. Tom braked hard so as not to get too close. He thought he glimpsed headlights in his rear-view mirror, but they disappeared as he rounded a corner. The grand piazza was deserted. Empty tables and chairs slumbered outside shuttered cafés. A stray dog padded over the damp cobblestones, casting a giant shadow across the floodlit facade of the City Hall. At the top of a tall column a bronze she-wolf suckled Romulus and Remus. 'Could it be true?' Tom mused as he saw the limousine turning down a side street. It was little more than an alleyway on a downward slope, with a blind turn at the end. He cut the Ducati's engine and killed its lights, letting it roll along, soundless and unheralded. Old-fashioned gas lamps guided the way around several sharp corners and bulging buttresses that propped up the ancient city walls. The Maserati was nowhere to be seen. For one anxious moment he feared the count had given him the slip. Then, as he rounded yet another right-angled bend, red brake lights briefly lit up a stone archway before emerging into another piazza beyond.

This piazza was much smaller than the first but was equally bereft of life. It was dominated by a marble monolith of a cathedral, which occupied the whole of one side of the square. More floodlights picked out the soaring Gothic tracery of its West Front. In stark contrast, the other elevations were covered in horizontal stripes of plain black and white marble, rising like alternating layers of icing sugar and liquorice. They reminded Tom of the witch's candy-coated cottage in Hansel and Gretel: he sensed a dark energy in that pied carapace.

The Maserati came to a halt beside the cathedral steps. A starry Sienese night greeted the seven Brothers of the Magi as they ascended the perron in their white hoods and habits, like phantoms doomed to keep some eternal midnight Mass. 'If only those tourists in the Uffizi could see this,' Tom grimaced in the shadows. Little did he know what far stranger sights the night had in store.

The Brothers paused at the top of the steps and looked back at the piazza below. All was quiet. The tallest among them flourished a black cane and led the way briskly along the south wall to a small door at the bottom of a lofty campanile.

Tom dismounted and, keeping to the piazza's unlit perimeter, ran to the far side of the campanile. In the darkness and in his black biker's leathers, he was all but invisible. Only when he made a dash for the small door did the flame-coloured wings blazoned on his black helmet momentarily catch the light. Inside the Maserati, the count's chauffeur could not decide whether he had imagined the flash he or not. But his quandary was quickly resolved: the red dot focussed on the back of his head from the unlit van which had pulled up behind him saw to that.

On entering the cathedral, Tom removed his helmet, and his senses went into overdrive. In the pitch-black silence, he saw and heard no-one, yet he felt a presence all around him. As his eyes adjusted to the dark, he spied a faint glow at the end of a passageway. His rubber-soled boots muted his footfalls as he crept towards the flickering light. Soon he was picking up the drone of lowered voices which drifted in and out of huge quatrefoil columns lining the nave. But it was impossible to pinpoint exactly where the sound was coming from; sometimes it seemed to come from several directions at once.

The silhouette of a massive pillar loomed just ahead. Tom was edging his way around it when, suddenly, there they were, just feet away, the white-robed members of the count's 'little club', formed into a circle at the crossing of the nave.

'Fratres,' the holder of a seven-branched candelabra summoned imperiously, 'Compagnia del Diamante, Brotherhood of the Magi, heirs of the Platonic Academy, welcome to Siena and to the Cathedral of the Assumption of the Blessed Virgin Mary.' In those few phrases Scala corroborated so much of what, to date, Tom could only guess at. He listened transfixed as the count went on to explain why he had brought his followers to Siena, so far from the home of the Medici and, for much of its history, an implacable enemy of Florence. It was, apparently, all due to Savonarola and his 'Bonfire of the Vanities'. 'That barbaric cremation of priceless manuscripts and works of art,' he said, 'was an attempt by the fanatical friar and his papal overlords to destroy the haystack in which they had failed to find the needle. But they were too late.' Scala let his words echo down the nave as if addressing a congregation of ghosts as well as his living brethren. 'For as I realised only this morning, Marsilio Ficino had already vouchsafed a secret copy of Hermes Trismegistus' teachings to Niccolo Borghesi, chancellor of Siena and trusted friend of my forefather Bartolomeo. That is why we are gathered here tonight in a place sacred to the Virgin or, as the Etruscans called her, Mernva, Goddess of Holy Wisdom.'

Ficino, Hermes, Bartolomeo: each name resonated with Tom and further confirmed his suspicions. He looked at the shorter, more slender, figure at Scala's side; it had to be Miranda. But what he could not see was the unease in her eyes, her growing realisation that the count's so-called 'little club' was engaged in something every bit as sinister as she had feared after he had rushed her away from the Uffizi, refusing ever since to let her out of his sight. Tomorrow morning, she promised herself, she would leave, even if it meant giving up on finding Cousin Frankie.

Scala lifted the candelabra high above his head. A thousand specks of light sparkled in the cathedral's vaulted dome. 'Above us, the Gate of Heaven,' he declared. Then, lowering the candelabra down to the marble pavement, 'And, below us, the Sibyls, the mysterious prophetesses who foretold the Coming of the Saviour.'

'And also the Last Judgement!' barked an unexpected voice.

Scala thrust the candelabra into the surrounding darkness but saw no-one. Then a single spotlight pierced the gloom. A black-hooded friar loomed over the Company of the Magi from an elevated stone pulpit. 'What's this?' he taunted as the count stared up in stunned silence. 'Does the grand Maestro of the Compagnia del Diamante have nothing to say?'

Although the friar's face was hidden deep within his cowl, Miranda was sure she had heard that pompous, squawky voice before – in the Vatican Library.

'Who are you?' Scala demanded. 'What are you doing here?'

'What am *I* doing here? It is you and your pagan brethren who must account for trespassing on Church property. Seize them!' No sooner had he spoken than arc lamps filled the crossing with a blinding light and Scala and his Brothers felt the points of seven sword blades jabbing at their backs.

'So, this is the bold Brotherhood of the Magi, is it?' cackled the friar with a derisory wave. 'See how the Medici spaniels cower before the Hounds of God, Savonarola's Swords of the Lord. Now you shall dance to my tune.' He plodded down the pulpit's spiral stairs and pranced along the line of his prisoners. With his black and white robes and raucous voice, he reminded Tom (who remained out of sight behind a pillar) of a plump, strutting magpie. 'Hold out your right hands!' he screeched. No-one moved. He waddled up to Scala and ripped off his hood. 'Hold out your hand!'

The count gave him a contemptuous glare and remained stock-still. Enraged, the friar turned to Miranda and tore off her hood too. 'What have we here?' he squawked. 'Have your Brothers all become Sisters, Count?' Loud sniggers went up from the Swords of the Lord. 'Do as I say or I'll put a scar right across your whore's pretty little face!'

'Touch a hair of her head and you'll wish you'd never been born,' Scala snarled as he stretched out his right hand and motioned his Brothers to do likewise. 'You dress like men of God,' he said, 'but you and your bully boys forget on what ground you tread.'

'On the contrary, my dear Count, it's you who forgot God's all-seeing eye. The sexton your man bribed for a key earlier today informed on you. This ground belongs to the Vatican, as do those diamond rings.' With that, the magpie grabbed Scala's hand and removed his ring, placing it carefully in a small metal box. Then he proceeded to remove the rest of the Brothers' rings, flitting from one to the other with a merry chirp. Six rings had been safely consigned to his little box, and he was just hopping round to Miranda – saving the best till last – when the knell of a solitary bell was heard. He checked his watch: it was midnight. With a shrug of his shoulders, he took hold of Miranda's hand. As she watched the chewed, nicotine-stained fingernails clawing at her ring, she knew beyond any doubt that this was Father Vincenzo, the sanctimonious cleric who had lied to her about her cousin and whom she had spotted on the Ponte Vecchio that very morning. Revolted by the touch of his sweaty paws, she instinctively lashed out with her free hand and sent his precious tin box flying. He clutched wildly at the air but it was too late. The box somersaulted out of reach and clattered to the ground, scattering its contents across the cold marble floor.

Vincenzo was apoplectic with rage. Screaming expletives, he slapped Miranda so hard that she was sent reeling to her knees, whereupon he punched her senseless to the ground. Scala immediately rammed the base of his candelabra into the face of the Sword of the Lord behind him and rushed to her aid. But, as he bent down to help her, another Savonarolan slammed the hilt of his weapon into the back of his head. Dazed, Scala slumped to the floor.

Fury surged through Tom's veins too. But to attack now would be futile; there were too many of them. However hard it was not to intervene, he had to bide his time if he was to stand any chance not only of rescuing Miranda but also of recovering the Gifts of the Magi.

Vincenzo meanwhile was scrambling around on all fours, frantically retrieving the scattered rings. As he popped the last one back into his little box, the midnight bell tolled for the final time. Something in the sudden stillness made both captors and captives catch their breath; but nothing happened. Vincenzo grunted and ordered one of his men to help him back on his feet. It was then that Tom witnessed the first of several weird happenings that night. The stillness became palpable, as if an invisible blanket had descended, deadening all sound and rooting to the spot friar and frater alike. At the same time, some unseen hand tore their weapons from the Swords of the Lord and flung them to the nether reaches of the nave. Then the marble slabs on which the luckless Savonarolans were standing melted into whirlpools of viscous liquid, sucking them down like quicksand, their mouths opening and closing in inaudible terror. When the last of them had been swallowed up, the paralysing stillness began to dissipate but, as it did so, the arc lamps exploded one by one and plunged the cathedral into total darkness.

Suddenly a blinding light burst from the high altar. It shone the whole length of the nave, revealing high, black-banded colonnades on either side and, above them, the mitred effigies of a hundred long-dead popes. Each face wore a different expression: stern, serene, frowning, forgiving, joyful, judgemental: a stone diapason of papal passions. But wait: were Tom's eyes playing tricks or did that chiselled pontiff just wink at him? And the one next to him, was that a grin cracking his frozen cheeks? No, he was not seeing things, all the heads were creaking into life: nodding, beckoning, swivelling. Then, turning their gaze as one towards the white-robed Brothers huddled in the crossing, they parted their lips and, in a deep Gregorian cadence, began to chant:

'Heed ye the threshold's warning:
Enter chastely the Temple of the Most Chaste.
Heed ye the Seven Stones of the Crossing,
Heed the Prophet Elijah,
Slayer of the Priests of Baal,

Slayer of the Seers of Ashtaroth,
The evil creatures of Jezebel.
For he spake the Word of God unto Ahab, king of Israel,
saying:
"In the place where dogs licked the blood of Naboth,
There shall dogs lick thy blood also, even thine."
As ye live by the sword, so by the sword shall ye perish.'

As the last notes faded away, the pontiffs fell once more beneath Medusa's spell and resumed their petrified poses. A bone-chilling wind howled down the nave like a pack of ravenous wolves, extinguishing the light from the altar before exhausting itself in the vault of the dome. Then, as the Brothers of the Magi shuddered in the icy darkness, they saw a strange, luminescence seep from the iron gratings which covered the cathedral's crypt. It slid across the marble pavement like an incoming tide, creeping over their feet and filling their nostrils with the stench of death. Soon they succumbed to the fumes and joined their maestro in semi-consciousness on the floor.

Tom, meanwhile, had taken refuge on top of a stone font, marooned in a sea of sulphurous smog. It was lapping at the vessel's rim when the tide suddenly reversed and the smog was sucked back to form a towering wave. He pulled down the visor of his crash helmet and braced himself against the imminent tsunami. But the crash never came. Instead, as the wave reached its zenith, it morphed into ten translucent figures who floated down the nave in two shimmering lines, like a miniature aurora borealis.

'We are the Sibyls,' began one, as they drew themselves up on opposite sides of the central aisle, 'the Sisters Ten, the number allotted to the Age of Men. Albunea is my abode. I the arrival of Christ foretold, when Taurus ruled and time grew old.'

The Sibyl opposite her next took up the refrain, speaking in the same ethereal whisper: 'I, the Prophetess of Persia, did the miracle of the loaves and fish foresee. O World, where are your miracles now? Where your gifts of prophecy?'

Then the other Sibyls followed, alternating down the nave:

'Your world looks but does not see, listens but does not hear. Your wounds are dressed with salt, and thorns crown your fear. So says the Samian Sorceress.'

'From Lydian Erythraea come I, whence too the old Etruscan race. All hail the Virgin full of grace.'

'Out of Heaven the trumpets sound; hell yawns beneath the ground. Thus warns the Phrygian witch.'

'On the wild Cimmerian steppe, I foretold His life and death.'

'Upon the Hellespont I sing my songs, where Europe pines and Asia longs. Behold the veil is rent in two, and day in night is lost to view.'

'Once at Delphi men questioned me: is God one, or two or three?'

'Innocence or iniquity: in despair shall be your hope. This is Libya's prophecy.'

The oldest of the Sibyls was the last to speak: 'Dreams of ivory, dreams of horn, do we die before we're born? The bard of Mantua sang of me, beside the deep Tyrrhenian Sea. Round and round the ages run, the end of time is thus begun.'

So saying, she and her sisters swooped low over Tom's head and hovered briefly above the crossing where Scala and his Brothers now struggled to their feet. An eerie laughter filled their ears as they watched the ten phantoms fly back to the far end of the nave. Here they joined hands around a mosaic depicting Romulus and Remus being suckled by the she-wolf. They began to dance and, as they danced, to sing:

'Romulus did poor Remus slay,
Shall brothers love, or love betray?
The First of Spring shall light the way.
Hear the music of the spheres,
Hear it echo down the years,
Above all joy, beyond all tears.
Keepers of the crystals seven,
By greed and lust the thief is driv'n,
Your treasure's lost, your purpose riv'n.
Seek ye, ere midnight's hour be crossed,
Our Father on these walls embossed,
And Hermes shall restore what's lost.
Then to Orpheus must you flee,
In the court of the Medici,
And so release Eurydice.
But nothing is for nothing won,
The wheel of time doth faster run:
Before they come, already gone,
Lost days of life beneath the sun.
The Hunter and his Dog draw nigh,
A New Year dawns, the Magi cry;
The stars revolve across the sky,
And mark the day to do or die.'

As their song melted away, the Sibyls too dissolved into wisps of smoke, leaving only their outlines traced on the cathedral floor.

39

'NOW WHAT?' GRUMBLED Hawkwood as the cathedral was plunged into darkness yet again.

'Quiet!' Scala hissed, still hurting from the blow to his head. Flicking his cigarette lighter open, he circled its flame through the dark. There was no sign of the ghostly witches, no sound of chanting gargoyles, no foul-smelling fog. He ordered the Brothers to remove their hoods: he needed to make sure who was there. An arc of bewildered faces met his gaze as he handed out candles which he relit from the candelabra on the floor. Hawkwood, Rossi, Jankovic, Sarachin and Gatti: all were present. But where was the one he most wished to see? Where was Miranda? Calling out her name, he ran to the spot where the fat friar had struck her down, but there was no sign of her, nor of her assailant and his box of stolen rings. Scala bowed his head: 'Not again,' he groaned, recalling the day he had stood at his wife's grave, scattering a handful of earth onto her coffin. How could he have lost both his love and his destiny in one fell swoop? Had he been too confident? Too trusting in the promise of history? Suddenly he felt a hand on his shoulder. 'Come on, man! We don't have much time,' Jankovic thundered.

Scala brushed him aside. 'Much time for what?'

'To find the bloody picture, of course. Didn't you hear those witches say we had to find their father on one of the walls before the midnight hour is over?'

Scala kicked himself. In his anguish, he had completely forgotten about the Sibyls and their prophecies. He looked at his watch: time was definitely speeding up. There were only seven minutes left before one o'clock.

'It's hopeless,' cried Gatti, wandering aimlessly around the crossing. 'The cathedral's packed with paintings and sculptures. Where do we begin? And who was the Sibyls' father anyway?'

'The Sibyls came from many different places, as we heard,' Rossi answered. 'They weren't sisters by blood. How could they share the same father?'

'Might it be,' suggested Sarachin, 'that the Sibyls' reference to "our father" was not meant in a biological sense?'

'Huh, trust a shrink to come up with that one!' Hawkwood scoffed. 'What other ruddy sense could "father" possibly have?'

'What about "Our Father who art in Heaven",' Sarachin replied with Californian calm. 'We are in a church, after all.'

'By Christ, I think he's got something!' Jankovic cried, as he and the rest of the Company of the Magi dashed off down the aisles, brandishing their candles at the walls, trying to find some representation of the Almighty. Yet, among all the paintings of saints, all the icons of the Madonna, all the depictions of Christ on the Cross, they could find not a single image of God Himself.

Scala looked on glumly: it was impossible to scour every wall of the immense edifice in time. With a sigh, he glanced across the nave and, noticing an expanse of white marble, walked towards it. As he got closer, he realised that it was the entrance to the Piccolomini Library, famed for its lavishly illuminated codices, bibles and prayer-books. Then he had a brain-wave. 'Pater Noster!' he exclaimed, his words echoing through the basilica. 'The Paternoster!' he cried again as the Brothers rushed to his side. 'It's "Our Father" in Latin. That's what the Sibyls meant.'

'What are you talking about?' Jankovic queried. 'The Paternoster's a prayer, not a picture of God.'

'There's a tablet,' Scala answered, 'taken from a tomb in Pompeii. It's engraved with a cryptic formula devised by early Christians to fool their Roman persecutors. When decoded, it reveals an invocation to "Pater Noster". It's on display here, in this cathedral.'

'Where?'

Scala shook his head. The slim guidebook in his study hadn't been specific. They would have to split up and look for it.

As he watched the Brothers' candles scurrying to and fro like crazed fireflies, Tom, with an aural acuity he had never experienced before, heard a distant click. The hammer of the cathedral's mechanical clock was cocked: any second now it would strike. Though desperate to rescue Miranda from the clutches of the magpie friar, he knew that, if Scala failed to find whatever secret this ancient building held, then his own mission too would fail. Instinctively, he closed his eyes and cleared his mind. At once, some inner compass directed him towards the south-west corner of the basilica. Racing through the darkness, a strange, noetic magnetism drew him to a spot near the great west door. He stopped, sensing that he was approaching a barrier. Inches from his nose, a group of letters appeared, glowing like fiery embers. They read as follows:

SATOR
AREPO
TENET
OPERA
ROTAS

It looked like Latin, but he could make little sense of it. A sudden chill ran down his spine: he felt an icy breath on the back of his neck. It was the Cumaean Sibyl. Her form was dim and oscillated in and out of focus, accentuating her haggard features and soulless eyes. 'Verily, thou art a true scion of Mercury,' she rasped in a voice that might have seeped from some fissure in the earth. 'So, my merry trickster, you have found the talisman. What does it say?'

Tom gulped: 'It's supposed to say "Paternoster" but I don't see how...'

'Look again!'

Tom did as he was bidden and watched in amazement as the fiery letters magically rearranged themselves:

```
            P
            A
            T
            E
          A R O
  P A T E R N O S T E R
          O O A
            S
            T
            E
            R
```

'Behold the Pater Noster!' cackled the Sibyl. 'Our Father above and below, across the Alpha and Omega of time and space. Now, Droplet of Quicksilver, touch the letter that binds all the rest, the key that turns the lock. Else, at the last toll of the bell, you and your fellow trespassers shall share Pompeii's fate and burn in hell.'

As the wraith finished speaking, Tom's keen ears heard the clock hammer lift to strike the hour. There was no time to think: he jabbed his finger into the centre of the tablet and onto the letter 'N'.

'Aiyee!' the Sibyl shrieked. 'Verily doth Minerva watch over her wolf.' And with that she was gone.

The cathedral bell chimed one o'clock, and then another, very different, sound assaulted his ears. Several yards away, at the bottom of the nave, a massive block of marble rose up out of the floor. It scraped and grated itself free of its moorings, floating on a cushion of light.

Scala and his Brothers came running to the scene. 'It's the Hermes Trismegistus panel,' Rossi panted breathlessly, 'the one in that guidebook you showed us earlier this evening, Maestro.' But before Scala could respond, the giant slab dropped back again into its vacant plot. Only the cushion of light remained, expanding now into a balloon which enveloped them all in a glowing luminosity. Then an even more wondrous sight met their gaze. A book lay on top of the marble panel. But it was no ordinary book. It was the size of a large bible and encased in finely tooled silver. The cover was embossed with a gold Medici shield, bearing the initials 'L.M.'. Scala knelt down beside it and read out the gilt lettering on its spine: '"Hermis Trismegisti Opera Omnia" – The Complete Works of Hermes Trismegistus.' He fingered the three chased metal clasps which nestled into six hollow tubes along the book's front edge. A pointed silver bolt passed through the tubes and slotted into a barrel lock, thus holding the clasps in place.

From beneath the collar of his robe Scala unclipped a fine chain and removed the golden key they had discovered at San Marco. His hand quivering with excitement, he inserted the key into the barrel lock: it fitted perfectly. But, as he was about to turn it, a gruff voice intervened. 'Thank you, Count. I'll take over from here.' He looked up. Professor Jankovic was standing over him, pointing a Stechkin semi-automatic pistol at his head.

'Traitor!' Scala yelled.

Jankovic broke into a broad grin. 'The omniscient Count Scala and his precious Brotherhood. You don't look so clever now.' He motioned the other Brothers to get down on their knees next to Scala. 'Did you really think we Serbs would kowtow to Medici capitalists?'

'Hypocrite! You decry the Medici but at least they put their wealth to good use. You're nothing but a common thief, motivated by greed and envy.'

The bristly professor growled like an angry walrus. 'Envy? What do you know about envy? You were born with a silver ladle in your mouth. You've never had to eke out an existence on the peanuts they pay astronomers in Belgrade. You've never slept in freezing mountains, shot at by Bosnian terrorists.' He rubbed a scar over his left eyebrow. 'But now it's my turn to live the high life. The Trismegistus and those diamond rings of yours will fetch truly astronomical prices.' With that, he thumbed a number on his mobile phone; a brief exchange in Serbo-Croat ensued. Tom, still unseen in the shadows, understood the gist of it, thanks to his fluent Russian. But one name was mentioned which needed no translation: 'Bargello', Florence's answer to the Tower of London.

The phone call ended. Jankovic ranged his gun along the line of kneeling Brothers. 'And now, gentlemen,' he said, 'I'm afraid it's time to say goodbye.'

'Wait!' Gatti cried out. 'Aren't you forgetting something, Professore?'

'What?'

'The diamonds. The friar took the diamonds.'

'Don't worry, Dottore,' Jankovic chuckled, 'my associates will take care of him.'

'Your associates?'

'They tailed us here, just as they have now tailed the friar to his lair. Very soon he will be joining the rest of you in hell.' Jankovic took aim at Scala. 'Arrivederci, Maestro!' he laughed.

Scala's heart missed a beat, but the expected shot never came. The Stechkin had jammed. The Serb pulled frantically at the trigger, cursing its Russian workmanship, but to no avail.

It was Scala's turn to laugh. 'Who's the clever one now, Professore? Didn't you see what happened to the swordsmen? You have defiled the Virgin's temple. There can be only one punishment.'

Jankovic stared at him wide-eyed. 'W-What do you mean?' he gulped.

The answer came swiftly. Scala turned the golden key in the Trismegistus' lock. A powerful spring catapulted the silver bolt into the air. It struck the professor straight in the eye, lodging deep in his cerebral cortex. Death was instantaneous.

40

'AH, SO GOOD of you to join us, Signorina Maddingley.'

Miranda blinked. She was lying on her side on a hard, cold surface, made still colder by the bucket of icy water which had just been emptied over her head. Her hands were manacled behind her back and her right arm felt numb from the weight of her body. She had been stripped of the long, concealing robe of the Brotherhood of the Magi, but her blouse and skirt remained thankfully untouched. A few inches in front of her the toes of two shiny black boots stuck out beneath the hem of a white habit. Craning her neck upwards, she saw Father Vincenzo's face leering down over his mountainous belly.

'I trust you had a pleasant nap?' he chirped. 'My car boot can't have been very comfortable, but I expect the chloroform helped. In fact, the drive back from Siena seemed to go by very quickly, now I come to think of it, but then my brain was racing with anticipation.' He bent down and brushed her long, wet hair away from her eyes. His breath stank of onions and stale cigarettes and made her want to throw up. 'Get your filthy hands off me!' she shrieked.

259

'Such ingratitude! I can see we shall have to punish you, my child,' he chuckled and slapped her smartly across the face.

Stunned, Miranda lay motionless for several seconds. But then anger restored her senses. Rolling onto her back, she glared at the friar. 'You pathetic coward!' she spat. 'You'll never get away with this. Count Scala will hunt you down.' And to aid her hoped-for deliverer, she started screaming at the top of her voice, straining at her bonds in a vain effort to break free.

'Ha, ha! What a wonderfully ridiculous spectacle you're making of yourself, counsellor,' Vincenzo laughed. 'Please go ahead. Shout and scream all you like. No-one's going to hear you down here. You see, this is the Bargello.' He opened his arms in an expansive wave. 'It was Florence's medieval prison. Its walls are three metres thick, soaked in centuries of blood and gore. Countless prisoners were tortured, tried and executed here, in the world's most cultured city.' He paused to savour the thought of evil lurking in the heart of beauty: it was so very satisfying. 'And here,' he went on, 'we are in the gaol's deepest, darkest dungeon. A place you won't find on any tourist map. The Gestapo were the last people to make proper use of it. They enjoyed the smell of hot coals on burning insteps, you know –' he kicked Miranda's bound and shoeless feet, grinning as she flinched in pain '– but, speaking for myself, I think the apogee of the torturer's art was reached in the Renaissance. I don't mean the commonplace thumbscrews and disembowelments, you understand, but methods truly worthy of Florentine refinement and sophistication.'

Miranda shivered as she watched her jailer purse his lips and frown in mock indecision as to what form her torture should take. Then his eyes lit up. 'I know,' he smiled.

'Have you heard of the strappado, my child? No? Well, it's actually quite simple, and therein lies its charm. First, a rope is attached to the victim's wrists. Then he – or, rather, she in your case – is hauled up to the ceiling on a pulley.' He pointed at the high, conical roof, soaring into the shadows which the dungeon's rusting strip-lights barely penetrated. 'Next, she's held in suspense (if you'll forgive the pun) for a minute, or perhaps two, until the rope is released and she plummets to the ground.' A cockroach scuttled across the flagstones in front of Vincenzo. There was a squidgy, crackling sound as he raised his boot and squashed it. 'Don't worry, my child, we will stop the rope just before you hit the floor. We wouldn't want you to miss the shock as the rope jerks your arms backwards and you feel the excruciating pain of your shoulders being wrenched from their sockets.'

Miranda shuddered, her lips quivering. Tears welled in her eyes.

Vincenzo stooped and stroked her cheek, like a farmer's wife stroking the chicken whose neck she's about to wring. 'There, there,' he cooed. 'Naturally we comply with health and safety regulations. We have a surgeon on hand to put your shoulders back in place, ready for another go. And you're in good company, you know: Scala's meddlesome Medici meted out the same treatment to our dear saint, Savonarola.' He heaved a sigh and crossed himself as he spoke the martyr's name. 'But nowadays,' he continued, 'only a few "aficionados", such as myself, make use of this chamber. So, you see Miss Maddingley, we shan't be disturbed down here, least of all by your beloved Count.'

Miranda let out another ear-splitting scream. It was all she could do, though she realised it was almost certainly in vain. More tears pricked her eyes but she refused to cry. That at least was one sadistic pleasure that she could still deny her tormentor. Averting her gaze as far as she could from his loathsome presence, she did not see him step back and give the signal to turn off the strip-lighting and turn on a semicircle of spotlights. Blinded by the intense glare, she heard movement all around her. Her flesh crept as she imagined a swarm of perverted sadists surrounding her. Screwing up her eyelids she could just make out someone fixing a camera on top of a tripod. Suddenly a figure in a carnival mask jumped out from nowhere and jabbed a grotesque nose into her face. She screamed even louder than before.

Vincenzo squealed with delight. 'Ah, screams of joy!' he mocked. 'It's so exciting to become a movie star, isn't it? And Count Scala will receive a special preview of your film debut.' Waving the man in the plague mask aside, he bent down and grabbed her hair, forcing her to look at him. 'But Scala will only see the first scene,' he said, pulling a sad face, 'just enough to persuade him to hand over the Gifts of the Magi so that his poor, sweet Miranda won't have to endure any further agonies. What a pity the hero will arrive too late to save his beloved. But that's show business, eh?'

Vincenzo let go of her hair and stood upright. Two more garishly masked men appeared and dragged her to her feet. A clip was attached to the steel cuffs that held her hands. She felt her arms rising behind her. Her shoulder muscles twisted awkwardly, the ligaments strained tight, the tendons stretched taut. And, when they would rotate no further, her whole body was lifted up, like a carcass at a slaughter house, until she was standing on tiptoe, desperately trying to relieve the searing pain that was coursing down her arms.

Vincenzo swaggered into the limelight, his head and face now hidden from the cameras by a wild ginger wig and matching beard. Stopping right in front of her, he pressed his flabby paunch against her midriff, sliding his hands around her waist, like a snake coiling round its prey. Then he locked his slobbering lips onto hers and inserted his tongue into her mouth. As she choked in revulsion and he sought to gorge his lust, neither was aware that, a few minutes earlier, a motorbike had screeched to a halt at the back of the Bargello.

***

Tom checked the time: the digital clock on the Ducati's speedometer flashed 4.10am. He frowned. How could that be? It was surely no more than half an hour since he had slipped unseen out of Siena Cathedral and raced like a bat out of hell down the deserted autostrada back to Florence. Anyway, whatever the time, there was no time to lose. He had gleaned from the late Professor Jankovic's brief exchange on his mobile that the Serbian mafiosi had tailed the thieving magpie friar to the Bargello Museum. Its towering walls now loomed overhead, the battlements etched against a starry sky like blunted teeth, gorged on centuries of blood and gaping for more. He continued along the deserted street. A black van was parked under a street lamp; a thuggish face stared at him as he passed: the Serbs, he assumed. He drove on. Fifty yards further down, he passed a car, parked opposite a side-entrance to the museum. Rounding a bend, he stopped, jumped off his bike and sneaked back up the road to the side-entrance. It was unlocked. Entering a large courtyard, he headed for a staircase which led up to the Bargello's first-floor loggia. Halfway across the open quadrangle he heard what sounded like a high-pitched squeak. A rat, he surmised. A couple of paces later, he heard it again, but louder this time. It seemed to be coming from an octagonal-shaped well which must have been the prison's original water supply. Leaning over the metal grill which covered the well, he heard the sound again, but now it was unmistakable: it was no rat, it was a woman and she was screaming.

A padlock secured the grill. He gave it a tug and, as he was now coming to expect, it fell open at his touch. Shoving the grill aside, he took off his crash helmet and climbed over the low wall into the narrow well shaft. He shimmied downwards, his biker's gloves and boots giving him additional purchase against the rough stonework. As he descended, however, the masonry became looser and wetter. A piece of mortar broke away and a distant splash echoed upwards. Suddenly his boot slipped and for a heart-stopping second he was plunging into the black abyss below. Fortunately, after a few feet, he landed on a jutting ledge and just managed to brace his arms against the walls of the shaft. Taking deep breaths to try to calm his shattered nerves, he felt a draught of cold air on his cheeks. With extreme caution, he inched his way along the ledge towards its source. Eventually, he reached a large, round aperture: he guessed it was the outflow of an old ventilation shaft. The sound of voices echoed in the distance. Tucking himself into the hole, he started to crawl on all fours down the sloping chute. The voices grew louder and the darkness lighter as he crept deeper and deeper, putting one hand in front of the other until, without warning, his right hand landed on thin air. The chute had run out. Somehow he stopped himself tumbling over the edge. His heart pounding, he poked his head out into the void. A stomach-churning sight met his gaze: he was staring into the vault of a beehive-shaped chamber with nothing between him and the ground, some sixty feet below. He flinched backwards, his whole body rigid with fear as he contemplated his predicament: there was no way down and there was no going back. He was well and truly stuck. Then, out of nowhere, he heard Rinpoche's calming tones: 'Make a friend of your fear, Tom. Embrace it, harness its awesome power.' Swallowing hard, Tom forced himself to look down once more. Far below, he saw what looked like a brightly lit stage set, complete with cameras, cables and microphone booms. And there, centre stage, was Miranda, her arms outstretched behind her back, in the grip of the magpie.

Suddenly the magpie sprang back, yelping in pain. 'Mmph! The 'ickle bish bit me,' he lisped in an almost comic falsetto whine. 'Now I'll teach you a lethon you won't forget.' Rushing from the stage, he returned seconds later, brandishing a horsewhip.

Tom had to act fast. Following the line of the rope attached to Miranda's wrists up into the shadowy recesses of the vault, he could see that it was suspended over a massive meat hook, bolted to the ceiling. But the hook was some six feet away and well beyond his reach. His only hope was to launch himself out of the ventilation shaft and try to grab the rope on the way down, using it to slide to the ground. The bookies would love these odds, he winced, as he braced himself for the jump. Having clocked the positions of the magpie's men – the cameraman, the two masked goons either side of Miranda, and a fourth man guarding the dungeon door – he leapt out into the void, every muscle of his body strained to the limit. He was in mid-trajectory when there was a flash and loud bang. A large brown rat shot through the air from a dark corner where the lighting cables had been plugged into cracked sockets hanging loose from the wall. The startled magpie and his film crew looked on aghast as the rat, burnt to a crisp, landed at Miranda's feet. A moment later, the spotlights blew out, hurling vicious shards of glass into the cameraman's eyes. For Tom it was the perfect distraction. As his outstretched fingers just grasped the rope, he held on tight, swinging his body until his legs and feet were firmly entwined around it. Then he slid downwards like a fireman down a pole. Only Miranda noticed the tug on her arms; she cried out in pain but her cries were drowned out by the cameraman's shrieks.

'Will thomeone thurn on the infernal light!' Vincenzo yelled into the darkness, as he fumbled with a torch. After several more lisped expletives he managed to switch it on, just in time for a black boot to slam into the head of the masked goon standing to Miranda's right. Vincenzo's torch followed the boot as it orbited 180 degrees into the back of the second goon, propelling him headlong into the blinded cameraman and leaving them both sprawled on the floor.

Vincenzo's hand shook uncontrollably as he flashed the torch hither and thither in search of the owner of the black boot. The last of his goons called to him to shine the beam towards the dungeon door, where the switch to the fluorescent strip-lighting was located. He managed to control his nerves sufficiently to do this, but as his minion entered the torchlight and reached for the switch, a black-gloved fist smashed his jaw and, for him, all the lights went out.

Panic-stricken, Vincenzo grabbed Miranda by the throat: 'Show yourthelf or I'll break her bloody neck!' he screamed, shining his torch into her terrorised face.

Tom rushed forwards. 'No! Don't!' he cried. Miranda recognised that young, manly voice at once, but it was the warmth of his plea which plucked at her heart-strings.

Vincenzo trained the torch beam on Tom. 'Aha! What knight in thiny black armour have we here?' he crowed as Tom's sleek biking leathers glistened in the torchlight. 'One of Thcala's brave band of brotherth no doubt?' Tom did not respond. 'No matter,' the newly cocksure magpie continued. 'Do ath I thay or the girl dieth.' Tom took a step forwards. 'Move another inch and she'th dead. And if you kill me, Thcala will never find the diamondth.'

'Don't listen to him, Tom,' Miranda screamed. 'I know where he's hidden them.'

'Shut up, you thtupid cow!' Vincenzo hissed. 'How could you know anything? You were drugged the whole time.'

'I came to before you threw the water over me, but I played possum. I saw you slip the box down the back of your hood.'

The magpie flew into a blind rage. 'Daughter of Eve!' he spat, as his sweaty fingers pressed ever harder against her windpipe. 'I hate you, you and all your kind. From Thalome to Delilah, you women are all the thame. I'll feed you to the dogth, like Jethebel! I'll...' But he did not finish his sentence. For a split second he had taken his eyes off Tom, and now a black glove was clamped onto the back of his neck, paralysing the brachial nerve. His arms slumped powerless to his sides and he was forced to back away from his choking victim. But, as Tom relaxed the pressure on his neck, he managed to wriggle free and plucked a dagger from the folds of his habit. Spinning round to plunge the blade into his nemesis' chest, he suddenly gasped as if some unspeakable terror had taken hold of him. Eyes bulging and foaming at the mouth, Vincenzo's dagger dropped to the floor, closely followed by his torch and then by the cleric himself, convulsed in a fatal seizure.

Whatever it was that had so terrified the perverted priest, now was not the time to speculate. Tom snatched up his discarded torch and quickly located the metal box tucked away at the bottom of his hood, just as Miranda had said. 'Are you okay?' he asked her, finally aiming the torch in her direction.

'Well,' she grunted after several gulps of air, 'I would be, if you'd hurry up and cut me loose, instead of standing there gawping like an idiot, Mr Stockton.'

Tom blushed. 'Sorry,' he said, as he sliced through the rope with Vincenzo's silver dagger – a dagger which, he noted, looked just like the one the hoodie had left embedded in the picture frame at the Uffizi.

'And the cuffs?' Miranda demanded with an impatient glance behind her.

Tom examined the manacles. She was in luck: they were spring-loaded. He pressed a small catch and her wrists were released.

She winced as she flexed her stiff arms, rubbing them vigorously to restore the blood flow. Then, overwhelmed with relief, she suddenly flung them around her rescuer's neck, laughing and crying at the same time. 'Thank you,' she sobbed, planting a big wet kiss on Tom's cheek. 'This is the second time you've saved my life.'

'All part of the service,' he snuffled into her soft, flowing hair. How he yearned for this moment to last forever, holding her, so joyously, in his arms. But reality promptly intruded. Loud Slavic voices and hurried footsteps could be heard approaching. The Serbs had given up waiting for Jankovic to arrive. 'Quick! Get yourself together!' he said, handing Miranda the torch and sprinting to the dungeon door.

'Who is it?' she asked, hastily slipping into the red moccasins which her kidnappers had cast aside nearby.

Tom did not answer; he was too busy trying to unbolt the door, hoping they still had time to escape. But it was too late: the Serbs were right outside. 'It's the Serbian mob,' he whispered.

She shone the torch at him. 'Who?'

'Keep your voice down,' he hissed. 'They'll kill us if they catch us.' He looked up at the ventilation shaft in the ceiling: there was no way they could climb back up there. They were trapped.

'What about this?' said Miranda, reading his thoughts. She pointed the torch towards a heavy iron ring which had poked her in the ribs when she was trussed up on the floor.

Tom dashed back. The ring was fixed to the flagstone beneath it. He grasped the cold metal and heaved. The flagstone rose an inch or two but then dropped back with a thud that echoed round the dungeon walls. The Serbs started banging on the door. He took a deep breath and tried again. This time the flagstone broke free of its footings. As it fell back, a spiral of stone steps came into view.

'Where do they go?' Miranda wondered.

Tom took her hand. 'Wherever they go, we're going there together.'

41

RICCARDO ROSSI HEAVED himself up from the rim of the ornamental pond on which he and the other Brothers had been perched for what seemed like hours. 'How much longer shall we be kept waiting out here in the cold?' he wailed as he arched his stiff back and watched his breath billowing in the crisp air.

'Good question!' snorted Dr Gatti, tugging the sleeve of his white cassock to check his watch. It was gone 3pm. 'Dio! Is that the time!' he exclaimed, jumping to his feet as if he was late for some urgent appointment.

Colonel Hawkwood leaned back, gripping the edge of the pond with his bear-like hands and transferring the weight of his considerable bulk from one numb buttock to the other. 'Calm down, chaps,' he barked in a tone familiar to every parade-ground squaddie. 'The count told us to hold our position here. He'll report back once he's fully recced the situation.'

Gatti glared at him. 'Perhaps you hadn't noticed, Colonel, but this isn't Afghanistan.'

'It might as well be,' groaned Rossi. 'We've lost two weeks of our lives, been attacked by fanatical monks, almost murdered by Jankovic, the count's chauffeur has been shot dead, and then we had to weave in and out of the backstreets of Siena to make sure we weren't being followed. What else would you call it but a war zone?'

'Quite right, Rossi.' Hawkwood nodded, gratifyingly vindicated. 'Scala did a bloody good job shaking off any more mobsters who might have been tailing us. Superb piece of night driving. Reminded me of the cat and mouse games we used to play with the Stasi in East Berlin…'

'Yes, yes. Fascinating.' Gatti butted in. 'But right now I'm more interested to know why the count has left us here, in this walled garden to which he just happened to have a key?'

'And where did he disappear to in such a rush, without a word of explanation?' added Rossi.

'There's a lot he hasn't explained, if you ask me,' Gatti grumbled. 'Didn't you notice how he kept the limo's communication window firmly closed all the way back to Florence – with the Trismegistus firmly at his side? And all the time we were cooped up like chickens in the back, in fear of our lives.'

'Oh, for Christ's sake, put a sock in it, Gatti!' Hawkwood boomed. 'Unlike some of us, the count's no backseat driver. He leads from the front. Always two steps ahead of the enemy.'

Gatti gave a hollow laugh. 'Really? So how come he didn't spot Jankovic as a traitor from the start?'

'Or anticipate the Swords of the Lord's ambush?' Rossi whined.

'Maybe he did for all we know,' Hawkwood blustered. 'They all ended up dead meat, didn't they?'

'Not all,' Gatti retorted. 'You're forgetting the friar – the one who got away with our diamond rings.'

Rossi wrung his hands. 'Ah, our gorgeous rings – lost! All lost! It's her fault, that woman he brought along with him. Why on Earth did he let a woman into our Brotherhood?' Hawkwood frowned. He had been wondering the same thing himself. Women were always trouble in his experience, especially pretty ones. 'And what became of poor Signor Radopoulos?' Rossi went on.

'Perhaps the colonel can enlighten us on that?' Gatti smirked.

The ex-soldier's eyes narrowed like a sniper taking aim. 'How the hell should I know? The point is we've given the Serbs the slip and we've got the book. End of.'

Rossi now seemed almost on the verge of tears. 'What use is the book without the diamonds?' he croaked. 'The Savonarolan fanatics or the Serbian mob have those. Either way, it's finished. I wish I'd never got mixed up in all this madness.' He sank back down onto the rim of the pond and gazed glumly into the muddy water.

Gatti meanwhile turned his attention to Sarachin. Something irked him about the man. He had spoken not a word since they left Siena, just sitting there in lofty silence, his grey eyes staring out unnervingly from his rigid mask of a face, like some actor from an ancient Greek tragedy. 'Rossi's right, isn't he, Leo?' he fired. 'Here we are, hanging around like lemons in these ridiculous robes, while Scala's disappeared with the one valuable object we had left. We'll never see either of them again, will we?'

The psychoanalyst regarded his petulant young inquisitor with weary disdain. 'Do you really think so, Dottore?' he asked pointedly.

Gatti tossed his lolling forelock impatiently. 'I need to piss!' he harrumphed, spinning on his heels and marching off down a narrow path that bisected the garden. Towards the end of the path he veered off and melted away among thick laurel and privet bushes. As he re-emerged, some minutes later, something slipped from his hand into the undergrowth, but he did not look back.

'I was just about to send out a search party,' Hawkwood guffawed as the dottore approached. 'Can't have you skulking in the count's shrubbery, now can we?'

'It's not his garden,' he replied sulkily. 'Can't you see the palle stuck on every wall? This is part of the Palazzo...'

'Medici,' a gravelly voice interrupted. Scala was standing at the wrought-iron gates which gave onto the palazzo's inner courtyard. He took a few moments to observe the remaining members of his Brotherhood. Was there another traitor among them? Jankovic may have brought the Serbian mafia to Siena, but he would not have had anything to do with the Savonarolans. No, it must have been someone else who led the Swords of the Lord to the cathedral, but who? The fat friar had pointed the finger at the cathedral's sexton, but that might have been just a ruse to protect his true source. Rossi was not up to it, surely? Or was his foppery merely an act? Hawkwood had proved his loyalty in helping to deal with the whistle-blower at the bank's London branch, as well as in assisting with the disposal of Radopoulos. Yet he was also a greedy, unscrupulous and quite ruthless mercenary. Then there was Gatti: he had an obvious connection with the Vatican, and his story about being under surveillance might be just a convenient cover. He may have seen enough of the Siena guidebook when he visited the count's study the previous morning to put two and two together and tip off the Savonarolans. Yet, Gatti was the one who had warned him about Jankovic. That just left Sarachin, he of few words and keen eye. A psychoanalyst was the most surreptitious of spies. On the other hand, the Savonarolans might simply have tailed them when they left the palazzo last night: the Serbs clearly had. He sighed; it was no good, all were suspect. 'This way, Fratres,' he said, unlocking the gates and waving them through a high, barrel-vaulted archway into a deserted courtyard. 'The palazzo is closed to the public this week, for renovation.' They made their way to the central arch of the loggia, where a statue of Orpheus gazed down from a lofty plinth. 'Welcome home, Brothers of the Company of the Magi!' he declared. In his white habit and sporting his trademark black cane, he seemed surprisingly calm for a man who had just lost the diamond rings that embodied his secret Brotherhood's whole raison d'être.

'Brothers be damned!' Gatti exploded. 'How can you stand there as if nothing had happened? Have you forgotten that the Savonarolans now have our diamond rings? That the Serbs are out to kill us?'

'And what about that woman in the cathedral?' Hawkwood joined in. 'Who was she? And what was she doing dressed like one of us?'

'Yes. And what's happened to Signor Radopoulos?' demanded Rossi.

'And the Trismegistus?' Sarachin threw in.

Scala tapped his cane sharply on the stone pavement. 'Brothers, you want answers and you shall have them.'

He explained that, in order to deal with the changed circumstances, he had needed to contact various people; these included his old friend, the superintendent of the Bargello, the museum which Jankovic had mentioned in his last phone call to his 'associates'. Sure enough, the superintendent had confirmed that there had been a security breach early that morning and unauthorised access had been gained to an off-limits part of the building. Five bodies had been discovered in a disused dungeon: a friar and four other men, all shot dead.

'That's five less to worry about then,' Hawkwood noted grimly.

Rossi turned very pale. 'Shot!' he gulped. 'But who...'

'The Serbs, of course,' Gatti cut in. 'But what about our diamond rings? Did your old friend find them too?'

Scala shook his head. Neither the rings nor the kidnapped girl had been found. It appeared that, in the melee which ensued after the Serbs broke into the dungeon, she had escaped down a disused drainage tunnel underneath the medieval prison. There were later reports of gunfire in a nearby street. The Serbs must have gone after her and that could only be because she had somehow retrieved the rings.

'Clever little Miss Maddingley!' Gatti snorted.

Hawkwood knotted his bushy eyebrows. 'Miss who?'

'She's a friend of mine,' Scala answered curtly. 'The dottore has met her. I asked her to take Radopoulos's place after his unfortunate demise.'

'Demise?' Rossi shrieked, all trace of colour now drained from his gills.

'Yes, Riccardo. I'm afraid his condition was more serious than we thought. The poor fellow had a weak heart. All that excitement at San Lorenzo, and then again at Villa Luna, was simply too much for him. My physician assured me that there was nothing anyone could have done.'

Rossi tottered backwards. He felt Hawkwood's hand steady his shoulder: somehow he did not find it reassuring.

'But where are Miss Maddingley and the diamonds now?' Gatti pressed.

Scala sucked his lips, finally betraying a little of the deep anxiety which was bubbling beneath that stiff, aristocratic exterior. 'I don't know. But Fabio and the rest of my staff happened to be in the area where the gunshots were heard. I've told them to search for her. All we can do now is...' Suddenly, there was a loud banging at the main gate.

42

AFTER SHUFFLING THROUGH the claustrophobic entrails of medieval Florence for what seemed like hours, Tom and Miranda reached the junction where the ancient passage they had been following debouched into a much larger tunnel. From the malodorous stench assailing his nostrils, Tom guessed this to be part of the city's main sewerage network. At the same time, a draught of much fresher air was wafting down from somewhere overhead. Just before Vincenzo's fast-fading flashlight gave out completely, he spotted a line of metal rungs going up the wall ahead of them. Taking Miranda's hand, he inched his way through the black void until his fingertips connected with the rusting ironwork. Trying not to slip on the damp metal, he ascended into a narrow chute. He could hear the rumble of traffic above him and soon realised that street level was closer than he had imagined. 'Ouch!' he cried as his head hit something hard and unyielding.

'Hey, watch what you're doing!' Miranda shouted from below as a hail of rust and dirt rained down.

Tom rubbed his sore pate. 'Sorry, it's a bit dark up here, you know!' Thrusting his hand upwards, he felt the circular, metallic surface of a manhole cover. He pushed it, but it would not budge. Retracting his arm, he rested for a minute. Angry shouts echoed along the tunnel behind them; the Serbs were closing in. Using both hands this time, he gave the cover a determined shove. Suddenly, it popped open and a crescent of brilliant sunshine momentarily blinded him. Poking his head above ground, he squinted at a hotchpotch of footwear passing to and fro, a few inches from his nose. He did not mind: the footfalls meant that the manhole was on the pavement, not in the road. With a final effort, he thrust the cover back; it came to rest against a wall which he correctly surmised to be the back of the Bargello. Hoisting himself aloft in a single lithe movement, he ignored the quizzical looks of passers-by as he quickly helped Miranda up into the open air. Her first concern was to get to her feet with as little indignity as possible, but that did not stop her admiring the strength in her rescuer's arms as he hauled her up from the underworld.

Ordinarily, the sight of a man, or even a woman, emerging from a manhole might not have attracted much attention, provided he or she was sporting a yellow jacket and a hard hat. But Tom and Miranda were very differently attired. He was clad top-to-toe in black leather biker's gear, whilst she, in dishevelled blouse and torn skirt, covered in dust and cobwebs, looked every bit the distressed heroine of a Gothic horror movie.

Say, will ya take a look at those guys!' cawed the outrider of a passing posse of American tourists.

'Gee,' trilled a buxom lady in frumpy culottes waddling beside him, ''dja reckon they're shooting one of those spooky vampire films?'

'Could be, honey. That gal sure looks like a movie star.'

Overhearing this exchange, Tom had a sudden inspiration. He quickly lowered the manhole cover back into position and stood on it. Then, beaming brightly at the small crowd that was now gathering, he turned to Miranda and said, in his poshest Hugh Grant voice, 'I say, dahling, do you think we're a little early for Brad and Angelina?'

Miranda stared at him as if he had gone completely insane but, before she could say anything, the American tour group rushed forwards as one, bombarding them with questions. 'Excuse me, sir, but did you mention Brad Pitt just now? Is Angelina Jolie coming? Could I have your autograph? Do ya need any extras?'

Tom and Miranda were surrounded and getting pinned closer and closer to the wall of the Bargello. His stratagem was in severe danger of backfiring. With an imperious wave, he called for order: 'Quiet! Quiet please!' The hubbub subsided; all eyes were glued to him. 'Thank you for your patience, ladies and gentlemen,' he said, conspicuously consulting his watch. 'The filming is due to start in five minutes' time. If you just wait right here where I'm standing, you'll have the best view of all the action. Meantime, if you'll excuse us, we need to go check on a few things. Have a nice day!' And with that, he grabbed Miranda's arm and fled.

When they were clear of the throng, Miranda pulled him up short. 'Hold on a minute!' she protested. 'What the hell was all that about – "Dahling"?'

Tom looked at her with an irritating grin. 'Don't you see?' he chuckled. 'The Serbian mafia now have several hundredweight of your fellow Americans standing right on top of them. We've gained a good five minutes' head start on them.'

Miranda glanced back at the excited mob. 'Tom, you're a genius!' she exclaimed, flinging her arms around his neck for the second time that day. For a moment the world stood still. But their rapture was short-lived. Loud screams suddenly erupted as gunshots exploded under the tourists' feet and bullets pinged against the bottom of the manhole cover. As the crowd scattered, men in dark suits emerged from the open drain, brandishing pistols.

'Come on!' Tom yelled, yanking Miranda's wrist. They sprinted to the end of the street. A huge parade was making its boisterous way up the main road in the direction of the Duomo. Hundreds of cheering, flag-waving men, women and children, dressed in colourful medieval costumes, were marching to the deafening accompaniment of kettledrums and bugles played by local bands. At the head of the procession, three men in ermine cloaks and golden crowns rode on prancing carthorses, acknowledging the cheers of onlookers and flanked by a troupe of colourful standard-bearers tossing banners high into the air.

Tom looked over his shoulder: the Serbs were less than fifty yards behind them. Their only chance of escape was to join the anonymous hordes bringing up the rear of the cavalcade and try to melt away into the crowd. The two fugitives wove their way as fast they could through the stately ranks of lords and ladies, maids and minstrels, pages and princesses until at last they plunged into the tide of humanity tramping along at the back like a column of camp followers.

Tom peeked out through fleeting gaps in the crowd: he could see the Serbs standing on the street corner, scanning the sea of faces. He and Miranda passed by unnoticed, and he was starting to relax as the Serbs receded into the distance when Miranda let out an ear-splitting shriek. A pony-tailed backpacker with size-ten hobnail boots had stepped on her toe. She was hopping about on one foot like a crazed kangaroo as people swerved to left and right to avoid her. Tom gave her his arm. 'We must keep moving!' he urged. But it was too late. Their pursuers had heard her scream and spotted the crowd eddying around her. A mountainous Serb was already bearing down on them through the sea of bobbing heads, like a shark scenting blood. Tom looked round desperately for a hiding place, but the bare walls and barred windows of the palazzi lining the street offered no refuge.

Suddenly, a gang of swarthy, unshaven men appeared out of nowhere and formed a cordon around him and Miranda. 'Fabio!' she exclaimed as one of the men grabbed her waist and bundled her like a rag doll through a nearby doorway.

'You know these gorillas?' Tom gaped in disbelief as he too was unceremoniously propelled through the same door.

'Sono il maggiordomo di Conte Scala, Signore,' Fabio retorted. 'My cousin is gatekeeper at this palazzo. You and the signorina must wait here till it's safe to leave.' And, with that, he slammed the door shut.

'Nice guys your boyfriend Scala employs!' Tom puffed as he got his breath back.

'He's not my boyfriend!' Miranda snapped. Her foot still throbbed, though the pain was slowly subsiding. She sat down, leaning her head against one of the columns of a graceful arcade which bordered the courtyard in which they now found themselves. Regretting his outburst, Tom sat down beside her. 'Sorry,' he said. 'I didn't mean to…'

She shot him an accusing glance. 'When do you plan on telling me, Tom?' she said abruptly.

His brow furrowed. 'Tell you what?' he asked, though he guessed what was coming.

'How you found me in that dungeon? Why you dislike Giovanni so much? What you're really doing in Florence?' He stiffened. She had seen that look before, in the eyes of clients who knew the truth but could not face it. 'Just spit it out, Tom,' she said. 'I'm a big girl, I can take it.'

He swallowed hard: it was time to come clean. As matter-of-factly as he could, he recapped the events of the last three months, bizarre and incredible though some of them were. When he finished, her face was a mixture of pity and incredulity. She had recognised at once the broken cufflink he showed her: it matched exactly the ones she had seen adorning Giovanni's cuffs. And she could well imagine that the secretive Italian count was indeed the mastermind behind a massive banking fraud. But the tales of ghostly Tibetan monks, wacky professors with magic mirrors, ancient maps and the lost Gifts of the Magi were too much. She watched his hand shake as he removed a bloodstained envelope from his pocket. It was, apparently, his only link to a father he had never known, and had once contained an incomprehensible letter addressed to the mysterious 'Dorje'. She put her hand on his arm: 'You need help, Tom,' she whispered. 'You're clearly having some sort of breakdown.'

'Huh, go see a shrink, you mean?' he said, snatching his arm away. 'That's the New Yorker's answer to everything, isn't it?'

'Yeah, well, that's what shrinks are there for, buster,' she bristled.

He drew a hand across his forehead. 'Why won't you believe me? You saw what happened in Siena. Was that just a hallucination too?'

She shrugged her shoulders: she had seen nothing. Vincenzo had knocked her out cold; when she woke up, she was in the Bargello. 'Anyway, whatever you think you saw was no doubt manufactured with the aid of lasers or 3D imaging or the like,' she said, employing the same logic with which she had dismissed the son et lumière show at San Marco.

Tom sighed: it was hopeless. How could he convince her of something he himself could hardly comprehend. He looked at his watch: how much longer would they be cooped up in this nameless palazzo? Then he had a brainwave. 'What time do you make it?' he asked.

She looked at her watch, blinked and did a double-take. 'That can't be right,' she frowned, checking to see if the second hand was still moving – which it was. 'But it was only midday when we got out of that drain, no more than half an hour ago.'

Tom pointed at the sky above the courtyard: a reddening sun was sinking towards the roof-line. 'The Wheel of time doth faster run,' he said. 'That's what the Cumaean Sibyl warned in Siena after you were abducted. Time is somehow speeding up, or at least it is for us. Like a ship leaving port, dragging us in its wake.'

She put her hand to her mouth. 'Oh my God,' she gasped as she remembered Fabio's odd remark at breakfast the previous morning ('It's good to have you home again'). 'What day is it?' she demanded.

'The 6th of January. That's what the procession outside was all about: Epiphany.'

Miranda turned deathly pale: how could two weeks of her life have just vanished? Fearing she was about to faint, Tom put his arm around her shoulders; he had forgotten how shocking this madness truly was. She turned and gazed into his eyes; there was a smudge of dirt, a memento of their tour of the Florentine drainage system, positioned rather comically on the tip of his nose. 'You look like a clown,' she giggled as she gently brushed it away with her finger. He chuckled too: it took guts to laugh in the face of such adversity. But it was not just admiration that he felt. Her touch had somehow united them: something had clicked between them. Miranda felt it too. Their lips were but a breath apart. She knew what was coming but did not resist. It felt like she had been waiting for that kiss all her life, a life whose brevity had just been so shockingly brought home to her. As their embrace loosened, she seemed to be floating on air in an almost trance-like state. She looked once more into those deep blue eyes. Somewhat bizarrely, they reminded her of another love, her old husky dog. 'But Smokey's eyes were an arctic blue,' she said, 'yours are more...'

'Himalayan?' The word came unbidden to Tom's lips, but it hit the spot. He saw a flicker of recognition in her face. He decided to rectify the only omission from his earlier disclosures. 'Stockton isn't my real name,' he confessed. 'I used my aunt's surname so as not to alert Scala to my presence. My real name is Talbot.'

'Talbot?'

'It's an old English name for a hunting hound.'

Miranda put her hand to her mouth. Suddenly, she was in the steppes of Central Asia, lying in the sand with blood oozing from an arrow wound in her back. And beside her a wolf howled at the moon. 'No!' she cried, reeling again from the overload of mind-blowing revelations. 'This is all too fast. I'm a lawyer from New York, you're a banker from London. Anything else is delusional, insane.'

Tom stroked her long auburn hair. Maybe she was right, maybe he *was* going mad: that was, after all, by far the easier conclusion. As his fingers reached the last glossy strands of chestnut, they lighted on a fine gold chain that wound around her neck and ended in a circular lump beneath the silk of her blouse. 'What's that?' he wondered aloud.

She looked down and grimaced: now it was her turn to raise the dead. She drew the chain upwards and let her uncle's bronze ring dangle in the air while she recounted her own personal journey of the last few months, from discovering the existence of Cousin Frankie to meeting Count Scala and joining in the escapades of his 'little club'.

When she had finished, Tom caught hold of the dangling ring. Suddenly, he leapt to his feet: 'Dolphins,' he declared.

She stared at him in alarm: was he having one of those weird visions of his?

'Look! Up there,' he said, gesticulating at the top of the column she was leaning against. 'Carved stone dolphins. I noticed them as I sat down.'

She pulled a face: surely they had more pressing things to think about right now than the local architecture. Still, to humour him, she did as he asked. There were indeed dolphins carved on the capital, not just of this column but, as she now observed, of every column around the courtyard. She scanned the rest of the masonry. There was not much to stay the eye: the building was elegant but plain, with very little ornamentation. Then, on a wall high above the colonnade, she saw something that brought her heart to her throat: there were more dolphins, but this time they were carved on a stone shield that matched exactly the seal on her uncle's ring. 'What is this place?' she cried, struggling to her feet and going to the palazzo's front door, where she found a notice pinned to the wood. She started to giggle. And the more she read, the more she giggled.

Tom wondered if she was cracking up. 'What's so funny?'

'It's the name, the name on the notice,' she blurted between snorts of laughter.

He came over and took a look for himself. The notice gave a potted history of the palazzo. The stilted English was quite amusing, as such notices often were, but it was not that funny, surely. 'I don't see the joke,' he frowned. 'Basically, all it says is that this palazzo was built in 1475 by the Pazzi family.'

But his comment only served to make her laugh even louder, so loud that her laughter echoed down the arcade, at which point she stopped abruptly. 'What was that?' she asked.

'Just an echo.'

'No, it was more an echo of an echo. A déjà vu of an echo, as if...' She broke off and turned to the funny notice again. 'Pazzi, what a ridiculous name,' she scoffed. 'It means "crazy" in Italian, you know. Giovanni told me.'

Tom nodded. He knew what 'pazzi' meant; he had picked up enough Italian after all, during his time at the Banca de' Bianchi. Yet, in this context, he had naturally taken it at face value, as the name of the Medici's arch enemies. In his drug-induced visions at Aunt Stella's, he had heard Il Magnifico swear to exterminate them for the savage assassination of his brother. But Miranda seemed unaware of the Pazzi's claim to infamy. 'I guess you don't know the story of Giuliano de' Medici's murder by Francesco de' Pazzi?' he said.

The nightmare image of her father's galleon, Amerigo Vespucci's *Bella Simonetta*, surrounded by predatory dolphins, flashed before Miranda's eyes. Yes, she had read about Giuliano's murder on the steps of the Duomo, but the focus of her interest had been Simonetta Vespucci and the love triangle with the Medici brothers. Only now did the real connection between her nightmare and her uncle's ring begin to dawn. She pinched herself: was she still in her nightmare? Losing two weeks in the twinkling of an eye, seeing ghosts in a Florentine monastery, tortured in a medieval dungeon, rescued by a guy who saw visions: it was *Alice in Wonderland* meets *Dracula*. And now there were the Pazzi to add to the mix: those bad, mad… she grasped Tom's hand: 'Did you say today is Epiphany?'

'Yes.'

'Well, I've just had one.'

At that moment, Fabio put his head round the door. The coast was clear; it was time to go.

43

COUNT SCALA LISTENED intently. One knock, a pause, then three, then one. He relaxed: it was his butler, Fabio. Doctor Gatti rushed to the Palazzo Medici's front gate and drew back the bolt. Miranda flew in, followed by Fabio and three of his 'cousins'. Tom slipped in behind them, hanging back in the shadows of the portico. Gatti eyed him suspiciously: from his pale complexion and biking leathers, he was clearly not one of Scala's Sardinian yokels.

'Miranda. Thank God you're safe!' Scala cried, throwing his arms around her in a display of emotion that surprised everyone present, not least Miranda. She handed him the small metal box in which Vincenzo had squirrelled away the Brotherhood's stolen diamond rings. Tom had quietly passed the box to her when Fabio had announced the all-clear and conducted them back to the count. The Serbian thugs, he told them, had continued to follow the Magi Cavalcade towards the Duomo, but sooner or later they would realise their mistake and double back to search for them. As Fabio had walked on ahead, leading them down narrow alleyways and deserted backstreets, Miranda had confided in Tom the shocking truth that had dawned on her in the Palazzo Pazzi. Her account of nightmares, model galleons, and family secrets had naturally resonated with him. Indeed, her tale had served to corroborate his own recent experiences. More than that, it had shed new light on them: a light so strange that he had shrunk from sharing it with her, though it illumined Miranda's past just as much as his own.

Scala took Vincenzo's box. In the gathering winter gloom, he moved back to the loggia, where automatic sensors had lit one of the large lanterns which now began to glow around the cortile. Carefully prising open the lid, his eager fingers raced among the sparkling rings, making sure all were present. Plucking one out, he slipped it on, lost in the depths of its cobalt-blue stone. When he looked up, Gatti was at his side. 'That one's mine,' he said, snatching a blood-red jewel from the box.

Scala nodded and proceeded to distribute the rest of the rings. Miranda was the last to be summoned. She approached slowly; her future lay with Tom, but now was not the time to tell Giovanni. 'Ecco qua,' Scala purred as he slid an amber solitaire down her index finger and gazed longingly into her eyes.

It was all too much for Hawkwood. 'What about Jankovic's ring?' he barked impatiently. 'Who's going to have that?'

'How about Miss Maddingley's handsome young companion?' Gatti chirped, aiming a mischievous grin towards the front portico. Tom had no choice but to step forwards out of the shadows.

Scala's eyes narrowed to slivers of ice. 'You again!' he scowled.

Miranda leapt to Tom's defence. 'He saved my life, Giovanni,' she said, withdrawing her hand from his. 'He rescued me from that sadist Father Vincenzo, as well as from the Serbian mafia.'

'But it was the Serbs who killed the friar. That's what you told Fabio, wasn't it?'

'Count Scala,' Tom interrupted. 'I can explain everything.'

The two men glowered at one another like a pair of rival tomcats. 'Everything?' Scala spat.

Tom took a deep breath. 'Yes,' he replied and proceeded to tell the story he had hastily concocted on the way from the Palazzo Pazzi. He had set out very early that morning to bag a good spot to watch the Magi Cavalcade. He was walking past the Bargello when he saw five men, one wearing a monk's habit, hauling what looked like a trussed-up body out of a car boot. He ducked behind a parked truck and watched. As they manhandled the bundle into the Bargello, a head bobbed out: it was Miss Maddingley. He was wondering what to do when a van came racing down the road and skidded to a halt. Several guys in dark suits and shades leapt out and also went into the Bargello. He followed them. When they caught up with the monk and his men, a fight broke out. In the confusion, he managed to free Miss Maddingley and they escaped together.

The count snorted. 'A truly remarkable tale,' he said. 'Let me see if I've got it straight. You just happened to be walking past the Bargello, just as Miss Maddingley was being hauled from a car boot. No doubt it was by a similarly extraordinary coincidence that you also happened to be in the Uffizi when that madman attacked the painting she was admiring.' Scala slammed the brass ferrule of his cane on the flagstone floor. 'What do you take me for? An idiot?'

'But it's true, Giovanni,' Miranda protested. 'Tom saved my life for the second time. I wouldn't be here – and neither would the diamond rings – if it wasn't for Tom.'

'Tom? Tom who?' Hawkwood demanded, his eyes boring into Tom's head.

'Stockton,' Tom lied, using his aunt's name just as he had when he first met Miranda in the Uffizi.

Scala's face turned to granite. 'Stockton?' he repeated as if he could not quite believe his ears. 'That's a very old English surname, is it not?'

Tom had no idea how old his aunt's surname was, much less why the count should find it so noteworthy. 'Well, er, yes, I suppose…'

'Yes,' Scala nodded. 'That's the name a Florentine called Canigiani adopted when he married Dame Elizabeth Stockton in 1472, instantly transforming himself into an English gentleman.' Tom bit his lip; this history lesson did not sound like it had a happy ending. 'Canigiani,' continued the count, 'had previously managed the London branch of the Medici Bank, which he single-handedly bankrupted by giving huge, unsecured loans to King Edward IV to squander on the Wars of the Roses.'

'Hang on a minute!' Hawkwood bellowed. 'I've seen this fellow before.' Everyone stared in surprise as the colonel marched up to Tom and pointed an accusing finger in his face. 'I thought I recognised you as soon as I clapped eyes on you,' he snarled. 'Your graduation photograph was on the mantelpiece at your parents' cottage. You're that blighter Talbot who caused all the trouble at the count's bank in London.' Tom lunged at the man who had just identified himself as Jasper's killer; but Fabio and his cousins quickly restrained him.

Scala gasped. When Woodcock had first mentioned Talbot's name at the Athenaeum back in September, he had dismissed it as mere coincidence. But now he saw the likeness between this young man and the English art historian whose murder he had procured twenty-seven years earlier. 'Cuff him,' he ordered as Fabio plucked a pair of handcuffs from his seemingly bottomless pockets and slapped them on Tom's wrists.

'What are you doing, Giovanni?' Miranda cried.

'He's deceived you, my dear. The man's a liar and a fraudster. He'll be handed over to the authorities as soon as this is all over.'

Just then, Fabio's mobile rang. After a brief exchange in unintelligible Sardinian, he whispered in the count's ear. Somehow they had been spotted entering the palazzo: the Serbs would be there in a matter of minutes. 'Quickly,' ordered Scala, 'everyone follow me.'

'But what about Jankovic's ring?' Hawkwood reminded him.

The count hesitated. Fabio would have been his first choice, yet now there was much to be said for Gatti's suggestion, facetious though it was. 'Bring Talbot to me!' The Sardinians pushed Tom forwards. Scala grasped his cuffed hand. 'Since you're here, you may as well be useful,' he growled, as he forced the last remaining ring onto his index finger. 'Welcome to the Brotherhood of the Magi, Mr Talbot. I'm afraid your membership will be short-lived.'

SPRING

—◦◦◦—

44

Scala sprinted up the stone staircase which led to the Palazzo Medici's piano nobile. 'Come and look at this,' he called excitedly to Miranda as she and the others followed him into a magnificent panelled library. With a backwards look at Tom, still in the grip of his Sardinian minders, she advanced through the sickly-sweetness of the wax-scented air. The count was standing by a window overlooking the cortile. Beside him, on an oak lectern, she spied a book bound in silver and felt a tingle run down her spine.

'Some say it was written by Zoroaster himself,' Scala enthused, seeing the wonder in her eyes. 'After being buried for the last five hundred years, Hermes Trismegistus is risen again.'

The name meant nothing to Miranda, but Tom had heard it before, in Siena Cathedral. He had guessed then that it was the same Hermes whose epilogue had been whispered of in the haunted gardens at Careggi. He watched as Miranda's hands glided down the book's silver spine, across the gold-embossed balls of the Medici crest, and over the purple of Lorenzo the Magnificent's initials. A strange magnetism seemed to hold her in thrall. Was it some memory transmitted in her genes, as her epiphany in the Palazzo Pazzi might now indicate? Or was there an even more ancient magic at work? A sudden jab in her ribs broke the spell. It was Gatti.

'Never mind the pretty cover,' he snapped, pushing her aside. 'It's the contents that matter.' He proceeded to flip off the book's clasps, now devoid of the pin embedded in Jankovic's skull. But, just as he lifted the cover, Scala's hand slammed it shut again. 'No need for that, Dottore,' he smiled thinly. 'I've already examined the contents.'

Gatti gave him a distrustful stare. 'And?'

'I found that, unlike Ficino's published version, the Siena Trismegistus contains a colophon.'

'What's that you say?' Hawkwood guffawed. 'The ruddy thing's got a phone? This I must see.' Pushing past Gatti, he stretched out his right hand towards the silver tome. But as soon as his skin came into contact with the cold metal, the solitaire on his index finger emitted a pulse of white light so intense it lit up every bone in his body. The flash lasted but a fraction of a second, yet it left Hawkwood shaking like jelly. Tom looked on in astonishment: unlike Miranda and the other Brothers, he was witnessing the power of their diamonds for the first time.

Fabio hastened to Hawkwood's aid, dabbing his blistered flesh with a special Sardinian liniment which both eased the pain and expedited the removal of his ring. This the assiduous butler handed at once to his master.

'What does it say?' Gatti and Rossi chorused as one.

Scala held the ring up to the windowpane and rotated it in the dying afterglow of sunset. Slowly, the words dripped from his lips:

'"CANDELIS... SAPIENS... SPECTAT... SECRETA... SACELLI... AEQ... VER."'

'Hmm,' Gatti pondered aloud. '"Sapiens spectat secreta" is simple enough. "The wise man observes the secrets".'

'And "Candelis" sounds to me like "candles", added Rossi. 'Maybe it means "by candlelight"? But I'm not sure what "sacelli" is.'

'We need a lexicon,' Gatti replied, surveying the library's shelves. Scala pointed to a thick volume already lying open on one of the tables. Gatti raced across to it and, with a quick lick of his thumb, began snapping through its wafer-thin leaves. 'Aha!' he cried triumphantly. 'I've got it. "Sacellus" means "a small sack or bag".'

Rossi frowned. '"By candlelight the wise man observes the secrets of a small sack,"' he translated dubiously. 'So where's the sack?'

Neither Gatti nor anyone else had an answer to that. Scala squinted at Hawkwood's ring again, but there was no mistake: the inscription was quite clear.

Miranda decided to see if she could shed some lawyerly light on the subject. 'Excuse me, Dr Gatti,' she said, approaching the table, 'may I take a look please?' With a disdainful toss of his lolling forelock, he thrust the dictionary towards her. Ignoring his histrionics, she calmly studied the minuscule text. 'Sacellus' was indeed Latin for a little sack. She scrolled her finger down the subsequent entries: 'Saccharon' – a sweet juice obtained from bamboo shoots; 'Saccibuccis' – chubby-cheeked; 'Saccularius' – a pick-pocket, and then 'Saccus' – a (full-sized) sack or bag. She paused: the next entry seemed to be out of alphabetical order. She read it aloud: '"Sacellum, genitive sacelli, a diminutive of Sacrum"...'

'Ah, that's why it comes *after* "Saccus", not before,' Rossi commented.

'"Sacellum",' Miranda continued, 'means a little sanctuary or chapel.'

'Huh,' Gatti sniffed, 'where does that get us?'

Scala slapped his forehead: the most beautiful little chapel in the whole of Italy was just along the corridor.

'Yes, that's right,' Rossi agreed enthusiastically. 'It's La Cappella dei Magi. And Gozzoli's exquisite fresco of the Procession of the Three Kings surrounds the chapel's walls.'

Scala nodded. 'Cosimo de' Medici had the chapel constructed at the very heart of his palazzo, where no daylight could damage Gozzoli's masterpiece. And when the Medici performed their private devotions...'

'It had to be by candlelight!' Miranda exclaimed.

'A round of applause for Miss Maddingley,' Gatti jeered. 'No doubt she can translate the date for us too.'

With a defiant glare, she asked the count to re-read the last words on the ring: 'Aeq. Ver'. They sounded like abbreviations. 'Could "Ver" be short for "spring"?' she wondered, recalling Botticelli's "Primavera" in the Uffizi.

'Well done!' Scala beamed, adding that 'Aeq.' might be short for 'Aequus', or 'equal' in Latin.

'Oh please, Count,' Gatti groaned, 'can we dispense with this tedious charade? You knew the answer already, didn't you?'

Scala smirked like an old fox watching the hounds race off in the opposite direction. 'Ah, Dottore, I believe you're referring to the colophon or, for Colonel Hawkeye's benefit, the epilogue to the Trismegistus. Yes, I must confess, I did already know the meaning of the abbreviation.' A murmur of discontent rumbled through the assembled Brothers. He patted the air, calling for silence. He had kept nothing back. The triggering of Hawkeye's ring had interrupted him, that was all. Time, as they all now realised, had somehow fast-forwarded since their gathering at San Marco. 'And, as the Cumaean Sibyl prophesied in Siena, it has continued to accelerate.' He pointed to the darkness which had now replaced sunset in the library window. 'The epilogue to the Trismegistus,' he said, 'confirmed that, for every diamond that is triggered, time passes faster. Thus we jumped from the winter solstice to the moon's first quarter at Epiphany.'

'And where has my ring jumped us to?' queried Hawkwood.

'From Epiphany to the Aequinoctium Vernum, or spring equinox, which this year is of special significance.'

Tom's heart missed a beat. Rinpoche's last instruction: 'Remember the equinox!' rang in his ears. What was its 'special significance' this year? Did it have anything to do with the Platonic Year he had read about on the internet? But his thoughts were interrupted by loud shouts coming from the courtyard. Scala peered through the window. Dark-suited figures were hurrying through the colonnade, their guns glinting in the lantern-light. It was the Serbs. Someone had left the palazzo's door unlocked. 'Hurry!' he cried, grabbing the Trismegistus. 'We must get to the Chapel of the Magi before they find us.'

45

THE BROTHERS FOLLOWED their maestro out of the library and across the passageway to the narrow door of the Medici Chapel. Tom watched Scala enter first with Miranda in tow. The blonde, bespectacled guy they called the 'dottore' followed close behind. Then came the other Italian: he of the Macassar hairdo and heady deodorant. Next up was Jasper's killer, Colonel 'Hawkeye', with his Lord Kitchener moustache and bulging eyes. Finally, the solemn, white-haired man who had not spoken a word so far, went in just ahead of Tom and his Sardinian minders. Fabio brought up the rear, bolting the chapel door behind them.

It was pitch-black. There were no windows. If they were lucky, Scala hoped, the Serbs might not find them; otherwise, they would have to trust to darker powers. He ordered Fabio to light some candles. A shuffling of feet and fumbling of hands ensued, interspersed with choice Sardinian curses. Eventually, a candle spluttered into flame, then another and another until, caught in the flickering chiaroscuro, a dappled kaleidoscope of colour revealed itself.

'Incredible!' gasped Rossi. 'I've been here numerous times, but never like this. Now, as if by magic, the candlelight has brought the whole room to life.'

'Pray continue, Riccardo,' the count exhorted him. 'Take us on a quick tour of the chapel. Somewhere it keeps a secret.'

Rossi's eyes lit up: his earlier panic attack in the palazzo's garden was quite forgotten, lost in a transport of aesthetic rapture. 'Gentlemen,' he commenced, ignoring Miranda's presence, 'the fresco you see before you depicts the journey of the Magi from Jerusalem to Bethlehem. The setting, however, is not the Holy Land but Tuscany.' Hill-towns and villas, cypresses and orange groves were lit up in swift succession. There were also some exotic touches: a camel here, a leopard there, as well as a hunting hound which, Tom thought, bore an uncanny resemblance to Buontempo. Indeed, according to Rossi, many of the figures in the Magi's train were portraits of real people, and of course they included the Medici.

Lorenzo Il Magnifico was apparently the idealised model for the youngest Magus, Caspar. He rode a snow-white horse, dripping with Medici insignia. But it was his equerry riding just ahead of him who caught Tom's eye. He was holding a gold, turret-shaped pyx containing Caspar's gift of myrrh, the symbol of immortality. Could this, Tom wondered, be an actual depiction of the real thing, salted away somewhere in the Medici vaults? He noticed Rossi glance apprehensively at his ring. Was he worried that it was about to explode just as Hawkeye's had done earlier, in the library? He fingered his own ring, the one which Scala had foisted upon him: was that too primed to detonate on some predetermined signal?

The second Magus, a black-bearded Balthazar, looked majestic on a muscular stallion. Clad in green and gold, this was apparently a portrait of a Byzantine Emperor.

'He seems rather sad,' Miranda remarked.

'They say the portrait was painted posthumously,' Scala answered.

'Or perhaps it's because his Gift is missing,' Hawkwood chortled. 'I can't see it anywhere in the painting.'

'That section of the fresco was destroyed,' Rossi sighed. 'A casualty of later alterations to the building.' He moved on to the third Magus, Melchior, an avuncular figure with a white beard and rosy cheeks, astride a mule.

'Looks more like Father Christmas to me!' Miranda quipped. Rossi gave her a snooty stare, but Tom smiled, as did Sarachin quietly.

Rossi's candle now caught the gold leaf of Melchior's gift: a gourd-shaped censer filled with frankincense, the symbol of prayer. Once again he eyed his ring anxiously but, again, he was reprieved. As the Brothers followed him to the fourth and final wall of the chapel, doubts began to take hold. Maybe they were mistaken and this was not the right chapel after all. Or maybe they had missed something in the glittering mural that forever travelled hopefully but never arrived. 'Time hasn't treated this part of the chapel kindly,' Rossi lamented, pointing to a plain rectangular apse with an altar at the back. 'At some point, some idiot decided to knock a window through the middle of the rear wall. Later on, it was bricked up again and covered with that incongruous bathroom wall-light,' he sniffed, pointing at a large disc of pearlescent white stone.

'Yes, I see what you mean,' Scala concurred. He had never really noticed it before, but the pearlescent disc did indeed seem out of place. He was about to take a closer look when the chapel door burst open.

'The Brotherhood of the Diamond, I presume!' bellowed a mountainous Serb as the door-bolts flew from their moorings. 'Sorry we're late. Have we missed the tour?'

'How did you find us?' Scala demanded, shielding his eyes from the Serb's powerful torchlight.

'Jankovic's mobile. It's got a tracker installed. One of you clowns must have made a call on it.' As he spoke, the giant Serb was busy squeezing himself through the chapel's narrow entrance, but the door suddenly swung back and thwacked him full in the face. Fabio had been standing behind the door and now threw his full weight against it. The Serb staggered backwards, scattering his accomplices and allowing Fabio to slam the door shut once more. His cousins immediately rushed forwards and braced themselves against it. For a moment or two, all was quiet. Then a hail of bullets hammered into the woodwork. Had the Serbs been armed only with pistols, the Sardinians might have been saved by the inch-thick oak. But against semi-automatic rifles it offered little protection. In seconds a dozen bullets had smashed into their backs. Fabio looked on in horror as his kinsmen's bodies slid to the cold marble floor. Surrounded by a cortège of kings, they lay before the chapel's altar like a blood sacrifice.

But there was no time to mourn. The Serbs were breaking in once again. The situation was dire. Scala felt as if he had been punched in the stomach. Stunned, he gazed down and saw a deep crater in the Trismegistus. The book's solid silver cover had taken a bullet for him. But he saw something else too: staring back him from the polished metal was a lamb. 'The Mystic Lamb!' he gasped. It was a reflection, he realised at once, but an impossible one. His eyes shot up to the lintel above the chapel door. On the other side of that lintel, outside the chapel, was a fresco he knew of old. It was of a scene from the Book of Revelations: the Mystic Lamb slain to receive divine power and to open the seven-sealed scroll of the Apocalypse. As if by some magical osmosis, the fresco had been transposed through the solid stone wall and now bathed the chapel in an unearthly iridescence.

Everyone froze, the Serbs included. The Lamb lay in profile on an altar supporting seven candlesticks, which spontaneously ignited, sending plumes of orange flame into the air. A single, blood-red tear dripped from the Lamb's all-seeing eye onto one of the seven seals arrayed beneath it and a voice like thunder spoke: 'The Gifts of the Kings, the prayers of the Supernal Spirits, the Mind of the Virgin, this most holy chapel guard. Let not the profane set foot in here.'

Immediately the seven seals crumbled into seven black and brooding voids, from which seven spouts of liquid night erupted, drowning the terrified Serbs in a cataract of impenetrable darkness. 'Their screams shall be like the squeaking of bats,' proclaimed the voice, 'and their cries but the rustling of leaves.'

Yet the dissolution of their attackers brought no respite for the Brothers of the Magi, as the black tide began lapping at their feet. Acting on instinct, Scala raised the Trismegistus, like an amulet, above his head. The Serbs had incurred the ultimate penalty by damaging it; maybe the same power that protected it would protect him and his Brotherhood too. The Mystic Lamb's reflection appeared once more on its silvery surface and, in an instant, the Stygian waters were sucked back within the seven seals from which they had sprung. Still following his intuition, the count now turned the Trismegistus towards Rossi's offending pearlescent disc. There was a loud click and the disc swung open. A golden chest slid slowly from a hidden cavity and fell with a thud onto the Medici family altar.

'The lost Medici reliquary!' Rossi exclaimed.

Overwhelmed with joy, Scala grasped Miranda's arm and walked her to the altar. 'One day very soon,' he whispered blissfully, 'we two shall do this to the sound of wedding bells.'

46

LETTING GO OF Miranda's arm, the count placed his fingertips beneath the golden reliquary's lid and opened it. There, as he had anticipated from his reading of the Trismegistus, he found a wooden casket. As he watched Scala raise it slowly out of its gilded container, Tom stifled a gasp: it was the very same casket he had seen in his vision of the Magi in the Persian desert, the casket which Rinpoche had entrusted to Yingsel and Dorje. He looked at Miranda, standing entranced at the altar. For a brief moment he saw not the feisty New Yorker he had fallen in love with, but Rinpoche's disciple, pale as death, an arrow in her back. He blinked and there was Miranda again, but now her eyes were locked on his.

Scala summoned Rossi and Sarachin, whose diamonds had not yet been activated, and told them to place their right hands on top of the casket. Warily, they did as they were asked. It was Rossi's diamond that reacted. He screamed as it pulsated with an emerald green light. A seven-pointed star, inlaid in ivory on the side of the casket, rose up briefly from the wood before sinking back again. As it did so,

Rossi's diamond ceased pulsating and he, like the others before him, was left nursing a badly burnt finger.

Fabio, as ever, went to Rossi's aid. 'The ring, Fabio, if you please,' Scala ordered as his butler eased it from the injured dilettante's hand. Holding it up to the candlelight, the Count read out the inscription on the ring's inner band:

'"SOL ABIT E GEMINIS, ET CANCRI SIGNA RUBESCUNT".'

'The Sun leaves Gemini, and the sign of Cancer grows red,' Gatti translated immediately.

'Gemini lies on the cusp of Cancer between June 21st and 23rd,' proffered Sarachin.

Gatti looked at Scala: 'But that's the summer solstice. I thought you said it was the vernal equinox that's the special date for us?'

'I did,' Scala agreed. 'And, as it happens, I recognise the inscription. It's from a poem by the Roman poet Ovid. But, as to the date, it does seem quite precise.'

'S-so my ring is unlike the previous ones,' quavered Rossi, still shaken by his ordeal. 'It just gives us a date, but no location.'

Silence ensued as they all tried to crack this latest conundrum. Then Miranda had an idea. 'Maybe it's a location as well as a date.'

'Go on,' said Scala.

'Well, the inscription could refer to a place where the solstice can be observed.'

'Or perhaps depicted in a painting or photograph,' Rossi threw in, as Fabio finished bandaging his burns.

Scala snapped his fingers. 'I know the very place! It's just across the road from here. Fabio, Dottore – bring the casket.'

They all piled after the count as, cradling the Trismegistus in his arms, he dashed like a man possessed through the bullet-riddled chapel door and down the stairs to the courtyard. However, on reaching the ground floor, he made not for the front gate but for the statue of Orpheus on the opposite side of the cortile.

'Why have we stopped here?' Gatti demanded breathlessly as he and Fabio put the wooden casket down in front of the statue. 'I thought you said we were going across the road?'

'So we are, Dottore,' Scala replied with an enigmatic smile. Then, flicking open the silver knob of his Malacca cane, he removed a small coin. 'Ask yourselves,' he said as the rest of his Brotherhood assembled, 'why does Orpheus, rather than Hercules, say, or Apollo, stand centre stage in the courtyard of the Medici?' His question drew only blank looks. 'Because he was a disciple of Hermes Trismegistus and sang songs such as even Cerberus here –' he pointed his cane at the three-headed hell-hound sitting at Orpheus' feet '– could not resist. Songs that – but for one fatal error – would have restored the dead to life. And therein, my friends, lies the answer to my question.' With that, he threw the coin into Cerberus' gaping jaws.

'An obol for the ferryman?' asked Sarachin.

'That's right, Leo. Charon's fee to cross the Styx. Just as the Sibyls prophesied in Siena.' Moments later, the front panel of the plinth opened inwards to reveal steps descending into the earth. Scala waved his cane: 'Time for us to visit the underworld.'

47

THE BROTHERS CLUNG precariously to a rusty handrail as they stumbled down a spiral staircase. The mini key ring torches which Fabio had handed round proved little better than glow-worms in the dank, pitch-black cellars of the Palazzo Medici.

'This way,' Scala called out as they reached the bottom of the stairs. The beam of his much more powerful torch was directed at what looked like the entrance to a cave, hewn out of the bare rock. Tom guessed from his recent experience of the Bargello's drains that this was a tunnel running beneath the main road outside the palazzo. 'Back into the bowels of Florence again!' he thought, tugging at his handcuffs.

'Don't try anything stupid, Talbot,' Hawkwood growled, giving him a sharp dig in the back. 'I'm right behind you.'

They had gone a hundred yards or so when Scala called a halt. There was a rattle of keys and a clanking of metal as an iron grill squealed its objection to being woken from an ancient slumber. Tom sensed the claustrophobic walls of the tunnel beginning to open out. The count shone his torch this way and that, trying to get his bearings in the cavernous darkness. Suddenly Miranda let out a scream. 'Where the hell are we?' she cried as skulls and skeletons danced in and out of the flashing light.

'Don't be afraid,' Scala reassured her. 'We're in the oldest crypt of the oldest church in Florence. Centuries of Medici remains are deposited here.'

'And you'll soon be joining them, chummy!' Hawkwood hissed in Tom's ear. 'That's a prom…' But he crashed to the ground before he could finish.

'What's going on back there?' Scala shouted.

'I tripped,' Hawkwood groaned. The subterranean procession came to a temporary halt while Fabio went to his assistance.

Tom stood to one side, quietly savouring the colonel's discomfiture. Suddenly, in the darkness behind him, a voice whispered: 'Don't turn round,' it said, as a small glass vial was pressed into his manacled palm.

'What is it?' Tom whispered back.

'An antidote. Drink it before the great diamond is set in place.'

'The great diamond?'

'Il Libro.'

He caught his breath. He had heard that name before, at Careggi. Savonarola's ghost had claimed it was a diamond taken from one of the Gifts. 'Who are you? Why should I trust you?'

'We've met before, in the desert beneath the stars.'

'I don't understand. What are you talk…'

'Right-ho, chaps,' Hawkwood's bluff tones broke in as

Fabio got him back up on his feet. 'Just a graze. Onward march.'

Tom glanced over his shoulder but, whoever the whisperer was, he had melted away into the darkness. He grimaced: just how was he supposed to drink anything with his hands tied behind his back?

48

A SOUGH OF AIR rustled in the stillness as a bronze door deferred to Scala's hand. The Brotherhood of the Magi had left the Medici crypts behind and now entered a very different space. All that was immediately visible in the encroaching gloom was a large crucifix hanging in subdued light above an altar carved in pure alabaster. Beautiful as this sight was, it could not dispel Tom's intense unease as soon as he set foot in the strangely claustrophobic chamber. The crypts had been macabre enough, but this was like nowhere he had ever been before. It possessed an inner tension, an oppressive energy that seemed far from benign.

Scala instructed Fabio and Gatti to put the wooden casket on what he called the 'vesting table', a great slab of white marble on four legs in the centre of the room, to which he now directed his torch. With the casket in place, Fabio pressed a button on the underside of the table causing uplighters to shine at intervals around it. Scala went to the head of the table whilst the others ranged themselves along its flanks. Hawkwood inserted Tom between Fabio and himself; Sarachin and Rossi stood opposite them, next to Gatti. Miranda made for the end nearest the altar, as far away from Scala as possible.

'Do any of you know where we are?' Scala asked, resting the Trismegistus on top of the casket.

'Isn't this the Sagrestia Vecchia?' Rossi ventured. 'The Old Sacristy of San Lorenzo?'

'So it is, Riccardo. We are in the earliest of the Medici chapels, first used by Cosimo himself. In the wall over there is the sarcophagus in which his grandson Lorenzo chose to be interred together with his murdered brother, Giuliano.'

'Weren't they both buried in the New Sacristy, Michelangelo's masterpiece?' Rossi queried.

'Their remains were transferred there later, but,' Scala added cryptically, 'not quite all of them.'

Gatti exhaled loudly. 'I thought we were in a hurry, Maestro.'

The count eyed him coolly; he was rapidly losing patience with the tiresome dottore. In fact, he was tired of all the Brothers, save one. He consoled himself with the thought that they would soon be history. If all went to plan, only he and the lovely Miranda would witness tomorrow's glorious dawn. He grasped the lid of the casket and gently lifted it. As it fell back on its ancient hinges, the Brothers gasped: there was nothing there. The casket was bare.

'Someone's stolen the Gifts!' Gatti cried, aiming an accusing look at the count.

'Don't be stupid,' Scala spat back. He turned to Sarachin: 'Leo, you and Talbot are the only ones left whose diamonds have yet to be activated. You must both approach the casket.'

Sarachin nodded and reached across the table until his right hand was hovering above the empty box. Meanwhile, Hawkwood unlocked Tom's handcuffs so that he too could stretch out his right hand, though he kept his left one tightly fisted around the glass vial he had been slipped earlier. On the count's signal, he and Sarachin lowered their index fingers towards the casket. At once their diamonds began to pulsate: one ruby-red, the other pearl-white. The two men immediately retracted their burning hands. Everyone held their breath. Suddenly, there was a sharp snapping sound and the front panel of the casket flew open to reveal a hidden drawer.

'So that's what Queen Ourania missed!' Tom thought to himself, recalling his vision at Aunt Stella's.

Scala gently eased the drawer from its housing. The further it opened, the wider the Brothers' eyes grew. And, when at last it was fully open, they gazed in awe at the Gifts of the Magi, not now in a fresco at the Palazzo Medici, but in reality. Yet, for Tom, there was something more: a realisation that he had seen all three of these objects before, though where and when he could not say. And as he wrestled with this unnerving insight, he felt a pair of eyes fix on him. He looked up: it was Sarachin.

Scala lost no time in removing the Gifts. He began with the golden pyx, the Magus Caspar's gift of life-preserving myrrh. This he placed on a disc of purple porphyry, inlaid on one side of the vesting table and bearing Lorenzo de' Medici's seven-palle crest. As he set it down, he quietly breathed in an invisible vapour through tiny vents in the pyx's crown. At once, a wave of rejuvenating vigour surged through his veins as every toxin he had ever imbibed, ingested, inhaled, absorbed or accumulated over five decades of mortal existence was washed away in an instant.

'Ah, the magic gum of Nubia,' Sarachin remarked. He alone seemed to perceive the myrrh's subtle effect. 'More biting than ammoniac, more soothing than tragacanth; the bitter-sweet mithridate against all disease and,' he added, looking straight at Tom, 'all poison.'

Scala, preoccupied with the Gifts, turned his attention to the gourd-shaped censer, the Gift of Melchior. This he placed on the opposite side of the table where an identical porphyry disc was inlaid.

Finally, he removed the third Gift, that of Balthazar, from its bed of straw. It was a pyramid of solid gold but with an odd, hollow dimple at its apex and an oblong indentation on one of its facets. Refusing all assistance, Scala set the weighty ingot down on a third porphyry disc between the pyx and the censer. Then, returning to the head of the table, he clasped the silver Trismegistus to his breast and fixed his gaze on the glittering axis of gold, sapphires, rubies and emeralds arrayed before him. 'Gold, frankincense and myrrh,' he declared, his voice reverberating in the sacristy's perfect symmetry, 'the first for a king, the second for prayer, the third for a divine physician. From the earliest days of Christianity the Gifts of the Magi were rumoured to possess magical powers: to heal the sick, to bring the dead to life, even to commune with God Himself.' He paused, revelling in the expectant faces ranged around the table. 'Half a millennium ago,' he continued, 'as I know from my family's archives, Ficino extracted traces of holy myrrh and particles of divine frankincense from these vessels.' He pointed to the pyx and the censer. 'These he secretly applied to the places where we have witnessed such extraordinary phenomena in our search for the Gifts. Yet, what we have seen thus far is nothing compared to what is to come.' He tapped his finger on the Trismegistus. 'The whole amazing story is written in here.'

'What does it say?' Gatti demanded eagerly.

Scala slapped him down. 'Patience!' He was not about to disclose to condemned men who had served their purpose the imminence of their execution. The game now was to string them along until their time was up. 'In Ficino's day,' he said, 'Hermes Trismegistus was believed to be a disciple of Zoroaster, who had lived over a thousand years before Christ. But Ficino, having translated the epilogue found only in this one special book, discovered the author's true identity. Hermes the Thrice Great, you see, was most aptly named, for he was not one man but three: the Three Wise Men to be precise.'

As a chorus of incredulity rippled around the table, Tom guessed that the 'epilogue' was the means by which the Magi had remedied the loss of the scroll they had spoken of in his vision. He listened intently as Scala explained how the epilogue had revealed the origin and purpose of the Gifts. How, at the end of the last Ice Age, beings from another world had visited the Earth hoping to take advantage of its unique position in the cosmos. Apparently, every two thousand years or so, a window in the fabric of space-time opened in the Earth's magnetic field, enabling interdimensional travel. But a volcanic eruption had destroyed the aliens' spacecraft, killing all but one of them. The lone survivor had hidden their precious instruments deep in a Himalayan cave, on whose walls he left a testament to their failed mission. 'Which is why,' Scala concluded, 'Cosimo de' Medici commissioned that.' He waved his black cane towards a small cupola above the alabaster altar.

Miranda, who was closest to it, looked up into the cupola's domed ceiling. What she saw was a brilliant depiction of the firmament: a cross between a modern planetarium and an astrological chart. There was her sign, Leo, its stars picked out as a lion roaring in the eastern sky. To the west, Taurus the Bull brandished his horns. And, just ahead of Leo, the sun blazed between a menacing crab and two twins. 'Oh my God!' she cried. 'It's the inscription on Rossi's ring: "The sun leaves Gemini and the sign of Cancer grows red."'

'Exactly,' Scala beamed at her. The ceiling was an astronomical map of the northern celestial hemisphere, bisected by the zodiac, whose belt was precisely calibrated in gilded decans.

'What's a star chart doing in a chapel?' Gatti queried.

Rossi knew the answer. 'That's easy. The cielo of the scarsella, to give the ceiling and the apse their technical names, commemorates the date when the schism between the Roman Catholic and the Eastern Orthodox Churches was healed at the Council of Florence on the 6th of July 1439, the Day of Union.'

'Yes, that is the politically correct answer,' Scala responded. Rossi looked blank. 'Think about it, Riccardo. Would Cosimo de' Medici really have wished to celebrate a union that ended in acrimonious failure even before the ink was dry?'

'Well, I suppose...'

'And, even if he had, wouldn't he have done so with traditional motifs – choirs of angels, prophets and saints

– rather than an abstruse astronomical chart covered in pagan astrological symbols? No, Brothers, as always with the Medici, appearance is very different from reality.'

'But I still don't see…'

'Remember the inscription on your ring, Riccardo.' Rossi rubbed his finger: how could he forget it. 'As I said before, it's from a poem by Ovid. In it, he associates the date of the summer solstice, the 24th of June, with the feast day of the god Summanus: the Etruscan version of Pluto, Lord of the Dead and hurler of nocturnal thunderbolts.'

'Ah yes, the 24th of June,' Rossi nodded, 'the birthday of John the Baptist, the patron saint of Florence. That is indeed another well-known interpretation of the scarsella.' But Scala shook his head: that was merely another example of the Christian Church appropriating pagan feast-days, just as it did with pagan places of worship.

'The count is quite correct,' Sarachin cut in. 'The 24th of June is the birthday of the Lord of the Dead, known as Osiris in Egypt or Mithras in Persia. It marks the heliacal rising of the constellation of Orion, the date when the Great Hunter of the Greeks first becomes visible at dawn in his annual passage through the skies.'

Scala raised an eyebrow: even for a Jungian psychoanalyst, Sarachin was surprisingly well versed in ancient mythology. 'That's right, Leo,' he said approvingly. 'Yet, we need to go even further back, long before John the Baptist or Osiris or Mithras or even Orion. We must return to the explosion that illumined an infinite darkness. That is the real subject of the star chart.'

'The Thema Mundi,' supplied Sarachin, his features graver than ever.

'Thelma Monday?' Hawkwood boomed, his head jerking upwards from the drowsiness which all the talk of gods and religion had induced. 'Who the hell's she?'

Sarachin gave him a pitying look. 'Not "she", Colonel. "It". The Thema Mundi is the horoscope of the world.'

'Right again,' said Scala, casting the Californian an even more curious glance. Very few people, in his experience, knew about ancient astrology's Holy Grail. And still fewer that, prior to the so-called Enlightenment, the vernal equinox was regarded as the birthday of the universe. He decided to probe further. 'Perhaps, Leo, you could also enlighten Hawkeye about the phenomenon known as the Precession of the Equinoxes?'

Sarachin obliged at once, succinctly describing how the position of sunrise at the vernal equinox had appeared down the millennia to regress through the signs of the zodiac at a rate of roughly two thousand years per sign. This, he said, was due to a gyroscopic nutation of the Earth in its orbit around the sun. The full cycle of the regression took around 26,000 years, the so-called Platonic Year.

As he listened to Sarachin's exposition, various threads came together in Tom's mind: Aunt Stella's 'liminal windows', the ghostly whisperings in the gardens at Careggi, and Rinpoche's final admonishment to remember the equinoxes. He felt as if he was standing on the brink of a precipice, about to discover at last the secret which had cost his father his life and thrown his own into chaos. Yet, Rinpoche had also told him that he would not face his destiny alone. He clutched the glass vial in his left hand: did he mean Miranda or was there someone else?

When Sarachin had finished, Scala took up his theme once more. 'And it was one such equinoctial transition which the alien makers of the Gifts were waiting for, eight thousand years ago. Namely, the transition from Cancer to Gemini.'

'But my ring said the sun was moving *from* Gemini *to* Cancer, not vice versa,' Rossi objected.

'True, Riccardo. And that's how scholars have always interpreted the scarsella's star chart. But didn't I just say that the Medici were masters of concealing reality in appearance? They wrapped the cloak of St John around the birthday of the universe: why not hide equinoctial night in a midsummer's day?' He pointed his cane at the apse behind Miranda. 'When people stand at that altar and look up at the sun moving through a painted sky, they are like those who look up at the real sky and think that the sun is moving round the Earth. They're looking from the wrong place, the wrong perspective.'

At this point, Gatti decided to take a closer look at the scarsella and its cielo. 'The clue is in the figure of Orion,' Scala called after him. 'Astronomical star charts always show Orion facing westwards, following the configuration of the stars in his constellation. But on that ceiling he aims his bow in the opposite direction.'

'Yes, okay, I see that,' Gatti conceded as he stood in front of the altar and stared upwards. 'But so what?'

'So, in order to view the cielo correctly, you need to look not up but down, into a mirror placed at the only point in this whole chamber that is aligned with the true perspective.'

Gatti looked back at the count. 'Where's that?' he asked, only to see the answer staring him in the face. There, reflected in the gleaming gold of the pyramid at the centre of the vesting table, was Orion facing west, with the sun slipping out of Cancer and into Gemini. For once, Gatti was lost for words.

'In fact, Dottore,' Scala chuckled, 'it was you that gave me the final clue.'

Gatti looked even more incredulous. 'Me? When?'

'In my study, when we deciphered the inscription on your ring. You mentioned the Babylonian moon god, Sin, the Lord of Wisdom, and his symbol, the crescent moon, marking the beginning of the Babylonian month. I was reminded of the crescent moon in the cielo.' Gatti looked again at the reflection on the surface of the golden pyramid. It was true; there was a crescent moon behind Orion, passing across the head of Taurus. 'And, when I read the Trismegistus,' Scala went on, 'I realised that the cielo actually represents the beginning of time itself. The moment when a flash of lightning turned midnight into midday and a cosmic clock started to tick to the heartbeat of God. And each time it beats, every two thousand years, a window opens, providing a momentary bridge between parallel universes. So, tonight, Brothers,' he declared, flourishing his cane theatrically around the vesting table, 'the sun will transit from Pisces to Aquarius. When it does, a new age will dawn and the glory of the Medici shall return to Italy.' Then, turning to Sarachin, he asked him to read out the clue which had no doubt appeared on his ring when he and Talbot had put their hands on the wooden casket.

Sarachin had eased the solitaire from his finger and was squinting at the inscription on its inner band when a scream ripped through the sacristy: Gatti had a dagger to Miranda's throat.

49

'WHAT MADNESS IS this, Dottore?' Scala thundered. 'Let go of her, or I'll…'

'You'll what? Kill me?' Gatti goaded, pressing the tip of his dagger into Miranda's neck until a drop of crimson blood trickled down its silver blade.

Tom tried to go to her aid but it was hopeless. Although Hawkwood had neglected to recuff him after his ring was triggered, the colonel still held his left arm firmly in an armlock and now gave him a sharp prod in the ribs for good measure. At the same time, Fabio, who was holding his right arm, kicked the back of his knees, causing him to topple forwards and hit his forehead on the edge of the vesting table. As he dropped to the floor in a daze, the glass vial with its whispered antidote slipped from his hand and rolled out of reach.

Meanwhile, Gatti dragged his hostage away from the table towards a bronze door on the left-hand side of the apse; this mirrored one on the right by which the Brothers had earlier entered the sacristy. 'Avanti, Gladii Domini!' he called, banging the door with his free hand. As it swung open, twelve Swords of the Lord, black in hood and cloak, stormed out with daggers drawn. Seconds later, the Company of the Magi was surrounded.

'Judas!' Scala raged. 'The Vatican wasn't spying on you; you were spying for the Vatican, weren't you, Dottore?'

A manic grin spread across Gatti's cheeks. 'Dottore? Calling Dottore Gatti?' He stopped and listened. 'Nope, nobody of that name here, Your Excellency.'

'Don't be ridiculous, you're Gatti. Who do you think you are?'

Gatti's grin disappeared. 'You know something, Scala? I've been asking myself that question all my life. Who am I? Then, last year, I finally found the answer.' He moved closer, shunting Miranda ahead of him. 'You've got no idea what it's like being a nobody. You, with your palazzi, your villas, your family archives. Not like me: the son of a drunken, two-bit actor who gambled and whored his life away, leaving my mother to rot in Rome's slums.' He sighed, lost for a moment in the rat-infested camps beyond the Eternal City's ring road. 'But then, last September, on his deathbed, the old junkie told me a little secret. A secret that turned a nobody into a somebody, a pleb into a patrician, a loser into a zealot.' He shoved Miranda further forwards until she was just a few inches from the count, so close he could smell the musk of her perfume and hear the pant of her breath. 'Gorgeous, isn't she?' the traitor sneered. 'The beautiful Miss Miranda "US attorney" Maddingley. Your one true love, my one lousy cousin.'

'Whaat?!' Miranda screeched, turning her head as far as her captor's knife would allow and matching his wild look with her own.

Scala tried to reach out to her, but the point of a Savonarolan dagger forced him back. 'You're mad, Gatti,' he spat. 'Utterly mad!'

'How right you are, Count, if only you knew it.' And, with that, the man known as Dottore Gatti tossed aside his thick black spectacles and tore off the unruly blonde wig which had, till then, concealed his bald scalp. All semblance of the bookish Vatican scholar was gone.

Scala looked aghast at the stranger who now stood before him. 'Who... who the devil are you?' he spluttered.

'The descendant of an outlaw who fled Florence and took ship for the New World five hundred years ago.'

'An outlaw? What was his crime?'

'To be the nephew of a hero who killed an infamous adulterer. An adulterer who had cuckolded the cousin of the ship's captain.'

Miranda's heart was pounding. She knew what was coming. It was the solution to her recurring nightmare, the reason why a model galleon was a family heirloom and the answer to the mystery of Uncle Ted's bronze ring. The epiphany she had experienced in the Palazzo Pazzi was about to be confirmed.

'The nephew settled in the New World,' her captor continued. 'Years later, his descendant married an Englishwoman and took her surname, just like that guy, Canigiani, you said became a Stockton. Only, my ancestor's new name was much closer to the Italian one: a direct translation, you might say.'

Scala's eyes widened in horror as an awful truth began to sink in. 'No,' he gulped, his eyes darting from his tormentor to Miranda and back again. 'You don't... you can't mean...'

''Fraid so, Scala. The ship that took my ancestor across the Atlantic belonged to Amerigo Vespucci, the man whose first name crowned a continent, and his last a courtesan.'

'Simonetta Vespucci,' Miranda gasped.

'Yes. And I'm your long-lost cousin, Frankie *Mad*dingley, the latest descendant of Francesco de' Pazzi, slayer of tyrants.'

Scala was speechless. Here, in the Medici Holy of Holies, at the very heart of their secret society, a scion of their mortal enemies had sprouted anew, like the spore of a fungus that had been lurking in the timbers of a long-buried coffin. Of all the things that might have marred his family's sacred endeavour, none could have been more abominable than this. And, yet, what pained him even more was the realisation that the girl he had fallen in love with was tainted by the blood of that detested clan. However things turned out hereafter, the future would now always be tinged with bitterness.

For her part, Miranda, though she did not share the love he professed for her, could not help feeling a twinge of sorrow for the man who had opened his home and his heart to her. A man who had also been betrayed by that same scheming cousin who had stolen her inheritance and who now held a knife to her throat. 'You bastard, Frankie!' she hissed.

'Bastard?' he laughed. 'Surely that's one thing I can't be accused of. And please call me Francesco, seeing as it was the Pazzi side of our family who actually put the mad into Maddingley.'

'I knew it,' she cried. 'I knew there was something wrong about you.'

'Really? I thought my act was pretty good. What put you onto me?'

'It was that morning when I first met you in Giovanni's study. I reminded you about a bottle of wine the hotel manager at the Villa Medici had put by for you. I said it was a cheap Frascati. It was actually a vintage Frescobaldi. You didn't correct me.'

Frankie snorted. 'Huh! You lawyers are so damn smart. What a shame lover-boy here isn't as clever as you.' With that, he thrust her bodily into Scala's arms. 'It's true,' he said, 'my education in the fine wine and luxury lifestyle department has been sadly lacking. But all that's gonna change when I get my hands on Uncle Ted's fortune.'

Scala grasped Miranda's shoulders with unaccustomed roughness. 'Fortune?' he growled. 'What's he talking about?'

'Oh didn't she tell you, darlin' Giovanni?' Frankie sneered. 'You don't think Little Miss Moneygrubber and her boy wonder over there –' he shot a glance at Tom, who was now back on his feet again '– came all the way to Italy just to say "hi" to poor Cousin Frankie, do you? No siree. They've come to stop me inheriting the $75 million bucks I'm due under our uncle's will.'

'That's a lie!' Miranda screamed. 'You've already received the bulk of Uncle Ted's estate.'

Frankie gave her a sly smirk. 'Hmm, so that shyster Winslowe did keep his mouth shut about the survivorship clause after all.'

'Survivorship clause?' she frowned.

'Yeah. I have to survive Uncle Ted by a year and a day, otherwise his whole estate goes to you, or whoever turns up with that old Pazzi signet ring he left you. My lawyers promised Winslowe fifty grand if he didn't tell you.' Miranda bit her lip in frustration: how had she let herself be hoodwinked by that Tennessee hick? 'Course,' her cousin added grimly, 'Winslowe didn't live to see the money; my Savonarolan friends saw to that.'

Scala's hands slipped from Miranda's shoulders. Her reasons for coming to Italy no longer interested him. Dealing with this Pazzi upstart was all that mattered now. 'What a clever little man you are, Francesco,' he smiled, his voice dripping with condescension. 'But aren't you forgetting something? We still don't know the clues on the last two rings.'

Frankie waved his dagger at Sarachin: 'Tell us what it says, old man,' he ordered.

Sarachin held his ring up to the light and proceeded to read out the inscription:

'"CHLORIS ERAM QUAE FLORA VOCOR: PRIMI DEA VERIS".'

'I was Chloris who am called Flora: Goddess of the First of Spring,' Frankie translated at once.

'So far so good, Francesco,' Scala acknowledged. 'But what does it mean?'

Frankie motioned to one of the Savonarolans. Moments later, a portable floodlight burst into life, revealing a large blue curtain draped across the back wall of the sacristy. Frankie strode across to it and tugged on a red tassel. The curtain swished aside and there, in all its pristine glory, hung the Primavera.

50

FRANKIE STRUTTED IN front of Botticelli's masterpiece like a TV art critic hogging the limelight. Revelling in the count's obvious consternation, he revealed that the Vatican had kept the Primavera under surveillance ever since the suspicious death of an Englishman who had helped to restore it over twenty-five years earlier. Scala glanced at Tom. He said nothing but his eyes betrayed his guilt and saw the hate ignited in Tom's. 'So,' Frankie concluded, 'when our spies heard that the painting was being moved here for a private viewing by Count Scala, Rome got ready for action.'

'You little creep, Frankie!' Miranda blazed. 'You were working for that beast, Father Vincenzo, all along.'

Frankie looked genuinely pained. 'Me? Work for that tinpot pervert? Give me a break. I acted the part he expected me to, just like I did with Scala and you. Acting was about all my father taught me.' He paused to take a theatrical bow. 'Vincenzo had no idea that I was the descendant of the first crusader knight to scale the walls of Jerusalem, the man who lit a torch at the Holy Sepulchre and then rode backwards on his horse all the way to Florence, to protect the sacred flame from the wind. People thought he was mad. That's how we Pazzi got our name and earned the honour of lighting the Easter candles in the Duomo.' Puffed up with reflected glory, he brandished his dagger at an imaginary Saracen. 'My Pazzi credentials took me way over Vincenzo's head,' he bragged, waving an arm at the Swords of the Lord who waited on his command. 'You see this ring,' he said, flashing his diamond solitaire, 'it once belonged to Botticelli himself. He betrayed the Medici, once Savonarola had shown him the light.'

Scala shook his head. 'Rubbish!'

'Is it? Why do you think he painted the Mystic Nativity with that mysterious inscription about the Devil and the Apocalypse? That was his confession. Those seven demons crawling in the rocks are the seven Brothers of the Magi, the seven accursed balls of the Medici. If only your girlfriend had been sacrificed in front of it, what poetic justice that would have been.'

Miranda and Tom looked at one another: her cousin had just confessed to attacking her in the Uffizi. 'Is that what you did with Gatti too?' she demanded. 'Killed him?'

Frankie ran a finger along his dagger, its blade glinting in the floodlight. 'The Doc was a fool,' he replied. 'When he first told me about the Tibetan scroll he'd found in the Pope's secret archive, I thought it was just another load of religious bunkum, the typical astrology bullshit he was obsessed with. But I changed my mind when I saw the power of Scala's diamond ring.' He laughed as he recalled following Gatti to San Lorenzo on the night of the autumnal equinox. After the Brotherhood's secret conclave ended, he had caught up with him on the banks of the Arno. 'He was shocked when I told him I'd been sent to spy on him and even more shocked to hear that I belonged to the great Pazzi dynasty. His last words were about the Pazzi chapel in Santa Croce church. I've been to see it. It's an almost exact copy of the one we're standing in right now, including the star chart in the apse.' He turned and pointed his dagger straight at Scala. 'Now why do you suppose my ancestors would have done that, Maestro?'

'Because they were too dumb to design one for themselves?'

'Very droll, but no. The Pazzi would never imitate the Medici without good reason. They must have believed that there was more to this chapel than meets the eye, something they were trying to replicate. Unfortunately, they never got the chance to find out: the Medici had them executed or banished before their chapel was completed.'

'What a pity.'

'The game's not over yet, Scala. I, Francesco de' Pazzi, have sworn to restore the honour of my once-proud family. The Pazzi dynasty shall return to greatness while the Medici rot in hell.' So saying, he raised his dagger heavenwards like some tragic actor, his eyes burning with the lust for vengeance. But, far from being awed, Scala broke into a slow hand-clap. 'Stop that! Stop that right now!' Frankie shrieked, hurling the blade at Scala's head.

With the razor-sharp reflexes of a man half his age, the count tilted his head. The dagger zipped past his left ear and straight into the eye of the Sword of the Lord standing behind him. The Savonarolan staggered backwards, blood spurting from his eye socket. But, before Scala could counter-attack, Frankie pulled a gun. Even so, the count seemed strangely unperturbed, leaning back on the edge of the vesting table, his hand resting casually on top of the Trismegistus. 'You've got it all so wrong, Francesco,' he said.

'Bullshit!'

A serpentine smile flitted across Scala's lips. 'Did you really suppose that by pointing the finger at Federov you'd put me off the scent? Sure, Federov showed his hand in Siena, but that didn't explain the charade at San Marco or the intervention of Vincenzo and these Savonarolan thugs of his.' He swivelled a look at the hooded Savonarolan who had stepped in to replace the one struck down by Frankie's ill-judged dagger. 'I knew there had to be more than one traitor amongst us. So, you see, none of this has come as any great surprise to me.'

'You could've fooled me. Or haven't you noticed that I'm the one holding the gun?'

Scala rapped his fingernails on the Trismegistus. 'Tut, tut, Francesco, don't you realise you've been fooled, you and your Vatican masters, all the way back to Savonarola himself? Sandro Botticelli didn't betray the Medici. Yes, he was swept up for a time in the wave of religious mania stirred up by that mad monk. But he could never be happy among the troglodytes who consigned Ovid and Pulci to the flames. Savonarola and his successors totally misread the Mystic Nativity.'

'You don't say.'

'Oh, but I do. The "Devil" Botticelli referred to, the one who roamed the Earth for three and a half years, wasn't Lorenzo de' Medici, it was Savonarola: the monster who terrorised Florence from November 1494 to his death in May 1498.'

Frankie's cheeks flushed with rage. 'What about the seven demons? Who are they if not the seven Brothers of the Magi?'

Scala arched his eyebrows in mock surprise. 'Why, Francesco, surely you recognise your own ancestors, the seven Pazzi conspirators whose wanted poster Botticelli famously painted on the walls of the Bargello?' Frankie said nothing. 'But you were right about one thing,' Scala conceded.

'What?'

'That the Medici are depicted in the painting. Remember the three men being embraced by angels? They are clearly idealised images of Cosimo, Lorenzo and Giuliano, risen from the dead, wearing crowns of olive, the Medici symbol of rebirth.'

'Crap! Nobody rises from the dead. Not the Medici, not Gatti, nobody.' With that, Frankie aimed his gun: there was a deafening bang. Fabio reached out to his master, but it was not the count who fell.

51

'**N**o!' Tom cried in horror as Miranda sank to the floor, her life-blood seeping onto the cold marble, just as it had seeped onto the hot sands of Central Asia two thousand years before. He wanted to go to her aid but, like Fabio and Hawkwood and the other Brothers, a Sword of the Lord held a dagger to his throat: there was nothing he could do.

Scala too felt torn. Even though she was related to that hated family and clearly preferred a younger man to himself, the fire that Miranda had reignited could not be so completely quenched. And he knew he had the means to save her, if he could escape his guard for just a few seconds. But to do so would give away too much of his plan and risk betraying all that he and his ancestors had lived for. That at least was one thing he and Frankie had in common: they were both prisoners of history. He looked away. Frankie was grinning at him like a hyena gorging on a rotting carcass. 'You were right, Francesco,' he said.

'I'm always right,' Frankie swaggered, blowing a puff of air across the barrel of his smoking gun.

'No, I meant about this sacristy not being what it seems.' Scala's words had the desired effect: Frankie was listening, not shooting. 'Notice how the walls and floor form a perfect cube.' Frankie scanned the room: it was indeed remarkably symmetrical. 'And do you also see how the vesting table stands in the centre with a circle of porphyry at its heart?' Frankie nodded: it reminded him of the pattern on Cosimo's tomb marker, only now in three dimensions. 'Well,' said Scala, 'that porphyry circle marks the point where all the diagonals of this chamber converge, where all its energies are concentrated, and where Ficino secretly applied a coating of cinnabar, the purple ore of mercury, five hundred years ago.'

'So?'

'So, do you suppose it was by chance that Cosimo dedicated the sacristy to St John the Evangelist, author of the Book of Revelations and supreme alchemist of Byzantine tradition?'

Frankie levelled his gun at Scala's head. 'I don't care if it's dedicated to Satan himself,' he snapped. 'Just get to the point, Scala, before I shoot you too.'

'It's an athanor,' Sarachin interrupted. Both Frankie and Scala stared at him: one confused, the other surprised.

'A what?' Frankie demanded, turning his weapon on the laconic psychoanalyst.

But the clinician's air of calm remained unruffled. He had treated too many psychotics not to know that any hint of fear would be fatal. He was also aware, like Scala, of the need to play for time. 'This sacristy,' he replied with slow deliberation, 'is a sort of cosmic oven, designed to cook up alchemical mercury, the sublime essence which, under the right conditions, with the right instruments, will transmute lead into gold.'

'And men into gods,' Scala added pointedly.

But Frankie's patience was at an end. 'No need for cosmic ovens, Scala,' he yelled, training his gun on the count once more, 'I can make you a god with just one bullet.' His finger tensed on the trigger and the hammer rose from its socket but, before he could fire, his diamond solitaire suddenly flared with a blood-red heat and rocketed into the air.

This was the moment Scala had been waiting for. He straightaway raised his right hand so that it was level with the face of his Savonarolan guard. A second later, his own solitaire shot from its mount, blasting into the monk's forehead and blowing out the back of his skull. Pandemonium erupted as all the Brothers' diamonds now hurtled around the sacristy, ricocheting off the walls in a kaleidoscope of pulsating colours: red from Frankie's, blue from Scala's, orange from Hawkwood's, indigo from Sarachin's, green from Rossi's and yellow from the one that flew from Miranda's limp hand.

Tom, however, was oblivious to the uproar going on around him. His gaze stayed firmly fixed on the ever-expanding pool of blood which oozed from Miranda's chest. As her life ebbed away, so his own also seemed to lose its meaning. Then a flash of coruscating silver zipped past his eyes. He watched as his diamond solitaire arced across the sacristy's dome like a comet, before plummeting earthward again. As it did so, the rest of the diamonds joined with it to form a corona of miniature stars revolving above the Gifts in the centre of the vesting table. Then his ring, though bereft of its diamond, started to glow ever more intensely until the inscription on its inner band burnt right through to the outer surface and projected a glittering thread of golden letters onto the vault high above his head. Scala was the first to decipher them, his voice trembling with emotion:

'"MAGNUS AB INTEGRO SAECLORUM NASCITUR ORDO."'

'At last!' he cried. 'The final prophecy of the Cumaean Sybil comes to pass in Virgil's immortal line: "The great procession of the ages is born anew". Now shall Lord Lorenzo rise again: the Perfect Man for the dawn of a new age.' With that, he stabbed his forefinger onto the Medici shield embossed on the front of the Trismegistus. The shield flipped open to reveal an oblong plaque of black jet. Snatching it up, he tossed it across the vesting table. Two Swords of the Lord rushed forwards to restrain him. 'Too late!' he laughed as the plaque landed on the golden pyramid, the Gift of Balthazar, and slotted itself into the matching indentation on the pyramid's side.

At once the floating corona of diamonds which had been circling the Gifts dropped, one after another, onto the black plaque, embedding themselves in its inky surface.

'First, red Betelgeuse, then blue Rigel,' intoned the count as though reciting a magical incantation, 'third, yellow Bellatrix and fourth, orange Saiph, bound by the silver belt of Alnitak, Alnilam and Mintaka.'

'What the hell are you raving about now, Scala?' Frankie screeched as he grabbed his gun from the floor, where in panic he had dropped it.

'They are the seven stars of Orion,' said Sarachin.

'Bloody hell!' Hawkwood suddenly exclaimed, gaping at the cupola above the altar. By some strange osmosis, the painting of the night sky on its ceiling had penetrated the sacristy's stonework and was converting the central dome into a huge, three-dimensional, celestial globe.

A spellbinding carousel of constellations, each delineated by the luminous outline of its eponymous hero or mythical beast, sailed majestically across the apex of the vault, which in turn, seemingly freed of material limitations, dissolved into the much vaster firmament that lay beyond the man-made architecture. Through the middle of the scene, arrayed in a sea of midnight blue, the signs of the zodiac glided on the gilded belt of a precisely graduated ecliptic. Leo roared at Cancer's claws, the sun's disc shone between the crab's shell and the twins of Gemini, who gazed warily at the tips of Taurus's thunderous horns. Outside the girdle of the zodiac, other figures ranged through the ether: Perseus carrying Medusa's head whilst rescuing Andromeda from a sea monster. To his left, a young man, robed like a Renaissance prince with shoulder-length hair, stepped purposefully down into the midst of the zodiac, carrying a kid under his arm. Below him, the unmistakable figure of Orion the hunter brandished a club at the Great Bear, whilst his dog, Sirius, pranced at his heels.

'Behold the conjunction of macrocosm and microcosm!' Scala announced rapturously as seven pencil-thin lasers shot from the seven diamonds on the golden pyramid and locked onto their counterparts high above, in the constellation of Orion.

Frankie tried to take pot shots at the starry figures but his blistered index finger was too swollen to pull the trigger.

'I told you, Francesco, it's too late,' Scala crowed. 'See how the sun already speeds westward from the dawn of time through Gemini into the horns of Taurus. How Aries fast approaches from the east. Thousands of years are passing in a matter of minutes. Soon the sun will reach the First Point of Pisces, where the vernal equinox stood at the birth of Christ. Even now the constellation of the Triangle, the luminous hand of the celestial clock, sweeps round the decans towards that very time.'

But Frankie was not listening. Transferring the gun into his left hand, he took aim at the figure of the Renaissance prince up in the dome and fired a volley of shots. But, as the bullets entered the twinkling vault, they exploded in harmless puffs of smoke.

'Hail, Auriga the Charioteer!' Scala cheered. 'Soul of the World who drives his chariot through the gate of each new aeon. Now at the Gate of Aquarius you stand, bearing in your arms Capella, the star of Amalthea, the goat whose horns flow with nectar and ambrosia. And from that cornucopia, you shall pour forth the soul of him in whose likeness you were painted so long ago: Lorenzo the Magnificent!'

Hardly had these words left his lips when a pulse of light, so bright that it lit up the entire sacristy, shot from the dog star Sirius and smashed like a meteor into the Primavera's gilded frame. Flames burst from the great painting's woodwork. Now it was Frankie who was laughing. 'You should have got a Pazzi to organise your firework display, Scala!' he jeered. But his laughter was premature: the flames quickly spluttered and died. A charred black hole, the size of an ostrich egg, appeared in the picture frame, directly above the tip of Mercury's wand where it pierced the clouds at the top left corner of the painting. As the smoke dispersed, a baleful glow began to emerge from the hole, gradually growing bigger and brighter until it became a shimmering brilliance on the surface of the frame.

'Mesmerising, isn't it, Francesco?' Scala taunted, as Frankie gawped at the giant diamond, just feet away. 'For centuries, it beguiled popes and emperors and lured collectors to the ends of the Earth. Thus the first secret of the Primavera, Il Libro, the Medici diamond, the Sirius of gems, returns to the light. Now it shall rejoin the seven stars of Orion and match the eight figures of the Primavera.'

Was that it? Tom wondered. Was it the discovery of Il Libro which had cost his father his life? But Scala had called it the *first* secret. How many more did the Primavera possess?

'I say, what's that hissing noise?' asked Hawkwood as a thick purple vapour billowed from the top of the censer, the Gift of Melchior. Moments later, the censer itself began to move, or rather the porphyry disc on which it stood began to rotate, as did the other discs beneath the pyx and the golden pyramid. As the Gifts spun round ever faster, the sound of pan pipes could be heard within the purple cloud. With every breath, exotic scents mingled with haunting music, altering consciousness, lulling all present into a blissful, dreamlike state where time slowed to a crawl. Then the Primavera came to life.

52

THE THREE GRACES, frozen for so long in their virtuous circle, shook off their painted pose at the centre of the Primavera and started to dance. Tom watched, bewitched like everyone else by the delicate glissando of their feet, the mesmeric undulation of their arms, as they tripped a roundel to the rhapsody of the Gifts. Zephyrs fluttered through the leaves of the orange grove and brushed across the carpet of wildflowers as infectious laughter spread through the magic glade and reached the ears of Mercury. A luminous sheen, the harbinger of life, infused his thick, mahogany hair, and simultaneously gave Tom the answer to the conundrum in his father's letter: the lock which had no key. Botticelli, he now realised, had mixed a lock of Lorenzo de' Medici's hair with the paint he used for Mercury's chestnut mane. *That* was the second secret of the Primavera, the discovery of which had been his father's death warrant.

As Mercury's eyes lit up and Il Libro sparkled at the tip of his wand, he leapt from the crusty paintwork, like a butterfly from a chrysalis, and landed, a young man of flesh and blood, on the floor of the Old Sacristy.

Scala stretched out his arms. 'All hail, Lord Lorenzo de' Medici, Il Magnifico!' he cried. 'At last you are restored to the bosom of your beloved Firenze.' Then, going down on one knee, he declared: 'I, Count Giovanni Scala, maestro of the Company of the Magi, descendant of Bartolomeo, high chancellor of the Florentine Republic, do humbly greet you, most noble prince, and hereby pledge my undying allegiance. Together we shall lead our city, our country and the whole world into a new Golden Age.'

Silence descended. Everyone was waiting on the response of a man who had not spoken in half a millennium. The prince, however, seemed in no hurry to reply. He looked bewildered as his eyes darted from Scala to Frankie, to the Primavera and back again. When at last he did speak, it was not in the strident, nasal tones which Tom had heard in his vision, but in those of a much softer, more youthful voice. 'What sorcery is this?' he said. 'Your words make no sense to me, Count Scala. I am not here to bring back any Golden Age. I have only one wish: to be reunited with my love.' He looked longingly at the figure of Flora, still frozen in mid-step. 'She who was so cruelly stolen from me in the bloom of her youth. She whose image has tantalised my soul all these endless ages, trapped in a limbo that I neither chose nor could escape until now.'

'But, surely, Lord Lorenzo—' Scala began.

'Why do you address me thus? I am not Lorenzo.'

Scala rocked back on his heels. 'Of course you're Lorenzo,' he insisted, 'Lorenzo, grandson of Cosimo de' Medici. You are the master of the Platonic Academy, the keeper of the secrets of the Trismegistus, the possessor of the Gifts of the Magi. Surely you must remember how you and Ficino and Botticelli planned your triumphant return in fulfilment of your grandfather's dearest dream?'

The young man's frown unfurled, replaced by a rueful smile. 'Truly, this is a jape worthy of that rascal Sandro,' he sighed. 'And yet he would not have done it unbidden.'

'A jape? What jape? I don't understand.'

'No, Count Scala, you do not. And neither did my grandfather. Few men really understood Lorenzo. I should know: after all, he was my brother.'

Scala covered his ears. 'No, it can't be!' he groaned.

'What a joke!' Frankie gloated, glorying in the count's chagrin. 'The great, all-knowing maestro taken for a ride by Il Magnifico himself. He pulled the plug on the whole pack of cards, betrayed his own family and disgraced the House of Medici. And now,' he said, pointing his gun at the prince, 'my moment has come. The moment when I, Francesco de' Pazzi, nemesis of the Medici, shall finish what my namesake began at the doors of the Duomo. Prepare to die a second time, Giuliano de' Medici. And this time for keeps!'

Giuliano stared at his assassin's reincarnation. He seemed to be reliving the horror of that sunny April morning long ago, when his blood spilled, warm and steaming, down the steps of Florence's new cathedral, assuaging – as some later opined – the sacrificial thirst of that ancient ground. Now, once again, he was face to face with the twin fires of envy and hatred burning insatiably in those insane Pazzi eyes.

The trigger clicked. The hammer struck. The bullet shot from the barrel. But, before it reached its target, a white blur, like a rush of wind, flew between it and Giuliano, stopping it in its tracks. Frankie exploded in a torrent of expletives. He was about to pull the trigger again when Mercury's diamond-tipped wand slammed into his mouth, slicing through the cervical vertebrae and lodging in the occipital bone. Frankie's legs buckled under him and he dropped to his knees. As his last breath rattled through his splintered teeth, he crumpled onto the shaft of the wand, his head propped up at an impossible angle and his arms dangling, like the limbs of a discarded marionette.

Giuliano too sank to his knees, cradling the body of his beloved Simonetta. For she it was whose soul had also come back to life, in the form of Botticelli's Flora, only to sacrifice that life at once for the sake of her lover. As he caressed her hair and planted a kiss on her dying lips, she lifted her hand and wiped away his tears, saying with her eyes what her voice could not. 'No! No!' he wailed as her hand slipped from his cheek and the smile he had waited half a thousand years to see smiled its final farewell. 'Why?' he raged, shaking his fist at the stars circling round the dome. 'Why was I reborn only to suffer the same sorrow yet again? Cruel fate! Now let me go where she is gone.' So saying, he drew the sword hanging at his side and thrust it into his chest. For a few moments the two lovers lay together, his arms entwined in hers. Then they returned to their painted paradise and, of their mortal forms, only two locks of hair remained. The stars in the dome stopped circling, the Gifts of the Magi ceased revolving and the music which had brought the Primavera to life was gone.

53

IN THE MIDST of the stunned silence which followed the Primavera's tragic reincarnations, a terrible groan rang out: Miranda was entering her death throes. The Sword of the Lord who was guarding Tom glanced at her a second too long and found himself flying through the air as Tom executed a textbook judo throw. 'The antidote,' he heard Sarachin cry. 'Give it to her now!' Snatching the glass vial from the floor, he leapfrogged across the vesting table and knelt down beside her. The whites of her eyes were swivelling up under her eyelids and he could feel no pulse. Wrenching the stopper from the vial, he poured the entire contents of sweet-scented oil into her mouth. The effect was miraculous. Frankie's bullet popped out of her chest like a champagne cork and the punctured flesh knitted back together without leaving the slightest scar. Miranda heaved a long, deep breath and, with the pain lifted from her cheeks, she opened her eyes. Tom lowered his lips to hers and their tears mingled in joy. But they were not out of danger yet.

'Look out!' Sarachin yelled as a Savonarolan prepared to plunge a dagger between Tom's shoulder-blades. He spun round just in time to seize his attacker's wrist and, with a sharp twist, plunged the dagger back into its owner's heart.

Meanwhile, taking advantage of the commotion, Fabio and Hawkwood had launched their own attacks. The brute strength and impervious hide of the Sardinian shepherd, combined with the hand-to-hand combat training of the ex-paratrooper, proved unstoppable. With Gatti skewered on Mercury's wand and half their number lying dead or disabled, the remaining Swords of the Lord decided to run. Two made a grab for the Trismegistus. Scala, dazed though he was amid the ruins of the Medici masterplan, automatically drew a slim, razor-sharp blade from his Malacca cane and despatched both men with two lethal thrusts. Other Savonarolans attempted to scoop up the Gifts of the Magi, but Sarachin threw a handful of black and yellow stones at them. Tom wondered what good that would do until he watched them frantically waving their arms around as if trying to fend off a swarm of hornets, as they fled, empty-handed, back through the bronze door by which they had entered.

'Now it's your turn, Talbot!' Hawkwood snarled, suddenly lunging at Tom with a blood-spattered dagger. Tom just managed to side-step him, tripping him up as he went past. The colonel fell heavily, dropping his dagger in the process; Tom made a grab for it but, as he bent down, Hawkwood's bear-like hands locked around his throat. Tom struggled for breath; his skull felt like a ripe melon about to burst. On the brink of unconsciousness, he swung his arms high above his head and slammed them down onto Hawkwood's elbows. The colonel's grip broke and a well-aimed headbutt sent him reeling.

Tom turned to check on Miranda, only to find Scala holding Mercury's diamond-tipped caduceus, which he had ripped from Frankie's corpse. 'Not so fast, Talbot!' he growled, hurling the wand straight at Tom. But, to their mutual amazement, it veered off to one side, as if guided by some invisible hand, and crashed onto the vesting table. Il Libro immediately snapped off and lodged itself neatly in the cavity at the top of Balthazar's golden pyramid.

'The fuse is lit!' Sarachin gasped as Il Libro began to rotate, emitting amber beams which scoured the sacristy like searchlights seeking out all mortal presence. Wherever they landed on human flesh, the skin burnt and the bones crumbled. First the fallen Savonarolans, then Frankie's body, were swiftly incinerated. Rossi ran around screaming, tearing his coiffed hair to shreds until, caught in a stray beam, he fizzled to nothing in a puff of smoke, like a fly on a hot blue bulb. Not so the fast-thinking Fabio: he escaped cremation by diving behind the altar, whose polished alabaster reflected the jaundiced rays.

'Quickly, Tom, the pyx!' Sarachin shouted, pushing Caspar's Gift across the vesting table. 'Inhale its perfume before it's too late!'

Tom rushed to the table and put his nose to the pyx's slender minaret. Inhaling deeply, just as Scala had done earlier, he felt the myrrh's healing balm fill his lungs, coursing through his veins and permeating every cell of his body. Seconds later, Il Libro's roving beams found him. To his great relief, he was left unscathed, as were Miranda and Scala: they were all immune. So too was Sarachin.

Suddenly, a hand clapped on Tom's back. 'For God's sake, Talbot, help me!' Hawkwood pleaded. 'You're a decent chap, I see that now. You can't let a fellow Englishman die like this. Let me hide behind you.'

Tom hesitated. Should he shield the ruthless mercenary from Il Libro's deadly rays? Should he let Jasper's killer live? He turned to the colonel, intending to reassure him, but Hawkwood stared at him in horror: the same horror which Tom had seen on Father Vincenzo's face when he had looked into his eyes in the Bargello.

'It's too late, Tom,' said Sarachin. 'He's beyond redemption.'

'What do you mean?'

'Your eyes. They are mirrors of eternity. When evil sees its own reflection, then like Medusa it becomes its own executioner.'

Tom nodded. As he stepped aside, he took a broken cufflink from his pocket. 'Remember this?' he asked. The colonel gasped but had turned to ash before he could utter a word. Tom tossed the cufflink onto the smouldering pile: Jasper was finally avenged.

54

'DAMN YOU, TALBOT!' Scala hissed. He was standing over Miranda, his sword an inch from her breast, as she lay on the floor still recovering from Frankie's gunshot.

'No, you're the one who's damned, Scala,' declared Sarachin with magisterial calm.

The count scowled at him. 'Sarachin, you snake! How did you…?'

'Know about Il Libro and its baleful rays? The same way I knew that you would use it to rid yourself of your erstwhile Brothers.'

'And me too,' Miranda piped up defiantly.

Scala slid the point of his sword up to her neck. 'Be quiet!' he snapped before turning his attention back to the vexing psychoanalyst. 'But you couldn't possibly have known about Il Libro's venom or how to counteract it unless…' he broke off: the very idea was too preposterous.

'Unless?'

'Unless you'd read the Trismegistus, which you can't have.'

Sarachin moved closer to the vesting table. 'Why should

348

I need to read it?' he asked, placing his hand on the ancient tome.

'Don't be absurd,' Scala scoffed. 'Only the Magi knew its contents and they've been dead for two thousand years.'

'But you said yourself that the Magi might still, to this day, visit Plato's tomb.'

'That was just a throwaway line, you old fool. I wasn't serious.'

'Perhaps not, but I am.' And with that, Sarachin raised his hand a few inches above the Trismegistus. As if by magic, the book opened and the pages turned in time to the motion of his fingers. 'I thought you were supposed to be one of "Those Who Know",' he said as the count stared in astonishment, 'yet you don't even know the Magi's names.'

'Their names? What have their names got to do with it?'

Sarachin gave him a pitying look. 'Poor Scala,' he said. 'From the very beginning, names have dogged your ill-starred venture. Your own Banca de' Bianchi concealed the name of the Banca de' Medici. The Company of the Magi was hidden within the Company of the Diamond and was itself a cloak for the Platonic Academy. The Pazzi masked themselves as Maddingleys and now a Maddingley has discovered, tragically for you, that Pazzi blood runs in her veins.' He paused, his grey eyes locking onto Miranda's, penetrating her very soul. 'Who's to say what other names she, or her friend here,' he gestured at Tom, 'have been known by in previous lives?'

The tip of Scala's sword crept up Miranda's neck, stopping just below her chin. 'Get to the point,' he growled, 'or Miss Maddingley will be in need of another new name for her *next* life.'

Sarachin slammed the Trismegistus shut. 'The Magi who wrote this book were named Caspar, Balthazar and Melchior by the Romans.'

'We all know that.'

'The Greeks, on the other hand, called them Apellius, Amerius and Damascus.'

'So?'

'In the original Aramaic, however, their names were different again.' He broke off for a moment or two before delivering the coup de grâce: 'In that tongue, they were known as Galgalat, Malgalat and…Sarachin.'

Tom was the first to react. 'So that's what you meant when you said we'd met before in the desert under the stars,' he exclaimed. 'You saw me that night when Queen Ourania brought the casket containing the Gifts to your encampment.'

'I heard you, yes,' Sarachin smiled. 'We have taken different roads, my young friend, but we travel the same path.'

'Liar!' Scala screamed, whisking his sword away from Miranda and pointing it at Sarachin. 'You're no ancient Magus, you're just another conjuror, a charlatan, like all you shrinks. How long have you been in league with Talbot and…' He glanced down, but Miranda had slithered to safety underneath the vesting table.

Sarachin shook his head. 'You refuse to see what's staring you in the face, Scala. Your blind loyalty to a dead dynasty has kept alive the threat of catastrophe: a catastrophe which we,' he said, waving towards Tom and Miranda, 'have sought in our different ways to avert for the last two millennia. And now, here we all are, standing on the edge of oblivion.' He pointed to the sacristy's dome. The magical projection of the heavens seemed unchanged: the same fixed stars, the same motionless constellations. But one thing was still moving: the sun. 'It was supposed to stop on entering the New Aeon of Aquarius,' he sighed. 'Unfortunately, when the astronomical chart in the apse was painted, Europe was still using the Julian calendar. The sun's ecliptic was thus wrongly calibrated.'

'Oh my God!' cried Miranda, who had meanwhile slid across to the opposite side of the vesting table and was now standing up, next to Tom. 'I was told that Doctor Gatti – the real one that is – used to spend a lot of time in the Vatican observatory where the Gregorian calendar was first proved correct. That must have been what he was investigating.'

'And, thanks to Frankie, he never got the chance to tell Scala,' Tom grimaced.

'Thus,' Sarachin concluded, 'time runs on unchecked. The sun will reach in minutes what should have taken millions of years: the end of its allotted span.'

'But wouldn't that mean curtains for the Earth as well?' Tom gulped.

'Inevitably.'

Scala turned ashen. 'The Trismegistus said nothing of this.'

'The Trismegistus is a guide for the wise, not a manual for fools. Even those who made the Gifts didn't appreciate what forces they would unleash, what demons wait at the gates of time.'

'But it can be stopped, can't it?' Miranda implored him, her heart gripped by an ancient fear.

For the first time, the voice of the Magus betrayed a quiver of fear. 'Not by me.' He turned and fixed his gaze on Tom: 'A.D. 2006 is the Lunar Year of the Dog. There is only one person here who can prevent the destruction of existence itself.'

Suddenly, a deafening thunderclap shook the sacristy and lightning flashed overhead as the sun sped on from Aquarius into the domain of Capricorn. A rushing wind blew through the centre of the dome, rending the celestial fabric in two and leaving a gaping black hole around which a whirlpool of stars began to form. As the constellations swirled precariously on the rim of the vortex, so from its inner core there a came a haunting cry. Nightmarish silhouettes emerged from the void, the stuff of the grimoire, the necromancer, the terra incognita of medieval maps. 'Now, Scintilla of Mercury,' Sarachin urged, 'now, Soul of Sirius, finish what was begun all those aeons ago.'

Tom instinctively raised his right arm. At once, Mercury's wand flew from the vesting table into his hand, like a hawk to the falconer. But the sight of the alien beings massing above him awakened a primeval memory. He recognised them and, in so doing, faced a paralysing dilemma. He turned to Sarachin, but someone else stared back.

'Hard isn't it, Tommy boy,' said Rinpoche, 'doing the right thing? That's what you chose to do when you saved those passengers on the train. But now it's the fate of the whole world that hangs on your decision. The hour is come: the Year of the Dog has begun and your spirit walks abroad. Do as your destiny demands!'

Rinpoche's words galvanised Tom's resolve. He touched Il Libro with the tip of his wand. Electricity crackled like quicksilver down the caduceus' stem as he aimed it into the dome. A bolt of unimaginable energy blasted into the demons' vanguard, atomising them instantly. But more kept coming, rank on rank with one relentless purpose: to snuff out the light.

'Keep firing!' urged Sarachin, now looking himself once more. He climbed onto the vesting table and, plucking Il Libro from the apex of the golden pyramid, began to intone a strange spell. Somehow understanding what he was saying, Miranda too leapt onto the tabletop, where an ancient Tibetan prayer flowed unbidden from her lips.

'What's happening?' demanded Scala as the vesting table suddenly emanated a three-dimensional image of itself and floated into the air, bearing away Sarachin and Miranda, together with the Gifts and the Trismegistus, like some magic carpet.

'The Gifts are going home,' Sarachin replied.

'Not without me, they're not!' Scala yelled, jumping up and throwing his arms over the top of the virtual table just before it rose out of reach. 'Goodbye, Talbot,' he laughed triumphantly. 'Save the world, if you can, but I've got the Gifts and the girl. Too bad!'

Tom immediately aimed his wand at the count as he dangled higher and higher in the air. Now his father's murderer would pay for his crime.

But Sarachin raised his hand. 'No,' he warned. 'The caduceus is too powerful. You'll kill us all and destroy the Gifts.'

'He's right, Tom,' Miranda cried. 'Forget about Scala. Fight the demons.'

Tom gazed up at her, his eyes glistening with tears. The fate of the world depended on him, but what was the world without Miranda? The sight of her receding figure was unbearable: he looked away. But, as Scala continued to hurl abuse at him, he spotted a dagger lying on the floor beside his feet. Snatching it up, he threw it skywards. Scala saw it coming and drew up his legs, but not far enough: the dagger sank deep into his thigh. His hands slipped to the very edge of the tabletop; he was clinging on by his fingertips. 'Admit it, Talbot,' he grunted as he struggled to get a firmer grip, 'you're no match for Count Scala.' Then, hearing Miranda's voice, he turned his head just in time to see the heel of her shoe slam into his face. 'Pride goes before a fall, Giovanni,' she shrieked as he plummeted onto the solid marble surface of the real vesting table, thirty feet below. There, above the tomb of the founder of the Medici dynasty, he breathed his last, his vacant eyes gazing up at the glory that might have been.

'Miranda! Miranda!' Tom called to her as she floated further and further away.

A name came to her lips which she had not spoken in two thousand years. 'Don't you see, Dorje?' she sighed. 'If the world is finished, so are we. That's the meaning of the Primavera. That's why Lorenzo sacrificed a second chance of life for the sake of his murdered brother and the woman he loved. It's the price we pay for love.' As she spoke, she tore the gold chain from her neck and let fall her uncle's bronze ring: once a totem of implacable hate, it was now a token of undying love.

With her words resounding around the sacristy like a battle cry, Tom summoned every last ounce of his strength and hurled the caduceus up into the dome. It shot like an arrow into the very heart of the black hole. There was a blinding flash and then nothing: no hole, no demons, no wand. Only the last susurrus of a whispered name lingered on the air.

EPILOGUE

Tom giggled. He could feel Miranda's warm breath on his cheek, a playful nuzzle in his hair, a provocative tongue in his ear. Then he woke up. A Jack Russell dog was grinning down at him as he lay surrounded by long grass. He sat up with a start. 'What the...'

'Come here at once, Tinker!' summoned a stout, middle-aged woman wearing a headscarf and tightly buttoned Barbour jacket. She was standing a few yards away, on a lane behind a hedge. 'Are you alright?' she enquired as her dog squeezed through a gap to be swiftly reacquainted with its lead.

Tom rubbed the back of his head. It was sore and he felt decidedly groggy. Looking around, he was startled to find Jasper's grave beside him and the sundial on the stone column next to it. 'Where's Miranda? What's happened to the Gifts of the Magi?' he asked, as much to himself as to the dog-walker.

She looked at him askance. 'Did you faint?' she ventured, more warily this time, eyeing a couple of beer cans which someone had discarded on the grass verge.

He shook his head. 'I'm not sure. I remember throwing the wand and watching the table fly away...'

She examined her watch hurriedly. 'Oh dear, is that the time? I'm late for my book club,' she muttered as she marched off down the lane, dragging the reluctant Tinker behind her.

Tom sank back on his elbows and stared up at the puffy clouds drifting across a pale blue sky. Was it all a dream? Rinpoche and Aunt Stella, Scala and his Brotherhood, Lorenzo and the Primavera, Sarachin and the Gifts? And what of Miranda: was she a figment of his concussion too? An overwhelming sadness washed over him. He lowered his gaze to the uncut grass: it smelled sweet and fresh with morning dew. Here and there, clumps of yellow daffodils nodded in the breeze. He frowned: daffodils? In September? Scrambling to his feet, he could see that it was not only the daffodils which were in bloom; there were primroses too and a profusion of white hawthorn along the hedge. In fact, wherever he looked, the signs of spring were evident. Then he realised that he was clutching something in his right hand. He opened his palm: it was an old bronze ring.

THE END

ACKNOWLEDGEMENTS

I WISH TO THANK Broo Innes, Dr. Nicholas Richardson and Carrie Williams for reading and commenting encouragingly on excerpts of this novel at various stages in its long and winding life. My thanks also to Stephanie Hale and the Oxford Literary Consultancy: their professional assessments of earlier drafts were packed with constructive advice which I have tried to follow, though there are no doubt places where the brass could be polished still further! Lama Shenpen Hookham of the Awakened Heart Sangha once kindly gave me her views on how she likes stories to end: I hope she may find this one entertaining. My fellow author, Julia Sutherland, has been the source of various practical tips on getting published as well as an additional spur to doing so. I shall be eternally grateful to Gareth Morgan for rescuing my magnum opus from computerised oblivion (and me from the slough of despond) with his encyclopaedic, technological wizardry. Fern Bushnell, my Production Controller at Matador, and her colleague, Emily Castledine, have guided me through the labyrinthine metamorphosis of word document to printed page with great good humour, helpfulness and efficiency. Above all, I thank my wife for her unfailing support, heroic patience and ever perceptive insights: without her, this would not be.

This is a work of fiction, but it is woven into a framework of historical fact, real works of art and actual locations. Ritual brotherhoods like the Compagnia de' Magi were common in Renaissance Florence. The Medici were patrons and leading members of several such confraternities, including that of the Magi, which seemingly was never legally dissolved, and morphed into the Compagnia del Diamante[1]. Marsilio Ficino and the other members of the Platonic Academy created by Cosimo de' Medici around 1462/3 can all be found in the history books,[2] as can Bartolomeo Scala and even Queen Ourania[3]. Savonarola did envision the "gladius Domini" ("the sword of the Lord") hanging over the earth[4], but of course the "Swords of the Lord", like all the novel's modern-day characters, as well as the Banca de' Bianchi, are pure invention.

The riddle of Botticelli's Primavera has long exercised the minds of art historians. It has everything: a masterpiece in its own right, the beautiful, yet tragic, figure of Simonetta

1   See Rab Hatfiled's article: *The Compagnia de' Magi* (Journal of the Warburg and Courtauld Institutes, Vol.33, 1970, pp.107-161 fn.141.)

2   I recommend *The Medici, Godfathers of the Renaissance* by Paul Strathern (Jonathan Cape, 2003), *Medici Money* by Tim Parks (Profile Books, 2005), and, for the Pazzi Conspiracy, *April Blood* by Lauro Martines (Jonathan Cape, 2003).

3   See Cambridge Ancient History (Cambridge University Press, 1952) Vol. X p.265.

4   See *The Burning of the Vanities – Savonarola and the Borgia Pope* by Desmond Seward (Sutton Publishing Limited, 2006, p.60).

Vespucci [5], her lover Lorenzo (Or is it Giuliano?) de' Medici, and the manifold interpretations of its meaning[6]. Similarly, the symmetry of the Sagrestia Vecchia in San Lorenzo and its esoteric, astrological ceiling have given rise to various theories, although not, as far as I know, to the Thema Mundi variation.[7]

Platonic and Neoplatonic belief in the soul and reincarnation/transmigration have striking echoes in Hinduism and Buddhism and perhaps they all ultimately derive from a common root[8]. Mysticism certainly appears to be a common aspect of all religions, and where could be more mystical than Tibet?[9]

The Teachings of Hermes Trismegistus were translated from the Greek into Latin by Ficino in 1471. Among the first translations into English was that of Walter Scott: no, not the author of *Ivanhoe*, but an Oxford don[10].

The Magi and their Gifts are mentioned in the bible only once, in St. Matthew's Gospel. Their images appear in the catacombs at Rome. Frederic Barbarossa had their relics

---

5   See Charles Dempsey's *The Portrayal of Love* (Princeton University Press, 1992).

6   See *The Primavera of Botticelli – A Neoplatonic Interpretation* by Joanne Snow-Smith (Peter Lang, 1993).

7   See *Cosimo de' Medici and the Florentine Renaissance* by Dale Kent (Yale University Press, 2000), pp192-3 and notes.

8   See *Eastern Religions and Western Thought* by S. Radhakrishnan (Oxford University Press, 1939).

9   See *Magic and Mystery in Tibet* by Alexandra David-Neel (Unwin Paperbacks, 1984).

10 *Hermetica. The ancient Greek and Latin writings which contain religious or philosophic teachings ascribed to Hermes Trismegistus* (Oxford University Press 1924-36). The very first English translation appears to have been that of G.R.S. Mead (The Theosophical Publishing Society, 1906). For the historical context, I recommend *The Egyptian Hermes* by Garth Fowden (Cambridge University Press 1986).

placed in a golden shrine in Cologne Cathedral in 1164. Their Hebrew, Greek and Latin names are given in *The Golden Legend* written by Jacobus de Voragine around 1260. The fate of the Magi's Gifts is not known, neither is their origin. But Pope Sylvester I did receive a delegation from the Nazarene Church in 318 and the antipope Baldassare Cossa (John XXIII) did pawn Vatican treasures to Cosimo de Medici's father in the early 1400s[11]. It is also the case that Cosimo, the consummate political pragmatist and architect of the world's ultimate banking dynasty, was paradoxically fascinated by mysticism and the Magi and spent many hours, alone with their fresco, in a cell at San Marco.

---

11   See *Medici Money* (note 2 above) p.53.